FORTUNE'S DAUGHTER

ALSO BY ALICE HOFFMAN

Property Of

The Drowning Season

Angel Landing

White Horses

FORTUNE'S DAUGHTER

ALICE HOFFMAN

G. P. PUTNAM'S SONS / NEW YORK

Published by G. P. Putnam's Sons,
200 Madison Avenue, New York, NY 10016.
Published simultaneously in Canada by
General Publishing Co. Limited, Toronto

The text of this book is set in Garamond.

Library of Congress Cataloging in Publication Data

Hoffman, Alice.
Fortune's daughter.

I. Title.
PS3558.0344F6 1985 813'.54 84-17750
ISBN 0-399-13056-X

Printed in the United States of America
2 3 4 5 6 7 8 9 10

To Jacob Martin
and to my mother

PART ONE

It was earthquake weather and everyone knew it. As the temperature hovered near one hundred degrees the days melted together until it was no longer possible to tell the difference between a Thursday and a Friday. Coyotes in the canyons panicked; they followed the scent of chlorine into backyards, and some of them drowned in swimming pools edged with blue Italian tiles. In Hollywood the tap water bubbled as it came out of the faucets; ice cubes dissolved in the palm of your hand. It was a time when everything you once suspected might go wrong suddenly did. For miles in every direction people just snapped. Lovers quarreled in bedrooms and parking lots, money was stolen, knives were pulled, friendships that had lasted a lifetime were destroyed with one harsh word. Those few people who were able to sleep were haunted by nightmares; those with insomnia drank cups of coffee and swore they smelled something sweet burning, as if a torch had been put to a grove of lemon trees sometime in the night.

It wasn't uncommon to have hallucinations in weather like this, and Rae Perry, who had never had a vision in her life, began to see things on the empty sidewalk whenever she took the bus home from work: a high-heeled shoe left at a crosswalk, a wild dog on the corner of La Brea, a black garden snake winding its way through traffic. Hollywood Boulevard seemed to move in waves. And at home, the white stucco walls in Rae's apartment shifted as if they were made of sand. It wasn't just the heat that was affecting everyone, it was the strange quality of the air. Every breath you took seemed dangerous, as if it might be your last. Even in the air-conditioned office where she worked for an independent producer named Freddy Contina, Rae found she had to take several deep breaths before typing a letter or answering the phone. Toward the end of the day the light coming in through the windows was a sulky amber color that made you see double. It was the season for headaches, and rashes, and double-crosses, and more and more often Rae Perry put her head down on her desk at work and began to wonder why she had ever left Boston.

But after she'd gotten home, and had sat for half an hour or more in a bathtub of cool water, Rae knew exactly why she had run away two weeks before her eighteenth birthday. As soon as she heard the Oldsmobile pull up, she ran to get dressed and open the front door. Sometimes she swore she was under Jessup's spell. He didn't even have to snap his fingers to get her to jump. All he had to do was look at her. Even in this weather Jessup seemed different from everyone else, as if he were above the heat. He had the kind of blue eyes that were transparent, and so pale that his mother had thought they were bad luck. For several summers she had kept Jessup out of the sun entirely, for fear his eyes would be bleached even lighter. But as soon as you touched Jessup you knew how deceiving his appearance was. He might have looked cool, but his skin radiated heat, and it got so that Rae had begun to wait for him to fall asleep so that she could climb out of bed and sleep alone on the wooden floor.

Since the time they'd run away from Boston, Rae had been afraid that one day Jessup would change his mind and ask her to leave. And the truth was something had been happening to him ever since they came to California. He actually went so far as to get an application to the Business School at U.C.L.A., though he never filled out the forms. He continually grilled Rae about Freddy Contina and even had her steal one of Freddy's résumés—Rae found him studying it one night when he thought she was still in the shower. It was as if the ghost of some ambition had suddenly appeared to Jessup. He had begun to want things, and it just wasn't like him.

In the past, Jessup's main ambition had been to keep moving. In seven years they had lived in five states. As soon as Rae began to feel comfortable somewhere, Jessup started to talk about moving to a place where there were more options. He never mentioned a new job or more money, just these unnamed options—as if the whole world would open to him as soon as they put a few more miles on the Oldsmobile.

Whenever Jessup reached for his stack of road maps, Rae had to remind herself that it wasn't her he was tired of, just the place they were in. This time there had been no maps and no talk of options, and yet Jessup's restlessness was so strong it had begun to affect Rae's dreams. At night she dreamed of earthquakes: glass shattered and spilled over the boulevards, the ground pitched and split open, the sky became a sheet of needles. When she awoke from one of these nightmares, Rae had to hold tight to Jessup or else, she was certain, she'd spin right out of the room.

She had been waiting so long for something to go wrong between them that it took a while before she realized that it already had. Each Sunday they went to the beach at Santa Monica, and as they drove along Sunset Boulevard Jessup's mood always grew worse. By the time they reached Beverly Hills it was impossible to talk to him. The funny thing was, it was Jessup who always insisted they take the same route. He claimed to hate the palm trees and the huge estates, but every Sunday he pointed them out as if seeing them for the first time.

"This is truly disgusting," he would say as they neared the same pink stucco chalet. "Who in their right mind would turn their house into such a fucking eyesore."

"Then when you have a house paint it white," Rae finally told him, and she knew as soon as she opened her mouth that it was the wrong thing to say.

"Do you have something to say about the fact that I don't own my own house?" Jessup said.

Rae looked straight ahead. "No."

"You think I'm a failure or something—is that what you're thinking?"

"Jessup, I didn't say one goddamned thing," Rae told him.

"You said paint it white. I heard you."

"Well, paint it whatever the hell color you want to." Rae was practically in tears. "Do whatever you want."

"I will," Jessup said. "I certainly will."

After that Rae had taken to riding with her head out the window of the car. She told Jessup it was because she loved the scent of jasmine in Beverly Hills, but really it was because Jessup's anger was heating up the car until the plastic upholstery just about burned you alive.

On the last Sunday in August they probably should have known enough to stay home. The temperature had risen above one hundred and there was a trace of sulfur in the air. When they pulled into the parking lot at Santa Monica, the asphalt beneath the tires turned to molasses. Jessup wasn't talking as they walked down to the beach; and when Rae spread out the blanket she wondered if there could possibly be another woman, someone he told all his secrets to, because he certainly wasn't telling Rae a thing. She watched him as she tucked her red hair under a straw hat, then rubbed sunscreen on her arms and legs. The water was so blue that it hurt your eyes, but Jessup stared straight at it. He wore a black T-shirt and jeans, and a pair of boots Rae had bought for him years ago. Everything around them shimmered with heat; every sound echoed. If you closed your eyes you could almost imagine that the cars on Route 1 were only inches away, or that the girls who cried out as they dove into the cold waves were close enough to touch.

Rae was flat on her back and nearly asleep when Jessup finally spoke.

"Guess how many Rolls-Royces I counted?" he said suddenly.

Rae had to crane her neck to look up at him; she kept one hand on her straw hat.

"Go ahead," Jessup urged. "Guess."

Rae shrugged her shoulders. She could barely tell a Ford from a Toyota these days.

"Two?"

"Eighteen," Jessup said triumphantly. "Eighteen fucking Rolls-Royces between Hollywood and Santa Monica."

For some reason that number frightened Rae. In the parking lot, their blue Oldsmobile baked in the sun. In the seven years they'd had the car they hadn't put a scratch on it. In fact, it had been one of the reasons Jessup had wanted to come to California in the first place. A car could last forever in Los Angeles, he had told Rae. No snow, no salt, no rust.

"I don't care about Rolls-Royces," Rae said. "I'd rather have our car any day."

She could see the muscles in Jessup's jaw tighten.

"God, Rae," he said to her. "Sometimes I swear you get stupider all the time."

He left her there on the blanket, just like that. Rae propped herself up on one elbow and watched him walk down to the water. He stood at the shoreline, looking far out into the Pacific, as if he were the only one on the beach able to see the cloudy edge of China. Rae was concentrating so hard, trying to figure out what was wrong, that she forgot to turn onto her stomach so she wouldn't burn. By the time they got home,

Rae's fair skin had burned to nearly the same shade of red as her hair, and that night Jessup had the perfect excuse not to come near her.

The following Sunday, Rae didn't dare ask Jessup to go to the beach. The heat was worse than ever, and people with respiratory problems were warned not to go outdoors. Jessup spent most of the day Simonizing the Oldsmobile; he tied a red bandanna over his mouth to filter the air, and took off his T-shirt. At noon, when Rae brought him a beer, Jessup seemed less upset; he stopped working long enough to pull down his bandanna and kiss her. That night Jessup insisted that they go out to dinner at a Mexican restaurant where the air conditioner was turned up so high you could actually feel brave enough to order the extra-hot chili. Rae wore a lavender-colored cotton dress and silver earrings. It seemed more important than ever before that Jessup notice how good she looked, and while he never actually said anything, he did reach across the table to take her hand.

In the dark booth of the restaurant, Rae managed to convince herself that the trouble between them was over. But when they got home, Jessup ignored her. He went into the kitchen, and, without bothering to turn on the light, he sat there and stared out the window. Rae wondered if it was just that Monday was so close. Jessup worked for several studios—he picked people up at the airport, he messengered film, he delivered platters of shrimp cocktail and pastrami up to the executives' offices whenever there was something to celebrate. On his tax returns Jessup listed himself as a driver, but whenever someone asked what he did, Jessup would smile and say, "I'm a slave."

At the beginning of the heat wave, when he'd first started to act so peculiar, Rae had made the mistake of asking Jessup how his day had been.

"How was my day?" Jessup had mimicked in a too sweet

voice. "Well, I spent most of my time picking up an order of cocaine that cost more than I've earned in my entire lifetime. That's how my day was. If you want me to continue, I'll be glad to tell you about my week."

She hadn't wanted to know any more. But when they got home from the restaurant no one had to tell her that Jessup was feeling cheated. He sat by the kitchen window and gave the parked Oldsmobile a murderous look. It was then Rae knew he was still thinking about Rolls-Royces, and that thinking about them was just about driving him crazy.

The worst part was that Rae couldn't think of a single thing she could do to make him happy. On Monday morning she got up early, so she could bring him breakfast in bed. The heat was still pushing down as she boiled water for coffee and switched the radio on to a low volume. Listeners were calling in to a talk show that followed the news, each with a way to predict the next quake. As Rae poured water through the coffee filter, she knew she shouldn't be listening to a program about earthquakes—she was so suggestible lately that she could already feel the buildings crumbling around her. But she was hypnotized by the heat, and by the scent of coffee, and as she put some bread in the toaster she continued to listen as a caller insisted that if birds were tracked by radar, entire cities could be saved. It was a well-known fact that birds always left an area long before any catastrophe. Rae found herself drawn to the window; at least there was still a line of blue jays on the telephone wire.

She took out the frying pan and heated some butter, but when she cracked two eggs into the pan she found blood spots in both yolks. Rae panicked and immediately poured the eggs down the drain, then washed out the pan with hot water and soap. But even after she had started over again with two fresh eggs, Rae kept thinking about the spots of blood. She actually had to sit down and drink a glass of ice water and tell herself that anybody could have brought those eggs home from the market—they just happened to have been in the carton she chose.

She watched the clock, afraid to wake Jessup. Although how he could sleep in this heat was beyond her. Other people tossed and turned, but Jessup lay perfectly still beneath a thin cotton quilt. Finally, Rae set out his breakfast on a white tray, then poured two cups of coffee. What was the worst that could happen? Freddy could fire her. Los Angeles could be devastated. Jessup could whisper that he'd found someone new.

"Why is it you people stay in California?" a long-distance caller from Nevada asked on the radio. "Don't you know that birds can't save you? Don't you know that by staying all you're doing is tempting fate?"

Rae climbed back into bed with a cup of coffee in either hand.

"Don't move," she warned Jessup.

Jessup opened one eye and reached for his coffee. Rae put her cup on the night table, then went back into the kitchen. By the time she had returned with the tray, Jessup had finished his coffee and had lit a cigarette. As Jessup tapped ashes into his empty coffee cup, Rae stood by the foot of the bed. There was one thing she knew for sure: Jessup had quit smoking two years ago, when they lived in Texas.

"You don't actually expect me to eat that, do you?" Jessup asked when he saw his breakfast.

"You're smoking a cigarette," Rae said.

"Golly, Rae, that's what I like about you," Jessup drawled. "You're so observant."

There had been a time when Rae had made it her business to find out everything she could about Jessup. Of course, that was when the really important things were whether or not Jessup liked long hair, or if he preferred her to wear blue or green. When Rae was fourteen she taped a photograph of

Jessup to her closet door so that she could memorize his face. This was one of the reasons Rae's mother, Carolyn, had decided to move the family out to Newton. It was one thing for Rae to moon over him when she was still in junior high, and quite another to continue this infatuation now that Jessup had graduated, and she was about to go into high school herself. They hadn't even told Rae until a week before the moving van was set to arrive. She locked herself in the bathroom and refused to come out.

"I'm not leaving Jessup," she told her mother through the locked door.

"Oh, yes you are," Carolyn had said. "And years from now you'll thank me."

"Oh, please," Rae said.

"It's not just that I don't like him," Carolyn said. "It's that he's dangerous."

Something in her mother's tone made Rae curious. She turned the lock and opened the door.

"Please believe me," Carolyn said, "because I know about dangerous men."

For Rae that was the limit. Her father was a lawyer who was home so rarely that Rae was actually surprised whenever she ran into him in the kitchen or the living room. Was he her mother's "dangerous man"?

"You can't tell me anything," Rae informed her mother. "You don't even know Jessup."

Once they had moved to Newton, Rae continued to see Jessup even more than before. Her friends found him threatening or mean, and they dropped away from her. It was just the two of them, and even Jessup's mother had to telephone Rae whenever she wanted to locate her son.

Rae had always been sure that if she knew anyone in this world it was Jessup, but now his suddenly starting to smoke again spooked her. Immediately, she had the sense that this was only one of the things he kept hidden from her.

"I'll tell you something else," Jessup said, as he lit another cigarette. "I don't eat breakfast any more—you should know that."

Rae tried to remember—hadn't they had pancakes only a few days ago?

"You have to watch out for things like breakfast when you get old," Jessup told Rae. "Otherwise you wake up one day and there you are—fat and over the hill."

Jessup still wore the same blue jeans he had worn when he was eighteen years old, but he was turning thirty this year, and the only thing that bothered him more than turning thirty was realizing that he cared about his age.

"I wish you would stop talking about getting old," Rae said. "It's ridiculous."

She was about to go into the kitchen and get Jessup a second cup of coffee, when he reached over and pulled her down on top of him.

"It's just a joke to you," he whispered. "You've got five more years. You've got time. I'm the one who has to hurry."

Jessup kissed her, and Rae wrapped her arms around him. Other women who had kissed only one man in their entire lifetimes might think they were missing something, but Rae certainly wasn't one of them. Instead, she found herself pitying women who had to settle for anything less.

"Wait a minute," Jessup told her.

Jessup walked down the hallway to the kitchen, and when he returned he was carrying a blue-and-white mixing bowl. As soon as Rae saw that the bowl was filled with ice cubes, she sat up in bed. He did have a mean streak sometimes, and the first thing Rae expected was that he'd dump the ice on her as a way of letting her know it was time for her to get up and get dressed for work.

"Oh, no you don't," she told him.

Jessup held the bowl of ice and grinned.

"I mean it," Rae said.

"You don't trust me any more," Jessup said. "And if you don't trust me, I don't see the point in staying together."

Maybe he meant it, maybe he was having doubts—Rae pulled Jessup back down on the bed. She closed her eyes and forgot about the ice. But later, when they were making love and Rae was so hot she couldn't stand it any more, Jessup reached for the mixing bowl. He took an ice cube in each hand and then traced the ice along Rae's skin. Nothing had ever seemed as delicious and cold, and Rae begged him not to stop. But there was something in the way Jessup made love to her that felt desperate; and what made Rae shiver wasn't the ice, it was noticing that, as he held her, he was looking at the front door.

It was nearly ten o'clock by the time Jessup started to get dressed. The phone had rung several times, but they hadn't answered. Jessup didn't talk to Rae. He pulled on jeans, then went to the oak dresser for a clean shirt. Rae sat up and watched him get ready. Jessup never bothered with a comb; instead he stared into the mirror and shook his head until his dark hair fell into place.

"I'm going to have to make up the time I just missed," Jessup told her.

He spoke into the mirror as he put on a white shirt. Rae found herself wishing that he would look over his left shoulder—then their eyes would meet and Jessup might see how much she wanted him to stay home with her. If he agreed, she'd be willing to take the whole day off. But that morning the temperature was already at one hundred and two, and the car exhaust on Sunset Boulevard had begun to form a pavilion of clouds, and Jessup simply didn't have the time to look over his shoulder.

"Don't bother to wait for me," he said.

⋙

Rae didn't know why she always had the feeling she'd been the one to force Jessup into something—he had been the one who kept coming to see her. Even on the coldest New England day, when the sidewalk was a sheet of ice, she'd look out her window and there he'd be, waiting. But then, after Rae had managed to get out of the house, he always seemed annoyed to see her. And so, Rae never really knew what it was that brought Jessup out to Newton so often.

That winter, when Rae was sixteen, was the last time Carolyn tried to separate them by force. When she realized who it was out there on the sidewalk nearly every day, Carolyn Perry called the police. After they'd taken him down to the precinct house, Jessup was threatened with charges that made him laugh out loud: loitering. But from where she stood in the driveway, all Rae could see was Jessup being hustled into the rear seat of a patrol car. She was certain they were driving him straight to the penitentiary. She ran upstairs, locked her door, and tried to slit her wrists with a nail file.

Carolyn, of course, gave up. She stopped questioning her daughter each time she left the house, and now whenever she looked out the living-room window and saw Jessup outside, Carolyn simply drew the curtains. Rae was delighted with her own courage, but when she told Jessup about the nail file, he wasn't impressed.

"You'll never kill yourself that way," he told her.

But the nail file had changed one thing—Rae and Carolyn no longer spoke to each other, they didn't even fight. In the mornings, Rae left for school before her mother came downstairs; at night she sat up in her bedroom on the third floor and waited for Jessup to call. Whatever shred of control Carolyn had had before disappeared. Now Rae did as she pleased, and whenever she wanted money she simply took it. If Carolyn noticed the dollar bills missing from her purse, she never said a word, and the silence between mother and daughter grew deeper and deeper, until finally, even if there had been anything for them to say to each other, it would have been impossible to speak.

Then one day, Rae couldn't find any change in her mother's purse and she decided to look through the bureau drawers in her parents' bedroom. In Carolyn's sweater drawer, between two wool cardigans, Rae discovered a red leather wallet. She knew she had found something important, but she had never expected so much—fifteen hundred-dollar bills, all folded neatly in half.

Without stopping to think, Rae telephoned Jessup and told him she had to see him. That night she ran all the way to the parking lot of the Star Market.

Jessup was crouched by a brick wall; as soon as he saw Rae he jumped to his feet. It had just begun to snow and the parking lot was deserted; it was the kind of night when you didn't go outside, unless your life depended on it.

"My mother has money hidden," Rae told Jessup breathlessly.

"Is that what you got me out here to tell me?" Jessup said. "Look, Rae, everybody's mother has money hidden. My mother has fifty bucks in a plastic bag in the freezer."

"No," Rae said. "I mean a lot of money."

"Oh, yeah?" Jessup said, almost interested.

"Fifteen hundred dollars," Rae whispered.

It was so cold in the parking lot that Rae could feel her toes freezing through her wool socks and her boots. But she didn't dare hurry Jessup; she just watched as he stood there and lit a cigarette and thought about her mother's money.

"I'll tell you what we'll do," Jessup said finally. "We'll keep that money in mind."

Rae didn't know whether to feel disappointed or relieved—

she had half expected Jessup to suggest she go right home and steal the money that night. But even if Carolyn's bankroll was safe for now, when Rae walked Jessup down to the bus stop, she knew she had betrayed her mother. She told herself it didn't matter; after all, her mother was her enemy now. And in no time Rae forgot all about the money—although maybe she let herself forget because she knew that Jessup was remembering. And two years later, when Rae was nearly eighteen and they were about to leave Massachusetts together, Jessup reminded her.

"I want you to take that money now," he whispered.

Jessup's arm was around her and they were sitting in the dark, on the bleachers behind the high school. Rae found herself wishing that she had never told him about the money in the first place. But when she suggested they didn't really need it, Jessup took his arm away from her, so quickly you'd think he'd been stung.

"Listen, I've had that money in mind all along," he told her. "If you want us to get a car we need that money." Jessup had been working at gas stations and construction sites ever since he left high school. "How much money do you think I earn?" he asked Rae now. "If you think I earn enough to buy a car, think again. Your mother doesn't need that money, Rae. We do."

Rae swore she would do it. But for days she put it off. If she imagined she was giving her mother some extra time to move the money to a new hiding place, it just didn't work. When Rae finally went to the bureau to check, she discovered that the wallet was in the same exact place, and there was more cash than before, twenty-two hundred dollars. The night before they planned to leave, Rae telephoned Jessup and told him she couldn't do it.

"Oh, great," Jessup said. "Here we go. This is just like when you tried to kill yourself with the nail file. You've got to learn if you're going to do something you've got to do it right. Do you think I want to hitchhike down south with some underage minor whose parents can have me put in jail? Think about it," Jessup told her, "and you'll soon see the attraction of having a car."

Rae admitted that she saw the attraction.

"If we leave Boston together we do it right, or not at all," Jessup said.

Rae could hear him breathing into the receiver. She knew that he had pulled the phone into the hallway so that his mother wouldn't overhear; he was standing there, waiting for her answer—and waiting was definitely something he did not like to do. There was no doubt in Rae's mind that, given one good reason, he would leave her behind.

"It's totally up to you," Jessup told her.

It was her decision, and she chose a night when the sky was so clear that the stars seemed no farther away than the rooftops. As her parents slept, Rae went into their room, carefully opened the dresser drawer, and took out the leather wallet. After that they were able to do it right, just the way Jessup wanted. They bought the Oldsmobile and drove to Maryland, and they never once went back. But even after seven years, whenever Rae couldn't sleep she blamed her mother. On those nights, Rae could open every window in the apartment and still feel haunted by the scent of her mother's Chanel perfume. The odor was everywhere, in the sheets and the curtains, in the dishwater and in every kitchen cabinet. And even though Rae knew it was impossible for Carolyn to have tracked her down after all this time, she found herself searching through the closets and kneeling to peer under the bed—and there were times when she actually believed she might find someone hiding.

The scent of Chanel was particularly strong on that Monday when Rae came in late to work.

"Did you have some woman up here?" she asked Freddy Contina.

"I wish," Freddy said.

Rae turned the air conditioner to fan and opened some windows. It was somehow much worse to smell that phantom perfume during the day; at night there seemed the possibility of an explanation: the woody scent of the bamboo outside the kitchen window, a neighbor's cologne filtering through the walls, the terrible power of nightmares.

"Speaking of someone being up here," Freddy said, "I don't want Jessup in my office while I'm gone."

Freddy acquired films in Europe and redubbed them; he was leaving that day for Germany, and whenever he was away Rae invited Jessup up for lunch. Although the last time, when Freddy was in Italy, Jessup didn't touch his food—he spent the entire hour going through the accounts file, and there wasn't a thing Rae could do to stop him.

"Never bring your personal life into the office," Freddy advised.

"What have you got against Jessup?" Rae asked.

The two men had met only once; Jessup had asked so many questions you'd think he was interviewing Freddy for a job.

"He's the mass-murderer type," Freddy said.

"What's that supposed to mean?" Rae asked, offended.

"Or maybe the lone-assassin type," Freddy reconsidered. "I can just see him up in his room, writing in his diary and polishing his rifle."

The idea of Jessup's keeping a diary made Rae laugh.

"You don't know Jessup," she said.

"That's just it," Freddy said. "I don't want to know him, and I don't want him in my office, Rae."

As soon as the car came for Freddy, Rae telephoned Jessup. She was planning to order up from the deli on the corner and put it on Freddy's account, but Jessup was out on a job and no one seemed to know when he'd be back. Rae could have ordered something for herself, but she felt the urge to escape from the office. She had found a woman's turquoise earring on the couch in Freddy's office, but the scent of Chanel was so unnaturally strong that even if Freddy had spent all night with a woman who had doused herself with perfume the aroma would have been gone by now. And yet there it was, in the filing cabinets and the carpeting, just as if Carolyn was in the office. And so Rae went out, even though the air itself was orange and so thick it seemed as if thousands of butterflies had settled above Hollywood Boulevard.

The minute she left the building, Rae knew she had made a mistake. It was noon, and so hot that the few people there were on the sidewalk seemed stunned. When Rae walked past a jewelry store she found herself staring at a tray of gold chains in the window. In all the years they had been together Jessup had never given her any jewelry, not even a cheap silver chain or a semiprecious stone. All at once, Rae ached for a ruby ring. She nearly walked inside and asked to look at a tray of uncut stones, but suddenly she felt as if she was drowning. On the hot sidewalk, in the middle of a city built out of the desert, she was going under. Maybe it was just that she couldn't get enough air in her lungs, or that the shadows along the boulevard were deep blue. The edges of things had begun to blur, and had she been submerged in ten feet of murky water it wouldn't have been any harder to take another step.

This had happened to Rae once before, when she was seventeen and had come down with pneumonia. Even after she was released from the hospital everything looked funny, as if bleach had been added to the air, and a hazy filter hung between Rae and the rest of the world. Jessup telephoned her every night, but after he'd called, he hadn't had much to say. They stayed on the phone for hours, in silence, as if the only way for them to communicate was by telepathy. But once, Jessup had actually said that he missed her.

"What?" Rae had said, certain that she'd misunderstood.

"Are you trying to embarrass me?" Jessup had said. "I said it once, don't ask me to repeat it."

There was something about her illness that made Rae fear she would never get well. She could only see white things: the sheets on her bed, the cream-colored walls, the ruffled curtains at her window. Everything else was fading; when she squinted, she couldn't make out the titles of the books on the shelf.

"I think I may be dying," Rae told Jessup one night when he called. She could practically hear him smirking. "I mean it," Rae said. "I think I may be going blind."

"I'll tell you what your problem is," Jessup said. "I'm not there, and the only thing worth seeing is me."

A few days later a dozen roses arrived. Carolyn considered throwing them out; even though there was no card, she knew who they were from. But she made the mistake of opening the cardboard box, and once she saw the roses she couldn't bring herself to put them in the trash. Instead, she filled a tall glass vase with water and carried them upstairs. As soon as she saw the expression on Rae's face when those flowers were brought in, Carolyn knew that she had lost her daughter.

All that week Rae watched the roses, and as they turned from scarlet to a deep, mysterious purple, she felt her vision returning. But when she was allowed to go out again, and she shyly thanked Jessup for the flowers, he acted as if he didn't know what she was talking about. By then, the roses had withered and Carolyn had tossed them into the trash, and Rae was left wondering if she had imagined the glass vase on her night table. After all, she had imagined other things when her fever was at its highest: a plane that was circling above the ceiling turned out to be just a buzz in her head; a green lion that sat by her clothes closet was only a sweater that had fallen onto the floor. It was possible that there had never even been flowers in her room, and once she was well again, roses really seemed too trivial a thing for Jessup to send.

Even though she had no fever now, Rae couldn't continue on to Musso Frank's, where she'd planned to put her lunch on Freddy's tab. The sidewalk was like quicksand, the next corner seemed miles away. Rae ducked into the closest doorway, the entrance to a place called The Salad Connection. When she leaned against the plate-glass window she could feel the shudder of an air conditioner's motor; each time a customer walked through the door a rush of cold air escaped, then was swallowed by the heat of the boulevard. Quickly, Rae began to count. She hoped that by the time she reached one hundred, she'd feel strong enough to walk back to the office and lie down in the dark. But she hadn't even gotten to thirty when she noticed a sign offering free psychic readings every Wednesday and Friday. And that was when Rae stopped counting.

Ten years earlier, when Rae and her mother were engaged in the worst of their fighting about Jessup, they had gone to a tearoom near the Copley Plaza Hotel to have their fortunes read. They'd been arguing about the curfew Rae always ignored, when Carolyn had thrown up her hands, turned, and walked into the tearoom. Rae had followed and they waited, side by side and in silence, until the fortune-teller signaled them to a table. The fortune-teller was hidden beneath fringed shawls and thick rouge; she offered them poppyseed cakes and mint tea, then proceeded with a reading that was dead wrong. To Carolyn, who had a real distaste for boats, she promised a sea voyage. For Rae, a miserable student, there was a scholar's future. Rae and her mother had looked at each other across the table; in spite of themselves, they smiled. Clearly, this fortune-teller would tell them whatever she imagined they wanted to hear. Of course Rae asked about Jessup. "What about my boyfriend? Will we stay together?"

"Oh, yes," the fortune-teller had said, and for a moment Rae saw her mother draw back. "Your boyfriend," the fortune-teller had gone on, "is tall and handsome and extremely shy. Polite, wonderful with children, could become a doctor or a lawyer—an all-around darling boy."

That misreading had made Rae and Carolyn so giddy that they'd fallen out the door of the tearoom and into each other's arms. Afterward it was a joke between them: when things seemed dark there was always a place near the Copley Plaza Hotel where it was possible to hear good news for only five dollars.

Good news was exactly what Rae wanted to hear right now, so she went to The Salad Connection, past a buffet table offering only the coolest food—lettuce leaves, cucumber, slices of avocado. Sitting in a leatherette booth, she ordered lunch and decided to skip dessert—if Jessup was thinking about gaining weight, she might as well think about it too. After she'd finished her salad, the waitress brought an empty cup and a pot of Darjeeling tea. There was a white business card on the edge of the saucer:

LILA GREY
47 Three Sisters Street
Readings and Advice - Limited Private Consultations
25 dollars per hour

Good news, Rae saw, had gotten more expensive.

After scanning the room for the fortune-teller, Rae realized that the psychic was at the next table. She had expected something more than a few silver bangle bracelets and a small silk turban. The psychic appeared to be in her forties, with thick gray hair cut on an angle at her jawline, so that when she leaned over to peer into a teacup no client could see her expression or her eyes. But across the aisle separating them Rae could see the psychic's hands resting on a tabletop, and the long, delicate fingers made Rae uneasy. A woman who picked up a teacup so cautiously might actually be searching for more than good news.

By the time the psychic sat down across from Rae it was nearly one o'clock, and Rae had the sense that if she weren't careful she might just believe anything she was told. Out on Hollywood Boulevard it was now so hot that the asphalt melted. Whenever people crossed the street their shoes got coated with tar, and the smell of tar made them remember summers in whatever town they grew up in, and they found themselves yearning for lemonade, just as they had on hot days back home when the air hung above them and clouds had the burning, sooty edge of August. Inside the restaurant the air conditioner was turned up higher, and as the psychic raised her arm to pour the tea, Rae felt an odd chill along the backs of her legs.

"You can ask me anything," Lila Grey, the psychic said. "Just don't ask me when the heat wave will break because I don't do weather."

The fortune-teller in Boston certainly hadn't asked them for questions; she had taken one look and had quickly decided what they wanted to hear.

"I'll bet everybody just pours out their whole life story to you," Rae guessed.

"Not really," Lila Grey said.

"I'll bet once they start talking about themselves, they can't stop," Rae insisted.

Lila Grey, who had three more tables to go, a dentist appointment in the late afternoon, and a stop at the market before she went home, was not as careful as she might have been. She might have at least looked at her client, but instead she glanced down at her watch. While she thought about having dinner with her husband that evening, out on the patio where it was cooler, Rae just couldn't seem to stop talking.

"You know, maybe they've got a boyfriend, and they don't know if he's really in love with them . . ."

Lila Grey cut her off. "Is that your question?" she asked.

Rae leaned her head against the booth and considered. "I guess it is," she said finally.

"If you don't drink your tea, we'll never know the answer, will we?" the psychic suggested.

As Rae gulped the lukewarm tea, Lila Grey finally took the time to look at her. The booth suddenly seemed uncomfortable, if only because there was now the odor of some strong perfume that was a little too sweet. When she had drained the cup, Rae offered it to the psychic. Lila Grey knew that something was wrong as soon as she touched the handle. She couldn't even bring herself to lift the cup. Already the tea leaves had begun to settle, and Lila was certain that if she hesitated, even for an instant, she would soon see the outline of the darkest symbol you can find at the bottom of a cup. She pushed the teacup away, then quickly reached for a saucer which she placed over its mouth.

Rae leaned forward. "What is it?" she said.

Lila had always been able to identify the women she had to avoid. The first time the symbol had appeared during a reading she'd taken it as a warning; the second time she'd been tricked by the absence of a wedding band on her client's left hand and by the dim light in her own living room. She shoved the teacup even farther away, and each one of her silver bracelets slipped down to her wrist. The effect was a sound like a wind chime, one you hear from a very great distance when you're in the center of the desert and are out of everything: water and hope and luck.

Rae's throat was dry. "It's something awful, isn't it?" she whispered.

Lila didn't answer. And after all, what was this woman's unhappiness to her; she had seen misery before, and she'd reworked it, turning bad luck into whatever fortune her client wanted to hear. But this was a fortune no one deserved.

Lila knew enough not to look at Rae. She concentrated and

closed her eyes. A wall of blue ice sprang up around her, it was hard as diamonds, impossible to penetrate. Lila was still there in the booth at the restaurant, but she was moving farther and farther away from Rae. She had thought she'd lost the ability to escape, but all Lila had to do was imagine that she was a crow. Her wings were so black they looked wet; beneath her the earth was a small blue globe. Her feathers were unfolding, one by one; and the air was as thin and cold and as pure as glass.

"Please, tell me what you see," Rae called to Lila, but her voice was tiny, as if she was standing at the edge of the planet calling up into the limitless sky.

"Even if it's horrible, I don't care. I want to know," Rae called.

Her words were pieces of crystal, and Lila was too far away to be pulled back down. To her, gravity was nothing. She could feel the moonlight on her feathers, that cold, white light. It was so beautiful and lonely; it was impossible to be touched by another soul. And with the compassion of one so very far away, Lila looked back down at Rae; she knew the mercy in not telling more than the smallest shred of truth.

"It's nothing so horrible," Lila Grey said. "It's just that I see you won't be able to sleep tonight."

⋙

That night, Jessup didn't come home. Rae tried to tell herself that the studio had forced him to work overtime, but she knew no one could force Jessup into anything, and they certainly couldn't stop him from making one phone call. If early in the evening Rae suspected Jessup might be cheating on her, by midnight it no longer mattered. She'd forgive anything, as long as he came home.

Turning on the radio just made things worse. People in

Hollywood were warned to keep their windows closed at night if they didn't have screens. A band of wild dogs gone crazy with thirst roamed the boulevards; they had begun to push open back doors and circle houses. On Sweetzer Avenue, in a backyard where birds of paradise grew, the dogs had attacked a six-year-old boy in a fight for his wading pool. By the time the police had arrived the boy's neck was broken. They had managed to shoot a collie, and when an autopsy was performed the oddest things were found in its stomach: a silk scarf; small bones, which had not yet been identified; blue water the color of sapphires; three gold rings.

At two in the morning, Rae was certain she heard the dogs outside her window. The trash cans rattled and fell, and something that sounded like claws hit against the cement walkway. Rae double-locked her windows, and she huddled in an armchair where Jessup usually sat to watch her undress for bed. Tonight, Rae didn't take off her clothes, because she could tell already, long before she watched the sky grow light, that the psychic had been right.

At seven the next morning Rae made a pot of coffee, and as she poured herself a cup she noticed that her hand shook. She went back to the armchair and waited, and at seven forty-five she finally got what she was waiting for. The telephone rang, and she picked up the receiver before the first ring was through. But after she answered, Rae found she couldn't speak; staying awake all night had robbed her of her voice.

"Rae, are you there?" she heard Jessup say.

She could tell from the metallic sound of his voice that he was calling from a phone booth. At the very least, he wasn't in another woman's bedroom.

"Are you going to speak to me, or what?" Jessup asked.

"I'll speak to you," Rae agreed, and she was amazed by how calm she sounded.

Whenever he hurt her, Jessup acted like he was the one who'd been wronged.

"I didn't come home last night," Jessup said now. "If you bothered to notice."

"Oh, I noticed, all right," Rae said.

Usually, not pressuring Jessup was the right thing to do—but now it backfired, and by the time Rae's voice traveled to the broiling metal phone booth where Jessup was standing, the cool flatness of her tone infuriated him. He decided it was his right to be cruel.

"I'll give you a hint as to where I am," he said. "I'm in the desert."

She knew he expected her to question him.

"Do you mind telling me in what state?"

"California," Jessup said. "Outside Barstow. You think it's hot where you are."

"Do you mind telling me with who?"

"With who what?" Jessup said. He was enjoying this, she could tell.

"Who are you with?" Rae said.

"Maybe I just wanted to see the desert," Jessup said. "Maybe I wanted to be by myself."

Jessup let her sit there in agony for a moment, and then he told her the truth—he was out with a location company that had needed a driver at the last minute. He actually seemed to think this announcement warranted congratulations.

"That's the reason you didn't come home?" Rae asked.

"Every jerk in the world is making a movie, and I'm driving them around," Jessup said. "Do you think that's fair?"

Rae found herself wondering if it was the coffee that now made her feel so sick.

"Rae?" Jessup said. "Are you still there?"

That was when she knew.

"You're not coming home," Rae said, "are you?"

"The shooting schedule is eight weeks, and I think that's enough time for me to set up my own deal with the producer. I don't see why I couldn't direct."

"Tell me right now, Jessup," Rae said. "Are you coming home or not?"

"Well, sure I am," Jessup said. "Eventually."

The future was so close Rae could feel it; it hung from the white stucco ceiling, and draped itself across the furniture.

"How can you do this to me?" she asked.

"Wait a minute," Jessup said. "Don't start pulling this guilt shit on me. Maybe I want to be somebody, Rae—this is a chance for me."

"Oh, really?" Rae said. "What about me?"

"What about you?" Jessup said, surprised.

She hung up on him. Even after she turned on the cold water in the shower and stood under the spray, Rae could still hear the crash of the phone receiver hitting against its cradle. She stayed in the shower until she was shivering, but after she turned off the water, she felt too exhausted to move. She sat down in the tub and cried. It wasn't so much that Jessup had left her, it was that after seven years together, Rae felt as if she had never had him in the first place. Outside, the bamboo that grew near the apartment building swayed in the hot wind; when the stalks rubbed together you could swear you heard singing. How could it be that Jessup now seemed like nothing more than a stranger who had telephoned from the desert? Unless he was someone she had dreamed up, and in that case Rae had been sleepwalking for seven years. And she could sit in that empty bathtub from today until tomorrow, and that still didn't change the fact that only the most dangerous of men would go off and leave you in Los Angeles, to wake up alone.

->>>

Outside the front door of a bungalow on Three Sisters Street was a white arbor where roses bloomed all year long. It certainly wasn't Lila Grey who took care of them; it was all she could do to remember to water the potted geraniums out on the patio. Her husband, Richard, was the one who took care of the yard, and the truth was, he didn't have much luck. The lemon tree out back was crooked, ivy crept into the windows, the hibiscus dropped its salmon-colored flowers on the walkway.

The entire block seemed ill-fated; once it had been an estate belonging to three young women, a gift from one of the early directors to his sisters. But the gift had not been enough for them; they'd withered there, grown old and sick, and finally they'd refused to leave their house. When the block was sold at auction in the thirties, the grounds were so overgrown that bulldozers had been brought in, leveling everything. Bungalows were built, and as the neighborhood slipped—more crime and more roofs that needed patching—the one thing that remained constant was that it was nearly impossible to grow anything on Three Sisters Street.

But Lila's husband was a BMW mechanic, and he insisted that plants had to be simpler than a German-made car. He refused to give up. During the heat wave, when the city allowed hoses to be turned on for only an hour each day, Richard became a maniac for water. He scooped out bathwater and soapy dishwater with a metal pail and rationed a little for each of the trees. He joked that working with plants was a part of his heritage—his father was a Shinnecock Indian who had long ago been a migrant worker, his mother a Russian Jew who could never keep a begonia alive on her window sill. When Richard was nine, his parents bought a gas station on the North Fork of Long Island, and Lila knew that the only things that had ever grown there were wildflowers and weeds.

Sometimes, when Richard was out mowing the grass, Lila could look out the window and actually see the grass turning brown beneath the blades. She had the urge to run outside and beg him to give up: they could brick over the lawn, extend the slate patio, chop down the twisted trees and use them for firewood on rainy winter nights. But Lila forced herself to keep quiet, and when she went outside it was only to take Richard a glass of lemonade. If he wanted to believe he could turn the lawn green and force strawberries to appear on the few spindly plants, who was she to tell him he was wrong? But anyone could see that the only thing that would ever grow in their garden were the huge scarlet roses, and they seemed not to need any care at all, not even water—in the neighborhood it was rumored that the roses had once grown by the Sisters' front door, that they were the last remnants of the hundreds that had once been on the estate.

Lila held with the idea of letting people believe whatever they wanted, no matter how foolish. Her husband believed at least a dozen false things about her, and that was just the way Lila wanted it. Just as Richard imagined himself to be the first man she had ever loved, he believed his wife to be psychic. If he came home early and found Lila giving a private reading in the living room—the lamps turned down, the red silk cloth spread out on the table—he tiptoed down the hallway. Lila didn't see any point in explaining that her readings depended less on the arrangement of a little water and Darjeeling than they did on the dark circles under a client's eyes, or the way some people twisted their wedding bands on their fingers, as though the gold irritated their skin. Those moments when she felt some sort of strange, pure knowledge she credited to intuition, no more and no less than anyone else might have. Privately, she felt her clients' preoccupation with the future was foolish, a sport for schoolgirls and lonely women. But the past, that was another matter. The past could press down on you until every bit of air was forced out of your lungs; if you weren't careful, it could swallow you up entirely, leaving nothing but a few fragile bones, a silver bracelet, ten moon-shaped fingernails.

Lately, Lila couldn't look in a mirror without seeing a young girl whose hair was so thick she had to brush it twice a day with a wire brush made in France. When she stood at the sink washing dishes, she could feel herself falling, pulled backward into a well so deep it might be impossible to ever climb back out once you let go. It was pure luck that Richard had managed to pull her back each time. He'd simply be looking for a magazine or a pair of pliers, he'd decide to have a piece of pie and slam the refrigerator door. That was all it took—his presence would bring Lila back and there she'd be, safe in her own kitchen.

But at night she was too far away for Richard to reach her, and Lila found herself dreaming about the apartment in New York where she'd grown up. It was a place where there were heavy drapes on all the windows, and at night the steam heat made a peculiar crying sound that quickened your heart. Lila was eighteen and still living at home. In the mornings she attended an acting class held in a deserted theater on the Lower East Side, but when her parents had had enough—talk of Broadway and Hollywood until they were dizzy—they insisted she find a job. Lila became a waitress at a restaurant on Third Avenue, and it was there, in the late afternoons, that an old woman named Hannie read fortunes in exchange for fifty cents. The cooks in the kitchen were afraid to tell Hannie to leave—they told each other that she wore long, black dresses to hide the fact that underneath she had chicken's legs. Instead of knees she had knobby yellow flesh, around her ankles there were white feathers. Her eyes, the waitresses all agreed, could put you under a spell and before you knew it you'd be barking like a dog.

Whenever Lila brought over the pots of hot water and raisin buns Hannie ordered, she made certain never to look the old lady in the eye. Lila couldn't help but notice that for every one in the restaurant who feared Hannie, there was a client who thought the world of her. In June so many girls about to become brides wanted to hear their fortunes that a line formed outside the restaurant on Third Avenue. Nearly all of her clients were women, and each had a slightly dazed look on her face as Hannie opened the purple tin in which she carried her tea. There were times when everyone in the restaurant had to work hard to ignore the weeping that came from that rear table, and on days when a bad fortune was read, everyone in the restaurant grew moody, and to cheer themselves the waitresses munched on chocolate bars, and butter crumb cakes, and figs.

Lila found herself drawn to the old fortune-teller. Each time she took a break, she wound up at a table in the rear of the restaurant, and as she drank a Coke with lemon and ice, she listened in to the tea-leaf readings. It was oddly thrilling to face in the other direction and still hear a tale of heartbreak or hope right behind your back. But though she could hear each client's complaints quite clearly, Lila could never make out Hannie's advice. The words were all garbled, too private and low; and Lila found herself moving closer and closer to the fortune-teller's table, until one day Lila realized that it wasn't the wall her elbow was resting on, but Hannie's bony spine. Lila moved away in terror, convinced that before the night was through she'd be howling at the moon. But the old woman smiled at her, then motioned for her to come to her table, and Lila could hardly refuse.

"As long as you're eavesdropping," Hannie said when Lila had sat down across from her, "you might as well sit here and learn something."

From that day on, Lila sat with the old fortune-teller whenever she could, and she no longer had to strain to hear Hannie's advice. Every time a new symbol appeared in a teacup during a reading, Hannie jabbed Lila's arm with her finger. On the back of a menu Hannie listed the most important signs: A flock of birds was always sorrow. The flat line of a horizon meant travel. A four-pointed star was a man who would betray you, and a five-pointed star was a man who was true.

Lila began to practice her new skill on her family and friends. She had a natural talent for guessing what was wrong with someone's life, and in no time she had a following. Some of her mother's friends slipped her a dollar for good luck when she read for them; the other girls who took classes at the theater brought in Thermoses of hot water and tins of loose tea and they offered Lila earrings and hair clips in return for their future. In the restaurant there were some clients who began to prefer Lila's readings to Hannie's, and they sat patiently, ordering cheese danish or mushroom soup, until Lila could take her break. But even after several months, whenever Lila looked into a client's cup she saw only murky tea leaves, never the future. She began to feel that each time she gave a reading she was committing a robbery. No matter how hard she tried, she couldn't see into the future, and when she asked Hannie why this was, the old woman made a sound in the back of her throat that startled Lila, for it sounded exactly like a chicken clucking.

"You could see the future if you wanted to," Hannie said. "You've just decided to ignore it."

Lila had just fallen in love with her acting teacher, and the future was practically all she did think about.

"Answer me one question," Hannie demanded. "Why do you think it is that after all this time you never asked me to do a reading for you?"

"Maybe I don't believe in readings," Lila admitted. "Maybe that's why I never really see anything."

"You think that's the reason?" Hannie said. The old woman's black skirt crackled as she leaned forward and took Lila's hands in her own. That day the luncheon special in the restaurant was pot roast, and the smell of burnt onions was everywhere. It stuck in your throat and brought tears to your eyes. All afternoon, Lila had been wondering if she'd have time to go home after work and wash her hair before she met Stephen. Stephen not only taught acting—he was the second lead in a play off Broadway, and every Thursday night they met in his small dressing room. Lila had already decided to wear a cotton dress with a lace collar, but now, with Hannie holding her hands, Lila wondered if she should wear something warmer. Suddenly she was freezing, and when Hannie closed Lila's fingers, so that each hand made a fist, Lila could feel the chill all the way from her fingertips to her heart.

"Let me give you some good advice," Hannie said. "Be careful—otherwise you may discover that you've lost the one you love best."

But at eighteen the only thing more impossible than being careful is listening to an old woman's advice. "You can see the future," Hannie had insisted. "All you have to do is open your eyes." There was the smell of burnt onions, the rattle of dishes in the kitchen, the rustling of the fortune-teller's black skirts.

And now whenever Lila dreamed, it was of New York. When she woke, she still heard the steam heat, and as she sat in the dark and watched her husband sleep she couldn't help but wonder if perhaps she did have some talent as a fortune-teller after all. There was no doubt in her mind that Rae Perry was the age her own daughter would have been. And she hoped that Hannie had been wrong all those years ago, because if this was what seeing into the future was like, Lila could do very well without that gift.

⋙

Jessup had been gone for a week when Rae began to suspect that even more was wrong than she'd thought. A rush of cool air swept the city, but Rae barely noticed the change in the weather—she still felt burning hot. She drank pitchers of water and took her temperature, convinced that she must have some terrible fever. During the day she couldn't stay awake: she locked the office door and curled up on Freddy's couch. Then at night, she couldn't sleep. She tossed and turned until the sheets were as twisted as snakes. She grew afraid of the dark, afraid of dreams and noises in the night, and clouds that covered the moon. No matter where she turned in her apartment she always found herself staring at the telephone, even though she already knew that Jessup wouldn't be calling her again.

On the day she went to see Lila Grey, Rae started out to go grocery shopping, and had made it as far as the vegetable aisle. But the checkout lines were all too long, and the peaches were bruised, and the milk not yet delivered, and Rae wound up deserting her cart near a display of radishes and scallions. After that it was easy—she didn't even have to think about it. Instead of turning right and walking home, she turned left, and in no time at all she found herself on Three Sisters Street.

Rae knocked on the front door, but as she stood on the porch the scent of the roses overwhelmed her, and before she knew it she was weak in the knees. By the time Lila opened the door, Rae was doubled over.

"I don't know what happened," Rae said as Lila helped her inside. "I just collapsed."

"And you decided to do it here," Lila said.

Actually, Lila felt panicky, and the only reason she went into the kitchen for some water was to get Rae on her feet and out of the house as quickly as possible. Lila stood at the sink and gulped down a glass of water herself before rinsing out the glass and filling it for Rae. In the living room, Rae took the water greedily, and she didn't notice that Lila was staring at her until she was done.

"I came to have my fortune read," Rae explained.

Lila was wearing blue slacks and a white cotton shirt. Without her turban and her silver bracelets she looked like someone you'd meet on line in the market, and Rae felt somewhat ridiculous asking her to see into the future.

"I work by appointment," Lila said sternly.

She would have said anything then to get rid of Rae.

"It's an emergency," Rae confided. "The man I'm in love with left me."

"If you consider that an emergency, half the women in Hollywood would be here right now."

Rae could feel herself sinking. "You won't believe this," she said. "I think I'm going to faint."

"Oh, no you don't," Lila said. "Not here."

Lila went back to the kitchen for a bottle of vinegar to hold under Rae's nose. When some of Rae's color returned, Lila went to the front door and opened it.

"You're right—I need air," Rae said gratefully. "And maybe some more water."

"Anything else?" Lila snapped, taking the empty glass.

"A cracker?" Rae called after her.

Lila brought out a box of Wheat Thins and a fresh glass of water. She told herself that in less than five minutes Rae would be deposited back on the street.

"This is fabulous," Rae said as she took out a cracker and bit it in half.

"I don't think you understand," Lila said. "I do readings by appointment only. I can't have anyone just walk in off the street."

"Oh," Rae said. She had the other half of her cracker in her mouth, but now she was too self-conscious to chew. The Wheat Thin expanded, swelling her cheek.

If Rae hadn't looked so pathetic, Lila might not have sat down in the rocking chair and reconsidered.

"When did he leave you?" Lila asked.

"A week ago," Rae said. "If I knew he was coming back I wouldn't mind waiting. I really wouldn't."

"Twenty-five dollars," Lila said. "And I don't take personal checks."

Rae reached into her purse and counted out two tens and a five.

"I hope you understand that you may not like what I have to say," Lila warned her.

"I don't care," Rae said. "I'm ready for anything. You can tell me everything you know."

Lila had no intention of doing that. This reading was not for Rae, but for herself. A simple thing like going into the kitchen and filling the teapot was suddenly an act of courage. Lifting the teapot onto the stove's front burner seemed to take forever; time was moving in that odd way it does when you are terrified of what may happen next, and your senses are slow and dull. As the water began to heat up, Lila looked out into the yard. Richard stood on a stepladder and picked lemons off the tree. A neighbor called across the hedge and Lila could hear the two men discuss fertilizer. But after a while Lila could no longer hear their voices; she couldn't hear the thud of lemons as they dropped into a wicker basket. Instead, she heard the flare of Hannie's stiff black skirts as the old woman shrank back and moved against the wall. Lila had brought Stephen to the restaurant just to meet Hannie, but now she could see that she shouldn't have. Hannie looked right through Stephen, even after he had given her his most winning smile, the one that worked on nearly everyone. When he asked the old woman for a reading, she laughed out loud—but it was a hollow sound that echoed in the kitchen and made the cooks put down the knives they were using to cut up potatoes for soup and stare at each other uneasily.

"Lila talks about you all the time," Stephen said to Hannie. "Don't tell me that now you won't tell my fortune."

Hannie hadn't answered. Instead, she gave him one long look, and the heat she threw off nearly burnt a hole right through him.

"I don't need tea leaves to tell you his future," Hannie said to Lila, just as if Stephen weren't there.

Stephen stood up; he went to the counter and didn't look over his shoulder. And there Lila was, in the middle. Now, Hannie wouldn't look at her either, and when Lila reached for the old woman's hand, Hannie's fingers seemed to retract, and Lila was left holding on to the table. Lila made her decision then and there; she got up and followed Stephen to the counter—although when he put his arm around her, Lila swore he was doing it for spite, more for Hannie's benefit than anything else. Of course, Hannie's rejection only made Stephen even more curious, and from that time on he was after Lila to read his tea leaves. But even then, Lila must have had some hint as to what would happen, because she refused him again and again.

Stephen had grown up in Florida, and when she was with him Lila found herself dreaming about oranges and salt water and endless white beaches where there wasn't a soul. There was nothing she would not do for him, and when Stephen decided that Hannie was a bad influence—a madwoman who could do nothing but harm an impressionable girl—Lila stopped sitting at the old woman's table during her breaks. Soon, Lila stopped telling fortunes; she threw away the tins of tea she kept in her mother's kitchen, she told her aunts and her girlfriends it had just been a game. But as she served customers in the restaurant, she could feel the old woman watching her and she grew clumsy, spilling tumblers of water and bowls of boiling-hot soup. What she missed more than anything were those late hours when business in the restaurant was slow, and she'd sit at Hannie's table, asking for another story about the village where the fortune-teller had grown up—a town nearly cut off from the rest of the world by forests where nothing but pine and wild lavender grew. Now she dreaded that time of the day, and although she tried to stand up to the disappointment on Hannie's face, it grew clear that the only solution to the distance between the two women was more distance. Lila quit her job at the restaurant and took another, at a Chock Full o' Nuts around the corner, where there wasn't the slightest danger that a waitress might talk to a customer.

Lila had to admit there were problems in her love affair: Stephen was married. But people did divorce, and all his marriage meant to Lila was that they couldn't go to his apartment. Instead, they met in a dressing room, or in the borrowed apartment of an actress friend who was often on the road. They stole things when they were in the actress's apartment: tins of sardines, pints of cream, earrings made out of glass. These small thefts bound them together, and when they were in the actress's bed Lila could almost envision their future together. They would sleep late on Sundays once he was free, a kiss would last forever, every cup of tea they drank would be sweetened with two spoons of sugar and utterly free of tea leaves.

But most of the time they were forced to meet in the dressing room, and whenever they were there it didn't seem to matter how hard Lila tried not to look—she always found herself staring at the small photograph of Stephen's wife. Not that he had ever lied to her or led her on. When the run of his play ended, Stephen planned to go to Maine for the summer—his wife's family had a house there. Stephen called it a cottage, but Lila had seen a photograph. It was a huge white house on the edge of a peninsula which jutted into a bay that froze solid from October to May. In her dreams, Lila was haunted by this house; a cold wind moved through the rooms turning every object to ice. Even the arms of the wooden rocking chairs on the porch were coated with frost. That summer house became

Lila's enemy, and she knew that it was just a matter of time before it claimed Stephen and Lila would be left with even less than she'd had before.

She did everything she could to prolong the run of his play. She used up her salary buying tickets which she gave away to distant cousins and neighbors. Every night she called the box office, and every night more tickets were available. At last, Stephen told her that the play was about to close. A part of Lila believed that if she just had time enough she could persuade Stephen not to leave her for that house in Maine. But the idea of battling that cold, empty house was simply too much, and her weapons too fragile—nothing more than desire and youth. Since she was about to lose him anyway, she decided she wouldn't ruin their last night together. But of course, it was ruined even before it began: when she got to the dressing room, Stephen had already boiled water for tea and he begged her to tell his fortune. Lila knew enough to be sure that if she refused him this time, they would argue and she would wind up in tears. And then Stephen would softly whisper that he could never stand to see a woman cry, and he would ask her to leave. So she sat across from him at a small wicker table and watched him drink his tea, although just the movement of his hand as he reached for the teacup nearly broke her heart.

"I especially want to know if I'll be famous," Stephen said. "Of course, I wouldn't mind being exceedingly rich."

He had come around so that he stood behind Lila. He put his hands on her shoulders and bent down. As he spoke, Lila could feel his breath on her neck. And she knew, even before she looked, that in the center of the teacup there would be a four-pointed star.

Lila told him exactly what he wanted to hear.

"I can see that you'll have everything you ever wanted," she told him, but then, the moment Stephen looked away, Lila dipped her finger in the teacup and stirred up the leaves. She still did not believe in the symbols Hannie had taught her, but it was so much easier to invent a future when the only distraction was the heat of her lover's breath. The predictions she offered Stephen were each more delightful than the next. His children would swim like fish and recite the alphabet before their second birthdays; his summers on that cold, glassy bay would be endless; and as for fame, his name would be remembered forever and ever.

To tease her, Stephen tossed a dollar down on the table, and then he pulled her down on the couch. But although she embraced him, Lila couldn't look at him. Instead, she stared up at a small window that was screened with heavy black mesh. That night the moon was so huge that it broke through the screen and filled the room with light. As they made love, Lila felt her spirit being pulled out of her. The sheet of moonlight was wrapping itself around her. Her bones were as brittle as ice, and the skin beneath her fingernails turned a startling blue. The tighter Stephen held her, the more lost Lila was. She was farther and farther away from the earth, up where the air was so thin it was always winter, and breathing alone hurt your lungs and left tears in your eyes.

When Lila reached up her arms it was the moon she reached for. To embrace this lover she had to leave her body behind. She could see herself on the couch with Stephen—her arms and legs covered with a watery film, her mouth wide open. It seemed a pity for Stephen to think she was there with him. Up in the air she was weightless, and her hair turned into feathers that were so black you couldn't see them against the night. That was when the light entered her, and as it did Lila could see the future. It unfolded to her cell by cell, second by second. At first she thought she heard the rapid flapping of a bird struggling for flight, but when Lila listened closely she knew it was the sound of another heart beating.

The very next evening, Lila waited outside the restaurant at closing time. She couldn't bring herself to go in like some customer off the street, and so she decided to follow the old woman home. It was a cool night, and the air was damp. Lila made sure to stay a block behind Hannie; she was frightened of being discovered, then having to beg for a reading on a street corner. They walked for a very long time, Hannie leading the way through a maze of streets, behind Chelsea, near the river. The streets were made of cobblestones—no one had ever bothered to tar them over. There was no traffic here, not even the underground shudder of the subway. No one lived here except for a few old women who carried their belongings in paper bags and pillowcases, and, in the abandoned buildings, feral cats, quick, underfed animals who hunted for pigeons on the fire escapes.

When Lila could no longer tell east from west, Hannie stopped outside the door of an old rowhouse and let herself in. Lila watched as the lights inside were turned on; in the window sat a huge, tawny cat—no relation to the wild cats on the fire escapes—and, Lila was sure of this, there was the impossibly delicious smell of bread baking. As she stood there, Lila imagined what it would be like to follow Hannie inside: the house would be warm and silent, there would be bread and butter and tea. You could sleep here all night and not even hear the wind. And if others missed you, they'd never find you unless you wanted them to. Not in a million years.

Lila began to think of her own mother, and of her own bedroom, where she had slept every night of her life. She could tell Hannie was waiting for her, but she felt a sudden wave of homesickness. She panicked and began to run. It was dark now, the sky purple at the horizon, and Lila thought she heard an anguished echo from the rowhouse, like a bird caught between wires. She was terrified that she was lost, but she never once stopped running. After a while she began to feel the rumble of buses, and she realized that she was looking up, and that the position of the stars had guided her back to Tenth Avenue.

That night, safe in her own bed, Lila couldn't sleep. The next evening she returned to the restaurant, but this time when she followed Hannie the fortune-teller disappeared around a corner after they crossed Tenth Avenue. Nothing seemed familiar to Lila, and she had to struggle so hard to get out of the maze of streets that by the time she stumbled across the avenue, she was in tears. She knew then that in turning away that first time, she had lost her chance. She was certain that Hannie had seen her and that she no longer trusted Lila, she didn't even want Lila to know where she lived. For weeks Lila tried to get up the nerve to go to the restaurant and see Hannie. She was obsessed with having her fortune read; she was desperate to know what her future would bring, and each day she grew more troubled, and ten times as lonely as she had been the day before. At night she dreamed of Stephen, asleep in a hammock on the porch of that house in Maine. She dreamed of birds and gold wedding rings, and she no longer felt safe in her own bedroom. She stopped taking classes at the theater. The new teacher was nothing compared to Stephen, and besides, Lila already knew, she hadn't any real talent after all. In July she went back to the restaurant, and although she didn't actually go inside, she felt a little braver. By the end of the month Lila was ready to face Hannie, to walk past the row of waitresses and the cooks, and ask to have her tea leaves read. Lila never once guessed that Hannie hadn't seen her and purposely avoided her in the alleys and cobblestone streets, just as she never knew that when the old woman squinted as she read tea leaves it wasn't in order to see the future more clearly, but because she was blind in one eye. Every day, when business was slow, Hannie sat at the rear table, waiting for Lila. But by the time Lila had the courage to come back she hadn't menstruated in two months, and she no longer needed to have her fortune told.

As she waited for the water in the teapot to boil, Lila tried not to think of the old fortune-teller. She watched through the window as her husband climbed down from the stepladder, but all she saw was moonlight, all she heard was the sound of cats' claws on the fire escapes, and the cool, damp air left her shivering.

Outside, Richard turned on the sprinkler. Now that the heat wave had passed, the city had lifted all water restrictions, and in every backyard there was the smell of damp earth. It was a heartbreaking scent, one that left you longing for everything you once had and lost. And although the tea was ready to be served, and Rae was waiting, Lila was really too cold to go back into the living room. Twice Lila had read for pregnant women; both times a small, still child had risen to the surface, before being pulled down into the center of the cup. She had lied, of course, and when she wept her clients had thought it was their good fortune that affected her so. If the symbol appeared a third time, Lila would again fail to mention that the child she saw was not moving, that it did not breathe or open its eyes. Whatever the shape of the tea leaves, Lila would advise Rae of her pregnancy, and tell her nothing more. She would fold her twenty-five-dollar fee into her pocket, and then, after Rae had left, she would stand with her back against the front door and cry. But there was never any hurry when you were about to tell someone that her life would be changed forever, and because the sunlight in the backyard was so warm and bright, Lila slipped out the back door, and she ran across the patio to throw her arms around her husband.

⋙

After the reading, Rae had no one to talk to. Jessup had never believed in friends.

"What's the point?" he had always said. "You get yourself a friend and the first thing they want is to borrow something from you. Next they want to tell you all their troubles. Then look out—because then they're mad that they owe you something, plus you know all their secrets, and they're not so sure they want you knowing so much after all."

What Rae wanted more than anything was a friend, a woman who would tell her that Lila's prediction had been all wrong. But when she really thought about it, she had to admit that there wasn't a friend on earth who could have convinced her that her swollen ankles and the wire stretched tight inside her stomach were anything other than signs of pregnancy. Her period was four weeks late, and she had lost her taste for coffee. What frightened Rae was not being pregnant, but having to tell Jessup about it. Jessup didn't even like to be in the same room with a child. He referred to children as midgets, and he had often suggested that orphans be put out on ice floes and left to drift into the cold, blue sea.

Once before Rae had thought she might have to tell Jessup he would be a father. They were living in a garden apartment in Maryland and it was so hot that September that you never saw any people—everyone stayed where it was air conditioned. It was their first home and Rae wanted it to be perfect. She taught herself how to cook, which was a real accomplishment considering she had learned nothing from her mother. Any time Carolyn started to cook she began to cry—just cutting up a leek or reaching for a bottle of olive oil was enough to set her off. She would have been astounded to discover that her daughter bought fresh blueberries for jam, grew her own tomatoes for gazpacho, melted bars of imported chocolate for mousse. By the time Jessup got home from work the table was always set and candles had been lit. But before she brought the meal to the table, Rae had to wait for Jessup to get ready. He was working with a construction crew building an addition to the local high school, and he came home caked with red dirt. Every evening, while Jessup soaked in the tub, Rae watched the candles burn down and she worried about the high-school girls Jessup was bound to meet. She was sure that if she ever lost him she would stay locked up in the air-conditioned apartment forever; and she always had the feeling she was losing him, no matter how hard she tried to please him.

One night, as they sat down to scallops and fresh string beans, Jessup picked up his fork and moved the food around his plate, as if he didn't know what else to do with it. His skin was dark from working outside, and his eyes were bluer than ever.

"Boy," he said as he touched a bean with the prongs of his fork, "you really go for this stuff, don't you, Rae?"

Rae had spent the morning searching for scallops; a raspberry tart was still baking.

"I thought you'd like scallops," Rae said shyly.

"Me?" Jessup said, surprised. "I'd rather have hamburgers."

Jessup ate a scallop, but Rae could tell he was forcing himself. She never used a cookbook again—after all, there was no point in cooking for someone who couldn't tell the difference between a *gâteau au chocolat* and a defrosted Sara Lee cake. But once she had stopped cooking there wasn't much for her to do but watch the clock and wait for Jessup. Each day when he came home after work, Rae was so relieved that she hadn't lost him that she didn't wait for him to take a bath—she pulled him down onto the living-room floor where they made love, and when they were through Rae's skin was streaked with the red dirt Jessup brought home. Afterward Rae stayed in the living room while Jessup went into the bathroom to run the water in the tub. She could never figure out why she felt so lonely, and whenever Jessup called to her, inviting her into the bathtub, Rae closed her eyes and pretended not to hear him. After a while he must have assumed that she liked to be by herself after they made love, because no matter how much he had wanted her, by the time they were through, he just walked away, as if she were a stranger.

It was right about that time that Rae began to think she was pregnant. There were certainly signs: her period was late and she had gained five pounds. But the oddest thing of all was that Rae suddenly had the desire to talk to her mother. One day, while Jessup was at work, Rae called home. When her mother picked up the receiver and said hello, the sound of her voice cut right through Rae, and she had to force herself to speak.

"It's me," Rae said casually. "I'm in a garden apartment in Maryland."

"I love it," Carolyn said. "Your father always insists you're in California. He's convinced that people like Jessup always wind up on the West Coast."

"Mother," Rae said, just as if a year hadn't passed since they'd last argued, "I didn't call you long distance to talk about Jessup."

"I've tried to understand why you'd run away with him, but I can't," Carolyn said.

"Stop trying," Rae said. "You'll never understand me."

"If you would just call your father at the office and tell him you're sorry. Tell him you made a terrible mistake."

"But I didn't!" Rae said.

"You're never planning to come home," Carolyn said suddenly, "are you?"

"I don't know," Rae admitted.

"It's just as well," Carolyn said. "Your father would never allow it—not unless you proved to him that you had changed."

Rae felt herself grow hot. "And you'd just agree with him?" she said.

Carolyn didn't answer.

"Mother!" Rae said. "Would you agree with him?"

"Yes," Carolyn said. "I would."

Rae could hear the Oldsmobile pull up. She dragged the phone over to the window and lifted up one venetian blind. Jessup got out of the car and took off his blue denim jacket.

"I have to go," Rae told her mother.

"I'm in the middle," Carolyn said. "Don't you see?"

Jessup was at the front door; he knocked once, and when Rae didn't answer he fumbled for the key.

"I just called to let you know I was all right," Rae said, but she wasn't—she'd never felt more alone in her life. Any second Jessup would walk through the door—if he discovered that she had called Boston there might be a scene. He might tell her to take the bus back home if she missed the place so much, and now Rae knew that she couldn't—by now they had gotten rid of the furniture in her bedroom, they had probably changed the locks on all the doors.

"Is that the only reason you called?" Carolyn said in a small voice, as though she actually expected Rae to say that she missed her.

"I really have to go," Rae said, and she hung up the phone and ran to get the door just as Jessup was letting himself in.

That night she couldn't sleep. She went into the living room and sat in the dark, the phone balanced on her lap. She dialed the area code for Boston, and then the number for the local weather report. It was much colder in Boston—forty degrees—and by morning a pale frost would appear on the lawns and between cabbage leaves in backyard gardens. On nights when she couldn't sleep, all Rae had to do was ask Jessup to hold her and he would; he might even sit up with her and watch a movie on TV if she asked the right way. But right then, the only person Rae wanted was her mother. If she closed her eyes she could smell Carolyn's perfume, she could feel how cold the windowpanes were in her third-floor bedroom on nights when the moon was full and a web of ice formed on the glass.

Later, when it was nearly dawn, Rae went into the bathroom. When she discovered a line of blood on her thigh, she sat down on the rim of the tub and cried. The sky had turned pearl gray and the crickets were still calling when Rae got into bed beside Jessup. She could tell he was dreaming; he held on to the pillow so tightly that his knuckles were white. As Rae pulled the sheet over them, Jessup woke up.

"I was dreaming," he said.

"I know," Rae told him. "I was watching you."

"It was summer," Jessup said. "There were a million stars in the sky and I was waiting outside your house, but you didn't see me."

Rae put her arms around him. "I saw you," she told him, but Jessup was already back asleep.

After that night, Rae risked the subject of children every now and then, but Jessup's reaction was always the same.

"Take a good look at me," he would tell her. "Do I look like somebody's father?"

Rae had to admit that he didn't. Even when she really tried she couldn't imagine him getting up at two in the morning, or changing a diaper, or shopping for a crib.

"All a baby will do is come between us," Jessup warned her. "Is that what you want? Because if that's what you want let's go into the bedroom right now and make the biggest mistake we ever made."

But this time there was a difference. This time Jessup wasn't around to convince Rae that it was a mistake. Jessup was out in the desert where the moonlight turned nights colder than any winter in Boston. He was turning in his sleep, unaware that Rae had already decided. Whether he liked it or not he was about to become somebody's father.

→>>

Rae took the bus to Barstow on a day when it was impossible to look at the sky and not think of heaven. After a while there was less traffic and the road opened up. Now, each passenger who got on brought some of the desert into the bus, so that a fine cover of sand drifted across the aisles. Even through the dusty windows you could tell how blue the sky was, and all along the roadside there were tuberous wildflowers that were so sweet they attracted bees the size of a man's hand.

At noon the sky turned white with heat, and Rae saw her first real mirage. There was a line of coyotes along a ridgetop, but when she blinked they disappeared. There was nothing in the distance but pink sand and low violet clouds, and of course it wasn't the right time of day for coyotes anyway. They waited for the temperature to fall before they came down from the mountains. Then they walked in single file, circling deserted adobe houses, making a noise in the back of their throats that made you think they were dying of loneliness.

When Rae got off the bus the air was so dry that it stung. She found a phone booth and called every motel listed; the film crew was registered at the Holiday Inn on Route 17, but the desk clerk told her that everyone had gone out on location. Rae took a cab to the Holiday Inn. She'd hoped to get into Jessup's room so she could take a shower and order room service before he got back, but the desk clerk refused to give her the key. After all, what rights did she have—they weren't even married.

By the time she had ordered a grilled cheese sandwich in the coffee shop, Rae was furious. It seemed as if Jessup had purposely not married her just so that one day she'd be kept out of his room at the Holiday Inn. She had wanted to get married all along, but Jessup felt it was a meaningless act. What difference did a piece of paper make—he pointed out his own father, who hadn't bothered with a divorce from Jessup's mother before disappearing, and then clinched his argument by bringing up Rae's parents, whom he called the most miserable couple on earth.

"We'd be different," Rae had promised. Carolyn had been married in a blue suit, as if she had already given up hope. Rae planned to wear a long white dress.

"We already are different," Jessup had said. "We're not married."

After thinking about it, Rae had panicked—if Jessup died she couldn't even legally arrange for his funeral. Dressed in black, she'd have to stand on a runway at Los Angeles Airport and watch as his body was shipped back to his mother in Boston.

"Don't worry about it," Jessup had told her. "If you're really concerned I'll send my mother a postcard and tell her you get to keep the Oldsmobile and my body."

Rae left the coffee shop and went to sit by the pool. Had she been allowed up to his room, she would have shown him. By now she would have ordered baskets of fruit and chilled champagne. Instead, she found some change at the bottom of her purse and got a soda from the vending machine. The heat rose higher and higher and no one dared to venture out of the air-conditioned rooms, but there she was, on a plastic chaise longue beside the pool—all because he had never bothered to marry her. The fact that he was out on location was what really upset her, because there was absolutely nothing worse than taking a long bus trip and having it end with no one there to meet you.

The last time Rae had taken such a trip, she was eight years old. She and Carolyn were going out to a rented summer house in Wellfleet; they had left a few days early so that everything could be in order by the time Rae's father drove down for the weekend. The trip had been a disaster—Carolyn got sick and the bus driver had to pull off onto the shoulder of Route 3. As the other passengers watched, Carolyn stood on the asphalt and tried to breathe.

"It's nothing serious," she told Rae when she returned, but Rae noticed that her mother was gripping the upholstered seat in front of them, and that her fingers were swollen and white.

By the time they got to Wellfleet, Rae felt sick, too. Carolyn had misplaced the key and they had to climb into the house through an unlatched window. Rae stood in the middle of the dark living room as her mother stumbled over to the wall to find the light switch. She could actually feel the goose bumps rise on her arms and legs. Later, Carolyn made up a bed for her with clean sheets, but Rae couldn't sleep. She could hear crickets and the hum that lightning bugs make when they're trapped in the mesh of a screen window. The walls in the house sagged and creaked, and there was an owl's nest in the chimney so that a muffled hooting echoed from inside the bricks. Carolyn couldn't sleep either; she came into Rae's room late at night and sat at the foot of the bed.

"It's not an accident that you have red hair," Carolyn said. She lit a cigarette, and in the dark the smoke spiraled up to the ceiling. "When I was pregnant with you I bought a pair of red high heels made in Italy. Even though I couldn't really wear them because my feet had swollen, sometimes when I was alone I put them on and just wore them around the house. That's the reason you have red hair."

"No it isn't," Rae said.

The hum of the lightning bugs was growing fainter, although Rae could still see patches of light caught in the window.

"I'll bet you anything it's the reason," Carolyn said.

"What if you had worn purple shoes?" Rae challenged.

"You would have had black hair that was so dark it would look nearly purple at night."

"Green?" Rae asked.

"Pale blond hair that turned green every time you swam in a pool with any chlorine in it."

By the time she fell asleep Rae had forgotten about the business on the bus, and the sound of the owls had become as regular as a heartbeat. But that weekend, when Rae's father drove down, Rae could tell that something was wrong between her parents. Usually, they argued—now they just didn't speak. The silence in the house was suffocating, but then, on Sunday, Rae found something on the front porch that made her think August wouldn't be so terrible after all. It was a cardboard shoebox, and inside was a pair of ruby-colored plastic beach shoes. When Rae slipped them on they fit perfectly, as if they'd been made for her.

She meant to go inside and thank her mother for the gift, but the shoes simply had to be used, so she walked past the salt marsh, down to the beach. Even when she ran into the water she kept her shoes on, and she walked for nearly two miles and didn't come home until dinnertime. Rae went around to the back of the house where she could rinse off her shoes under a metal faucet, but she stopped by a mock orange shrub that was covered with white flowers. Carolyn was out there on the back porch, and she was breathing in that same way she had when she'd asked the bus driver to pull over. Rae's father was standing behind the screen door to the kitchen, looking out.

"If you're so miserable why don't you leave," he told Carolyn.

The sky was as blue as ink, and when Rae licked her lips she could taste salt. There was a slight wind, and Carolyn's skirt rose up, like the tail end of a kite. Right then what Rae wished for more than anything was that her mother would have the courage to take Rae and get back on the bus and leave him.

"But if you stay," Rae's father said through the screen door, "I don't want to hear any more complaints. I'd just as soon not talk at all."

In the shadows by the side of the house, Rae crouched even lower and held her breath. She expected Carolyn to call out her name, and when she did Rae would stand up and her mother would grab her hand; then they'd run past the high white dunes, and keep running until they reached the center of town.

But Carolyn didn't call out her name, she just stood at the porch banister, then she turned and went inside, and the screen door slammed behind her. Even then, Rae could tell when someone had given up, and as she stood out in the yard she felt betrayed. Later, when she went inside, Carolyn was setting the table for dinner as if nothing had happened, and Rae's father was starting a fire in the fireplace to get some of the chill out of the house. As they ate canned soup and tunafish sandwiches, Rae could hear the sand crabs outside, scrambling through the dunes. When a log in the fireplace popped Rae was certain that Carolyn shuddered. That was when Rae decided she would never trust her mother again; she could never love someone so weak, someone who couldn't even tell her husband not to light a fire because on the top of the chimney there was an owl's nest made of sea grass and straw.

All that summer Rae kept to herself, even during the week when her father wasn't there. She hid the red shoes at the back of the closet in her room, and when they left Wellfleet at the end of August, Rae left the red shoes behind, relieved to know that even if they rented the same house again, those shoes would never fit her the following year.

As she waited for Jessup by the pool Rae fell asleep and she dreamed about the house in Wellfleet. In her dream, Carolyn stood out on the back porch. It was late at night and the sky was black. As Rae watched, her mother disappeared, slowly dissolving in the salt air until there was nothing left on the porch but some fine white powder. When Rae woke up it was after five and the lounge chair had left ridges all along the side of her face. There was absolute silence, except for the wind and the sound of metal chimes hung along the outdoor balcony.

Every room on the second floor opened out to a painted blue walkway, and each room had a view of the pool. But when Jessup had gotten back an hour earlier, he hadn't bothered with the view. He had picked up a bottle of tequila after work, and as soon as he got into his room he pulled the drapes closed and ran a bath. When Rae knocked on his door, Jessup was sitting in a tub of cool water, his feet propped up on the far rim. He was drinking tequila out of a Dixie cup, and wondering why lifting a few pieces of sound equipment had left him feeling like an old man. He heard the first knock on the door but decided to ignore it. Tonight he didn't care about extra pay, he wasn't working overtime. He leaned his head against the cool ceramic tiles behind him and listened to the echo of water running through the pipes as someone on the floor above him ran the shower.

The longer she stood out there in the sun, the more Rae felt like crying. She had promised herself she would be calm; she had gone over this a hundred times in her head, and she planned to argue her case reasonably. But she didn't feel reasonable. She was certain that Jessup was in because the desk clerk had assured her he had picked up his key, and Rae wound up pounding on the door. When Jessup finally answered he had a towel wrapped around his waist and he was dripping wet. Rae walked right past him and sat in a tweed armchair. The room was small enough for her to lift her legs and reach the bed; she rested her shoes on the clean bedspread and looked up at him. Jessup had closed the door behind her, and now he was trapped. The only way for him to get anywhere was to jump over Rae's legs. And there was something else in Rae's favor—Jessup wasn't wearing clothes and somehow that made things fairer.

He sat down on the bed and put a hand on Rae's ankle. "Look who's here."

"You bet I'm here," Rae said.

The air conditioner was on, and the sound got between them. It was difficult to hear, and neither of them wanted to shout. In spite of herself, Rae thought he looked better than ever—he certainly wasn't wasting away.

"I wish I could explain some of the things I've done lately," Jessup said. "But all I can say is I'm going through some sort of crisis."

They both laughed at that, and Rae laughed a little too long. Before they knew it, she was crying.

"Come on, Rae," Jessup said. "Please."

"Goddamn you," Rae said.

Jessup shook his head sadly. "I know," he agreed.

Rae took a shower while Jessup got dressed. She rehearsed the right way to tell him she was pregnant, but the thing was she didn't quite believe it herself. She didn't look any different; it could very well be a mistake. When Rae got out of the shower and dressed again there was sand in her clothes and it stuck to her damp skin. She couldn't stop herself from imagining the worst. What if a monster was growing inside of her, something made out of blood and flesh that wasn't quite human. It might be her punishment; it had to happen to somebody—somebody's baby had to be misshapen, somebody had to die in a delivery room and be wrapped up in a stained sheet, somebody's lover had to leave her when he found out she was pregnant.

That night they went out to dinner; they ordered hamburgers and played the jukebox and tried to pretend that nothing was wrong. On the drive back to the Holiday Inn a wind came up suddenly; sand whipped around the Oldsmobile and Jessup had to switch on the windshield wipers in order to see the road. Rae heard the sound of wind chimes each time they passed a house or a trailer, and even though Jessup told her that people in the desert believed the chimes brought good luck, the sound put Rae on edge. The temperature had dropped nearly twenty degrees, but when they reached the motel the wind had begun to die down and Rae saw millions of stars above them. Jessup opened the door to his room, but Rae just leaned over the balcony railing. The night was black and white and so breathtakingly clear that she felt she had never seen the sky before.

Finally, Rae went in. She took off all her clothes and got under the covers. Jessup left a wake-up call for seven, then took off his boots, undressed, and turned out the lights. After he'd gotten into bed he didn't touch her.

"I've been trying to think of ways to explain what went wrong," Jessup said. He reached for his cigarettes in the dark, and when he lit a match Rae blinked in the sudden light.

"It's like I've been dreaming all these years and I suddenly woke up," Jessup said. "And here I am. Almost thirty."

The window in the room was open. It was the time when coyotes came down from the ridgetops; you could hear them howling as the moon rose higher in the sky. As she lay in bed Rae listened to the wind chimes out on the balcony; cars pulled into the parking lot, they idled, then cut their engines.

"I'm glad you woke up," Rae said bitterly.

"Don't take it personally," Jessup told her. "You know what I mean."

"Well, if you're planning to leave me we may have a problem," Rae said. She could feel Jessup's weight on the mattress; each time he breathed they shifted a little closer together. "The problem is," Rae said, "I'm pregnant."

Jessup reached for a glass ashtray and stubbed his cigarette out. When he put his head back on the pillow, Rae knew it was over.

"Are you saying you think you're pregnant or you know you're pregnant?"

"I know," Rae said.

"There are plenty of times you say you know something, and then I find out you've made a mistake."

"Jessup," Rae said. "I know."

Jessup sat up in bed with his back toward her. In the room next door someone turned on the television and muted voices drifted through the wall.

"Look, I'm sorry," Jessup said finally, "but this is impossible. I'm not ready for this."

Lately, Rae had the sense that everything that was happening to her was really happening to someone else. She pinched her thigh until she could feel the bite of her own fingernails.

"I appreciate the fact that this is a serious situation," Jessup said. "I really do. But what the hell do you expect me to do about it?"

She didn't have an answer.

"I'm not going to be somebody's father."

If he were anyone but Jessup, Rae would have sworn he was about to cry.

"Here I am in the middle of some sort of crisis and you come and tell me you're pregnant."

She knew it for sure now, he was crying. She was glad the lights were out and she didn't have to see it. She wasn't angry with him any more, just tired.

"We don't have to talk about it now," Rae told him. "We'll talk tomorrow." She put her arms around him and pretended not to know he was crying.

"It's not like I don't miss you," Jessup told her. "I don't want to, but there doesn't seem to be anything I can do about it."

She held him until he fell asleep, and then she moved back to her side of the bed. Long after midnight, when she was finally able to sleep, Rae dreamed that she left Jessup in bed and went to the window. She opened it wider and climbed outside. She dropped down two stories, and her feet landed in the sand with a thud. Right away, even though it was dark, she saw the pawprints and she followed the tracks far into the desert. The sand was the color of moonlight and the cactus grew eight feet high. All she had to do was sit down, and the coyote came right over to her, curled up by her feet, and put its head in her lap.

It didn't seem to matter if the coyote was her pet, or if she'd been captured. When she reached down she could feel its heart beating against its ribs, and she felt elated to be so close to something so wild. She stayed in the desert all night, and by morning she had learned all of the coyote's secrets: she knew which cactus were rich with hidden water, and how to follow a path along sharp, bone-colored rocks. She knew how to stand so still on the top of a high ridge that rabbits ran right past you, and hawks mistook you for stone and tried to light on your shoulders. At last she knew the moment when the night was so pure, you could fight it all you wanted and still—sooner or later—you'd throw back your head and howl.

When she got back to the motel she climbed up the railing, then crouched on the window ledge. Everyone in the Holiday Inn was asleep, covered by white sheets, dreaming of home. There was sand all along the window ledge and it spilled onto the wall-to-wall carpeting. Once Jessup turned in his sleep, and Rae held her breath. But even though he opened his eyes briefly, he didn't see her at the window, and he never heard her climb down onto the carpet, where she slept curled up at the very edge of the room.

When Rae woke up it was dawn, and she knew that she had to get out. She needed fresh air, and breakfast, and a change of clothes. Jessup didn't wake up when she ran the shower; he didn't hear the window close, he didn't hear the door. She would think about losing him later, but this morning all she wanted was to get across the desert before noon. She left the motel room exactly as it had been before she arrived. The air conditioner was still on; the pipes in the walls made a murmuring sound; in the bathroom there were a bottle of tequila, a package of disposable razors, a plastic container of Dixie cups. Only two things were missing when Rae left: the car keys were no longer on top of the night table, and out in the parking lot the space where Jessup had left the Oldsmobile the night before was empty. By the time Jessup woke up the asphalt in the parking lot was already beginning to sizzle. By noon it would reach a hundred and fifteen degrees. But by then Rae was already out on the freeway, and with all the windows in the Oldsmobile rolled down, the only thing she could feel was a perfect arc of wind.

PART TWO

On the night Lila gave birth to her daughter she had already walked up two flights of stairs before she realized she couldn't go any farther. She held on to the iron banister and slowly sank to the floor. In the middle of a terribly cold winter, there had been an oddly warm week, with rain instead of snow, and everyone in the city seemed sluggish and out of sorts. Lila's parents had come to agree that their daughter's strange behavior was caused by a combination of the weather and the mysterious pains of being eighteen. Ever since autumn, Lila had refused to wear anything but the same wide, blue dress, which hung from her shoulders like a sack. She refused suppers and lunches, yet she looked heavy and she walked as if off balance. At night, the next-door neighbors could hear her crying, and when she finally slept nothing could wake her, not even a siren right outside the apartment building. No one had dared to ask Lila what was wrong for fear she might tell them. And so, it had not been very difficult for her to keep her pregnancy a secret. But on that day in January, when her legs gave out and she sat huddled on the second-floor landing, Lila knew there was just so much you could hide.

Lila was expected home for dinner, but she sat in the stairwell for nearly an hour. Outside the sky filled with huge white clouds. The weather was changing that night, dropping five degrees an hour, and Lila tried to convince herself that the sudden shift in the atmosphere was what made her feel so exhausted and sick. In her calculations she had at least six more weeks to go. Lila was still stunned by what had happened to her, and every time the baby moved she was amazed all over again. On those rare days when she accepted that she was indeed pregnant, she could never quite believe she would actually give birth. Perhaps after nine months of pregnancy the process would reverse itself: the baby would slowly dissolve, forming, at the very last, a nearly perfect pearl, which Lila would carry inside her forever. But there on the stairs, Lila knew that something was happening to her. When she found the strength to stand up a wave began somewhere near her heart; it traveled downward in a rush, and then, without warning, exploded. Suddenly, Lila's dress was drenched, from the waist to the hem, and as she climbed up the stairs a trail of warm water was left behind that would not begin to evaporate until the following day.

Lila managed to get into the apartment unnoticed, then she undressed and crawled into bed. When her parents realized she was home they came to knock on her door, but by that time Lila's voice was steady enough to call that she was really too tired to join them for dinner. She closed her eyes then, and waited, and she was in her own small bed, in that room where she'd slept every night of her life, when her labor pains began. At first it was nothing more than mild cramps, as if she had pulled the muscles in her back. But the cramps came and went in a regular pattern, and no matter how hard Lila willed the pain to stop it rose upward; it was climbing to the roof. The movement of time changed altogether; it seemed as if only two minutes had passed since Lila had managed to sneak into her room—but it was more than two hours later when the pain began to take on a life of its own. There was a steady rhythm it complied to, and as the pain gained control, Lila panicked. She jumped out of bed, pulled a blanket around her, then ran out of her room and into the hallway. Lila's parents had long finished dinner, but her father was still at the table reading the newspaper, and her mother was returning the dishes to the cabinet in the dining room. When Lila's mother saw her daughter in the hallway with a wool blanket wrapped around her and her dark hair flying wildly, she dropped a large platter which broke into a thousand pieces on the wooden floor.

"Something's wrong," Lila screamed. Her voice did not sound at all like her voice, and though her parents were only a few feet away, Lila was certain that she had to yell to be heard. "I have to go to a hospital," she cried. "Something's happening to me."

Lila's mother ran over and put a hand on her daughter's forehead to check for fever, but a strong contraction came that made Lila drop down and crouch on the floor. Through the wave of pain, Lila could hear her mother shrieking, and the moment she was able to stand again her mother slapped her face so hard that Lila could feel her neck snap backward. It was then Lila's parents began to argue and accuse each other of stupidity, lunacy, and every other parental crime possible. They nearly forgot that Lila was there in the room with them. At last, her mother and father both agreed that an ambulance's siren was too deep a shame for them to endure, and so Lila's cousin, who was a nurse in the emergency room at Beekman Hospital, would have to be called.

At that point, Lila didn't really care what was decided. It didn't matter that her mother was crying hot tears as she telephoned Lila's cousin, or that her father had already left the apartment, even though he had no place to go—too humiliated to sit in the lobby or ask a neighbor for a glass of water or tea, he went to the stairwell and sat there, and prayed that no one he knew would see him. Lila let them make all the decisions. When they refused to take her to the hospital, she went back to her room and knelt by the side of the bed. After a while, she put her face down on the cold sheet and gripped the mattress with both hands. She felt herself slipping into something dark, and each time a contraction came her waist was ringed with a band of fire. Each time the band grew hotter, until finally it threatened to burn right through her spine. One thing Lila knew: she could not live through this kind of suffering. But even now, she didn't dare scream and bring the neighbors running. She simply begged for someone to help her, and although her mother must have heard her she did nothing more than come into the hallway and quietly close the bedroom door.

The night grew so cold that when it began to rain the drops froze the moment they hit the sidewalk. There were hundreds of accidents: cars and buses skidded on the icy avenues, lights in hotel rooms flickered as generators came to a halt, pipes froze and then burst, and every frail tree in the city was hidden beneath a shower of ice. Up in her room, Lila was surrounded by black fire. She might have slipped into the darkness forever if her cousin Ann hadn't arrived a little after midnight. The bedroom door opened slowly, and the scraping of wood against wood sounded like the flapping of some huge bird's wings. Lila gasped when the sudden light from the hallway filled her room. For one calm moment Lila wondered if she had imagined the pain, and she watched as her cousin took off her gray wool coat and her leather boots. Before the bedroom door was closed Lila had enough time to look out and see her mother peer into the bedroom. At least, Lila thought it was her mother—she wore her mother's clothes, and was her mother's shape and size. But if it really had been her mother, wouldn't she have run into the room and thrown her arms around her daughter and tried to save her? Lila blinked and strained to see, but the figure in the hallway just grew shadowier, and when Lila's cousin walked toward the door she blocked the light, and then there weren't even any shadows. There was nothing at all.

When the door closed the sound echoed. Lila could actually feel the sound somewhere beneath her skin. Immediately the room was airless; the heat in the radiator poured out until it was impossible to breathe. That was when Lila knew she couldn't have this baby.

"I'm sorry," she told her cousin. "They made you come here for nothing. I've changed my mind. I'm not going through with this."

Ann had been a nurse for eleven years—long enough to know she had better not tell Lila that every woman in hard labor had made the exact same pronouncement.

"I can't do this!" Lila screamed.

Every neighbor on the floor above could hear her now for all she cared. Her contractions had been coming two minutes apart for some time, but now something changed. She could no longer tell the difference between one contraction and the next; the pain began to run together in a single line of fire. As each contraction rose to its highest peak, hot liquid poured out between Lila's legs. She couldn't sit, or lie down—she couldn't stand. Ann helped her onto the bed and examined her. By the time she was through, Lila was so wet that the sheets beneath her were soaked.

"Give me something," she begged. "Give me a shot. Put me out. Do anything."

The pain owned her now; it owned the earth and the air and at its center was an inferno. She was in the darkest time before birth, transition, and even though she didn't know its name, Lila knew, all of a sudden, that she could not go back. There was nothing to go back to, there was only this pain—and it was stronger than she was. It was swallowing her alive.

She wanted Hannie, that was all there was to it. In the past few weeks she had considered going to see her a hundred times, but a hundred times her pride got in the way, and now it was too late. She tried to imagine the stiff black skirts, and the clucking sound Hannie made in the back of her throat, and couldn't. There was nothing but this room, and inside the room there was only pain. And even if Hannie had been right beside her, Lila would still have been alone. That was the unbearable part of this pain—no one could accompany you, no one could share it, and the absolute loneliness of it was nearly enough to drive you mad.

Ann went to the bathroom to dampen some washcloths, and when she came back she found Lila standing by the window, looking out. The sidewalk was three stories down, and from this distance the ice that had formed on the cement seemed as cool and delicious as a deep, blue bay in Maine. Ann ran and turned her away from the window. It did no good to think of an escape, or even to wish for one. This was the center of it, and all you had to do was stand your ground—you could not even think about giving up.

When she saw the damp washcloths, Lila grabbed one out of her cousin's hand and sucked out the water. She was dying of thirst. She would have given anything for a piece of ice, a lemonade, a cool place where she could drift into a deep and dreamless sleep.

"Please," Lila said to her cousin.

"Just remember," Ann said, "I'm not going to leave you. I'm going to stay right here with you till the end."

"You can't leave me!" Lila cried, terrified and misunderstanding.

"I won't," Ann told her. "I'm right here."

Lila threw her arms around Ann's neck. She had never wanted to be closer to anyone. Again and again she whispered "please," but she knew there was no one who could save her. And then something let loose inside Lila, and it was simply beyond her powers to hold it back. She felt a terrible urge to push this thing inside of her out, and when Ann told her she couldn't push yet, she started to cry. Ann showed her how to pant—it was a trick to fool her body into believing it was breathing that she must concentrate on—but even then Lila's tears ran into the back of her throat and nearly made her choke. Nothing was working, she couldn't even pant; she took in more and more air until she started to hyperventilate. Ann began to breathe along with her, and eventually Lila was able to slow her panting to match her cousin's. Lila stared into Ann's eyes and the room fell away from her; the city no longer existed. She fell deeper into those eyes—they were the universe, filled with energy and unbelievable light. Lila heard a voice tell her to get back onto the bed. She didn't feel herself move, and yet there she was, on those damp white sheets with her legs pulled up.

"It's time," Lila heard someone say to her. "Now you can push."

For a moment everything was clear. Lila recognized the ceiling in her bedroom, and the face of her cousin who was a hospital nurse. It seemed that a serious mistake had been made. This could not possibly be happening to her.

It was day now, but the air was so cold that the dawn was blue. Lila sat up in bed; she leaned back against the pillows and pulled her legs up as far as they could go. She pushed for the first time, and when she did she was horrified to hear her own voice. Surely, a sound like that would tear a throat apart. She pushed again, and again, but after more than a hour there was still the same enormous pressure. The only difference was now Lila was so exhausted that she couldn't even scream. All she wanted was for this horrible burning thing inside her to come out. She found herself thinking the same odd phrase over and over. It's only your body, she told herself. It was her flesh that had betrayed her, her blood that was on fire. The solution was simple and took only an instant. As her cousin leaned over her and wiped her face with a washcloth, as dawn reflected through windows all over the city, Lila left her body behind.

Her spirit leapt up into the pure white air. The utter joy of such a leap was almost too much for her. Lila rose upward, guided by a perfect beam of light. Below her, she could see her body propped up on two pillows, she could see that her eyes were closed, and that she held her breath as she pushed down with all the strength she had left. But how could she be concerned with a body that twisted and groaned, something that was so far away. Up here, in this strange new atmosphere, everything was silent. The air was so cold it crystallized, and each time Lila opened her mouth to breathe it quenched her thirst. There was the scent of something much sweeter than roses, and Lila wasn't the least bit surprised to find that her spirit had taken the shape of a bird. What else but a blackbird could swoop so gracefully above a room of pain?

"So now you're free," someone was saying to Lila. "Now you know that absolute freedom of leaving your body behind."

"It was so easy to do," Lila said. "How could anything be this easy?"

Far below her, Lila could hear her cousin ask who on earth she was talking to. But Lila didn't bother to answer. Any moment she might have to return to her body, each second was too precious to waste. The blue dawn was nothing compared to the white light that Lila had discovered. And when the time came for her to return to her body, Lila felt such a terrible sorrow that for an instant she thought she might choose not to return at all. She was floating just above herself, still undecided, when she suddenly found herself moved by the struggle beneath her. Her body's shallow breathing and the beat of her own heart filled Lila with pity; with one tender motion she slipped back inside her own flesh.

This time when she pushed, something hard moved so that it was nearly out. Lila reached her hands between her legs and felt the soft hair on the very top of the baby's head.

"Oh, my God," Lila said.

"The next time you push you may feel as if you'll explode," Ann said. "You may feel like you're burning."

But Lila had already been a spear of flame; she could dance

on red coals now and not feel a thing. She bore down harder, and suddenly the baby's head was free. Lila panted again to stop the urge to push while Ann untangled the umbilical cord from around the neck, and then, with the next push, the entire body slipped out in a rush.

Blood poured from Lila, but she felt strangely renewed. She leaned her elbows on the pillows and lifted herself up so that she could watch as Ann cleaned off the baby and wrapped it in a white towel.

"Is it all right?" she whispered.

"It's perfect," Ann told her. "And it's a girl."

Lila's father had come home from a night spent out on the stairway, where it was so cold it could freeze your soul. He and his wife sat on the couch in the living room, rocking back and forth as if in mourning. Behind the closed bedroom door, Ann placed the baby in a dresser drawer on a bed of flannel nightgowns. It wasn't until after she had delivered the placenta that she told Lila that her parents had already had her contact a doctor who arranged private adoptions.

"But I have to have your approval," Ann told Lila.

Lila leaned her head back on the pillows and closed her eyes while Ann lifted her legs and put down a clean sheet.

"You have to tell me," Ann said. "What do you want to do about this child?"

What amazed Lila was how fast it was over, how far outside herself she had gone and how quickly she had returned. Already, the pain she'd felt seemed to belong to someone else. How strange that now she didn't want it to fade—she wanted to grab on to the pain and claim it for her own.

"I'll be honest with you," Ann said. "I don't really see how you can keep this baby. If you do, your parents won't let you stay here. Is it fair to keep her, when you can't even take care of yourself?"

Even though the steam heat in the radiator made a gurgling

noise, and buses trapped in the ice strained their engines, Lila swore she could hear her baby breathing as it slept in the dresser drawer. It was at that moment that her heart broke in two: she knew she could not keep this child.

"I want to see her," Lila said.

"Take my advice," Ann told her. "If you plan to give her up, don't see her. Let me just take her away."

"I know what I want," Lila said. "Let me see her."

As soon as her daughter was brought to her and she held her in her arms, Lila knew her cousin was right. But instead of turning her away, Lila held the baby even tighter. Her skin was as soft as apricots, her eyes were the color of an October sky. Lila could have held her forever. She begged for time to stop, for clocks to break, for every star to remain fixed. But none of that happened. Up on the fourth floor the neighbors ran the water in the bathroom, in the hallway outside the apartment there was the scent of coffee.

When Lila gave her daughter up to her cousin's outstretched arms, the room grew darker, as if she had given away a star. The dresser drawer where her baby had slept was still open, and it would be days before Lila would be able to close it again. But now, as her child was taken out into the coldest winter morning ever recorded in the city, wrapped in nothing but a white towel, Lila did manage to get one last look, and for the first time she knew the loss she would feel from that day onward, every morning and every night, for the rest of her life.

⋙

They sent Lila away because she just gave up. By the end of February her milk had gone dry, and the bloody sheets had been cut into pieces and thrown into the incinerator, but Lila still refused to leave the apartment. She couldn't even sit too close to her open bedroom window, because the breeze from outside stung her lungs. She had grown so used to the still air in the apartment that she had come to dread fresh air and light. You couldn't tell the hour of the day in Lila's bedroom when the curtains were drawn. It no longer mattered if it was day or night. If anyone had asked what future she saw for herself at the bottom of her own teacup she would have said endless days without purpose or plans. But then, on a day when the sky was as gray as cement, Lila found herself alone in the apartment. She went into the bathroom and closed the door behind her. And when she opened the medicine cabinet above the sink, it seemed as if she'd had a plan and a purpose all along.

As she slit her wrists with her father's razor she felt nothing at all. Although when she imagined them finding the body she had to smile: her mother could scrub the floor for weeks with every cleanser on the market, and the blood would still never come off the black-and-white ceramic tiles. But Lila didn't cut deep enough, and before she could correct her mistake, she fainted and hit her head on the tub. When her mother came home from the market where she'd bought codfish and potatoes and lettuce, Lila was still alive. Most of the blood had spilled neatly into the sink. But although the bathroom floor wasn't ruined, when the ambulance drivers carried Lila out a trail of blood stained the oak floor in the hallway, and it never washed out.

Two weeks later, when Lila's wrists were still bandaged in white gauze, they sent her out to East China on the Long Island Rail Road. As Lila handed the conductor her ticket a bit of gauze peeked out from the wristband of her glove, and all the way out to East China she kept her hands clasped together in her lap. Her destination was the home of her great-aunt, Belle, a woman in her seventies who was so hard of hearing she was never quite sure if Lila's mother had whispered baby or lazy when she called to ask for a room for her daughter.

Certainly, Belle never asked what the problem had been, she just sent a taxi to meet Lila at the small wooden railroad station, and her only demand was that her great-niece never use salt when it was her turn to cook dinner.

All through March, Lila tried to feel something. But everything around her seemed bloodless and cold: the bare maple trees, the sound of bats up on the roof in the middle of the night, the empty two-lane road called the East China Highway that ran right by the house and seemed to go nowhere at all. In her cold bedroom in the attic Lila could sleep, but she had no dreams. Each night before she went to bed Lila went to the window and longed for the deep oblivion of the sky. She had no energy, nothing left to give. Just speaking a few words to her aunt was an enormous effort—afterward, Lila always had to go back to her room where she slept on the old rope bed, covered by a quilt Belle had sewn when she was not much older than Lila.

There was only one thing that attracted Lila, and that was death. The one time she agreed to do readings for her aunt's old friends—having foolishly admitted that she used to tell fortunes—she saw nothing but symbols of death in their cups: hearts that refused to beat, black dogs, poisoned apples and pears. And although she continued to think about Hannie, she never once missed Stephen, the lover she'd thought she couldn't live without. Stephen was a ghost; compared to death he was nothing, and it was death who called to Lila now. He was there with her every night when Lila ran her fingertips over the knives as she stored them in the silverware drawer; when she washed the dishes he was by her side, telling her that under just the right amount of pressure the glass she held could shatter into shards that would cut right through her skin. What was wonderful about these dark whispers was that they left very little room for Lila to think about her child. But at night, when the wind rose off the Long Island Sound to sweep through the potato fields and rattle down the chimneys, the cold air sounded like a baby's wailing. And even when Lila put a pillow over her head and covered her ears with her hands, she could still hear the baby crying, and it cried from midnight till dawn.

Lila became convinced that she wouldn't last through the winter. She lost twenty pounds and her dark hair fell out in clumps—she found it all over her pillow in the mornings, as if a molting bird had visited her in the night. And then quite suddenly, without any warning, it was spring. The ice disappeared, the earth was left steaming, and all over East China the air was silvery, like steam from a kettle. Puddles formed on either side of the East China Highway, and in them were small dark fish and green turtles. Laundry was hung outside on thick rope lines, and as soon as the snow melted there were white flowers and wild strawberries in every backyard.

No matter how hard Lila tried to resist she was drawn outside her room. Even when she closed her window, she could smell lilacs from the tree out in the yard that had not yet bloomed. There was the scent of seaweed in the air, and a feeling of longing in everyone, even in Lila. Early in April, more than a month after her milk had dried up, Lila awoke one morning to find that her breasts had been leaking all night—her nightgown and bedclothes were drenched, and they smelled so sweet that bees came in through the window and followed Lila all through the house until she took a broom and chased them out the front door.

Hannie had once told Lila that a long time ago, in the village where she had grown up, a separate cottage had been built for women who had lost their children at birth. Every morning people brought presents to leave outside the mother's door: bunches of lavender, sunflowers, caged birds, hot black bread. For six nights the mother who had lost her child was not allowed to go any farther than the front door where the collection of gifts had been piled. No one was allowed to see her weeping; anyone who heard her cries in the middle of the night was to light a candle and then think of other things. On the seventh day everyone went out to collect wood, and a fire was lit outside the cottage. As the flames moved closer and closer to the rickety front steps no one could interfere, no one was allowed to run to the pond for a bucket of water. In moments the flames circled the cottage; nesting birds flew away, dragonflies who lived in the eaves darted into the sky. And then came the hardest part—waiting until the flames leapt up to the roof.

The woman inside always ran out to join the others, although sometimes it was not until the very last minute, just before the cottage collapsed into a heap of flaming twigs. It was in this way that the mother discovered that she still had the will to live, even now, and she was usually the first one to help when the cottage was rebuilt.

Lila could not stand for April to affect her this way. Every day she felt more alive, but if anything this made her more bitter about her own ability to survive. There was nothing that did not remind her of her daughter: the new bark on the lilac tree outside her window was the exact same color as her daughter's newborn slate-gray eyes. The moss that grew near the back steps was as soft as her daughter's hair. It did no good to stay inside because there the lace doilies on the easy chair felt like baby blankets and the small silver teaspoons were exactly the right size for a child to hold as she ate cereal and pears. And so, one day in the middle of April, Lila left her aunt's house for the first time since she'd arrived at the railroad station in February. Each time Lila took a long walk she felt more hopeless: for no reason at all she was terribly alive. In town people smiled at her, as if she was some young girl with her whole future ahead of her. And so, Lila made certain to walk away from town, out by the potato fields where there were nothing but sea gulls, who were so brave they actually swooped down to take bread right out of her hands. And if it was early enough, the time of day when fog rose along the white line in the center of the highway, there were sometimes small deer who stood perfectly still for a moment, before turning to run back into the woods.

What Lila hoped to find, as she walked along the East China Highway, was a reason to go on living. She had turned nineteen only a few weeks earlier, and she'd been surprised to realize that she was still so young. The days were long now; sunlight lasted past suppertime. At night there were falling stars, and even when armfuls of lilacs were cut from the trees more and more blossoms appeared.

Lila was faced with her past each time she chose a long-sleeved blouse from her closet to hide the scars on her wrists. But spring distracted her, she began to feel that her scars were not enough, and so each day she devised a new way to remind herself of her suffering. When she sewed she made certain to jab her fingers with the needle, when she cooked she picked up pots by their handles without bothering to use a potholder. All that remained pleasurable in her life were the long walks she took, until she realized that she could ruin these, too. The very next time Lila left the house she slipped her shoes off and left them underneath the porch of her aunt's house. She would have to walk far, but by late afternoon the tar on the road would be hot enough, and Lila knew that her feet would burn.

She had walked more than eight miles, and was halfway between East China and Riverhead, when Lila stopped at a gas station. She had come so far on the burning tar that there were blisters on the soles of her feet. She bent down and dusted off some of the pebbles and dirt, and when she looked up she saw Richard sitting in the shade outside the office of the gas station. He was twenty-one, and even from fifteen yards away, Lila could tell how handsome he was. She lowered her eyes immediately, angry at herself for imagining she had the right to look at a man.

"The best thing for hot feet is to pour cold water on them right away," Richard called to her.

"I don't happen to have any water with me at the moment," Lila called back. Even though she wasn't looking at him, Lila felt herself grow embarrassed.

When Richard stood up, the metal chair he had been sitting on creaked, and Lila felt herself shudder, as if she'd been touched. Richard walked over, and as he passed the gas pumps he picked up a pail. He handed the pail to Lila, then stood there and watched as she emptied it onto her feet. The water was so clear and so cold that it made her gasp.

"Is something funny?" Lila said, annoyed when she looked up and saw that Richard was smiling.

Richard backed away from her, stung by her tone. He was more than six feet tall, but he was terribly shy. And right now he was also confused—he didn't know what on earth had made him call out to Lila, it just seemed like something he had to do.

"Nothing's funny," he said. "It's just that you're so beautiful I can't stop looking at you."

Lila turned and she ran all the way home. She ran so fast that by the time she reached her aunt's house her feet were bleeding. That night she locked herself in her room, and she swore that she would never again walk west on the East China Highway. But as she sat in her dark bedroom, the constellations in the sky were so bright they burned through the cotton curtains, and Lila knew that if she saw Richard even one more time, she'd be in danger. If she wasn't careful she might just fall in love with him, and that was one thing Lila did not intend to do.

At first, when she heard her aunt's friends talk about Richard's family, Lila assumed it was no one she knew. These friends were old Russian women who had come to East China by accident. All of them had immigrated long ago with hopes of being in Manhattan, but all had in common a cousin who helped pay their fare, and then insisted they come to live in East China. This cousin had raved about the soil that was so rich potatoes seemed to grow overnight, and it was he who first brought a band of migrant workers to the area. Even though their cousin had been dead for nearly thirty years, all of the relatives he had helped to bring over were still in East China. Every one had planned to move into the city after his death, but Manhattan had faded until it was nothing more than a dream; it was less than a hundred miles to the Midtown Tunnel, but it might as well have been on the other side of a black forest guarded by wolves.

Of course there was one woman, the daughter of a distant cousin, who had managed to leave East China, although she hadn't gone any farther than the outskirts of town. Twenty-five years earlier Helen had married a migrant worker, a Shinnecock Indian whom the Russian women referred to as the Red Man. The Red Man had taken Helen to a small unheated farmhouse where the pines were so tall and their shadows so dark that not even potatoes could grow. When Helen came to town to do her grocery shopping everyone said hello, but nobody really talked to her, and there wasn't a soul in East China who didn't know that Helen's mother had died of shame.

In the winter, when the ice was treacherous, many of the old women didn't venture out of their houses. When April came and the old friends were reunited, gossip flowed. On a particularly clear night, when Lila's feet were still bloody and blistered, four of Belle's distant cousins came to visit, and the conversation turned to the Red Man and his wife. It was a well-known fact that Helen had been cursed with a curious inability to have children, except for one, the son. Everyone wanted to know what had happened to the son during the winter—for years the old ladies had been waiting for him to be shipped off to the penitentiary, and none of them would have been surprised if he had murdered both his parents with a shotgun and then disappeared into Connecticut or New Jersey. However, there was not much news, even after the winter: Helen's son was still working at the gas station his father, the Red Man, had somehow managed to buy. And later in the evening, one of the old Russian women admitted that after an ice storm in January, when she was stranded and out of groceries, Helen's son had come to fix the engine of her Ford, which wouldn't turn over. After having a cup of tea laced with whiskey, she shocked them all by adding that he really was quite handsome.

Lila served the tea that night, but when her aunt's friends asked her to read their tea leaves, she excused herself—she said she had a headache and couldn't possibly see into the future that night. But really, Lila was simply too excited to sit still in a room full of old women. She was nineteen years old, and in spite of everything, very much alive. That night, Lila slept better than she had in months. For the first time since the birth of her child she dreamed. In her dream she found that lilacs were growing in the middle of winter, their blue petals pushing through a slick cover of ice. In the morning, when she woke up, Lila got dressed while it was still dark. She went downstairs quietly, even though her great-aunt wouldn't have heard if she had slammed the doors. Before she left, she stood out on the front porch for a moment, not yet ready to leave her sorrow behind. In the middle of nowhere, between East China and Riverhead there was a man who might be able to make her forget. Suddenly there seemed to be a reason for everything, and although Lila started off walking slowly, she wound up running down the two-lane road which for the very first time seemed like a highway that led you somewhere you might want to go.

⋙

They were married on the edge of East China, in the parlor of Richard's parents' house. It was July and orange lilies were blooming everywhere, even beneath the huge pine trees where the shadows were deep green. Richard's mother, Helen, cried from the beginning of the ceremony to the very end. The only guest was a high-school friend of Richard's, a boy named Buddy who was so nervous about his duties as best man that he nearly fainted during the justice of the peace's speech about fidelity.

After the ceremony Helen took Lila aside in the kitchen and she held her hand. "I hope you understand that no one in town will ever speak to you again," she told her new daughter-in-law.

In fact, Lila's own great-aunt had asked her to leave the house as soon as she was told about the marriage, and Lila had spent the last week and a half at a motel in Riverhead. But after losing both her child and her parents the disapproval of neighbors was meaningless.

"Richard's the only person I need," Lila told her mother-in-law as she reached up into a cabinet for some plates. There was a luncheon following the ceremony, but with the exception of the still shaky Buddy, there were no guests.

"Just wait," Helen said ominously. She took a tub of potato salad from the refrigerator, then sat down at the kitchen table, as if the weight of the potato salad was too much for her. "You'll be the object of every conversation in town. They'll find out every piece of gossip about you and spread it all over the Island."

The screen door was open and they could hear the sound of bees. Lila stood still and held the china plates to her chest. She had not stopped to think about her past resurfacing out here in East China; she had not even thought how she would explain the scars on her wrists when she undressed in front of Richard that night.

"Don't get me wrong—I'm not complaining," Helen said. "But my life hasn't been easy. What saves me is I'm in love with my husband. But sometimes," she admitted, "I'd like to hear another person's voice."

Lila was no longer listening to her mother-in-law. She was sure that if Richard ever found out about her past he would leave her, and she vowed then and there never to let him know about her baby. She came to him without a past, as if she herself had been born on the day she first saw him.

Richard's father, the Red Man who was gossiped about in so many living rooms and parlors, came into the kitchen for champagne and glasses. He was the same height as his son, although Richard was convinced that his father was several inches taller. No one in town cared, but his name was Jason Grey, and when he saw how sad his wife and new daughter-in-law looked he popped the champagne cork right there in the kitchen and the sudden noise and gush of dry champagne made both women gasp and then laugh out loud.

That night Lila and Richard moved in to the bedroom on the second floor. Jason Grey had put up new wallpaper, and Richard had refinished the pine bed. But even after the lights were turned out, Lila refused to get undressed. It was impossible to see any stars through the pine boughs outside the bedroom window, but somehow the moonlight managed to get through. The room was so well lit Lila was certain that the moment she took off her clothes, Richard would be blinded by the scars on her wrists.

As Lila stood by the window, Richard sat down at the foot

of the bed and took off his boots. He was so much in love that he was actually afraid to blink, even once, as if Lila might just disappear. Lila's back was turned to him, and in the moonlight Richard could see that her posture was as straight as wire. All of a sudden she seemed shy, and because she was, after all, a new bride who had just moved into her in-laws' house and because she had promised herself to a man who was really still a stranger, Richard felt his heart go out to her. In that moment he fell even more deeply in love.

"I'll tell you what," he said softly. "Since we're married and we've got the rest of our lives together, we don't have to make love yet if you don't want to."

Lila wanted to more than anything. She knew that she was about to cry, and she couldn't imagine an explanation that would satisfy her new husband once he saw that she had tried to take her own life. Because she did not know what else to do, Lila quickly unbuttoned her white dress, let it slip to the floor, then stepped out of it. She held up her hands, wrists together like a hostage. She had not yet unpacked her suitcase, and if Richard insisted she tell him about her past, she had decided she would have to leave him.

When Richard came over to her and held her, Lila closed her eyes and arched her neck, as if getting ready for some great pain.

"I can't believe how beautiful you are," Richard said.

Lila opened her eyes and backed away. Just then she wondered if she hadn't married a fool.

"You're not looking at me," Lila said sharply.

Richard bent down and kissed her. "Oh, yes I am," he said.

Lila pushed him away and she raised her hands until her wrists were directly in front of his eyes. The jagged lines along her wrists grew whiter and whiter; no one in his right mind could ignore them.

"Look at me," Lila urged her husband.

Richard had spent his whole life in the odd circumstance of being both well loved and lonely. His parents were so much in love that no matter how deeply they cared for him, Richard was somehow excluded. He didn't care if he was considered an outcast in East China, all he needed was one person, someone of his own. Now that he had found Lila, he didn't intend to lose her, even if the scars that she now showed him meant he had gotten a little more than he'd bargained for. Richard Grey wasn't a fool, and he certainly knew something about death. When he was ten he accidentally saw a man kill himself. It was out in the woods behind the deserted army barracks used as a camp for migrant workers. Richard had been born in the barracks, and even after his parents had bought the gas station and moved into the house they still lived in, Richard felt drawn to the migrant camp, if only because there seemed to be more deer there than anywhere else in East China.

He was in the woods, late in October, sitting motionless so that he would not frighten off any deer, when he saw a migrant worker walk into a clearing in the woods with a shotgun in his hands. Richard assumed that this man was an out-of-season hunter searching for deer. But then, quite suddenly, the migrant turned the gun on himself and fired.

Even after he had run for miles, Richard could still hear the shot. And when he had to go to the district attorney's office to testify to what he had seen, Richard humiliated himself by crying in public when he was questioned. Afterward he couldn't seem to make himself go into the woods; he stood at the edge of the backyard where the lawn disappeared into brambles and pines, unable to take another step.

And then one day Jason Grey came out to the yard.

"Let's go for a walk," he said to Richard. He pushed some brambles aside, stepped into the woods, and signaled to his son.

Richard swallowed hard, but he followed. It was darker in

the woods than he'd remembered, and each time a branch broke under his father's boots, Richard shuddered. It didn't take long for him to realize that his father was leading him right back to the exact spot where the migrant worker had shot off his head.

"Come on," Jason Grey said when he noticed that his son had stopped walking. "What's keeping you?"

In the shadows of the pine trees, his father suddenly seemed like a stranger. "You can't make me go there," Richard said.

Jason walked back to him. He reached into his jacket pocket and took out a cigarette. "I guess you're wondering what made him do it," he said.

"I don't care," Richard said.

Jason Grey inhaled on his cigarette and then coughed, and his cough made Richard ache with the sudden knowledge that one day his father would be old and sick.

"If we wanted to," Jason Grey said, "we could find out everything about that man who shot himself. We could find out how much money he owed, and if his wife had left him for somebody else. But we'd never really know what went on in his mind. It's not our right to know what goes on in another man's mind. But whatever it was, we know one thing for sure—he just couldn't fight it any more. And that's his right, too." Jason finished his cigarette and motioned to his son. "Come on," he said.

Together they walked the rest of the way to the clearing. The few leaves left on the trees had turned yellow, and when the sunlight filtered through them the air seemed to shine. Richard felt the urge to grab his father's hand; instead he stood in the clearing and watched the yellow light.

"People have private places in their minds," Jason Grey said. "That doesn't mean they're crazy. It doesn't even mean they're cowards if they run from something awful."

They could hear leaves falling. Jason Grey stared straight

ahead, but he reached down and took his son's hand.

"You just remember there's a big difference between not being able to fight it any more and feeling like you're all alone sometimes," he said.

"Even when you're married?" Richard had asked, surprised that his father knew so much about being alone.

Jason Grey couldn't stop himself from smiling. "Especially then," he had said.

On his wedding night, Richard knew exactly what his father had been talking about. There was a private place in Lila's mind that was somehow the same as that migrant worker with the shotgun. But if anything, this made Lila seem more precious. When Richard touched the white scars on Lila's wrist he was dazzled by hope—it was as if Lila had died and come back to him, and he held her tight for a moment, before he stepped away.

"I am looking at you," Richard said. "And all I see is my wife."

The rest of that summer seemed to last forever; the air smelled like strawberries and the sunlight was unusually thick. Helen was delighted to have another woman in the house, and she taught Lila all her secret recipes, for cabbage soup and jam cake and sweet potato pie. Just before supper Lila always went outside to wait on the lawn for Richard and Jason Grey to come home from work. At that time of day the sky was deep blue, and under that sky Lila felt brand new. For a brief time she was a woman without a history—even her dreams were filled with ordinary things, fireflies and pearl-edged clouds, and teapots made out of copper. She didn't question her good luck—she didn't dare to. All she knew was that someone had fallen in love with her, and, amazingly enough, that was all she needed.

But when autumn came, something changed. At night, after they had made love and Richard had fallen asleep, Lila found herself shivering with fear. She was certain that she would lose Richard: one day when she went out to wait for him Jason Grey's Chrysler would pull up in the driveway and only her father-in-law would get out. She began to dream about her past; her womb tightened as it had for days after her baby had been born, and the contractions kept her up all night and made her afraid to sleep in the same bed as her husband.

One night, Richard woke up sometime near dawn to find Lila huddled on the floor. He started to get out of bed, but Lila held up her hand, warning him to stop.

"Don't come near me," she said, and the coldness of her own voice filled her with grief.

"Come back to bed," Richard said quietly.

"If you really knew me you would never love me," Lila told him.

"If you're referring to the fact that you once tried suicide, I know that and I don't care," Richard said.

Lila threw back her head and laughed, and the sound went right through Richard.

"Come back to bed," he urged.

"You really think you know me," Lila said contemptuously.

Richard could tell that after only a few months of marriage Lila was drifting away from him, and for the first time he raised his voice to her.

"Then go ahead and tell me the reason why you tried to kill yourself. You obviously want to tell me, so you go right ahead. Tell me."

"I don't want to," Lila said in a small voice.

"Then don't," Richard said. "But either do it and get it over with or let it go, because we can't keep on this way, Lila."

Lila got back into bed and put her arms around him.

"I thought when I met you you said you could read the future," Richard said.

"I said tea leaves," Lila whispered. "That's all."

"Well, I can see into the future," Richard told her. "You might as well stop fighting it, because we're going to be together for a very long time."

Lila wished she could believe him, but by the time winter came she was convinced that if they stayed in New York State they had no future at all. Someone in East China might manage to find out the truth about her; someone might tell Richard. She felt as if the past were right on her heels, and it got so bad that whenever she went into town to shop for groceries with her mother-in-law she wondered if perhaps the doctor had arranged for a couple in East China to adopt her baby. It became impossible for her to look at a child of any age; she swore her breasts were filling with milk again—at night they ached so badly that she had to sleep on her back. As her own child's birthday grew near, Lila thought she might be going mad. Every night the sky was orange and black, and the days were as gray as stone. She grew more certain that if she stayed in East China through the winter something terrible would happen. She began to talk about leaving, but Richard imagined that what she wanted was a house of their own. He promised that in less than a year they'd find a house with a view of Long Island Sound and move out. But then one day when it was cold enough to make her shiver and remember the ice storm, Lila walked to the gas station to take Richard and Jason a Thermos of hot coffee and some lunch. There was a car idling by the gas pumps; in the passenger seat was a little girl. The girl's mother had gone into the office to ask Richard for directions and a map, and when she came back out she found Lila with both her hands on the passenger window, weeping as she stared inside.

Lila forced herself not to run after the car. It hadn't mattered that the child wasn't hers, Lila wanted her. She'd had the terrible urge to get behind the wheel of the car and kidnap her, and if the child's mother hadn't come out of the office when she did Lila might have already been driving west. She would have turned the radio on to a low volume, and the heat up to high, and the little girl would have been right beside her, her sleepy breath filling the car with a deliciously sweet odor.

That was when Lila decided that California was the answer. Once, she had imagined that she and Stephen would go there together and live high above Hollywood, in the hills. Now all she wanted was a place to start over, a place so free of history that the past barely existed. She started talking about going west that evening at supper, and once she started talking she couldn't seem to stop, not even after the others had put down their forks and turned to look at her.

"Are you and Richard planning to leave New York?" Helen asked in a frightened voice. For the first time she began to know the dangers of having a daughter-in-law.

"No," Richard told her, although he realized that something was about to happen. "We're not planning anything," he told his mother.

Helen was relieved, but when Richard glanced over at his father he didn't look quite sure of himself, and Jason Grey could tell that his son wouldn't be in East China much longer.

Every night Lila begged him to leave. She talked about palm trees and pelicans until Richard began to dream about the Pacific Ocean. In his dreams the ocean was amazingly green, like a thin piece of jade held up to the sun, and blue-eyed pelicans dove into the waves. One night when the snow was falling and Lila was turned away from him, Richard sat up in bed.

"All right," he told his wife. "We'll go to California."

Lila kissed him until his cheeks and his eyelids were wet.

"But you're the one who has to tell my mother," Richard said.

Lila backed away. "You're her son," she said. "You tell her."

"You're the one who wants to leave. You tell her."

Richard put his arms around Lila and pulled her close.

"You don't understand," he told her. "I'm her only child and as far as she's concerned she'll be losing me forever."

Richard felt his wife move away from him, even though she was still in his arms.

"I understand perfectly," Lila said coolly. "And if you're too afraid to tell her, I will."

But that night Helen was already being told. Jason Grey turned to her in their bed and asked, "How would you like for it to be just you and me again?"

"You and me?" Helen said, confused. Then she realized what Jason meant. "Oh," she said, and she started to cry.

"All you had to do was say no," Jason teased her.

"What makes you so sure they're leaving?" Helen asked.

"I'm sure," Jason said. "They just don't know how to tell us."

"Well, if that's what they've decided," Helen said, still crying, "I can think of a lot worse things than being left here with you."

Helen might be losing her son, but she didn't intend to make it easy for Lila to take him away. First of all, she was sweet as pie—every time Lila began to talk about California Helen offered her a wool sweater that just didn't suit her any more, or a new recipe, or a piece of china, until—piece by piece—Lila had an entire service for eight stored in a cardboard box in the attic. Every day Lila swore she would tell her mother-in-law about their plans, and every day she put it off. Richard unpacked their suitcases, convinced that Lila's obsession with California had been nothing more than a reaction to a particularly cold winter. But when Lila stopped talking about leaving it wasn't because she wanted it any less.

One day in January, Lila went up to the bedroom and didn't come down. She stayed in bed for three days and nights, and every time she breathed she felt a terrible pain in her abdomen.

She refused to speak to Richard, and she would not see a doctor. Richard couldn't bring himself to go to work and he wasn't allowed in his own room. He sat for hours at the kitchen table, unable to eat, not understanding why he felt as though he had lost his wife.

On the fourth day Helen spent the morning crying, then she went upstairs. She walked into Lila's room without bothering to knock and sat at the foot of the bed.

"You don't have to tell me what's wrong," Helen said. "Just tell me—is leaving New York the only thing that will cure you?"

Lila hadn't talked for such a long time that when she spoke her voice was thick.

"It's the only thing," she told her mother-in-law. "If I stay here I'll die."

Helen took the suitcases out of the closet and packed Lila's and Richard's clothes. She telephoned Jason at the gas station and asked him to bring home the station wagon he'd been working on to replace their old Chrysler. Then Helen went downstairs to the kitchen and closed the door behind her. While Jason Grey and Richard packed up the station wagon and helped Lila down to the car, Helen baked a honey cake. She used almonds, and sweet brown pears, and when it was done she carefully placed it in a tin that she carried out to the car. She handed the cake to Lila through the window of the station wagon, and she kissed Richard twice before she let him go. Lila held the cake tin on her lap, as if its heat could make her well. When they had been on the Long Island Expressway for over an hour, she suddenly begged Richard to drive into Manhattan.

"I understand," Richard had said. "You want to see your parents before we go."

But that hadn't been it at all. It seemed so simple now—Lila would run into the apartment and shake her mother by her shoulders until she divulged the name and address of whoever had stolen Lila's daughter. Then all Lila had to do was go back out to Richard and tell him that her mother had insisted they take a little cousin with them to raise as their own. Once they reached the house where her daughter was being held, Lila would slip through the front door, wrap the child in a warm blanket, then run as fast as she could. All the way to California she would hold her daughter on her lap—she wouldn't let go of her, not until the western sky opened up in front of them as they sped past black hills and corrals full of half-wild horses.

When they got to the apartment building, Richard couldn't find a parking space, so he circled the block. Lila got out of the car, but once she was standing on the sidewalk her sense of expectation disappeared. She went inside the building and climbed the three flights of stairs, but when she reached the apartment and knocked on the door there was no answer. She knocked again and again, but each time she did she felt more defeated—in the cold hallway her plans to kidnap her daughter seemed ludicrous, and in the end, when she walked downstairs and back out on to the street, she was relieved that no one had been home.

She could see the station wagon half a block away, stuck in traffic. It was then that she happened to turn back to take one last look at the apartment building, and when she looked upward she saw the curtains moving in the window of the parlor. Up on the third floor, hidden behind lace curtains, Lila's mother gazed downward. As soon as she realized Lila saw her, she dropped the curtains and moved away. But even then Lila could see her mother's shadow, a line of black pressed against the white curtains.

When the station wagon pulled up to the curb, Lila got in, leaned her head against the seat, and wept.

"They may not be the best in the world, but they're still

your parents," Richard said. "It's not easy to leave people behind."

Lila reached down and lifted up the hem of her dress to wipe her eyes.

"Are you sure you want to do this?" Richard asked. "We don't have to go to California—we can still turn back."

Without bothering to look, Lila knew that her mother was still watching her. She moved over so that Richard could put his arm around her, then she closed her eyes as they drove toward the Lincoln Tunnel, and in no time at all they had left New York behind them for good.

->>>

At first it seemed as if it was only a matter of time. But a year passed, then two, then three, and Lila still hadn't gotten pregnant. She bathed in tubs filled with warm water and vitamin E, she forced herself to eat calf's liver twice a week, she gave up caffeine and chocolate and spices. Every morning, before she got out of bed, she took her temperature, and she kept a chart of her ovulation taped to the back of her closet door. But in her heart, Lila knew that she'd never be given another chance; each time Richard talked about the child they would someday have Lila grew more desperate, and by the time she turned thirty she had given up hope.

The nights they made love, Lila could never sleep. She waited until Richard's breathing grew deep, and then she carefully got out of bed. On these nights she went out to the garden, and she sat in a black wrought-iron chair beneath the lemon tree. She never bothered with slippers, even though the patio was cold and snails moved across the slate, leaving slick trails behind. There had been something wrong with the garden from the start; the neighbors had warned them that everything you wanted to grow simply wouldn't, but renegade plants would reappear each time you pulled them out by the roots. At the rear of the yard, along a low wooden fence, the previous owner had foolishly planted a passion flower vine that was now so tangled it had begun to strangle itself with its own flowers. At the time of night when Lila went to sit in the yard it was almost possible to hear the vine growing, wrapping itself tighter around the fence.

In the mornings Lila climbed back into bed, and Richard never seemed to notice that she'd been gone all night. He still talked about the son they would have someday, the daughter who would look just like Lila, but each year he sounded a little less convinced. When they had been married for fifteen years, Richard said, "Let's say we can never have any children. Is that the worst that can happen to us?"

She told him it wasn't, but secretly Lila believed that it was. Childless women began to disgust her—she could sense their brittle presence in the supermarket and the bakery, she could look right through them and see white dust and bones. The worst times were when Richard's parents came out to visit. The older they got, the more they wanted grandchildren, but even they knew enough to stop asking when. The year Lila turned thirty-nine was the first time Helen Grey visited without advising them that the guest room would make a perfect nursery. But every now and then during that visit, Lila would look up and find her mother-in-law watching her, as if she were the only person who really knew just how badly Lila had cheated her son.

That was when Lila began to do readings again. It wasn't for the money—Richard had bought his own shop—it was because of the comfort she found in reaching into someone else's sorrow. She began carefully, starting with her neighbors, who were shocked by her sudden interest in them. In time, Lila's clients swore by her. Her advice was noncommittal but sound, and Lila actually found she was pleased when her clients grew to depend on her, waiting to make travel plans or give a husband an ultimatum until Lila could read their tea leaves. It was one of her regular customers, Mrs. Graham from around the corner, who brought her niece to Lila's one afternoon. The red tablecloth was set out and the water boiled by the time the two women arrived. Lila read for Mrs. Graham first—the question of whether or not to put her ailing dog to sleep was evaded until next time—and then for the niece. The niece had come from a bad marriage in Chicago, and she was already reconsidering the separation from her husband.

"What I want to know is will he walk all over me if I go back?" she asked Lila. "I give in to him a lot, and that's my problem. If he tells me he's spent his paycheck I say, Why that's all right—but inside I'd like to kill him."

Lila nodded and poured the water over the tea leaves; she could tell that the niece was going back to her husband to give him another chance. She watched the leaves float to the surface without much interest, but when the niece had finished her tea Lila took one look inside the cup and immediately began to cry. Lila's clients sat on the edge of their seats, and they both let out a whoop when Lila informed the niece that she was pregnant.

"Wait till I tell my husband," the niece said. "He is going to flip out when I tell him."

After they left, Lila went into the bathroom and ran the cold water, and from then on she refused to open the door if Mrs. Graham came for a reading. All the rest of that month, Lila felt shaky, and each time she closed her eyes she saw the small motionless child in the center of the cup. It was not as if she had not seen death during readings before, but this was different, this was enough to break your heart. She grew careful; if a client even mentioned that she was considering pregnancy, Lila never read for her again. But she was tricked the following year by a high-school student who had accompanied her mother to a reading. Lila had carelessly poured a cup of tea for the girl so that she'd be occupied during her mother's reading. It wasn't until the reading was over, and Lila reached for the girl's cup to carry it into the kitchen, that she saw the symbol again. At first she was paralyzed, but when the mother went out to start her car, Lila found an excuse to pull the girl back into the house. After she'd told the girl she was pregnant, Lila was so upset she was the one who seemed to need comforting.

"I'll be okay," the girl promised Lila. "Really."

"Did you know you were pregnant?" Lila asked her.

"I sort of thought I was," the girl admitted.

Lila simply couldn't bring herself to tell any more of what she'd seen, and she couldn't bear to listen as the girl confided that she planned to enter a special high school program for mothers, not when she was so certain that the child would not live.

That night Lila had a fever of a hundred and three and when she woke up the next morning the bed was soaked with tears. After that she almost gave up the readings altogether, particularly at times when she happened to look in the mirror and saw how much she looked like the old fortune-teller in New York. But she continued to see her clients. She managed to convince herself that it was just a job like any other and that she couldn't possibly know what the future would bring, although now and then she still seemed to know more than she wanted to.

Late one night, in the middle of a warm, dry winter, the telephone suddenly rang. Lila felt certain that something had happened to Helen. She sat up in bed, rigid, while Richard ran to answer it. The air was so warm that the clothes Lila had hung up to dry overnight were no longer even damp, but when Richard came back into the bedroom he found that Lila had wrapped a heavy woolen blanket around her shoulders.

"It's my mother," Richard said. "She's in the hospital."

He sat on the edge of the bed, but when Lila went to sit next to him he didn't seem to notice.

"She's dying," Richard said.

"Oh, no," Lila said, but what she really meant was *Please don't leave me.*

"I have to go tonight," Richard told her. "Otherwise it may be too late for me to see her again."

Lila called the airline for a reservation; then she took out the suitcase and packed a week's worth of Richard's clothes.

They were standing by the front door, waiting for the taxi, when Lila thought she heard the sound of bees.

"Come with me," Richard said to her.

But for Lila New York had dissolved; it wasn't even on the map any more.

"It's better if you go alone," Lila told Richard. "You're her only son. You're the one she wants to see."

"I'm going to give my father hell," Richard said. "He should have told me before."

"Don't do that," Lila said. "You know your father."

That was when Richard started to cry.

"Oh, don't," Lila begged him. "What good will it do you?"

"I just don't see how he's going to go on without her," Richard said. "That's the part that really gets me."

When the taxi came, Lila walked Richard out to the porch, but she couldn't watch him drive away. It was the first time since their marriage that they had been apart. But although she dreaded being alone, Lila needed this time by herself: this was the week her period was due, and if she missed it again it would make three times in a row. Every morning Lila checked to see if the sheets were stained. On the fifth day there was one wild moment when she actually thought she might be pregnant, but of course she was not. She sat by the open window, and as night began to fall she grew flushed, and her nerves seemed much too delicate—she could feel them jump beneath her skin.

She should have been relieved; for years she had tried to get pregnant just to please Richard, she had never really wanted any child other than the one she had lost. An early menopause simply saved her from trying to love another child in a way she never could. But now that it was truly over, Lila cared much more than she should have. She went into mourning: when neighbors knocked on the door, she didn't answer, she didn't even bother to get dressed, and when Richard phoned from New York, Lila no longer recognized his voice. Eight days later, when Richard returned, Lila knew that neither of them would ever be the same.

It was early evening when the taxi pulled up. Lila was already in bed asleep when Richard came to lie down next to her. He woke Lila by watching her, and she came to him from a dream where all the furniture in her parents' apartment had been replaced with woven mats, and tea was being served from a silver samovar in the middle of the floor.

"Was she in pain?" Lila asked when she woke.

"She didn't remember me," Richard said.

"Of course she did," Lila told him. "You're her only son."

Richard didn't have the strength to unbutton his shirt—he had been wearing the same clothes for two days.

"The hedges are all overgrown," he said. "I noticed it first thing when I got out of the taxi."

"She knew you," Lila said.

"No," Richard told her. "She knew my father and she called him by name, but she didn't remember me."

"You don't understand," Lila said. "The worst thing in the world for a mother is to leave her child. She couldn't bring herself to remember you, because if she did she'd have to leave you behind."

In the morning, when she woke up, the first thing Lila

heard was a jet overhead. But when she listened carefully she could hear the rhythm of an ax. She got out of bed and reached for her robe. In the kitchen, the back door was ajar. A few hours earlier it had begun to rain; puddles had formed, and when Lila walked out to the patio the sudden rush of cold water on her feet left her confused for a moment. In the rear of the yard Richard was cutting down the vines that covered the fence. The ax he used had been stored in the garage for years, but it was still so sharp that in no time a huge pile of vines had collected on the ground. There were white flowers with green centers all over the yard, as if an earthquake had torn them from their vines.

At this time of year in East China, nothing grew. Lilies were deep in the frozen ground, peach trees and azaleas were bare. It had been the dead of winter when Lila and Richard left New York, but the sky had been deep blue. The cake tin Helen had given Lila was red metal, and because the cake inside was still warm, the tin seemed to shine. The one time Lila looked back, Helen was following their car. She went as far as the end of the dirt driveway, where in the spring there would be so much deep mud that Jason would have to shovel for hours before he could move his car. Helen stopped, and she stood there waving. Up on the porch, Jason Grey lit a cigarette, then leaned over the wooden railing. He stayed right where he was as they drove away, watching his wife and waiting for her to come back to him.

Out in the rain, Lila pulled her bathrobe tighter around herself. Somehow, she had become forty-six years old, and she didn't know quite how it had happened. She wondered if there was something about California that made the time move so quickly. Without winter to shock you into another year, entire seasons had dissolved in the sunshine; and no one could manage time in a place where even the roses were so confused that they bloomed year round.

Richard was almost through clearing the fence. He worked

harder than ever, as though his life depended on the steady rhythm of the ax. Later, Lila would make him a pot of hot coffee. She'd sit on the rim of the tub while he bathed, just to be near him. But for now, she waited. In their own backyard, as the rain washed all the snails out of their garden, Lila and Richard crossed over an invisible line together. Impossible as it seemed, they had become older than Helen and Jason Grey had been on that day in East China when ice was everywhere and the sky was so cold and so blue.

PART THREE

In November, when the moon was clear and white and the acacia trees gave off a bitter scent, Rae began to believe that she had lost the baby. It wasn't just that odd look on the psychic's face as she read Rae's tea leaves, it was that she felt so absolutely well. During the first three months she had been exhausted, and so queasy that she couldn't stand to look at boiled eggs. Now she could stay up past eleven, she could eat hot chili if she wanted to, and she had so much energy that she found herself cleaning out closets on her days off from work. The better she felt, the more she sensed something was wrong, and there was one thing she knew for certain: in all these months she had not once felt the baby move.

She went through lists of birth defects and diseases, but in the end she decided that she herself was at fault. She had taken too many hot showers, eaten too much salt, she'd lifted her arms high above her head so that the umbilical cord had wrapped itself around the baby's neck. In her heart she knew that each time she gained another pound it was only because her body had been cruelly tricked. Her pregnancy was a farce, it would never last full term; eventually someone would cut her open and remove whatever was inside her, and that would be the end of it. She put off going to see an obstetrician, and at work she refused to answer any of Freddy's questions about her health. But Freddy had already guessed, and one day he took her out to lunch at a Chinese restaurant and offered her five hundred dollars.

"You're kidding," Rae said. "You want to give me money?"

"I was thinking of it as a loan," Freddy said. "For one thing, Rae, you need new clothes."

"Are you going to fire me?" Rae said.

She and Jessup had managed to save four thousand dollars—the bankbook was hidden in the silverware drawer, under the forks and spoons—and if she really had been having this baby she could have used the savings to cover the hospital bills if Freddy fired her.

"Of course I'm not going to fire you," Freddy said. "But I'll tell you the truth—I'm real uncomfortable about this whole pregnancy thing."

"So am I," Rae said.

"You know what I'd like to know?" Freddy said. "Where's that assassin now that you need him?"

"I'm not interested in your money," Rae said stiffly.

"Oh, come on," Freddy said. "I'd charge you less interest than a bank would."

Rae couldn't help laughing.

"Seriously," Freddy said. "It's a gift."

Rae knew that Freddy was feeling sorry for her, and somehow that made her feel sorry for herself. She put down her chopsticks and watched him write out the check, unable to stop him, unable to tell him the baby would never be born. If she and Jessup had only left California things might have been different. For a while they had talked about using their savings to go to Alaska. Actually, Jessup had been the one doing the talking.

"This country feels too small for me," he had told Rae one night.

"Oh, really?" Rae was amused by the idea.

"Yes, really," Jessup had insisted. "Everything's been overdone and overused in this country. There are no options any more."

"What about Alaska," Rae had teased. "Is that too small for you, too?"

The moment he looked over at her she thought, Oh, shit—he's serious about this.

"Admit it," Jessup had said. "It's not a bad idea—even if it is yours."

"Not Alaska," Rae told him.

"I'll tell you what," he said. "Let's just consider it—that's all."

They had been in bed, and Rae wrapped her arms around him. "All right," she'd agreed. "But that doesn't mean we'll really do it."

Now she wished they had. If it had been just the two of them somewhere in Alaska, they might still be together. Snow would reach the rooftop of their cabin, and at night the ice outside would turn everything blue—everything, the glaciers and the white wolves and the owls that lived in the eaves. A child born there would be so healthy it would reach out its arms to hold you the moment after its birth.

"I think I have to go home," Rae told Freddy.

She took the rest of the day off, and when she got home she opened all the windows in the apartment. She had suddenly begun to miss Boston, and although she had always hated the winters there, she yearned for a real November, and clear, cold air. Once, on the Tuesday after Thanksgiving vacation, she had been sitting in the kitchen, drinking coffee, when Carolyn came downstairs, wearing her camel's-hair coat and a black wool hat.

"Listen," Carolyn had said to Rae, "don't go to school today."

Rae looked up from her coffee, but her mother didn't explain any further. They still weren't really talking to each other, except for those things that had to be said: Pass the butter, Pass the salt, The telephone's for you. But Rae had a math test that day, and everyone suspected a surprise quiz in French class.

"All right," Rae agreed.

They drove downtown, to the Museum of Fine Arts. In the parking lot Carolyn turned to Rae after she took the key out of the ignition.

"I've been thinking about going back to school," Carolyn said. "Maybe even law school."

Rae had heard this before. "Do it," she advised.

"I don't know if I can," Carolyn said.

"Then why do you always talk about it?" Rae snapped.

"You know what my problem is?" Carolyn said.

It had begun to grow cold in the car; Rae shifted uncomfortably.

"I was always afraid to be alone."

"Oh, yeah?" Rae said without interest.

"Now I see you making the same exact mistake with Jessup as I did with your father," Carolyn said.

"Oh, for God's sake!" Rae said. "Could we just go to the museum?"

She got out of the car and slammed the door behind her, then walked ten paces ahead of Carolyn to the door of the museum. All through the Grecian ruins Rae stayed far enough away from her mother to prevent any conversation between them.

"I'm sorry," Carolyn finally said.

They were walking through a room filled with Japanese kimonos. "I don't mean to insult you," Carolyn said. "It's just that I see you running after Jessup."

"I am not running after him," Rae said.

"Well, going after him, then," Carolyn said. "And once he wrecks your life there'll be nothing I can do about it. I'm warning you—don't come running to me."

A young couple had come into the room, and now walked past them. Rae moved away from her mother. Carolyn followed her daughter to the next glass case of kimonos. The material had been painted by more than two dozen women; willows and water lilies washed over gold- and rose-colored silk.

"The one time I didn't feel alone was when I was pregnant," Carolyn said. "After you were born I couldn't imagine how I had managed to live all those years without you. How did I survive before? Who did I love?"

In the gift shop, before they were about to leave, Carolyn had insisted on buying Rae a gift, a poster of Monet's water lilies, which somehow seemed crude after the delicate kimonos. "Perfect for your room," Carolyn had whispered as they waited for the cashier to wrap the poster in brown paper.

Rae had agreed, she had even politely thanked her mother, but she knew that before long she and Jessup would be leaving, and the Monet poster would hang in her empty bedroom.

When they left the museum it was four, and very nearly dark. Rae carried the rolled-up poster under her arm and kept her hands in her pockets. If she had gone to school that day she would have already been home for a half an hour, waiting for Jessup to appear on the sidewalk.

"I don't know why it is, but November smells like smoke," Carolyn said. "Maybe I'm crazy, but I think it's delicious."

When Rae breathed in she realized that her mother was right, the air was delicious. For some reason Rae had the sudden urge to put her arm through her mother's arm, to feel the weight of the camel's-hair coat that Carolyn stored in a cedar closet every summer. But by then they had reached the car and Carolyn was humming as she reached into her coat pocket for the keys. Rae felt something in her chest, and she forced herself to take several deep breaths. As Carolyn unlocked the car, Rae wondered why it was that she should have to feel sorry for her mother, and why, as she breathed in the smoky blue air, one visit to the Museum of Fine Arts could make her feel so lost.

In Massachusetts, Rae could look out her window and see chestnut trees, white stars, clouds that covered the moon. Here, from her kitchen, she saw only the empty street. But the dogs were out there, she knew it. Ever since the heat wave they had been wandering through the neighborhood, looking for water and bones. And sure enough, when Rae pressed her face up against the glass she saw a large black Labrador in the courtyard; she quickly pulled down the shade. Late that night, at ten minutes after twelve, she telephoned Lila Grey.

"Are you crazy?" Lila said after Richard had handed her the phone. "How dare you call me at this hour. I'll tell you something right now—I don't intend to read for you ever again. Got that?"

Richard sat up in bed, concerned.

"It's nothing," Lila told him. "Go back to sleep."

"This is the thing," Rae said slowly, as though she hadn't heard a word Lila had said to her, "I think there's something wrong with my baby."

Lila leaned up against the headboard; she could feel her mouth grow dry.

"Don't ask me why, because I can't tell you," Rae said. "I just know something's wrong."

"Do you want my advice?" Lila asked. She was shaking, and she wished Richard would turn on his side and stop watching her. That motionless child in Rae's teacup refused to disappear. "Go see a doctor," she told Rae.

"I can't do that," Rae said quickly.

"Tomorrow, as soon as you get up, call an obstetrician and make an appointment," Lila said.

Rae didn't answer; she lifted the windowshade and watched the black dog stretch out in the courtyard for the night.

"Are you going to listen to me?" Lila said. She could hear the edge of panic in her voice, and she took Richard's hand to reassure him; under the sheets their fingers intertwined.

"Yes," Rae said.

"And I don't want you to call me again," Lila said.

"You hate me," Rae said. "Don't you?"

It was really much too late to be talking to strangers, it was the time of night when mothers went to their children who had nightmares, and they held their sons and daughters close, and stroked their hair until they fell asleep.

"Call a doctor," Lila said gently.

"All right," Rae agreed.

"Good girl," Lila said.

After she'd hung up, Rae couldn't sleep, and in the morning, when she called for an appointment at a clinic nearby, her voice was so hoarse she had to struggle to whisper. They made room on the schedule that afternoon. In the waiting room, Rae tried to imagine that Jessup was beside her, but she knew he would have never come here with her. She considered leaving, but before she could the nurse called her name and took her into a small office for blood tests. Rae didn't panic until she walked into the examining room. The doctor was a woman who seemed much too young—and really, Rae knew, this visit was pointless.

"I don't think this is the best time for me to be examined," Rae said.

"You're right," the doctor said. "The best time would have been two months ago."

Rae took off her clothes, put on a paper smock, and lay down on the examining table. She closed her eyes during the internal, and when she was told that everything looked fine, she was sure this doctor was a fool.

Rae answered all the questions for a medical history, but as she did she could feel herself growing colder. If she really thought about it, it was better this way. She wasn't meant to have a baby alone, it was fate; and if there was a good time to lose a baby it was now, before she began to feel it move inside her, before she started to wait for the rhythm of its turning in its sleep.

"Is something wrong?" the doctor asked her. "You just don't seem interested." She had been going over a food chart and discussing the vitamins she was about to prescribe.

"How long have you been a doctor?" Rae asked.

"Four years—is that long enough for you?"

Rae felt herself grow embarrassed. "Oh, it's enough, all right," she said. "It's just that you missed something. My baby is dead."

"I see," the doctor said. "You're positive?"

Rae was so cold that she was certain her blood had begun to freeze. When she looked closely at herself she noticed that the skin on her arms and legs was faintly purple.

"Don't you think I know?" Rae said. "Don't you think I can tell?"

"Lie down," the doctor said.

Rae knew now—this was the moment when she would be cut open: the doctor would reach her hands deep inside and lift the baby out, then hide it as she sewed Rae back together.

"You'd better not touch me," Rae said.

She could not believe her voice. Her real voice didn't sound that way. The doctor rolled over a tall, metal machine, and when she moved closer to the examining table, Rae sat up straight.

"Don't come near me," she said.

It was her voice after all. God, she was practically squeaking. It wasn't so much being cut open that terrified her, it was the fact that it was now. Now the operation would begin. Now she would lose her baby.

"I don't know what you think I'm going to do to you," the

doctor said. "But all I'm going to do is listen to your baby's heartbeat."

Rae nearly laughed out loud; this was supposed to comfort her? A wild search for a heartbeat that wasn't there.

"Okay?" the doctor said.

Rae looked at her coldly, then shrugged. She lay back down on the table and closed her eyes.

"This amplifies sound," the doctor explained as she rubbed some gel on Rae's abdomen.

With her eyes closed, Rae could feel the ice in the room, and it made her think of the time she and Jessup had taken a bus to Rockport one winter. The harbor had been frozen solid, but as they stood by the docks they could see the tide moving beneath the ice, and when they knelt down and peered beneath the dock they could see that the ice itself was shifting.

"That's the placenta you hear," the doctor said.

"If I lived in this town I'd go crazy," Jessup had said. "Imagine trying to sleep with the sound of the goddamn ocean ringing in your ears."

"I'd love it," Rae had said. It was one of the few times she had disagreed with him. She didn't look over at him, but could tell he was studying her.

"Yeah, well, maybe you get used to it if you hear it every night," he had finally allowed her.

"I think I've found it," the doctor said.

Rae opened her eyes. She leaned up, resting on her elbows.

"I don't hear it," she said.

"Just listen," the doctor told her.

That was when she heard it, and at the moment she heard it she started to cry.

"That's it," the doctor said. "That's your baby."

Rae was hit by something as immediate as lightning, but more piercing, whiter, a thousand times more perfect. The heartbeat seemed to come from a very great distance away. She had to remind herself that it was inside her. If she'd ever said she didn't care about this baby she'd been a liar. When the amplifier was turned off and she could no longer hear it, she sat on the edge of the examining table and wept. Later, she apologized to the doctor and got dressed. She filled out her medical forms and drove back to her apartment, but if anything it was all more of a mystery than it had been before: how anything as fragile as a body might suddenly be so strong it could carry two hearts, and not even feel the weight.

⋙

In less than a month, Rae found that she could come home from work, spend the entire evening in Jessup's easy chair reading Dr. Spock, and actually enjoy it. There was a whole new language to learn: colic and cradle cap and expressed milk. She began to wake every night at three a.m., as though she were in training. She bought milk by the quart and drank herbal tea. When none of her clothes buttoned any more, she decided against a secondhand store. Instead, she took two hundred dollars out of the bank account, went to the maternity department at Bullock's, and then spent more money on clothes in forty-five minutes than she had in the last five years. By the time the saleswoman had handed her two shopping bags, Rae was so out of breath that she had to go out to the parked Oldsmobile and lean her head against the steering wheel. There, in the parking lot, Rae felt something move for the first time. It wasn't at all what she had expected, and she picked her head up from the steering wheel and waited for it to come again. She'd been expecting an actual kick, but what she felt was more like fluttering, as if a pair of wings were deep inside her. When it happened a second time Rae realized that she had been feeling the exact same thing for weeks.

"Oh, Jesus," she said to herself in the Oldsmobile. This was really it: her child was moving.

She decided on natural childbirth and discussed it with her doctor. But when the subject of a labor coach came up, Rae found herself lying—her husband, she said, was currently on the road, selling truck tires. It was a career so unlike the ones Jessup dreamed of that for a moment she almost felt as though she had gotten back at him. She imagined him in a VW van, with a load of oversized tires, and she left him stranded on the interstate in Nebraska with a blowout and no tire small enough to fit his van.

The first person she asked to be her coach was Freddy, and he told her it was out of the question. For days afterward he was afraid to talk to her. Finally, he offered her money to hire a labor coach, and he couldn't understand why she refused him.

"It would be totally different to have you as my coach," Rae told him. "I wouldn't be paying you—you'd be there because you wanted to be."

"Oh, no I wouldn't," Freddy said. "Believe me. I wouldn't want to be there. Rae, I don't even want to hear about somebody's birth. I don't want to see a photograph. Is that the kind of coach you want?"

She nearly asked the woman next door, an actress she sometimes arranged to do her laundry with so they wouldn't both have to sit in the laundromat alone after dark. But when Rae met her out by the mailboxes one evening and mentioned natural childbirth, her neighbor looked stricken. She couldn't even step inside a hospital, she told Rae—if she were ever to have a child, they'd have to knock her out at the door.

And so it wasn't as if Rae wanted to ask Lila Grey—she simply didn't have anyone else.

"It's pathetic, isn't it?" Rae said, after she'd phoned Lila and explained what she wanted. "That I have to ask you."

What was infinitely worse, Lila thought, was to be stupid enough to get trapped on the stairwell, and to have your water break right there, in a place that was so dim it was difficult to find your way on an ordinary day. No one had been there to help her on that stairway—but there were times when Lila liked to think that Hannie grabbed at her own side at the very same moment she did, searching each rib for the pain.

"Don't you have anyone else?" she asked Rae. "A friend?"

"If I did would I be calling you?" Rae said.

"I told you not to call me," Lila said, but she didn't sound convincing, not even to herself. If she had only had the nerve to walk into the restaurant on Third Avenue she might not have been in that awful hot bedroom when her labor began, curled up in a bed that had been too small for her since she was twelve. She could have been safe in Hannie's house, and for days afterward someone would have brought her hot tea and thin slices of toast, and she wouldn't even have had to get out of bed, she could have held her daughter close, and watched as she slept.

"Just think about it," Rae said. "That's all I'm asking."

For two weeks Lila thought of nothing else, but she didn't return Rae's call. She simply couldn't bring herself to say no, not when she knew what it was like to be alone in a room that was so dark it sucked you into itself and filled your throat with so much darkness that every time you took a breath a dozen black plums pushed down on your tongue. When the door to Lila's room had opened, the light from the hallway had saved her. She could still feel the sensation of the light on her skin as her cousin had walked into the room, she could feel each footstep as her cousin came closer, then mercifully put her arms around Lila and helped her up from the floor.

If that symbol hadn't appeared in Rae's cup, if it hadn't been so clear that her child would be either stillborn or so damaged that a future was impossible, Lila might have agreed to help her. But instead, Lila stopped answering her phone. She told Richard she'd been getting crank calls, and the two of them lay in bed, still as stones, whenever the phone rang late at night, with a ring so piercing it cut right through your dreams. Lila's readings suffered—not just because she missed appointments when she didn't answer the phone, but because she had used up so much energy in not telling Rae the truth that she now couldn't seem to lie to anyone else. She told one bad fortune after another: old clients began to cancel their appointments for weekly readings, new clients at the restaurant fled from their tables in tears and complained to the management. But Lila couldn't seem to stop herself. She told old women to draw up their wills, and young women wept when they heard that the lover who was absent on holidays was not with a sick friend but with a wife. The manager of The Salad Connection gave Lila one more chance, and when there were three more complaints in a single afternoon—a divorce, failure at a job, and possible drug abuse—he fired her.

In a way it was a relief. That very same day Lila took all the tins of loose tea from her cabinets and poured the tea down the drain in the sink. She had Richard call the phone company and change their number; she cut up her white silk turban with a pair of garden shears and threw out the red shawl she always used as a tablecloth during readings. When she decided to go into the auto shop each morning and take over the books, Richard was shocked, but Lila explained that she couldn't stand another moment of listening to someone's troubles; adding up the repair bills for BMWs and Audis was exactly what she needed to clear her head. But in the afternoons, when she was alone in the house, Lila was so uneasy that she couldn't sit still. And when she looked out her window one day and saw Rae sitting in her parked car, Lila's throat went dry, but she wasn't surprised. She had been expecting her to appear for days, and, what was worse, she had wanted her to. Lila put on a sweater and went outside; she got into the passenger seat next to Rae and slammed the door shut.

"I've been trying to get up the nerve to come in and let you have it," Rae said. "You could have at least answered the phone. You could have told me that you didn't want to be my labor coach." She stole a look at Lila. "Unless you haven't decided yet."

"I'm not the right person," Lila said.

"It hardly takes any time," Rae insisted. "There are only six weeks of Lamaze class, and they don't start until February. You wouldn't even see me again until then."

Lila shook her head. "You need somebody else."

"Don't you understand?" Rae said. "I don't have anyone else."

They both looked out through the front windshield. Rae was close to tears, but Lila was the one who was afraid: if Rae reached out during labor and put her arms around Lila's neck, she might be pulled back into the darkness. Already, she could hear the flapping of huge wings.

"I'll tell you what I think," Lila said evenly. "You may not need me after all. Your boyfriend may come back."

"My boyfriend!" Rae said. "That'll be the day." But she looked over at Lila, interested. "What makes you say that?" she asked.

"I just feel it," Lila said. "He's not gone yet."

Lila found herself agreeing to be Rae's labor coach if Jessup failed to return—that's how sure she was that she wouldn't be needed. But afterward, when Rae had driven away and Lila was walking up the path to her front door, she felt a peculiar kind of regret, almost as if she wanted to witness the birth. She stood on the porch, between the two rose bushes. Even though the front door was open, she stood there a little longer, and she looked down the street. But Rae had pressed down hard on the accelerator—just in case Jessup had already come home—and the Oldsmobile was gone. There was nothing to see on Three Sisters Street except for a line of blue clouds in the western sky, a sure sign that before long the weather would change.

The following week it rained every day, but in spite of the weather the superintendent of Rae's apartment complex strung white Christmas lights in the courtyard. The baby seemed more restless than usual, shifting its weight and throwing Rae off balance, so that she had to grab onto furniture and walls to stop herself from falling. It was the worst time of the year, those weeks between Thanksgiving and Christmas when being alone can send you over the edge. Rae had just about given up hope that Lila's prediction was right—expecting Jessup to come back left her lonelier than ever before. Every morning when she got out of bed Rae switched on the TV, just so she could hear someone's voice. After a while she moved the set into the kitchen and propped it up on the counter so she could watch as she ate dinner. It was some time before Rae realized that this was exactly what her mother used to do, and it drove her wild to think that now that she finally was no longer haunted by the scent of Carolyn's perfume she had to go and take on her habits. Once, she actually added mustard to her egg salad before she remembered it wasn't she who liked egg salad that way, but her mother. Too much time alone was what was making her watch the news while she ate dinner and add mustard to things. When she was with Jessup she used to count the hours till the weekend, now weekends meant nothing to her, and there were times when Freddy had to remind her what day it was.

It was a Friday, and still raining, when Rae ran through the courtyard to get to her apartment before she was soaked. The door was slightly ajar, and she knew right away that Jessup was inside. She could hear the sound of the TV and she smelled fresh coffee. For a moment as she stood in the courtyard it was almost as if everything was the same as it had been before that awful heat wave. But as soon as she went inside and saw Jessup in the kitchen, she knew that it wasn't the same. He didn't even look as if he belonged any more: he seemed too big for the wooden chair he sat in, his boots stuck out from under the far side of the table, his denim jacket was hung over the back of the other chair, dripping water onto the linoleum. The oven was turned on so that his jacket would dry, and Rae felt uncomfortably warm. She stood in the kitchen doorway and stared at him and was surprised to find she had nothing to say.

Jessup cleared his throat. "I made some coffee," he finally said.

Rae looked at the table now and saw that he had set out a ceramic mug for her and filled it with coffee. She could not remember his ever doing that for her before, not in seven years.

"I can't," she said. "I'm staying away from caffeine."

"Oh," Jessup said, as if he suddenly remembered her condition. He looked at her dead center, and Rae immediately pulled his old rain slicker more tightly around herself.

"Why don't you sit down?" Jessup said, as if it was his place to invite her in.

Rae stayed exactly where she was.

"I've got myself a room in a place outside Barstow," Jessup said.

"You don't even have the decency to tell me what you think," Rae said.

"Think about what?" Jessup said uneasily.

"About the way I look," Rae said.

She really had to watch herself; she could hear her voice cracking. She went to the refrigerator and poured herself a glass of milk.

"You look great," Jessup said.

"What a liar," Rae said.

She sat across from him at the table and she knew that he hadn't come back for her.

"After the movie wrapped I figured I had two ways to go," Jessup said. "I could try and get my foot in the door of the movie business, which is a joke because once you're a driver they think you're an imbecile. Or I could get involved in a business proposition with a guy I met in Hesperia."

"What business?" Rae said.

"I got lucky for once," Jessup said. "It's an estate sale. Some old guy died and his family is selling the property cheap. Three thousand dollars up front for me, and three thousand for my buddy."

Rae had never heard him call anyone his buddy. She thought of the four thousand they had saved and her mouth tightened.

"You didn't ask me how I've been feeling," Rae said.

"You didn't give me a chance," Jessup actually had the nerve to say.

Rae picked up the carton of milk and threw it at him. He hadn't expected it so he didn't even try to duck. The carton hit him on the shoulder and milk poured down his shirt.

"Oh, Christ," Jessup said. He jumped up and wiped off his shirt. "It doesn't take much to get you hysterical these days, does it?"

Rae realized that she was exhausted. She reached for her glass of milk and finished it, wondering if they were having some kind of divorce here.

"There are plenty of things you didn't ask me," Jessup said. "Like what kind of business I'm considering." When Rae didn't ask, he told her anyway—it was forty acres with a trailer and a barn. "You know why the barn's there?" Jessup grinned.

Rae couldn't even begin to guess. "Why?" she asked.

"Because I'm going to be raising horses."

She couldn't help but laugh. When they had first run away together Rae had found a cabin for rent in Maryland, but, when Jessup had come to look at it, all he had to do was hear the squirrels running back and forth inside the attic walls and he'd fled. They had rented the garden apartment in Silver Spring instead.

"Laugh," Jessup said. "But they're not any old horses. They're midget horses," he informed her.

Rae let out a shriek that was so piercing Jessup ran over to her. It took a few seconds before he realized that she was hysterical with laughter. He shook his head and poured himself another cup of coffee and glared at her. He watched her, waiting for her to stop, but every time Rae even thought the words *midget horses* she burst out laughing all over again.

"Go ahead," Jessup told her. "But you'll take me seriously when I'm rich."

Rae wiped the tears from her eyes and instantly felt sober. He actually believed in this.

"I swear to God, Rae," Jessup said, "they're no bigger than Saint Bernards."

He spooned sugar into his coffee.

"I need this ranch," he said.

Now she knew exactly why he'd come back. "Not on your life," Rae said.

"Look, you took the car, now let me have the bankbook."

"I would rather give that bankbook to a total stranger than give it to you," Rae said. "I'd tear it in half first."

"You won't give me an inch," Jessup said.

"I gave you a little more than that," Rae said. "Like, try everything. I was in love with you."

"Was?" Jessup said. He came up behind her and put his arms around her.

"Cut it out," Rae said. "I really mean it."

"I could stay here tonight," Jessup said.

Having his arms around her reminded her that the room was much too hot. She stood up and turned off the oven. "I don't want to pay the gas bills to dry your jacket," she said.

They stood facing each other. It was getting dark, but

neither of them went to turn on a light. There was still a puddle of milk on the floor, Jessup hadn't bothered with it when he cleaned off his shirt, and the milk looked blue, as if someone had spilled a bottle of ink. Rae could feel the baby shift, and she put one hand against her ribs.

"I could stay," Jessup said.

Rae shook her head. She couldn't bring herself to look at him until he turned away, then she watched as he rinsed out his coffee cup and put on his denim jacket.

"I guess I'll take the bus back," Jessup said.

"I guess you will," Rae shrugged.

You couldn't see a thing out the kitchen window, but Rae could tell from the sound of the rain—it was bad weather for taking the bus back to Barstow, alone.

"I don't want there to be any bad feelings," Jessup said.

"Why should there be?" Rae said. "Because you care more about some horses than you do about your own child?"

"It's all in my head," Jessup said. "Nothing that's happened lately has anything to do with you."

"Nothing you've ever done has had anything to do with me," Rae said.

"You're wrong about that," Jessup told her, and after he'd left she almost believed him. On some of those days when he stood outside her parents' house, it was so cold even Jessup must have felt it. When she couldn't manage to get out of the house she could see him from her bedroom window, waiting for hours. She couldn't help but think of him there on the bus back to the desert; his legs were so long he'd have to stretch them out in the aisle and he wouldn't get to Barstow until after midnight. In all the years they spent together Rae had believed that if she just kept working at it, she could keep him. But she just didn't want to work that hard any more.

That night she didn't have any trouble sleeping: her bed seemed softer than usual and the rain continued till dawn. In the morning, Rae cleaned the milk off the floor and washed out the coffeepot. But she didn't open the drawer in the kitchen and reach beneath the silverware until two weeks later. She felt like a total fool to just be discovering that the whole time he'd been sitting there with her he'd already had their bankbook in the pocket of his denim jacket, and that his asking had only been a formality—he'd planned to leave her with nothing at all from the start.

->>>

When Rae didn't call back Lila felt herself grow more and more anxious. She wanted to hear for herself that their bargain was sealed, she wanted to know the exact hour of the day when Jessup had come back. Rae's unborn child had begun to haunt Lila: in the shop she thought about foolish things—baby smocks with pearl buttons, tiny silver spoons, bibs embroidered with lace—and each time she added up the columns of figures in the books she added wrong and charged Richard's customers too little or too much. At night she dreamed of stillborn babies whose fingers and toes were as cold as ice. But what terrified Lila most was that there were actually times when she found herself making a list of names, as if this baby was hers.

If she was wrong—if Rae's boyfriend didn't return—Lila knew that she wouldn't keep her part of the bargain. Every day she waited for the phone call that would release her, but the call never came. Richard could tell how upset she was; he asked so often what was wrong that finally Lila told him. But Richard didn't understand; he thought Lila would make a wonderful labor coach, he urged her to keep her promise to Rae. His praise only drove Lila away from him, and it made her realize that if you haven't told someone the truth for a long enough time, after a while you can't tell him anything at all and expect him to understand.

So many days went by that Lila began to wonder if perhaps she was free of Rae at last. But then one night, as she was washing the dishes after supper, Lila closed her eyes for a moment and saw a tall man sitting in the very last row of a bus, his head tilted back so he could sleep. It seemed to be very late at night and the sky above the road was so clear Lila could see the Milky Way. Lila turned the water off in the sink and went to sit down. When Richard saw the look on her face, he dropped the magazine he'd been reading and sat up straight in his chair. Lila looked up at him; her eyes were so dark it was impossible to tell their true color.

"I've just seen something," Lila said.

Richard tried to get her to explain, but she wouldn't. He thought what she had seen was the problem, but that wasn't it. It was the fact that she had seen anything at all. It was simply that on this night Lila knew that she could find out things she didn't want to know. And she could feel it—it wasn't the future she was seeing, but the past, and she grew so frightened that she couldn't even go back into the kitchen alone, she had to ask Richard to walk in there with her and hold her hand.

They finished the dishes together, but Lila wouldn't talk to Richard, and later when he said he was going to bed she didn't seem to hear him. He stood in the doorway, waiting; when he called her name sharply, the way you call to people you can't seem to waken, Lila told him to go on without her. And as Richard walked down the hallway he had the distinct impression that it was Lila who was walking away from him, even though she was still in the kitchen, staring out into the yard.

When Richard got into bed, Lila could hear the springs creak; the light from the crack under the bedroom door disappeared as he turned off the lamp. Lila called Rae at a little after eleven. Rae had already been asleep for an hour, and her voice was thick, but Lila could tell, right away, that Rae had been sleeping alone. She didn't whisper the way she would have if her boyfriend had been there with her. You could hear the raw sound of betrayal in her tone.

"He came back all right," Rae told Lila. "Only he left that same night, and he took all my money with him."

"How could you let him do that to you?" Lila said.

"I didn't let him!" Rae said. "He just took my bankbook and left."

Lila sat down in a kitchen chair. She intended to tell Rae that she couldn't go through with it—Rae would have to find another labor coach. But out of the blue she started thinking about names again, and the most beautiful of the names—Catherine and Jessica and Claire—made her feel like weeping.

"You think I should go after him and get that money back, don't you?" Rae said.

"I don't know," Lila said. She felt dizzy, she really didn't feel very well at all.

"You know, you're right," Rae said admiringly. "I let him get away with everything, but I'm not going to do it this time."

After she'd hung up the phone, Lila put some water up to boil. She needed something comforting and plain: a packaged teabag, two spoons of sugar, a chipped blue cup and saucer. As Lila poured the water in, the teabag split apart, and she had to wait for the tea leaves to settle before she could drink. She sipped the tea slowly and listened as the rain began. At first there were only a few hard drops hitting the highest leaves in the lemon tree, and then it came down faster. The weeds on Three Sisters Street had gone wild this winter; each time it rained they crept farther into the vegetable patches, they wound themselves around the chain-link fences and around the lowest telephone wires. Tonight, the birds in the trees shivered, and husbands and wives turned to each other in bed beneath extra blankets and quilts. It was the kind of night when no one should be up past midnight, alone in the kitchen.

Lila had finished only half the cup when she realized that there was something wrong with the tea. It left a strange aftertaste in her mouth; her tongue was coated and numb. When she looked down into the cup, the outline of a child was already forming. Lila ran to the sink and spilled out the tea. She stayed there, leaning against the sink for balance. The rain was coming down harder than ever, but Lila couldn't hear its echo on the roof or in the rain gutters. She suddenly knew exactly what she wanted; she didn't even have to think about it, she felt it the way a mother feels her baby's cries somewhere just beneath her skin. It seemed so simple now, she could hardly believe she had waited this long. She was going back to get her daughter, and before the rain slowed down, before the moon returned to the center of the sky, Lila went into the bedroom, and she quietly dragged her suitcase out of the closet and packed nearly all her clothes.

That night Richard dreamed of his mother. She was in the parlor of the old house in East China, with her hands in front of her face, weeping. Somehow, sparrows had gotten into the house; they flew everywhere and got tangled up in the drapes. There was nothing Helen could do to help them; she could only watch as more and more were caught in the heavy fabric, trapped inside billows of linen. As Richard dreamed, Lila packed her suitcase. Then she left the bedroom and closed the door behind her. She put her suitcase in the front hallway and went to make coffee. At exactly three a.m. the birds outside began to sing, and Lila went to the window. But already she was seeing only the things she imagined her daughter saw: bare white birch trees, a thin layer of ice smoothly covering the cement, the morning star in the east.

She was still thinking about her daughter when Richard woke up in the morning and found she wasn't in bed. He went into the living room. Lila was sitting on the couch; her coat was draped over the rocking chair. Richard sat down next to her, but instead of taking her hand he kept his own hands folded in his lap.

"What's happening to us?" Richard said.

Lila knew she should have told him the day she met him, or the night before they got married. She should have asked him to take a walk with her on the East China Highway or told him in the car on the way to California. There were a half dozen times when she nearly begged him to turn back to New York—every time they saw a little girl, in the back seat of a car, at the counter of Howard Johnson's, on a billboard high above the interstate. On each anniversary, during every full moon she could have told him. But all of those chances slipped away, just as this one was slipping away from them now.

Lila turned to him and rested her head against his shoulder. Richard was wearing a blue bathrobe that Lila had given him for his birthday one year. He began to stroke Lila's hair, and each time he did Lila held him a little tighter. But by the time the blackbirds in the yard had flown to the highest branches of the lemon tree, Lila had missed another chance completely. All the way to the airport, in the back seat of the taxi, she kept one arm on her suitcase and thought about the way he'd asked her, at the very last minute, not to go. He never asked why she was leaving, just asked her not to go. After the taxi dropped her off, Lila stopped thinking about Richard, and, after all, she had to. Once the jet had taken off, it didn't really matter if she missed him or not: in less than six hours she'd be back in New York.

⋙

It took Rae three full days to track him down, and at the end of that time she felt as though she could commit murder. It had been bad from the start—when she drove out to Barstow there were dead animals all over the road: snapping turtles with their shells cracked open, lost dogs, hawks with wingspans of nearly two feet. Every time she passed something dead on the road, Rae closed her eyes and pressed her foot down harder on the accelerator. Then, when she got into town, she found he wasn't listed in the phone book, and she had to waste forty dollars on two nights at a motel where the lumpy mattress made sleeping impossible.

He didn't have a box at the post office, and there wasn't a car registered in his name at the Department of Motor Vehicles. It was almost as if he had never existed. By the third day Rae had just about given up hope of ever finding him again when she heard a waitress mention his name at Dunkin Donuts.

"Is that my Jessup you're talking about?" Rae said without thinking.

The waitress turned from her friend and looked Rae up and down; even when she was seated anyone could tell Rae was pregnant.

"I don't know," the waitress said carefully. She was eighteen years old and she had the feeling that she might have gone out with a married man. "It's the Jessup that took me out to dinner last Saturday night."

"How many of them do you think there can be?" Rae said.

"One," the waitress agreed.

It didn't take much to talk the waitress into divulging Jessup's Hesperia address, and once she'd gone that far the waitress went on to give Rae exact directions, writing them down on the back of a paper napkin.

On the drive over the hills Rae saw two coyotes turning over crushed turtles with their paws, inspecting the shells passively. It was night when she finally got to Hesperia, and she had to pull over and switch on the light so that she could study the directions. For a while she thought she was lost, but after another twenty minutes of driving in the dark she knew she had found the right place—she saw a flash of silver. Jessup's trailer. She pulled the Oldsmobile off the road, then cut the lights and headed down the long dirt driveway. It was so quiet that she felt herself straining to hear something. There was an old Ford convertible parked near the trailer, and Rae thought bitterly, Jessup's buddy's car. She parked and turned the key in the ignition, and when her eyes adjusted to the dark she made out Montana license plates on the Ford; she could see a row of shovels and hoes leaning against the trailer, and Jessup's old leather boots, the ones she'd bought him, caked with mud, set out on the porch.

A huge antenna was balanced over the trailer, but the air out here had to be too thin for TV frequencies, and when Rae turned on her radio to find out the time, all she got was static. Whatever time it was, it felt late. The lights in the trailer were out, and anyone could tell that whoever was inside was already asleep. Still, when Rae listened carefully she could hear noises. Beyond a small barn was a corral; Rae leaned toward the windshield and narrowed her eyes to see the horses. Jessup was right, they weren't any bigger than dogs, but somehow that didn't seem funny now. They moved in a group along the wooden fence, restless, raising a thin layer of dust. Rae found herself wondering what would happen if somebody opened the gate for them. Probably they would race toward the hills and you'd be able to hear them for miles as they moved like one dark creature, the sound of their hoofs steady in the night.

After two nights of not sleeping well, she just couldn't face Jessup yet. While she was deciding on the best place to look for a motel for the night she fell asleep behind the wheel, and it was Jessup's partner, Hal, who found her when he went out to feed the horses at five thirty the next morning. He hadn't had his coffee yet, and it was still dark, so he didn't notice the parked Oldsmobile until after he'd dragged the bales of hay out of the barn. The horses were waiting impatiently at the gate; Jessup had shut off the alarm clock and turned over, leaving everything to Hal, just as he did every morning. A stranger's parked car just meant one more thing for Hal to attend to while Jessup slept, but when he walked over and saw it was only a woman asleep, he couldn't wake her. He went to feed the horses, and it was the sound of their running to greet him that woke Rae. She knew right away she shouldn't have slept in the car: her legs were riddled with cramps and her ribs hurt, as if the baby had been pressing against them all night long. When she got out of the car she stamped her feet; it was much colder than she'd expected and she wrapped her arms around herself. She went over to the corral, leaned against it, and watched Hal drag the hay inside. The air smelled like peaches, but it was cold enough to give you goosebumps.

"I'm Rae," she said when Hal faced her, but she could tell from his puzzled look that her name didn't mean anything to him.

Inside the corral, the horses were so excited as they ate hay that their bodies seemed to shake. They were shaggier than most horses, and even when they ate they stayed crowded together, as though they were afraid to be alone. Rae couldn't take her eyes off them; the longer she watched them, the more difficult it was for her to breathe.

"It takes a while to get used to the air out here," Hal said after he'd walked out of the corral and shut the gate behind him.

He took her inside the trailer. The place was a mess—kitchen cabinets left open, clothes tossed all over the floor—and everything was so tiny that Rae felt more uncomfortable than usual about her size. She had to turn sideways to get into the kitchen and sit down. At the rear of the trailer was a set of bunk beds; Rae could tell that the person asleep in the lower bunk was Jessup just by his shape beneath the blankets.

"I can't believe this is what he spent my money on," Rae said.

Hal poured himself a cup of coffee and offered one to Rae, but she refused with a wave of her hand.

"I could kill him," she said.

Hal handed her the sugar bowl. "We're out of milk," he said. "We've got Cremora, but I never use it. It always gives me a terrible headache."

Rae looked at him as if he were the stupidest person on earth. "I'm upset," she said. "Can't you tell how upset I am? Don't you talk to me about Cremora."

Hal took some orange juice out of the small refrigerator and poured her a glass. He sat down across from her without saying a word and watched her drink.

"We've been together for seven years," Rae said. "That's not even counting high school. I don't suppose he ever mentioned me?"

Hal shook his head. "The longest I ever lived with someone was two years and seven months," he said. "Her name was Karen."

Rae nodded, expecting more, but Hal clammed up.

"I left her," Hal said finally. "I guess I'll always regret it."

Jessup moved in his sleep, and Rae and Hal looked at each other.

"He never gets up on time," Hal said. He took a sip of black coffee. "And of all the things he never told me, he certainly didn't mention a wife who was pregnant."

"We're not married," Rae said. And to herself she thought: This is really it. I really could kill him.

In his sleep, Jessup heard Rae's voice, and he dreamed that he was talking to Rae on the telephone in his mother's apartment in Boston. Whenever he used to talk to her, he'd felt as if there was nothing he could not do. Back then, all they'd needed was enough money for gas. Everything was out in front of them, possibilities were endless. Jessup woke up, but he lay in the lower bunk bed without moving and he counted the weeks until his thirtieth birthday. He had been born in the dead center of March, in one of the worst snowstorms ever to hit Boston. He just couldn't wait to be born, his mother had told him. She could feel his head moving downward as the taxi drove to Brigham and Women's Hospital, and he'd been born in the elevator, between the third and fourth floors.

Rae had admitted to Hal that she was starving, and he'd decided to drive into Barstow and get food. Jessup stayed in bed until he heard the trailer door slam and Hal's car start. Then he got up and pulled on a pair of jeans and a sweater. Rae heard him coming up behind her, but she didn't look at him, not until he navigated around the table and faced her.

"I was just thinking about sending you my new address," Jessup said.

"I'm here for my money," Rae told him. "You couldn't possibly have spent it all on a down payment for this."

"I'm just curious," Jessup said. "How'd you find out where I was?"

"If you really want to know," Rae said, "from a waitress in Barstow."

"Paulette," Jessup said. "Well, I think I ought to tell you that she's nothing to me."

"Look," Rae said, "I don't care what she is. I want my money."

Jessup lit a cigarette and leaned against the refrigerator. "I don't have it, Rae. I used half as a down payment, and the rest went to fix this place up. We're going to build a new corral, and we're buying a pickup truck—we've got expenses."

"Get the money back," Rae said stubbornly.

"Let me just tell you my plan."

"Get it from that waitress," Rae said. "She must save her tips."

"I told you already. She's nothing," Jessup said. He seemed pleased every time Rae mentioned Paulette. "Let me just explain my plan. These horses we've got are the perfect pet for people with money. Compared to one of these horses, a dog is nothing. What I'm saying is you'll have to just wait a while for your money. But I intend to pay you back."

"How could you do this to me?" Rae said. "What did you think I needed money for, a trip to Tahiti? I'm having a baby, Jessup."

"Let me just show you the place," Jessup said.

He got her a heavy sweater and opened the trailer door.

"Come on," he urged. "Just take a look."

They went out to the corral; the horses were now huddled at the far side. When he showed her the barn, Rae put her hand to the small of her back and rubbed the muscles that had been aching all morning. She realized then that the baby was pushing down on her bladder and that she'd never make it back to the trailer. She went out behind the barn, crouched down, and peed, and when she got up she saw Jessup watching her.

"Don't look at me," she said.

"Why not?" Jessup said. "You look really good. I never saw anybody pregnant look so good."

"What's that supposed to mean?" Rae said.

"It's a compliment. But then I always thought you looked good," Jessup said. "I picked you, didn't I? Didn't I ask you to leave Boston with me?"

Actually, he had, and afterward she'd wondered if she'd imagined it. He was walking her home one night; as usual they had stopped on the corner before Rae's block. That was the night he told her that he planned to leave Boston. He hadn't been looking at her, but as she watched Jessup, Rae felt as though she could see the shell around him crack open, and for a second she could see inside him.

"I mean, it's totally up to you," he had said casually. "I'm used to being alone, but if you want to go I'm not going to stop you."

"Maybe I will leave with you," Rae said, trying to sound just as casual. After that she kept sneaking looks at Jessup, searching for that crack in his shell, and at certain angles she could almost see it. But she never again had the sense that she was looking inside him, and it began to seem ridiculous that she had once imagined she could see past his skin to a thin band of light.

Whatever had happened, she had certainly never felt chosen by Jessup, and now it didn't matter who had done the choosing.

"I'll never forgive you for this," Rae said.

"I guess not," Jessup said.

They were at the corral when Hal drove up with the groceries. They turned to watch him carry the bags into the trailer.

"Don't you care that this is your baby?" Rae asked Jessup once Hal had gone inside.

"What if I did?" Jessup said. "What good would it do me? Even if I wanted to *be* his father, how could I be? I'd just ruin it—I'd end up disappearing and the guy would hate me in the end, so I might as well get all that over with now." Jessup lit a cigarette. It was windy, so he had to cup the lit match in his hand. "If we had planned it, it might have been different," he said. "I could have gotten some place like this ranch before, and by the time the kid was born I would have been rich."

She knew he wasn't going to give her any of the money back, and somehow Rae didn't even care any more. She gave him back his sweater and walked over to the Oldsmobile. The engine took a while to turn over, and once it did Rae had to pump the gas to keep it going. Through the closed car windows she could still smell the horses. If she hadn't been pregnant she might have actually considered moving here, in spite of the waitress and the fact that he hadn't even asked her to stay. Usually, she didn't take up much space—she could have slept beside him in the bunk bed, her spine against the metal wall. It would have been easy enough to wash all the dirty dishes with boiling-hot water, and the clothes left strewn on the floor would have taken a half hour at most to hang up. At night, the horses would run in circles, and the coyotes would come down from the hills to watch them, a little braver and a little closer to the corral each time. But, of course, she was no longer really alone, and Jessup would never be able to understand her putting somebody before him.

Just as she was about to leave, Jessup walked over and tapped on the window. After Rae rolled it down, he surprised them both by taking her hand. For a moment Rae swore she could see the stream of light just beneath his skin, but she forced herself to look away.

When Rae put the car in gear Jessup let go of her hand. But before she drove back onto the dirt driveway Rae turned to him and smiled.

"You're going to miss me," she said, and she didn't even give him a chance to disagree.

In Barstow, Rae stopped at a diner and got herself a sandwich to go, which she ate as she drove over the mountains. There was a thin cover of snow on the ground, and even though the altitude was higher, it was already easier to breathe. By the time she reached the flatlands it was possible to pick up L.A. radio stations. The air grew warm enough to turn the car heater off. She wasn't thinking about Jessup, she was thinking about those horses, and the more she thought about them the more relieved she was that she didn't have to spend another moment watching them move along the wooden fence. The whole time she had been with Jessup she had been seeing those horses. Even when she wasn't looking she could still see them out of the corner of her eye, like a shadow that kept getting in the way of her line of vision.

She got home in the middle of the afternoon. After she'd parked the Oldsmobile and gotten out she noticed a Volkswagen parked in front of the entrance to the apartment complex. As she walked by she could tell that the man in the driver's seat was watching her, and halfway across the courtyard she knew that he was following her. Rae walked faster and kept her keys between her fingers, sharp edge out. When she heard him clear his throat she started to run. For the first time in weeks she wished desperately that Jessup were in the apartment and that all she had to do was shout his name and he'd open the front door.

"Are you Rae?" she heard the man behind her call.

She kept running.

"Rae?" he called.

She turned and faced him. He was standing in the middle of the courtyard watching her.

"What if I am?" Rae said. She was less than fifty feet from her own door, and if she ran she could make it there before he had the chance to move.

"I'm Richard Grey," he told her. "Lila's husband."

Now that he was here he felt slightly ridiculous. He'd found her address in Lila's phone book, but it was really none of his business.

Rae looked over her shoulder, at her front door. Being afraid had started her wishing for Jessup, and now she found she couldn't stop. It was almost as if the man she wanted was someone other than the one she had just left in the desert. The Jessup she wanted was waiting for her at home. Together they felt so safe they could keep the door unlocked at all hours of the day and night and not feel as if they were in any danger.

"Is something wrong?" Rae managed to ask.

"Lila's gone," Richard told her.

"What do you mean—gone?" Rae said.

"She went to New York," Richard said. "I knew you were counting on her to be your labor coach, so I thought I'd better tell you. I've been trying you on the phone, but no one's ever home."

"Wait a second," Rae said. "She promised me."

"Well, she's back in New York," Richard said. In the empty courtyard his voice sounded hollow. "That's where we come from," he added, as though it explained something.

Rae felt her face get hot. "You can't depend on anybody," she said.

"So what do you think?" Richard said to her now. "Do you think she's coming back?"

Rae looked at him carefully and realized that he was crying. She looked away, embarrassed, but she couldn't help wondering what it would be like to be loved that much.

"Sure," Rae said. "She'll come back."

She was certain that after she'd left this morning Jessup had gone on with his plans for the day. He wouldn't start to miss her till later, and then he'd borrow Hal's car and drive to Barstow. He'd look up that waitress or somebody new, and the whole time he was missing her, he'd be holding somebody else.

Richard had collected himself, and he was particularly grateful that Rae hadn't looked at him while he'd been crying.

"I guess I'll go home," he said.

"That's a good idea," Rae agreed. "Maybe she'll call you."

They looked at each other then and laughed.

"It's hell waiting for a phone call," Rae said.

"How about a drink?" Richard said suddenly, and then he seemed flustered. "I didn't mean alcohol," he explained. "I was thinking about something cold."

Actually, Rae knew that what he wanted wasn't a drink. It was just some company.

"Sure," she said.

Richard followed her across the courtyard, then waited while she unlocked the door and went to turn on the lights. His pain was so evident that Rae almost forgot her own as she led him into the kitchen and poured them both glasses of cold, blue milk. It made it a little easier to come home when someone was sitting across the table, and because neither of them wanted to leave, they drank two glasses of milk apiece, and after a while Rae had to admit she could use a little company, too.

PART FOUR

It was snowing when Lila first got to New York, and that made her arrival easier. Everything was white, and when she took the limousine from Kennedy Airport into Manhattan she could have been anywhere: in the middle of a frozen city in Europe, deep in the iciest part of Canada. She was dropped off at the Hilton, and it felt so anonymous there that she stayed. She ordered room service and had her dinner at a table by the window on the twenty-third floor. Below her was a grid of lights. Each time a building dared to seem familiar it was swallowed up by snow; this high up above the city it almost seemed as if Lila was farther away from New York now than she had been for the past twenty-seven years.

At midnight Lila got into bed, but every time she closed her eyes she thought she heard something, and at a little after two she got up and turned off the steam heat. In the morning it was so cold that ice formed inside windowpanes all over the city. Lila ordered breakfast from room service, and then, when the waiter had left her alone and her coffee had been poured, she took out the Manhattan Telephone Directory. Her parents were no longer listed, and when she dialed the old number, which she was surprised to find she still knew by heart, a stranger answered and insisted she'd had the number for more than fifteen years.

She would get the information out of them no matter what. She didn't care how old they'd become: she would shake her mother by her shoulders until her fragile bones snapped, she would stare her father down no matter how sightless his eyes had become. She got dressed and went down to the lobby at a little after ten. Her wool coat was much too thin for a New York winter, and even after she had gotten into a cab she was still freezing. She gave the driver her old address and sat on the edge of the back seat. The city seemed much more complicated, and there was so much more of everything: traffic, and lights, and fear. When they got there Lila made the driver circle the block four times before she admitted that her building was gone. The old brownstones had been knocked down and a new co-op had taken their place, and it was the oddest feeling to be back on her old street without really being there at all. She had the driver circle the block one last time while she tried to decide what to do. She could feel herself begin to panic. All she could think of were the smallest details from her past: the numbers of the buses that used to run crosstown, the varieties of flowers their neighbors used to keep in a window-box, how many cracks in the sidewalk had to be stepped over and avoided when she walked from the front stoop to the candy store.

"This is costing you money," the driver reminded her. "Not that I'm complaining."

"The building's gone," Lila said. Her voice sounded higher than it should, as if she were still eighteen and so shy she could barely bring herself to ask customers in the restaurant what they'd like for lunch.

"Yeah, well, that happens," the driver assured her. "How about trying another address?"

They drove to Third Avenue, but when they reached the corner Lila told the driver not to stop. As they passed by the spot where the restaurant used to be, Lila rolled down her window. Hannie always walked west when she left the restaurant in the evenings; if Lila worked late she could sometimes look out and see Hannie looking through the wooden boxes of vegetables in the market down the block, choosing the right head of cabbage or pointing to three perfect apples with a bony finger before she reached for the change purse she kept pinned to the inside pocket of her black skirt.

All the time Lila had been away she had imagined New York to be exactly as she had left it. Pigeons still sat on the ledge outside her bedroom window, her mother made pot roast every Friday night in the cast-iron roasting pan she had inherited from Lila's grandmother. At night the sky was inky, apartments were always overheated and hallways much too cold, and on Third Avenue, at the rear table, you could find out everything you ever wanted to know for fifty cents. It was almost as if Lila had truly believed that she could be eighteen again, and that one ticket on a jet from Los Angeles to New York could buy back all the things she had lost. There was only one more address that might be worth something—her aunt and uncle's apartment on 86th Street. They were her cousin Ann's parents, and by now they'd be quite elderly. Lila had spent holidays at their apartment. The adults had always sat in the living room, drinking wine and eating small apple cakes. The children had been relegated to the bedroom, where they could make as much noise as they liked.

Ann, older than the rest of the cousins, would lock herself away in the second, smaller bedroom. They could hear her radio through the bedroom wall, always the same thing, Frank Sinatra, and the cousins made fun of her behind her back and called her Frankie's girl. Once, when the cousins were being particularly obnoxious, opening the windows and tossing crumpled newspapers onto anyone who happened to walk by, Lila had gone out into the hallway, pushed open her cousin's bedroom door a bit, and looked in. The radio was on and Ann was lying on her bed, writing in her diary. When she saw Lila at the door she rushed over and slammed it shut, so hard that it made Lila jump. Lila was twelve years old, and because she felt that nobody wanted her, she stayed right there in the hallway. Then and there she decided that she would never come to another family get-together again, and when her parents were ready to go and called out her name, they were surprised to find her waiting by the door, already wearing her coat and her hat.

She had never gone back to that apartment again, although when the driver now pulled up it seemed as if she had been there only days ago. She went in through the first set of doors. It was dark in the foyer, just as it had been the last time she'd been there, when her hair was so long it fell to her waist, even after it had been braided. Her parents had been arguing, so Lila was the one to ring upstairs, and she'd stood on tiptoes to reach the buzzer.

All morning Lila could feel the chances of finding her daughter slip away; and there were times, when the taxi was stalled in traffic, when she could not quite remember why she had come back in the first place. Here in the foyer, the black-and-white tiles echoed when you walked across them. The glass shade that covered the overhead light made things seem fuzzy and shapeless, and Lila had to look twice before she allowed herself to believe that the name Weber—her mother's maiden name—was still on the tenants' directory. She had found someone.

She rang upstairs; there was the sound of static as someone on the sixth floor picked up the intercom.

"Yes?" a woman said.

"It's me," Lila said, right away, as though she'd been expected. "Lila."

There was static over the intercom, and then suddenly, the buzzer rang. Lila grabbed the door open and ran all the way to the elevator. She went down the long hallway on the sixth floor, and then knocked on the door, once. She could feel her heart racing, and when someone came to open the door Lila could feel the click of the lock inside her own body, like a bone breaking.

There was a chain inside the door, and a woman looked out, examining Lila. For a moment Lila recognized her aunt; she was just as she had been when Lila was twelve years old.

"It is you," the woman said.

It was Lila's cousin, not her aunt, and for the first time since she'd come to New York Lila felt that same sense of expectation she had had when she had begged Richard to drive into Manhattan one last time. She could actually feel herself getting closer to the past when she walked into the apartment, and if her teenaged cousin had run past them, to lock herself in her bedroom and listen to records, she wouldn't have been the least bit surprised.

"I guess I must look old to you," Ann said. "You get this way living in Manhattan, but when my parents moved to Florida I couldn't pass up a rent-controlled apartment, so I moved back here."

Lila tried to listen to her cousin, but she couldn't. Again and again she reminded herself that she didn't have to scream—all she had to do was ask; she simply wanted a name or an address. She wanted her daughter.

"I was married and divorced and I took back my own name," Ann was saying. "If I were still living in Connecticut you would have never found me. His last name was Starch, which should have warned me right from the start."

Lila wanted to interrupt, but she couldn't bring herself to speak.

"It's just my mother now," Ann said. "My father died two years ago." She looked at Lila carefully. "Do you want to know about your parents?" she asked.

"No," Lila said.

The force of that word felt like a piece of glass under her tongue, and when Ann asked if she wanted a drink of water or juice, Lila nodded. While Ann was in the kitchen Lila realized that she was sitting where her mother always sat when they came for a visit. On holidays her mother never had more than two glasses of wine, but that small amount did something to her, and on the way home from this apartment she always told Lila family secrets: how her brother had been in love with another woman but had settled for his wife, how her father had been such a big drinker they used to hide the wine in a boot kept in the front closet.

"Are they alive?" Lila asked when Ann came back with tall glasses of orange juice.

Ann shook her head. "I'm sorry," she said.

There was a plate of cookies on the table, and that reminded Lila that her mother had packed her a lunch to take along on the train out to East China. She had been unwrapping the cheese sandwich that her mother had made in those last moments before they took her to Penn Station when the train reached the outskirts of East China. She put her sandwich down and moved closer to the window and saw the spot where the potato fields begin, where the earth is so sandy you can feel it whenever you rub your fingers together, and at night the sand gets in between the sheets on everyone's bed, and each time you kiss someone you can feel sand on the edge of your tongue.

"Cancer," Ann said. "Both of them."

They sat on couches facing each other, a coffee table between them.

"I know why you're here," Ann said. "It was all my fault. When they asked me about adoption I should have kept my mouth shut."

"I want her back," Lila said.

It was such a simple thing to say that it was hard to believe it could hurt so much to say it.

"Sometimes I wish I had taken her for myself," Ann said.

"I've wanted her back from the minute you took her," Lila said.

"I thought about keeping her when I had her with me in the cab," Ann said. "She was wrapped in one towel, and it just seemed so cold that night."

That night when she had walked out to the living room both of Lila's parents had turned away, terrified to look at the baby. Out on the street, she couldn't get a cab, so she kept the baby warm inside her coat and walked to Eighth Avenue. The baby was crying and Ann could feel her shivering. The ice storm had stopped everything: no buses were running and telephone lines were out. Stores that were usually open twenty-four hours a day were shut down behind iron bars, trucks were abandoned on the roads, pigeons froze in midair, and their shattered bodies lined the sidewalks.

Some people who were stranded had managed to get cabs, which were driven by only the bravest drivers. They skidded and careened down the avenues, and each time one passed Ann hailed it, but no one would stop for her. She had called Dr. Marshall from Lila's parents' apartment and arranged to meet him in his office at the hospital as soon as the baby was born. Now, she wasn't sure if he'd still be there or if he'd gone home once the ice storm had begun. But where else was there to go? Although her feet were numb and a coating of ice formed around her ankles, she continued walking downtown. After a while the baby stopped crying, and that was what really scared Ann—as long as it had been making noise she knew it was alive. She shook it, but there was no response, and she could tell it was the silence of someone who has nothing more to lose. She had to get to the hospital immediately, and the next time a taxi passed Ann ran out into the street and stood right in front of it. The taxi skidded to a halt when it couldn't avoid her, and as soon as it had stopped, Ann ran to the passenger door and got inside.

"What do you think you're doing?" the cabbie said. "You can't just jump in front of a cab and get in."

"I have to get to Beekman Hospital," Ann told him.

Now that she was sitting down she could feel that, tucked inside her coat, the baby was still breathing.

In the back seat was a couple who had been stranded uptown; because all the hotels were full, they had offered the cab driver a hundred dollars to take them home to Brooklyn. Ann looked slightly crazy to them—every strand of her hair was covered by ice, and under the yellow light of a street lamp they could see that there was dried blood on her hands.

"Take her wherever she wants to go," they advised the cab driver, and that was when Ann considered not giving the baby up, that was when it just seemed too cold.

Dr. Marshall was asleep on the couch in his office. Ann woke him, then stood by the desk as he called the couple on Long Island whom he'd promised the baby to earlier that night. She didn't hear a word he said to them; she was listening to the baby's even breathing from deep within her winter coat. Finally, she handed the baby to Dr. Marshall so that he could examine her and put her footprint on a birth certificate made out in the adoptive parents' names. He wanted to take the baby upstairs, but Ann wasn't ready to hand her over. She asked if she could be the one to carry her to the nursery.

That night there were nearly a dozen other newborns in bassinets, and for some reason none of them were crying. A night nurse sat in a rocking chair, but she had fallen asleep, and when Ann placed the baby in an empty bassinet there wasn't a sound in all of the nursery. She walked all the way to the apartment she shared with three other nurses. By now, it was a beautiful night, so clear that you could see Orion just above the roofs of the tallest buildings.

After that night Ann just couldn't bear to see Dr. Marshall any more. When he came into the emergency room the next morning to admit one of his patients who had gone into labor, Ann hid in the toilet until he was gone. Later, she went up to the nursery, but the baby was already gone. Whatever spell there had been the night before had been broken—all the babies were crying in unison, and the attention of five nurses couldn't soothe them. A few weeks later, Ann applied for a job at New York Hospital and moved uptown. There were times when she simply refused to meet old friends downtown. And when she got married and was living in Connecticut, she was grateful that she no longer had to walk past the maternity ward or the nursery and feel she had helped ruin somebody's life each time she heard a baby cry.

"I need to know their name," Lila said evenly.

Ann looked over at her, confused.

Lila's voice rose dangerously. "Tell me the name of the people who took her to Long Island."

"I already told you," Ann said. "I didn't listen when Marshall phoned them. It didn't seem to matter."

"It does matter," Lila said. "Can't you remember?"

"I can't," Ann said. "But I know who could—Dr. Marshall."

They went into the kitchen together, and Lila stood right next to her cousin as she called Beekman Hospital. Marshall hadn't been affiliated with Beekman since his residency, but if they waited the address of his private practice could easily be found. Lila couldn't wait; she went back out to the living room and stood by the window. She was so close that she could hear her daughter breathing, buttoned up inside Ann's winter coat; she could hear the taxi skidding across the avenue as the driver stomped on his brakes. If she had been the one in that taxi she would have never let that driver stop, she would have persuaded him to drive all night, and by the time they reached New Jersey her daughter would have been sleeping and the ice on the highways would have melted and refrozen into daggers, so that anyone who tried to follow them would have gotten no farther than the first dangerous corner.

Ann wrote Dr. Marshall's address and phone number on a yellow slip of paper, and Lila quickly folded it and put it in her coat pocket. When Ann walked her out to the elevator neither woman could look at the other; it was as if what had once happened to them was so private they couldn't allow themselves to acknowledge it. But when the door to the elevator opened, Ann put a hand on Lila's arm to stop her.

"I always wondered if you blamed me," Ann said.

"Of course not," Lila said, and when she kissed her cousin goodbye anyone could tell that the only one she had ever blamed was herself.

It was late afternoon and already dark when Lila walked back to her hotel. But once she got to the Hilton, she didn't stop, she continued walking, west and downtown. Each time she put her hand in her coat pocket to feel the slip of paper there, she felt a jolt; she was on the very edge—if she took one more step forward, she could never go back. Each time she tried to imagine going to see her daughter she couldn't seem to get any farther than the front door. When she reached for the bell she was put off by some terrible heat, and when she finally forced herself to ring the bell it left its burning black imprint on her flesh. She was so terrified of her daughter's reaction that she simply disappeared, and each time her daughter opened the door there was no one on the front porch, just two black feathers and a rush of cold air.

If she backed off now she could take the limousine back to Kennedy and be home tonight. She could watch Richard prune the rose bushes and then lead him into the bedroom and lie down beside him as though she had never been gone. And so each time Lila passed a phone booth and considered stopping to phone Dr. Marshall she kept on walking, and she knew that once she had her daughter's address she would have to go on and that nothing would ever be the same again. She walked until it grew too late to call the doctor's office; the streets became crowded with people on their way home from work, and in apartments above her lights were turned on, and ovens were lit to cook supper.

Tenth Avenue was exactly as she remembered it; when the wind came up across the river on a dark January evening it was still the coldest place in the city. If you stood on the corner facing west you could be sure your eyes would tear as you felt the pull of the river. It was colder by only a degree or two, but it was enough to make you feel it, enough to make you shiver as you waited for the first stars to appear in the sky.

If she could have found her way on the cobblestone streets beyond the avenue, if Hannie were still alive, she would have begged the old fortune-teller for advice. She needed someone to tell her what to do: this way hope, this way despair. She stood on the corner for longer than she should have, and when she finally hailed a cab the palms of her hands had turned blue. That night she was still undecided; she phoned the airlines for times of departures to L.A., she took out the slip of paper with Dr. Marshall's address and looked at it a thousand times. She couldn't eat dinner, and she was afraid to sleep. But when it was very late she had to lie down, just for a moment, and as soon as she closed her eyes she could feel herself begin to drift. When she dreamed, she dreamed of Hannie. They were two crows, high above the earth. Lila tried to hide it, but the scent of fear was all over her, and she was ashamed for Hannie to know what a coward she was. They were flying over a place where there were black hills; below them women prepared for a birth. From the air they could see that white sheets had been raised on poles to form a tent. There were ripples in the sheets, and the women had left footprints in the earth that looked like marks made by crows. There were more than a dozen women below them, and even though they seemed not to hurry, they were a hundred times faster than the crows flying above them.

"I can't do this," Lila called to Hannie, but the air was so thin she couldn't be heard. All anyone could hear was the sound of the wind. In the center of the sky the sun grew hotter and hotter, and the wind began to smell like fire.

When the women reached the tent, each one knelt on the ground. In the air, Lila struggled to keep up with Hannie. When the old woman flew lower Lila followed her, even though the air currents were against her and she could feel tiny bones in her wings breaking.

She thought to herself, It's too late, and she watched as Hannie took to the earth so quickly that her feathers were set on fire by pure speed. The women had begun to sing; the sound was closer all the time, and it went right through Lila. She was falling; it was a drop of twenty stories below her. The tent seemed much more beautiful than clouds, whiter than stars. She just gave in to it then, she let herself fall without a fight, even though the heat was getting stronger all the time. She could actually smell the burning feathers, and then the scent of black earth. Above her the air was cool and blue and so much easier to breathe. But it was such an enormous relief to finally let go that she couldn't stop herself from weeping as she floated into her own shadow and, once and for all, gave up struggling against the delirious pull of gravity.

⋙

She needed to get in to see Dr. Marshall without his suspecting anything, and because he wasn't taking any new patients, Lila had to lie to his secretary. She insisted that she had been a patient years ago, that she had just moved back to the city and was desperate: she had found a lump in her breast. She had to wait four days until he could fit her in. She should have been nervous, there was enough empty time to imagine the worst: medical files lost in a fire, doors slammed in her face, a squad car called to oust her from the doctor's office. But instead, Lila began to feel calmer, and each day she was more convinced that it was only a matter of hours before she would have her daughter back again.

Each time she closed her eyes Lila could see the blue inlets of Connecticut that her daughter must have seen when they first brought her out to Long Island. At night her daughter heard gulls overhead, and in the summertime mimosas grew outside her bedroom window. At the far end of the hallway, in a room where there was a double bed and heavy pine furniture, the people who claimed to be her parents slept, never guessing that in her small white room Lila's daughter closed the door and dreamed about her real mother.

In the morning, when the smell of bacon filtered through the house and they called upstairs to her, Lila's daughter was still dreaming: somewhere there was a woman with blue eyes who had to brush her hair a hundred strokes each night, just as she did, so that the knots would untangle. She was always polite to them at breakfast, but they could tell she wasn't really with them. On days when there were snowstorms or when she had the flu, she felt particularly trapped—the couple at the far end of the hallway became, momentarily, her keepers. But all she had to do was look up into a night that was filled with stars and she knew that she was leaving them: in her mind she was already with her true mother.

When they finally sat her down in the living room to tell her that she'd been adopted she nodded and smiled; she didn't want to hurt them by telling them she had always known she wasn't theirs. She just continued to do what she'd done all along: wait for her mother to appear. On the day of her high-school graduation, on her wedding day, on the morning after the birth of her first child, she waited. Soon she had another child, and her son and daughter were so talented they could swim like fish and recite the alphabet backward before their second birthdays, and when you held them their skin gave off the scent of oranges. On dark nights she kept a candle in the front window and she had her husband put a spotlight up over the garage so that the path to their house was well lit. Every year on Mother's Day she sat out on the front porch, even when it was pouring rain, and she waited for her mother until long after dark, still hoping that this might be the day.

When they were reunited Lila would give her daughter everything she hadn't been able to before. She bought a cashmere sweater at Lord & Taylor, a silk scarf at Bloomingdale's, a pair of small opal earrings at a jewelry shop on Madison Avenue. She kept writing checks and didn't even bother to enter the amounts on the stubs, and at night she sat on the floor in her hotel room and carefully wrapped each gift in imported wrapping paper that was so delicate it shredded if you unfolded it too quickly. Only on the day of her doctor's appointment did she begin to feel a sense of dread. She was in the shower, with the water turned on very hot, when she distinctly heard a train whistle. She held on to the metal railing in the shower stall, but the train was so close that the railing had begun to rattle. It was one of the old trains that the Long Island Rail Road still used on routes that were no longer well traveled. There was a long stretch of frozen tracks, and the snow was so blinding that Lila had to reach for her sunglasses. But once she got to East China, once she was standing in the front yard of her in-laws' house, it was so warm that she didn't even need a sweater. She could see herself right there, under the pine trees, but when she opened her mouth to speak nothing came out but a stone.

Lila turned off the water and got out of the shower as fast as she could. She could still taste the cold weight of that stone in her mouth. She quickly got dressed and went down to get a cab, but when she got into the back seat she found that she'd lost her voice and it was a few moments before she could tell the driver where she wanted to go. In the doctor's office she filled out a medical history with false information, then waited for nearly half an hour. A nurse led her into the consultation office, and that was when Lila realized how unsteady she was.

Dr. Marshall had already begun to read her invented medical history. Lila sat absolutely still in a chair across from him; outside, in an alleyway, the garbage was being collected and metal cans hit hard against the pavement.

"You've found a lump in your breast," the doctor said, concerned.

Lila kept her hands folded in her lap, but she could feel the blood running through them until each finger was amazingly hot.

"No," Lila said. "I haven't."

Dr. Marshall was confused, and he looked back down at her history.

"I'm looking for my daughter," Lila said. "You placed her with a family on Long Island twenty-seven years ago, and I want her back."

"I think you've made a mistake," Dr. Marshall said.

"It was during the ice storm," Lila told him.

The door to the office had been left ajar; now the doctor got up and closed it. Lila sat calmly in the leather chair, but she could feel her heart racing.

"What do you want?" Dr. Marshall asked.

"I told you," Lila said. "Just give me an address."

"You don't understand," the doctor said. "I couldn't even if I wanted to."

"You can," Lila insisted.

He told her that it was too late; her daughter was a grown woman, with parents, a history, a life of her own. But he couldn't talk Lila out of it. Nothing he could say would erase her small bed drenched with milk or the three weeks afterward when she bled every time she walked down the hall to the bathroom, and everything she owned became stained with blood.

"You think I don't have any sympathy for you, but I do,"

Dr. Marshall said. "If you had come to me the next day, or even the next week, I might have been able to do something."

"I was eighteen years old," Lila said. "I couldn't."

"I don't think you're listening to me," the doctor said.

She tried to explain what the moments just before the birth were like, how it was to touch your belly and know that inside there was a perfect mouth, eyes that already blinked, fingers that opened and closed, searching for something to hold on to. Inside your own body was another, you could feel the pressure of its head until the moment when it was half inside you and half lost to you forever, slipping farther and farther away with every second, with each heartbeat.

"I don't see how I can do what you're asking," Dr. Marshall said.

Lila put one hand on her forehead and rubbed her temples.

"I don't see how you can't," she said.

When the nurse in the reception room buzzed the intercom, Dr. Marshall picked up and told her he wasn't taking calls. Then he turned to Lila.

"I have two daughters myself," he said.

Lila looked at him carefully. He leaned back in his chair and took off his glasses, and Lila saw that something was wrong with one of his eyes—it was milky and unfocused. She forced herself to look away so she wouldn't feel anything for him. Lila could tell, already, that he was about to reveal something, and she also knew that afterward there wouldn't be a day when he wouldn't feel he'd compromised himself.

"I raised those girls and I still have times when I feel like they're total strangers. I'm just warning you—you don't know how disappointed you can be after twenty-seven years."

"You don't know how much you can still regret something after twenty-seven years," Lila said.

"How about a cup of coffee?" Dr. Marshall asked Lila.

Lila shook her head no, but the doctor stood up and took

two ceramic mugs from the top of one of the filing cabinets behind his desk.

"I strongly recommend some coffee," he told her.

Lila looked up at him. "All right," she said.

"Their last name was Ross," the doctor said. "Naturally, I'm trusting you not to go through my files while I'm out of the room."

"Naturally," Lila said.

"I don't approve of this," Dr. Marshall said.

"I know," Lila said.

"Cream and sugar all right?" he asked.

"Perfect," Lila told him. "Thank you."

He went to the kitchenette down the hall, giving her ten minutes. When he came back to the office, carrying two mugs of coffee, she was gone. The file drawer on the far left had been opened and Dr. Marshall closed it. Then he drank both cups of coffee, even though he never took cream. He was tired, and his left eye was acting up so that things looked blurry. He had four more patients and a train ride to go before the end of the day, and it was one of those winter afternoons when the day already seems over at four o'clock, and everyone is tired and ready to quit much too early. Still, he wished he could have seen the look on her face when she'd finally gotten what she wanted. He never once guessed that Lila didn't even look at the file after she'd found it. She just took it out of the drawer and slipped it inside her coat. She didn't look at it out on the street, or even in the cab back to the hotel. She waited until she could sit down in the chair by the window. She waited until the sky was dark and the lights below her were turned on. And if the doctor had been able to see the look on her face, he would have been disappointed. Lila's face didn't give anything away. And when she really thought about it, she wasn't the least bit surprised to find that her daughter had been given to a couple in East China, and that she had spent her first day on the same train Lila later took out, in that particularly cold winter when the Sound froze over and you could walk over the waves, all the way to Connecticut.

⋙

Jason Grey picked her up from the train in a Ford station wagon that had no muffler and no shock absorbers. Lila walked right past him and went to stand out on the platform. But as soon as she saw the old Ford she knew it was his, and after she turned back toward the station she realized that an old man was watching her. It had been five years since her in-laws' last visit to California, and in that time Jason's hair had gone completely white. But that wasn't what made him seem so much older—it was that he was no longer as tall. When Lila walked over and hugged him they seemed exactly the same height.

"This is one of the best surprises I could have," Jason Grey told Lila as he lifted her suitcase into the rear of the station wagon.

They drove out to the East China Highway. There was no heater in the car and their breath fogged up the windshield. Somehow, he didn't really seem surprised to see her. He took her out to breakfast and they both ordered coffee and eggs, and as they ate they watched the traffic on the highway.

"If you've left Richard, he must have deserved it," Jason Grey said in an offhand way.

"Maybe I just decided I wanted to see you," Lila said.

Jason laughed and paid their bill; he had seen the way she was staring out at the East China Highway, and he knew he wasn't the one she was there to see.

Outside, the air was so salty and cold that it burned. A new layer of ice had formed on the windshield, and Jason took most of it off with a plastic scraper. They drove out to the house, then went down the rutted driveway and sat there staring at the place. The pine trees were taller than Lila had remembered; beneath them the house was drowning in a pool of black shadows. It was too dark even to see the wooden front door.

Jason got her suitcase out of the back, and Lila followed him up to the house. The air was even colder underneath the pines, and it smelled sweet. Lila could feel something in her throat, and she forced herself to swallow hard.

"I hope you're not here to feel sorry for me," Jason Grey said. He had pushed open the unlocked front door, but now he kept her standing out on the porch.

"Absolutely not," Lila said.

"Good thing." Jason nodded as he led her inside.

He carried her suitcase up to the second floor and gave her the bedroom that used to be his and Helen's. When Lila's mother-in-law was first sick she couldn't manage the stairs. They had moved into the parlor, and ever since Jason had kept the heat in the rest of the house shut off and he'd remained in the parlor bedroom. Now he got out a portable kerosene heater and started it up so that Lila's room would be warm by the time she went to bed. While he poured in the kerosene Lila went to the window and wiped the fog off the glass. Out in the back the lawn had disappeared and the woods now came right up to the back of the house.

"I started to have my doubts about mowing the lawn," Jason explained when he saw her at the window. "It just seemed silly after a while."

Lila had come here without any real plan. She never imagined she'd waste a whole day with her father-in-law. But now that she was in this house, she felt strangely tired. After they'd gone back downstairs she sat down on the couch next to a hospital cot in the parlor. In no time three hours had gone by.

She knew no one could do it for her. She had to walk out the door, start up the Ford, and drive to the other side of town. She was only five miles from her goal, and she was paralyzed. All the time the day was slipping away from her Lila kept thinking: I can do it anytime. But the horizon grew dark, and the birds mistook the parlor windows for the sky, beating their wings against the glass. Lila began to wonder if she would ever be able to leave this house. When she tried to lift her arms she couldn't move. At dinnertime, Lila managed to follow Jason into the kitchen, but then her knees felt weak and she had to sit down.

"This is my big secret," Jason Grey said. He opened the refrigerator and pulled down the freezer compartment. "I eat frozen dinners."

Lila found that if she really tried she could pretend to speak.

"I won't tell," she said, and she managed to stand up, light the oven with a wooden match, and slide two frozen dinners onto the lowest rack.

They ate in the kitchen with the oven left on to heat the room. Every time she swallowed Lila swore the dinners hadn't defrosted and that she was swallowing pieces of ice. Jason Grey seemed to be having no trouble with his turkey and mashed potatoes, although every once in a while he stopped eating long enough to fiddle with the stove.

"I can't stand to give the oil companies any more money than they already have," he explained. "The oven in here isn't too bad, and I put the woodstove in the parlor three years ago."

Lila really didn't know what was happening to her. She put her fork down and covered her eyes.

"I'll freeze to death before I give the oil companies another cent," Jason said cheerfully. "I'll bet you think I can't make good coffee," he added. "Well, you're wrong."

He got up to start the coffee, and he let Lila cry.

"Thanks," Lila said when he brought over the coffeepot.

"I don't like to see you upset," Jason said.

"Oh, well," Lila said.

"I mean it," Jason said. "I don't like to see it."

He got some milk and sugar and took down two cups from the top cabinet. "We don't have owls any more around here," he told Lila. "Remember how there used to be owls all over East China—in the trees and everywhere? They just took off, and now the only thing you hear at night is traffic. You never used to hear traffic around here."

They drank coffee and Lila took off her boots and lifted her feet up to warm them by the oven. Sitting here with Jason, she could almost forget why she had come back to East China in the first place.

"We should have asked you to live with us," she told her father-in-law.

"Not me," Jason Grey said. "I'm never going to California."

It turned out that Jason wasn't paying for hot water any more either, so Lila boiled some water to wash the coffee cups and spoons. By the time she finished and went into the parlor, Jason was already asleep on the couch, and Lila covered him with a wool afghan her mother-in-law had crocheted. Then she turned off the lights. She went upstairs and got into bed, but when she turned off the lamp on the night table there was still a glow from the kerosene heater. In that bedroom, beneath a heavy quilt, Lila felt perfectly safe. It was quite possible, she knew, to stay here forever. Especially in winter, when it was dark by four and there was wood to be brought in, salt blocks to be dragged out to the yard for the deer, ice on all the windows. She hadn't known quite how much she'd missed winter, and now that she was back she almost felt young in this season, in this house. That night she brushed her hair a hundred times with a wire brush she'd found on the bureau, and she slept deeply as the ice on the windows grew thicker. By midnight you couldn't have seen outside even if you'd wanted to; it was as if nothing existed on the other side of the glass but snow and an old road that led nowhere in particular.

In the morning, Lila woke suddenly. The heater had run out of kerosene and the room was freezing. She reached for her clothes and got dressed under the covers the way she and Richard used to on mornings when it was too cold to get out of bed. Sometime during the night Jason Grey had woken up, put more wood in the parlor stove, then gone back to sleep on his cot. When he came into the kitchen at six-thirty Lila had already made coffee and French toast, which was staying warm on a plate in the oven.

Jason smiled when Lila brought his plate to the table. "I never knew you could cook like this."

Lila turned the oven up higher, then put on a second borrowed sweater, and watched her father-in-law eat. She couldn't quite believe she had been in the house for less than twenty-four hours. In a little while she planned to fix the wallpaper that was coming down in the hallway; all it needed was some masking tape and glue.

After breakfast, Jason insisted on doing the dishes.

"I guess you're going somewhere today," he said when he'd finished. He had used cold water and the cups and plates were streaked.

Lila could feel a tightening in her throat.

"I was thinking about getting some groceries," Lila said.

"That's not what I mean," Jason Grey said.

Lila had the sudden urge for a cigarette. There was a pack of Marlboros on the table; she lit one, but the smoke only made her throat feel worse and she handed the cigarette to her father-in-law. She just wasn't ready to go out. Maybe after some time in this house, after the winter when there was something else in the world besides snow, maybe then she could think about it.

"We both know you didn't come out here just to see me," Jason Grey said. "I'm not asking why you're here, you understand."

Jason sat down across from her and Lila pushed a glass ashtray toward him. He smoked only half the cigarette before he stubbed it out and coughed for what seemed too long a time. If Lila didn't go after her daughter soon, she would never do it. And if that happened she would never be able to leave this house; she might be able to go as far as the driveway, but then a feeling of pure terror would force her to run back inside and lock herself in the upstairs bedroom.

"I figure you'll need my car," Jason Grey said. "Just remember to pump those brakes before you make a stop. They work. They just work better if you pump them."

Lila pulled on her boots and left the house. The thermometer nailed to the porch was at fifteen degrees. It took ten minutes for the car to heat up enough so that it wouldn't stall out every time she put it into gear. Jason had always said that it was an auto mechanic's duty to have a car that always needed repairing—that way if he had no business he could always give himself a job. As she sat in the idling car, the smell of gas made her sick to her stomach. She drove down the driveway carefully, and when she pulled out onto the East China Highway she skidded; if there had been oncoming traffic she wouldn't have been able to pump the brakes in time.

She had forgotten how small the place was—two long streets and a marina, then the circle of residential streets on a hill above the harbor. On one of these streets was a small housing development that had been built the year before Lila first came to East China. It was easy to find the right address, but, once she had, Lila turned the key in the ignition and just sat there, looking at the house. All along she'd imagined a two-story house, and here it was a ranch in a neighborhood that was so deserted that when Lila finally got out of the Ford and the car door slammed behind her, the sudden noise made her jump.

The ground was frozen and there was a cover of ice on the asphalt driveway. Lila tried to tell herself that the worst part was over—she had found the house where her daughter had grown up. But already it felt wrong to her. She walked up to the door and knocked. She could hear something inside—a dishwasher or a washing machine. She realized then that she had expected some signs of children—a bicycle or a set of swings. The idea was ridiculous—it was winter, and her daughter was a grown woman—she probably only came back to this house on holidays, two or three times a year.

Lila could hear someone walking down the hallway, but it wasn't until the door opened that she believed it was finally happening. A woman stood looking at her through the storm door. The sound of water was even louder, and Lila could tell now—it was a dishwasher.

"I'm Lila Grey," Lila said right away, as if that explained anything.

The woman nodded, expecting more, a sales pitch for cosmetics or vacuum cleaners. Lila could tell that she had already decided to say no and was just being polite.

"My father-in-law used to own the first gas station on the highway," Lila said. She was talking too much and too fast, but she couldn't seem to stop herself. "He lives just past the station, in that old green farmhouse you can see from the road, and that's his car out there. I knew I shouldn't have borrowed it, but I did, and now I'm stuck and I have to call him."

When the woman looked out at the parked Ford it was easy to believe that Lila had indeed had car trouble. And then she actually did it; she unlocked the storm door and let Lila inside.

"Everything's a mess," the woman said apologetically as she led Lila to the kitchen. There was a wall phone above the table, and the woman turned the dishwasher off so that Lila could hear. Her name, Lila knew from the file, was Janet Ross, and she had been thirty-three years old when cysts were discovered in both her ovaries. When the cysts were removed the surgeon found that the walls of her ovaries were depleted and thin. Janet Ross had come to see Dr. Marshall for a second opinion, and she had broken down in his office when he told her she'd never be able to have a child. When the doctor phoned her a few months later to tell her he had found a baby for her, it was late at night and the ice storm had made driving impossible. They took a train into Manhattan at five that morning. By seven they were in Dr. Marshall's office at Beekman, and the doctor couldn't help but notice that Janet Ross had dressed so quickly she was still wearing a nightgown underneath her dress and the flowered hem hung down past her knees to the tops of her boots.

Lila held the phone down with her finger and dialed; she kidded Jason for lending her a wreck of a car and suggested he bring his tools and meet her out on the street.

Janet Ross was at the table, polishing a silver creamer when Lila got off the phone.

"He'll have to take a cab over," Lila said. "I guess I'll wait in the car. I just wish the heater worked."

"No heat," Janet Ross said sympathetically.

Lila kept looking for a sign: a Mother's Day card taped to the refrigerator, a photograph hung on the wall.

"How about some coffee?" Janet Ross asked.

"Great," Lila said. "But why don't you make it tea. I read tea leaves," she explained.

Janet Ross put some water up to boil, but she gave Lila a look.

"It's a hobby," Lila explained. She waited just the right amount of time before she spoke again. "Why don't you let me read yours?"

"I couldn't ask you to do that," Janet Ross said, taking two teacups out of the cabinet.

"Oh, you have to let me," Lila said. "I'll feel much better about barging in on you."

She took the teabags Janet Ross had put in each cup and tore them open with her fingernail. As water was poured into the cups Lila realized how uncomfortable she was in this kitchen; she had expected it to be much nicer than it was: the walls were covered with something that was supposed to look like slate, and the appliances were all a too bright yellow.

"Lovely place you've got," Lila actually said.

"Do you really think so?" Janet Ross said, pleased. "We moved out here from the city thirty-two years ago—right after we were married."

Lila held up her hand. "Don't tell me any more about yourself," she warned. When Janet looked puzzled, she added, "Otherwise, what's the point in having your fortune told?"

The women smiled at each other, but all the time Lila was thinking what a fool Janet was. First she pretended to be someone's mother, and now she was about to tell Lila everything she wanted to know.

"Can I add milk to this?" Janet Ross asked. Used to coffee, she was having a hard time with the bitter taste of tea.

"Just drink it," Lila said.

She sounded harsher than she'd planned, but Janet quickly finished her tea, as though, for a moment, she'd been frightened of Lila. Lila held the cup and peered into it.

"I see the letter L," she said. "A man who is very close to you."

"I can't believe it," Janet said. "That's Lewis. My husband."

Lila smiled; she had her now.

"This Lewis," Lila said, "he's an engineer someplace where they make airplanes?"

Janet Ross grew rigid. "How did you know that?" she asked.

Lila pointed to the teacup. Dr. Marshall's files were very complete. "See this," she said. "This little airplane in the corner?"

Janet Ross looked and couldn't see a thing.

"Well, it takes years to understand the symbols," Lila said. "Take this one." She briefly passed the cup in front of Janet. "This is clearly the symbol for your daughter."

"My daughter?" Janet said, confused.

"I see here that she is twenty-six—no, twenty-seven years old this month."

She looked at Janet Ross out of the corner of her eye, and kept her voice as even as possible.

"I can't quite make out where it is she's living now," Lila said. "Is it East China?"

Janet Ross seemed to be having trouble breathing. "I don't know what you're talking about," she said.

"Your daughter," Lila said impatiently. "Where is she?"

They looked at each other across the table, and Lila could feel something passing between them.

"I don't have a daughter," Janet Ross said.

Lila sat straight in her chair; her head snapped back, as though she'd been slapped. She had the file in her suitcase and she knew this was the right house. This was the right woman—you could tell she was a thief just by looking at her.

"Wait a minute," Lila said. "I see the symbol for your daughter in the tea leaves, and the tea leaves never lie."

It was all a show for Janet Ross, and so it was even more terrible when Lila looked into the teacup and really did see something. There were arms and legs surfacing, and then, for a moment, a child's face.

"Oh, my God," Lila said. "She's right there."

In the fluorescent lighting of the kitchen Janet Ross suddenly looked much older than she was.

"What do you want?" she whispered.

Lila knew that she could lose it all now; one more outburst

and she might never find out where her daughter was. "You don't have to be nervous now that we've begun to talk about children," she said. But she could tell that Janet Ross wasn't quite as stupid as she'd thought.

"There's nothing wrong with your car," Janet said.

"Of course there is," Lila said quickly. "Just take a look at it."

"I don't want you here," Janet Ross told her.

"You're the one who invited me in!" Lila said.

She could feel the edge of Janet's hysteria as Janet stood up and reached for the phone.

"I'm calling the police," Janet Ross said.

Lila leapt up and grabbed the phone receiver out of her hand.

"Don't you dare call the police," Lila said, and when she let go of the phone Janet obediently hung up. Lila had no time to waste. She went into the living room and began to search for signs of her daughter. Janet followed her and watched as Lila tore through the house. She went through the bureau drawers and found nothing—not a photograph, not an address. She went through the bedrooms, the closets, the medicine cabinet in the bathroom, and all the while Janet followed her, watching. By the time Lila had finished with the last room—a den in which there was a fold-out couch for guests—she was shivering.

"I don't know what you're looking for," Janet said. "We don't have anything worth stealing. Take the color TV if you want it." She took off her wristwatch and her diamond ring and held them out to Lila. "Here," she offered. "Take these."

"There's nothing here," Lila said weakly.

"I could have told you that," Janet Ross said. "You picked the wrong house."

Lila went to the front door and let herself out. It was freezing cold, and Lila just couldn't wait for the car to warm up, so every time she shifted into gear, the engine stalled. She should have known from the minute she walked through the door that no child had ever lived there. If her daughter had grown up in that house she would have left some sign for Lila: a framed picture of a robin, bronzed baby shoes, fingerprints that Janet Ross could never get off the kitchen door. Lila immediately blamed Dr. Marshall for giving her the wrong address to throw her off the track, but maybe it was an innocent mix-up of his files, and after all these years what could anyone expect? Files got lost, names misplaced, children disappeared on cold, clear days. And as Lila drove away she had only one wish: that she had come here last night at midnight with a pack of matches and some kerosene and burned this house to the ground. Then, at least, there'd have been smoke and ashes, and when Lila had picked through the rubble she could have imagined that everything she touched had once belonged to her daughter.

Lila went back to her father-in-law's house and sat down in the kitchen with her coat still on. Jason Grey was in the back, putting out salt licks for the deer. When he heard the Ford pull up he finished and came inside. As soon as he saw Lila he knew she hadn't gotten whatever it was she'd wanted.

"Do you want me to ask you what's wrong?" he said.

Lila shook her head no.

He made her a pot of coffee and set it down on the table, then he left her alone. Lila sat in the kitchen all afternoon. She could hear the TV turned on in the parlor, she could hear footsteps in the hallway every once in a while when Jason came as close to the kitchen doorway as he dared, just to check on her. When it started to get dark, Lila didn't bother to turn on the light. She could sit there in the dark forever, and the colder it got in the room, the less she felt like moving. She let the cold get into her bones and if she waited long enough, if she really tried, she might be able to feel nothing at all.

It was seven in the evening when the phone rang, and by then Lila was so cold that she could barely move. Jason came in from the parlor and they both watched the phone, set out on the kitchen counter, as it rang five more times.

"You know who that is," Jason Grey said. "He always calls me on a Friday night."

Jason went over and turned the oven on.

"You shouldn't be sitting here," he told Lila. "It's too cold."

The phone began to ring again.

"I take it you don't want to talk to him," Jason said. He lit a cigarette and leaned against the sink. Bent over that way he was actually shorter than Lila.

Everything seemed to have a hard edge; when Lila looked at her father-in-law she could see only his skeleton.

The phone had stopped ringing, and this time Jason went over and pulled the plug out of the wall.

"You don't have to talk to him if you don't want to, Lila," Jason Grey said. "But I'll tell you one thing you do have to do—eat dinner. And I'll tell you what I have in mind." He was talking to her as if it were the most natural thing in the world for them to be there together in the dark with her not saying a thing. "Helen never liked for me to have Italian food, she was sure it was bad for your heart. But I've been thinking about going to a restaurant in town. And that's what I'm going to do—I'm going to take you out to dinner."

They left the kitchen oven on, so that the house would warm up. Jason Grey put on his down jacket, and his high boots, and then they walked arm in arm down the dirt driveway toward the Ford. Lila held on tightly to her father-in-law, so that he wouldn't slip on the ice. The stars were brighter than they'd ever been and the sky was so huge it made you aware of how fragile you were, how easy it would be to slip on the ice and break something. As they walked past the pines it grew even colder, and Lila breathed in deeply, but she didn't dare speak. Already, she could feel that the stone had formed and was waiting to drop from her tongue.

⇛

On the day of her daughter's birthday it was fifty-eight degrees, one of the warmest days in January anyone in East China could remember. By now Lila couldn't go any farther than the end of the driveway, and she knew it was pointless to try. It was as if there was a sudden drop in the oxygen out there, or a pack of half-starved wolves roaming the East China Highway, out for blood.

Of course there were things she could have done: hired detectives, made phone calls, pored over school records in the basement of the elementary school. But nothing outside the yard of Jason Grey's house seemed very real, and California seemed most unreal of all. Richard kept calling. Twice, Lila had overheard Jason Grey talking to him on the telephone, and each time she had been startled by the idea that you could talk to someone who was three thousand miles away.

"I'm telling you she's all right," she had heard her father-in-law tell Richard on the Saturday after she'd been to see Janet Ross. But Richard refused to believe him; he phoned again and again, and when he called one night after midnight, Lila could tell he was thinking about following her. She stood in the kitchen doorway, near the cabinet where the brooms were stored; she dreaded the possibility that Richard might come after her. Jason sensed her presence in the room and turned to her. Lila couldn't seem to blink, and Jason was reminded of the deer who edged closer and closer to the house each season, as the woods claimed more and more of the yard.

"Don't argue with me," Jason had said to Richard. "Sometimes people need to be alone and you can't take it personally."

Richard stopped calling after that. Lila tried to thank her father-in-law by baking him a cake, but she ran out of flour, and she couldn't go into town any more, not even to the grocery on Main Street. Each day she stayed closer and closer to the house, but on her daughter's birthday the weather was so seductive that even Lila went outside. She pulled on a pair of Jason Grey's old boots and began to rake the mud in the front yard. She had been working for nearly an hour, and had broken two fingernails when she heard the car pull into the driveway, its wheels spinning in the mud. The birds had gone crazy with the sudden warmth; there were so many of them searching for worms that from certain angles the earth looked blue. At the far edge of the yard were the shells of two Chryslers waiting for spring when Jason would rebuild them. If he worked slowly enough, he had told Lila, those Chryslers might keep him busy for the rest of his life.

When the car pulled in, Lila stood up and put one hand on her hip. Every time she licked her lips she tasted salt; she had lost so much weight in the past two weeks that her wedding band slipped up and down her fourth finger easily. But now she held on to the rake so tightly that the ring stayed in place. She knew, right then, as the car pulled over and parked, that she was about to find her daughter. The first thing she did was make a quick list of things she had to do: wash her hair, file down the nails that had broken while she raked, look through her mother-in-law's closet for a leather belt, polish her one good pair of shoes.

Janet Ross didn't see Lila out in the yard, and Lila let her walk to the house without calling to her. She enjoyed watching from a distance as Janet navigated through the mud and knocked on the front door and she stood still as Jason Grey invited Janet inside. Lila wanted this exact moment to go on and on. She wanted the same sound of the birds, and the thud of the front door as her father-in-law closed it, and the air so surprisingly warm and sweet it made you feel like crying. And when she finally walked back to the house, Lila made certain to take her time—because, after all, she had been waiting for this moment for more than half her life.

She took off her boots in the hallway and hung her sweater on a hook by the door. It was still chilly in the house, from months of freezing weather. Lila could hear voices in the parlor and, standing in the hallway, she was reminded of the first time Richard had brought her here. Then it had been Helen Grey's voice she had heard, and the sound of it had made her frightened to go in. She'd had a strong sense of interrupting something, of stepping inside a place where she didn't belong.

"Don't worry," Richard had whispered to her, and he had taken her arm to give her courage. "They're going to be crazy about you."

Janet Ross was sitting on the couch, still wearing her coat, when Lila walked into the room. Jason had just put out a cigarette and was coughing. His cough, Lila couldn't help noticing, was getting worse.

"I guess you lied to me," Lila said, right away, not willing to give Janet Ross an inch.

"I'll bet you ladies are thirsty," Jason Grey said. He had been sitting in the old chair that faced the couch, and now he stood. "What if I offered you both some bourbon and water?"

Lila and Janet Ross were staring at each other.

"None for me," Lila said to her father-in-law.

"None for me," Janet echoed.

"You'll excuse me if I get some for myself," Jason Grey said, and he left the room. They could hear him in the kitchen, but then the back door slammed, and Lila knew that what he'd wanted wasn't a drink but an excuse to leave them alone.

"I guess your father-in-law lives here by himself," Janet

Ross said. "You can always tell just by looking at a room."

Lila sat down in the armchair. She could still hear the birds outside, even through the closed windows.

"You can tell from a room when something's gone wrong," Janet said.

She looked at Lila then.

"As soon as I saw you I knew you were Susan's birth mother," she said.

The name cut right through Lila. That was definitely not her daughter's name, not Susan. All during her pregnancy, and even after the baby was born, Lila had not once thought of a name for her daughter. It was only lately that she felt her daughter had to have a name, and she certainly wasn't about to let someone like Janet Ross choose it.

"Not her birth mother," Lila said. "Her real mother."

Janet Ross looked toward the doorway of the parlor after Jason Grey. "Maybe I will have that bourbon," she said.

"I don't think there is any," Lila told her. "He just wanted to get out of the room."

"Well, I don't blame him," Janet said. She unbuttoned her coat, but she was so nervous that she couldn't get all the buttons undone. "It certainly was a different kind of January back then," she said. "It was so cold that when you stepped out for a second to get the mail your eyelashes froze together and you couldn't see a thing."

"I know what it was like," Lila said.

"When the phone call came I thought I was dreaming," Janet said. "I was half asleep, and my husband had worked late the day before so he was exhausted—he didn't even hear it ring."

"Look," Lila said, "I don't care about you or your husband. I don't care about anything you have to say. I just want to know where she is."

"I know that's what you want," Janet said. "That's why I'm

telling you this. Because I remember everything about it. I remember thinking, This is going to be the best day of my life. Even before it happens to me, I know it can never be any better."

They were in Dr. Marshall's office when he brought her in to them. At first Janet was afraid to touch her; she had wanted her so much that now if she reached out a little too quickly the baby might dissolve into smoke. Of course, once she did hold the baby she refused to let go. She held her all the way back to East China and refused to speak. Even when her husband asked her a direct question, she just couldn't answer. It was all too perfect to talk about. From the window of the train they could see that the sound had frozen solid, each wave had turned into green ice.

That first night Janet sat in the rocking chair in the nursery, fed the baby a bottle, and sang her to sleep. Lewis had wanted to call the baby Deborah, after his grandmother, but the name Susan came to Janet the moment Dr. Marshall put the baby in her arms, and she insisted upon it.

After that first quiet night Susan couldn't seem to sleep, and Janet had to rock with her for hours. The baby slept peacefully during the day, but as soon as it grew dark she was restless. All the books assured Janet that this sort of fretting was normal, but sometimes, after Susan had finally fallen asleep and her mouth was still puckered from crying, Janet wondered if it was something more, if Susan simply couldn't bear the dark. After a while, they settled into a routine, but Janet still felt drawn to the nursery at night. She stood in the doorway, and even from a distance she could see that Susan's skin was luminous. She nearly shimmered beneath her woolen blanket, and even on moonless nights the nursery seemed brighter than the rest of the house, as if the baby had managed to chase away the night.

Janet's husband, Lewis, may not have been a model husband—he worked overtime too much, and he sometimes didn't listen to a word she said—but he was a good father to Susan. He brought home dresses and toys, and when the baby came down with a cold in February he took turns rocking her back to sleep. Susan's cold lingered for more than a month. It seemed to wrap her in a cocoon, and Janet had the feeling that the baby was far away, even when she was holding her. Janet had Lewis hook up an intercom to connect their bedroom with the nursery, and whenever she heard a hiccup or a cough in the middle of the night she sat up in bed, eyes riveted to the intercom until it was quiet again. She was overanxious, but what had she expected? She had been afraid of losing this baby even before she had her, and now she couldn't escape the uneasy feeling that Susan was somehow on loan to her, and that sooner or later she'd have to give her up.

In early April the weather turned warmer and Susan's lingering cold disappeared. Janet began to take her everywhere, first to the market, and then for drives in the car. They went to towns where Janet had never been before, to restaurants and diners where Susan sat in her infant seat, propped up on the table quietly drinking her bottle without any fuss at all. For the first time in her life Janet began to talk to strangers, and when she did, she lied. She pretended that she was Susan's natural mother; she described her labor to waitresses, she discussed her nursing problems with women at the next table. And all the while she felt Susan watching her, studying her carefully with her wide eyes.

At three months, Susan had smiled for the first time. A few weeks later she actually turned over and both her parents were so overcome they had tears in their eyes. Susan watched everything now, and she looked so knowing that Janet sometimes felt uncomfortable. She had gotten into the habit of talking to Susan all day long, calling out each ingredient as she added to the batter of a chocolate cake, reading aloud from the morning newspaper. Sometimes Janet marveled at her own nerve. How had she ever dared to think she could take care of this child? How could she have pretended to be someone's mother?

Janet felt proud whenever Susan did anything new, as if she had something to do with the child's brilliance. She could sit for hours, rapt, as Susan studied the mobile above her crib, or carefully examined her toes. They were a closed circle, the two of them, and even Lewis sometimes felt like an intruder. It may have been because of those colds Susan continued to have; though none was bad enough for a trip to the doctor, Janet was so protective that even she began to be amazed at how fierce her love had become. There was something about sitting up late at night with Susan that made Janet totally surrender to the child. Each time her daughter reached up and put her arms around her neck the world outside the nursery evaporated, the nightlight on the wall became far brighter than the moon.

There had been a two-month visit to the pediatrician, and there would be another at six months. But even if someone had suggested that something was wrong, Janet Ross wouldn't have believed it. She didn't even notice how small Susan was until the child was five months old. It was June; the mimosa trees were in flower and the air was silky. Janet took Susan down to the playground near the harbor for the first time in her new stroller. That day Susan was dressed in white cotton tights and a yellow dress, and Janet felt she had never seen a more beautiful child. At the park she sat on a green wooden bench with the other mothers. She took Susan out of her stroller and held her on her lap; together they watched two ten-year-old boys on the swings who were making themselves dizzy with height. Across from them, on another green bench, were two other mothers whose children were in strollers identical to Susan's. They waved to Janet and she waved back gaily, and she didn't even have the urge to lie to anyone about her labor and delivery. That's how right she felt sitting there with the other mothers. That's how perfect the day was.

When it was time to go home, Janet put Susan back into the stroller and walked past the mothers on the bench across from theirs.

"Look," one of the women said to her child, "a brand-new baby!"

The children in the other strollers stared gravely at Susan.

"Not all that new," Janet smiled.

"God, I can barely remember when Jessie was that small," the woman said.

"I don't think Paul was ever that small," her friend said. "He was ten pounds two ounces at birth."

Janet bent down to the stroller and smiled. "Hear that?" she said to Susan. "But just you wait till you're as old as these babies are now. I won't even be able to lift you up."

Susan looked so beautiful in her stroller that Janet could hardly bear it. She had the urge to pick her up again; instead she smoothed down Susan's skirt.

"How old is she?" the first mother asked Janet. "About six weeks?"

"Six weeks!" Janet laughed. "She was just five months. She's already wearing size six months clothes."

The two mothers on the bench looked at each other; both knew that a newborn child could fit into that size.

"She was only five pounds six ounces when she was born," Janet said, flustered.

Susan had untied her hat and the two mothers were studying her.

"How old are yours?" Janet said stiffly.

"I love that hat of hers," one of the mothers said. "I never saw anything so cute."

Janet looked closely at the two other children in their strollers; both were twice Susan's size and Janet guessed they were somewhere between a year and eighteen months old.

"I'd really like to know," Janet said now. "How old are they?"

"Jessie is four months this week, but Paul is already six months," one of the mothers said quietly.

"My daughter is very petite," Janet said quickly. She felt as though she'd been slapped.

"That's right." The other mother was just as quick to agree. "Five foot two, eyes of blue. She'll have all the boys chasing after her."

Janet walked home then. Susan fell asleep on the way, and Janet left her out on the porch in her stroller. She went inside and sat down on the couch, but after a while she went and got her baby. It just didn't seem right to leave her out there, asleep and defenseless, because it now seemed that the air was a little too silky, and the sky was almost threatening, it was too bright and too blue.

That night Janet asked her husband to measure Susan. They held her down on the couch and lined up a tape measure. Janet looked up the growth chart in the back of one of the baby books and she found that Susan's length was that of a six- or eight-week-old baby. She had just stopped growing, and they hadn't even noticed. She had been getting four bottles of formula a day and she'd never cried out or complained that she was hungry, but when they weighed her now, sitting her down on the bathroom scale, she was only ten pounds.

Janet could feel something inside her snapping, but after she put Susan to sleep and Lewis wanted to talk about it, she couldn't.

"There's nothing wrong with her," Janet insisted.

But she lay in bed awake all night, and she could tell Lewis was awake, too.

"I've thought it over," he told her in the morning. "There

probably is nothing wrong with her, but maybe she has a hormone deficiency or something. I just want to take her in and get her examined. I want to be sure."

He was right, and Janet nodded her head, but she just couldn't stand it. Lewis took the day off from work and they drove to see the pediatrician. When the doctor saw Susan something in his eyes changed. It passed in a moment, and he calmly examined Susan, but Janet knew then that something was wrong. He never accused them of anything, although now all Janet could think of was why hadn't they thought to weigh her, why hadn't they brought her in one of those times she was coughing and feverish? By the end of the exam the doctor had made an appointment for a chest X-ray that afternoon at Central Suffolk Hospital.

"That's impossible," Janet found herself saying. "Susan takes a nap in the afternoon."

"Janet!" her husband said.

"I don't think you understand," the doctor said gently. "There may be a problem with her heart, and that's what may have affected her growth."

But Janet understood perfectly. They were about to take Susan away from her. When she was taken into the X-ray department Janet had to look away. The technicians had fitted Susan into a sort of glass tube to keep her from moving, and inside the glass Susan looked tinier than ever and so beautiful it nearly broke Janet's heart. She tried to think of a reason why she would be punished this way, and she knew it could only be that she hadn't been a good enough mother. Not a real mother. She had resented the crying in the night sometimes, she had been overwhelmed by the sheer amount of dirty laundry one baby could generate. And now she was being punished, and what's more, she deserved it.

They discovered a congenital heart lesion. It had stopped Susan's growth and made her delicate enough to catch so many colds. The valves of her heart were beyond repair. Janet and Lewis took her to Mount Sinai for a second opinion, but the second opinion was the same as the first. Susan would not last through her first year. The strange thing was that, if anything, Susan became more beautiful, and when Janet took her for walks in her stroller people turned and stared and some of them couldn't stop themselves from coming right up to tell Janet what a lovely daughter she had. Janet herself looked much older. Lewis told her to take it easy, not to work so hard, to sleep more. But Janet just didn't feel she had the time to waste on things like sleeping and eating. She only wanted to be with Susan. She spent all day playing with her, and didn't bother with supper for Lewis or vacuuming the rugs. She taught Susan to eat cereal off a tiny demitasse spoon, to clap her hands together, to wave goodbye. One afternoon, when they were sitting together on the floor, Susan stopped playing with the soft rattle she held, looked up at Janet and said "ma." Janet felt her heart break in half, and all that night Susan ran her new sound together, "amamamamam," and even after she had closed her eyes, when Janet went into the nursery to check on her, Susan turned in her sleep and called out to her.

In July Susan had a cold, and then a stomach virus; she just didn't have the defenses to fight it off. And then, when it seemed that the virus had subsided, it suddenly got worse, and it happened so fast there was no time to think. One moment Susan was well enough to take solid foods, and the next she'd begun vomiting and her eyes had rolled upward so that all you could see was a milky white line beneath each lid. When they rushed her to the emergency ward she was absolutely limp, like a small doll who occasionally took a deep breath, and Janet thought to herself, This is a test. This is to get me ready for all I have to bear. Only a few hours after she was hooked up to an IV Susan revived, and as they took her home Janet realized that she hadn't once allowed herself to cry. Even Lewis could do that, she had heard him in the bathroom, with the water in the sink running to mask the sound. But somehow, crying was an admission of what was happening to them, and Janet would never be ready for that.

She died on the second Sunday in August, when the sky was cloudless and the temperature eighty-two degrees. Janet woke up at five in the morning and, lying next to her husband in bed, she knew. The light that morning was pearl-colored and soft. It was the sort of morning when summer is everywhere, in all the rooms of the house and in every backyard. Janet slipped out of bed, leaving her husband asleep. When he got up at seven, he found Janet in the nursery, rocking back and forth in the chair, holding the dead child. There were always blackbirds in East China, but this morning they called so loudly in the trees that they set all the neighborhood cats howling. Lewis sat down on the carpeted floor of the nursery and put his head in his wife's lap, and because there was no longer any reason not to, Janet finally let herself cry.

They couldn't find a coffin small enough, so they had one specially made. By the following morning all signs that a child had been in the house were gone: the crib and all the boxes of clothes were taken up to the attic; the photograph albums and toys were stored in the cellar behind an old metal sink. But all that first night Janet swore she heard a baby crying for its mother.

The day that Lila had appeared at the front door Janet was suspicious, and as soon as Lila began to question her about her children, she was a hundred percent sure. It wasn't unexpected—why shouldn't Susan's birth mother come back after all these years? Why shouldn't she accuse her of murder? But Janet wasn't about to admit anything, and when Lila finally left the house Janet double-locked the front door, and she didn't dare take another breath until she heard Lila drive away.

But even though she had tricked Lila into leaving, Janet

couldn't stop thinking about her, and that night she went down to the cellar and for the first time in twenty-seven years she opened the cardboard boxes. It was cold in the cellar, but when she opened the first box Janet felt a rush of heat, as if some of the air from that August had been trapped inside when Lewis first sealed the boxes. She put her flashlight down on the floor and took out the photo album. She had to force herself to go on past the first picture, taken the first week after they had brought her home. How could they have thought that anything so beautiful, so perfect, could last? In every photograph Susan seemed to be leaving them behind, calmly departing, and it suddenly seemed silly to Janet that she had ever thought of Susan as hers. It was just that for a little while she had been allowed to take care of her, and even if she told Lila the truth she couldn't lose someone she had never really had.

They could hear the scrape of the rake outside as Jason Grey cleared out the driveway. Lila sat perfectly still and although she thought to herself over and over, She's a liar, she knew it was all true. It was the kind of truth you feel in your bones. The sudden knowledge that there was nothing at all wrong with Rae's child nearly made Lila cry out loud; it was her own child who had surfaced from the bottom of the cup. It was her own bad fortune.

"Maybe I've been waiting for you to come back for her all this time," Janet Ross said quietly. "But you don't have to tell me how I failed. Believe me. I know."

That August had been the best time in Lila's life. The sunlight had been so bright you could see only certain things: a thin gold wedding band, the reedy stalks of orange lilies that grew by the back door, the line of Richard's shoulder when he turned to her in bed.

Janet Ross slid a photograph album across the coffee table between them.

"I brought this for you," she said.

Lila planned to say, I don't want it, my daughter is twenty-seven years old, today is her birthday, she lives somewhere right here in this town, she has children of her own, and she's been waiting for me, every day she opens the back door and looks out across the lawn and expects to see me. But when she tried to speak she couldn't, and though she tried to stop herself she reached for the album on the coffee table. The baby nearly jumped out at her. She was sitting in the backyard, on Janet Ross's lap underneath a mimosa tree, and her eyes were so alive they couldn't be held back by the confines of the paper. Lila could feel a sharp pain all along her left side. The child was stunning, but Lila had already decided—she was not her daughter.

"She doesn't look anything like me," Lila said, and as she spoke she could feel the cold, round shape of the words drop from her mouth.

"I brought this, too," Janet said. She took a small white sweater out of her pocketbook and gently placed it on the coffee table. "She looked beautiful in anything you put on her, pastels, stripes, anything at all."

Jason Grey had never believed in using anything stronger than a sixty-watt bulb, though the pines made the parlor dark all day long. But even in the dim light, even though Janet Ross had turned her face away, Lila could tell that she was crying. Lila closed the photograph album and went to sit next to her on the couch. Janet wiped her tears with the backs of her hands and laughed.

"If my husband goes down to the cellar before I clean up he'll probably wonder if a robber's been there. He'll wonder why anyone in their right mind would pick those old boxes to go through.

Lila couldn't take her eyes off Janet, and she found herself calmly thinking: *So that's how it feels.* Janet's sense of loss was all over her, in the way she buttoned her coat to leave, in the angle of her shoulders. When she compared her absolute lack of feeling to Janet's grief, Lila couldn't even bring herself to feel guilt—only uselessness. Outside it was even warmer than Los Angeles on a winter day; the earth had begun to steam, giving off moisture in little gasps. And Lila knew one thing for certain: She was not about to lose her daughter this way.

When Lila slid the photograph album back onto Janet Ross's lap, Janet looked over at her, confused.

"I brought it for you," Janet said.

Maybe she should have felt grateful: here was the woman who sat up nights mixing formula, rocking back and forth in the rocking chair, not daring to go back to her own bed, even though the baby's breathing was fine and the intercom was switched on. But the truth was that the one time in her life when Lila was about to do something that seemed selfless, she was feeling nothing at all.

"You take this all home with you," Lila insisted. "She was your daughter."

That evening Lila and Jason Grey sat in the kitchen and had a supper of coffee and sandwiches. They could feel the drop in the temperature and they knew it was about to snow.

Jason had been watching her all evening and now he said carefully, "I liked that visitor of yours. Nice lady."

For the first time since she'd come back Lila realized just how cold this old house was.

"I think I might go back to California," she said.

Jason nodded. "They're predicting a hell of a February. Wherever you look you're going to see snow."

"I don't see how you stand it," Lila said, and they both knew she wasn't talking about the snow.

"I'll tell you what the hard part is," Jason Grey said. "It's not feeling Helen's not with me—I feel like she's with me all the time. It's letting her go. After all, it's pretty selfish trying to keep her here with me in this house, so every once in a while I just remind myself to let her go."

That night, before she went to bed, Lila went around the

house, turning off all the lights. In the parlor, her father-in-law was already asleep, and when Lila went over to turn out the lamp near his cot she saw that Janet Ross had left behind the small white sweater, neatly folded on the coffee table. Lila hesitated, but then she picked it up and discovered that the sweater was warm, as if it had just been worn.

She went upstairs, brushed her hair, and undressed; and when she got into bed she took the sweater in with her and held it against her chest. Everything in the room was faintly orange from the light of the kerosene heater, and outside the window, above the pine trees, the moon had a hazy ring around it, promising snow. Lila brought her knees up to her chest, and she rocked back and forth; in no time at all she was holding her daughter in her arms. She hadn't changed since the day she was born, she wasn't one minute older. And as Lila rocked her baby to sleep she closed her eyes and couldn't help thinking that Jason Grey could do whatever he wanted. It wasn't her baby that Janet Ross had been talking about, and she wasn't about to let her daughter go.

By morning nearly a foot of snow had fallen; the drifts reached the center of the front door and it took Lila and Jason Grey nearly two hours to dig the car out so that Jason could drive her to the airport. The last thing Lila had packed was the white wool sweater, and once they had gotten the car started, she kept the suitcase on her lap. At the edge of the driveway, just before they turned left onto the East China Highway, Lila felt a brief surge of pity for Janet Ross. But then, it didn't really concern her. She had found her daughter after all, and all the way to the airport she kept her left hand on her suitcase and she swore she could feel a heartbeat, as if she had hidden inside her suitcase a child so perfect and small no one else could see her, a baby who needed to be held all night, and gently rocked to sleep.

PART FIVE

They were on the floor in the living room, so intent on their breathing techniques that they hadn't heard her come in. As she watched from the hallway, Lila felt a coldness settle around her. Rae lay on a bed of pillows, her knees drawn up, eyes closed. She exhaled rapidly, as if she were blowing out an endless row of matches. Richard was right beside her, staring at his watch and counting out the seconds. On the coffee table there was a tape recorder, but instead of music there was the echo of wind chimes, brittle and cool and clear. It was the kind of sound that went right through you and made you realize that if you weren't lonely already, you would be soon.

When she had had enough, Lila dropped her suitcase so that it fell to the floor with a thud. They both sat up, startled, and turned toward the hallway. It was late afternoon, and so quiet you could hear air currents move through the room. The light that came in through the drapes was opalescent; everyone got lost in its shadows, you had to blink twice just to see straight. Except Lila, to whom everything was now obvious. For the past six hours, as she traveled between New York and Los Angeles, Lila had been wondering how she could walk in and resume her old life. Now, in an instant, she saw that she simply could not.

"Don't let me interrupt you," she told them.

She turned and went into the kitchen, but once the door had closed behind her, she didn't know what she was doing there. She didn't notice that it was too warm to still be wearing her wool coat and her boots. She had a confused, weightless feeling, as if she had stumbled not only into the wrong house but into the wrong time. When she had imagined coming home she had imagined feeling guilty, not betrayed. And she nearly forgot that even though she had not found Richard alone, she also was not alone. She had brought her daughter home with her.

By the time Richard followed her into the kitchen, Lila had decided to act as if nothing was wrong. She filled the tea kettle and put it up to boil. But every casual movement was difficult. The atmosphere was pushing down on her, the way it does in a jet, just after takeoff when the pressurized air suddenly turns fierce.

"Is this it?" Richard said to her. "After all this time you just walk right past me without a single explanation?"

Lila took a lemon from the window sill and cut it into quarters. She looked down and saw that her hand was shaking, and she quickly dropped the knife into the sink.

"Why didn't you talk to me when I called?" Richard asked. "Why did my father act like everything was a goddamned secret?"

They could hear Rae straighten up in the living room, picking up pillows from the floor, putting on her shoes, rewinding the relaxation tape on the recorder. In the kitchen, the sound of the rewinding tape was exactly like the sound of someone drowning.

"I should have guessed you'd get involved with her," Lila said.

"What is that supposed to mean?" Richard said. "You left and she was stuck without a labor coach."

"Are you sleeping with her?" Lila asked.

"Are you crazy?" Richard said.

"I don't know," Lila said. "Is it crazy to want your husband to remain faithful?"

"How are you doing this?" Richard said. "How can you manage to make it seem like I'm the one who's done something wrong?"

Miles above the earth, somewhere above Michigan, Lila had been struck with the sudden knowledge that she was about to lose someone. If she had to choose, Lila knew who that someone would be. The cabin of the jet had been flooded with light; to look at the clouds or the earth below, you had to wear sunglasses and squint. It was like the instant after you flip a coin, and your heart rate lets you know what you really wanted all along.

"Are you going to tell me why you left?" Richard said.

The tea kettle had begun to whistle, and Lila got a cup and saucer from the drying rack. If she had brought back a young woman she could have introduced her as her daughter, she could have explained. A long time ago, she would have told Richard, on a night that was so cold you couldn't light a match without having the flame freeze, she had given in to something so powerful it was impossible to fight it. She could hold on to the mattress until her fingers turned white, she could scream until her throat was raw, but all the time she did she knew she was just about to surrender. The surrender was unconditional, it lasted forever. But it didn't really matter that she had no proof, no flesh-and-blood child, no one to introduce to him. She was someone's mother, and there was no way to explain that her daughter was a ghost.

"Just tell me what's going on," Richard said. "Is that asking too much?"

Lila opened the cabinet above the stove. She took one look and could feel their marriage dissolving. When she thought now of their wedding day, she couldn't even remember what kind of flowers had grown outside by the kitchen door. There were no longer any teabags in this cabinet; he had rearranged things without once guessing that putting down new shelf paper and moving a few boxes and bowls would make her believe that it was over between them.

"What did you do?" Lila said.

Richard reached for the cabinet nearest the refrigerator and pulled it open. A box of teabags was now stored next to canned vegetables, soup, salt shakers, silverware.

"It's a lot more convenient this way," Richard began to explain.

"How could you do this to me?" Lila said. "How could you go ahead and do this?"

Richard looked at her carefully. He ran one hand through his hair. "This is crazy," he said. "This is true insanity."

It wasn't just the whistle of the kettle that caused the high pitch in the room. It was the tension between them; they couldn't take their eyes off each other, and both of them knew that if they weren't careful someone was about to go too far.

Out in the living room, Rae knew that she had to get out of there, but she didn't know quite how to do it. She had been waiting for someone to come out of the kitchen and dismiss her, preferably Richard. But now she could tell, from the sound of their voices, they had forgotten her. So she did what she thought was only polite. She went to the kitchen door and gently knocked.

"I think I'm going to go now," she called in to them.

"Oh, God," Lila groaned. She could feel Rae draining her energy, just as she had the first time they met. "Will you get her out of here?" she said to Richard.

"She has nothing to do with this," Richard said.

But through the closed door Lila could feel Rae's weight, and the slow movements of her baby as it turned in its sleep. Worst of all she could feel Rae's happiness, and it was that sense of expectation that burned right through Lila, like a jolt of electricity. Without thinking twice, Lila turned to the open cabinet and threw everything on the floor. Salt and silver trinkets saved in a box with a dog's tooth they had found in the garden, three silver knives, a fistful of black tea torn from two teabags, a wishbone, dust. And as Richard watched, horrified by the mess, Lila bent down and mixed it all together, and as she did she secretly wished Rae a labor exactly like her own. Right there in her own kitchen Lila called up pain, fear, suffering, blood, loneliness, and deceit.

Richard backed her into a corner and said her name three times. But she still wouldn't listen to him.

"Get her out!" Lila said.

Richard swallowed hard, then he went out to the hallway and helped Rae find her coat in the closet. Lila could hear their voices. Richard was apologizing, she could tell from his tone. He walked Rae to the door, and then Lila heard his footsteps returning. She was pacing the floor when he came back; her nerve endings were so raw that the air against her skin hurt.

"She's gone," Richard said. "We can talk now."

Lila looked at him from the corner of her eye and laughed.

"Please," Richard said. "Just talk to me."

He was begging her, really. But Lila forced herself not to look at him. She couldn't be distracted, not by him or anyone else. When she concentrated she could force her energy out through her fingertips in a flow of heat. She could bring back the ghost of the child who had died in East China.

It was dangerous business. It was walking on the thinnest sort of ice where one false move can make you stumble. And once your foot broke through the ice it was only seconds before you fell through to that place where lost children call to their mothers but can never be found, and even their voices disappear after a while, each cry swallowed whole by the dark. Lila refused to let anything she felt for Richard get in her way, and so she held her breath and she slowly and purposely stepped right over the line of forgiveness.

"Don't you understand anything?" she said to him. "I don't care enough about you to talk."

Richard instantly drew back. Lila had known that he would, but she hadn't expected it to hurt so much. Hannie had had that same wounded look the first time Lila refused to speak to her. Lila had brought over her order of hot water and raisin buns, but when the old woman invited her to join her at the table, Lila pretended not to hear. She had walked away instead, and she hid in the kitchen, near the crates where they stored lettuce. But every time the swinging doors to the kitchen opened, Lila could see out to the rear table and, as she watched, the look on Hannie's face turned to despair—it was a look that assured you the other person knew it was over between you.

Out in the backyard three jays circled the bird feeder before they perched on its farthest edge. Richard stood absolutely still, just as he had on that day she first met him, when the tar bubbled up on the road and sea gulls dared to eat from the palm of her hand. When he left her, Lila tried to hear only one thing—the thin wail of the kettle. But when the front door slammed the sound echoed. And as she stood there, alone in the kitchen, she could not believe what she had done.

She ran after him, but Richard had already gotten into his car and put it into gear. Lila pushed open the screen door and said his name, but he couldn't hear her now, and she knew it. It was the time of day when the horizon above the city turns violet, the time of year when the air itself is blue and unpredictable. It was easy to forget how deceiving February could be in California—it pretended to be one season just long enough to fool you, then turned itself inside out and delivered what you least expected—a heat wave or a storm. Tonight it felt exactly like summer. There was that lemon-colored light you usually saw in August, and the scent of dried grass and eucalyptus. But for the first time that Lila could remember there wasn't a single rose on the bushes outside the door, and when she looked carefully she could see a milky substance on the leaves, a sure sign of aphids and neglect.

After a while, Lila went inside. She pulled the screen closed and locked the door. Then she carried her suitcase into the bedroom and began to unpack. She had a headache, a bad one. Bad enough so that when she closed her eyes she swore she could see Richard. His car was idling in the parking lot behind the liquor store on La Brea and the radio was turned on. Everyone who walked past could hear it, and it made them self-conscious about going into a liquor store alone. They all wound up buying more to drink than they'd intended, and they thought it was the Ray Charles song on the radio that made them feel like getting really drunk. But it wasn't. It was seeing somebody who looked desperate parked out there in the lot on such a beautiful night that could really get to you, if you let it. Even if the big decision Richard was working on at that moment was a choice between bourbon and scotch.

Lila took two aspirins from the medicine cabinet in the bathroom before she came back and took off her coat and boots. A jet passed by overhead, and out in someone's yard a dog began to howl. When Lila had unpacked she went to her bureau and picked up the three silver bracelets she had left there. She put them on and they hit against each other, like pieces of ice in a glass. She thought, then, of her father-in-law. It was late in New York, and he was certainly already asleep in the parlor. Richard had told her that on the afternoon of Helen's funeral, Jason Grey had locked himself in a closet and cried. Afterward, they'd had dinner together, a casserole sent over by the wife of the fellow who'd bought Jason's gas station a few years back. Richard had continually looked over at his father, waiting for him to break down again. But he hadn't—he ate some of what was on his plate, had coffee, and went to lie down on the couch in the parlor at a little after eight. Richard slept in his old bedroom. Near midnight he heard something out in back of the house and woke up. He went to the window and saw that his father was out there, digging a hole in the ground with a shovel. The first thing he'd thought, he'd told Lila later, was that his father was digging his own grave. That night the moon was orange and full and Richard had been certain that the reason his father had not appeared to be grieving during dinner was that he'd been planning to bury himself alive.

Richard had stood at the window, unable to move. Outside, Jason Grey stopped digging; he leaned on his shovel and looked up at the sky. That was when Richard could see that the hole his father had been digging was much too small for a grave, even for something the size of a small dog. Jason took something out of his pocket. Richard pressed his face against the window and he could see that his father held a palm full of jewelry. It was Helen Grey's jewelry—her wedding ring, a small aquamarine brooch, a strand of seed pearls, a silver locket in the shape of a heart. Jason Grey knelt down and carefully buried the jewelry in the ground. But then he didn't go away—he just stood there, and he was standing there long after Richard had turned and gone back to bed.

When he'd come home to Los Angeles a few days later, Richard told Lila that at the moment when his father knelt on the damp ground, he'd had the sense that something was about to begin. It wasn't until the following morning that he realized what he'd felt was the start of his father's grief, the beginning of something that would take years to complete.

Lila sat on the edge of the bed and took off her silver bracelets. She felt terribly moved by the thought of her father-in-law out in his backyard, in the dark, opening his hands and trying to let his wife go. But, the truth was, it wasn't the same. Outside, the dog who had been chained up tugged on his lead and whined. The sky was dark now, you couldn't even see the birds who were nesting in the lemon tree for the night. There was simply no loss that compared to the death of a child. It was the one death that contained a thousand more within itself. An unbreakable ring, the end of everything your child might have been, the girl of ten, the woman of twenty, the one loss you just cannot bring yourself to believe.

If Lila had been there, if she'd felt her daughter grow cold, if she'd been the one forced to search all over East China for a coffin small enough, she might have accepted it by now. She might have been able to take her father-in-law's advice to let the dead go, even though afterward there would have been marks on her palms from the wrenching of letting go, small pinpoints that let in air and never seemed to heal. But instead of mourning what had been lost, Lila reached into her suitcase and took out her daughter's sweater. She held it in her hands and she closed her eyes until she couldn't see anything but white light. And as she sat there on the edge of the bed she could feel the material in her hands begin to grow warmer—so she closed her eyes tighter and willed her daughter to come to her.

Richard came home after eleven. He'd had more to drink than he could ever remember. He parked his car in the driveway and carefully maneuvered his way up the dark path. There wasn't a sound in the street, just his unsteady footsteps on the cement. When he got to the front door he just couldn't bring himself to go inside. He sat down on the porch steps, between the two rose bushes, and tried to figure out what had gone wrong.

Lila knew that he was back. She realized that all she had to do was make one move and all the others would follow. Just get out of bed, then put on her robe, then walk down the hallway and unlatch the front door. But she couldn't do it, she couldn't let her thoughts be swayed for a second. Her thoughts had to be as pure as light. And so she didn't move when she heard him push the latch up on the screen door, then unlock the front door.

He stood outside the closed bedroom door for a while, and then he went to the linen closet in the hallway and got some sheets. He undressed in the living room, in the dark. Just before he was about to lie down on the couch Richard realized that he smelled something burning. He followed the smell into the kitchen, where it turned overpoweringly bitter. The kitchen was dark, except for a circle of blue light that seemed somehow dangerous. For a split second, Richard found that he was afraid. But then he switched on the overhead light and saw that the blue circle was only the gas burner on the stove, turned on and forgotten. The water in the kettle had boiled away and the tin bottom was charred and smoking. Richard turned off the gas and put the kettle in the sink. He turned on the cold water and there was a rush of steam as the hot metal sizzled. When the kettle had cooled down, Richard tossed it in the trash, but even after he had opened the window the burning scent was still there, clinging to the curtains and the walls.

Richard didn't bother to put the sheets on the couch. He lay there, unable to sleep, imagining the way Lila used to look. The first time he saw her he knew there could never be anyone else, and the first time he had made love to her, he had actually cried—that's how much he'd wanted her. Every night he watched as she brushed her hair a hundred strokes with a wire brush. And he simply couldn't stop watching her, not even after she had fallen asleep. As she slept she reached out for him, she did it every night, just as every night Richard pulled her a little closer until it seemed there was only one person asleep in their bed and only one heart beating.

But on this night Lila didn't reach out for her husband, she didn't even think about him. She lay in their bed and concentrated so hard that she could feel the room spin. Her blood moved faster and faster; her fingertips began to burn. After a while Lila could feel herself growing weaker, and she knew she didn't have much more to give. The sheets beneath her were soaked with sweat and she could feel she was just about to break—her bones were rising up to the surface like fish, her skin simply couldn't contain energy like this. And just as she was about to give up, Lila felt something move in her arms.

She ground her teeth and refused to give up. She concentrated even harder, imagining every tiny finger and toe, recalling each second after her baby's birth—the shape of her cheek, the dark eyelashes, the odor of blood and milk. At last, Lila felt a weight on the bed next to her. She held her breath and when she opened her eyes she could see, even in the dark, that her daughter was finally beside her.

The baby's eyes were closed, her eyelids as white as stones. Slowly, the lids fluttered, and two perfect slate-gray eyes stared up at Lila. There was an outline of light all around the baby. Even when Lila held her tighter underneath a white sheet, the outline remained. And Lila wept when she realized that her daughter knew her, she cried so many tears that in no time at all both she and her child were coated with salt.

Out in the hallway you could see the light that surrounded the baby escape from under the bedroom door. It spread out all along the floor, into the other rooms of the house. Richard might have seen it if he hadn't been on his back, staring at the ceiling. He wished that he were holding his wife, but by now it was after midnight and Richard wouldn't have dreamed of disturbing Lila, any more than Lila would have thought to call out his name. Richard fell right asleep, maybe because he knew that he'd be sleeping out in the living room for a long time. And every night after that, before he went to sleep, Richard stood outside the bedroom door for a moment, and every night Lila heard him. But neither of them could go to the other; a thin sheet of glass had sprung up between them, and it separated them until they were as distant from each other as they were from the stars.

->>>

At the beginning of her eighth month, Rae woke up one morning and decided that she wouldn't go through with it after all. It wasn't being pregnant, she had gotten used to that—the insomnia, the heartburn, the pressure on her bladder, the way she had to get down on her knees every time she wanted to pick her shoes up off the floor. It was the idea of labor that terrified her. Throughout her life there had been a conspiracy, and there was still a secret she'd never been told. Lately, women with small children had begun to smile at her for no reason at all. Rae had thought it was sympathy—she was so lumbering and huge—or a particularly sweet memory of the time when their own child was about to be born. Now she realized it was something more—a moment of compassion for the uninitiated, a spinning backward through time to their own innocence. No one had ever told Rae the truth about childbirth. Not her Lamaze instructor, not her doctor, not her own mother. No one had bothered to suggest to her just how much it might hurt.

She'd done the practical things—read child-care books, renewed her insurance coverage, interviewed day-care mothers, even gone to a parenting course at U.C.L.A., where she'd given a doll a bath in a plastic washtub and pretended to insert a thermometer to check for fever. Still, the idea of holding an infant in her arms scared her. She had never even changed a diaper. The one time when she had baby-sat, she'd been lost. She'd sat for a nine-month-old boy who lived down the block from her parents' house, and he'd been asleep when she arrived. Rae was sixteen, and madly in love with Jessup, and she'd arranged for him to come over an hour after the child's parents had gone to the movies. They were on the couch, kissing, when the baby woke up. There'd been no warning, no slow escalation of louder and louder cries—suddenly the baby was screaming his head off, as if he had been stuck with pins.

"Oh, shit," Jessup had said. He sat up and threw his head back against the couch. "Why did I bother to come over here?"

Rae ran upstairs and peeked into the nursery. A nightlight gave off a purplish glow. From the doorway, Rae could see the baby standing up, holding on to the bars of his crib, screaming in a way that turned her blood cold. Rae stood there for a moment, then ran back downstairs. She found Jessup in the kitchen, looking through the refrigerator for a beer. When he saw Rae he was surprised.

"Why didn't you shut him up?" Jessup asked.

"I don't know how to," Rae said.

Jessup found a six-pack. He took out a can and pulled off the tab. "Did you change his diaper?" he said.

Rae could feel the baby's screams inside her skin. "I can't," she admitted. "I never did it before."

"You can't?" Jessup said. "You took this job and you don't even know how to change a diaper?"

Rae looked away from him and shrugged.

"What about feeding him?"

"I don't know how to," Rae had said in a small voice.

"Jesus Christ, Rae," Jessup said to her. "Don't invite me to any more of your jobs, all right?"

He slammed his beer down on the counter, got a bottle of formula out of the refrigerator, warmed it, then left her there in tears. She felt absolutely desperate—the pitch of the baby's cry had grown worse, and Rae imagined covering his mouth with her hand and shaking him until he stopped. But after a few minutes, the crying stopped, and Rae took off her shoes so she could creep back upstairs. By the time she got to the nursery, Jessup had changed the baby's diaper and he was sitting in the rocking chair feeding the baby his bottle. Rae stood in the doorway and listened to the squeak of the rocking chair and the greedy sound of the baby's swallowing. After a while she felt like an intruder, so she went back downstairs and sat on the couch.

Jessup came down after the baby was asleep. He got his beer, sat down next to Rae, and put his boots up on the coffee table.

"How did you do that?" Rae said to him.

"Do what?" Jessup said, as though he had never left her side.

They'd heard the key in the lock then, and Jessup had immediately leapt to his feet. He ran into the kitchen and was out the back door before the baby's parents had set foot in the house. But they saw the open beer can on the coffee table and, to Rae's great relief, they told her they'd see to it that she never baby-sat for anyone in the neighborhood ever again.

Afterward she tried to get Jessup to explain how he'd known what to do.

"I've got a couple of cousins," Jessup had said with a shrug. "Every kid is the same—when they pee you change their diaper. Then you give them something to eat so they can pee again and you can change their diaper again. It's no big deal."

Still, there was one thing Rae couldn't figure out—how Jessup had known to put the baby over his shoulder after he'd had his bottle, and gently rub his back until he fell asleep. Rae had been right there, standing in the doorway, but the room had been dark and there had been that purple, misleading glow of light, and after a while she guessed that she'd been seeing things. Maybe Jessup hadn't been as gentle as she'd imagined. Maybe he hadn't actually been humming, and she had also imagined the sound of a lullaby that was so sweet you knew you weren't meant to overhear.

She was missing him more these days, she was even dreaming about him. She dreamed that she was out in the desert, late at night, when there wasn't a soul around. The Oldsmobile was parked in a dusty field, and Rae sat on its hood, looking at the sky. She heard hoofbeats then, and she knew even before she saw it that it was one of Jessup's horses, smaller than a pony, with a coat that was the same blue-black color as the night. The horse came up right alongside her, and Rae could tell that Jessup had sent him to her. She waited, and after a while the horse spoke to her and told her that Jessup was being held captive. They stood there in the dark and both of them began to cry. Their tears formed a pool, and when Rae bent to look she saw that there were silvery fish swimming in circles, shimmering in the dark water. And when Rae looked even closer she noticed that where each fish's gills should be there was a tiny arm, and a hundred babies' hands paddled in the water.

Another time she dreamed that she and Jessup were making love, and when she woke she missed him more than ever, and all that morning she was weak in the knees, as though she had just come from her lover's bed. Missing Jessup was bad enough, what made it worse was that everyone around Rae was so distant and preoccupied. Freddy Contina didn't even go home any more. He worked till midnight and slept in his office, and he still couldn't figure out why no theater would release the films he'd brought back from Europe. Rae couldn't talk to him, and she couldn't talk to Richard any more either. Something was so wrong with Richard you could feel it just by touching his hand. When he knelt down beside Rae in Lamaze class his unhappiness interrupted Rae's concentration, and she often lost count of how many breaths she had taken. After class, as they walked out to the parking lot together, Rae always felt as if she were alone. She tried to talk to Richard about Lila, but he refused. "Don't even think about her," he told Rae. "Don't be concerned." But Rae couldn't help it, she was concerned. And sometimes, late at night, Rae wondered if she might have to pay for the sorrow on Lila's face when she walked in and saw them in the living room, a look that made Rae think of the way she used to look at Jessup when she knew he was about to go somewhere and leave her all alone.

She still couldn't quite believe Jessup wasn't coming back. She began to actively try to erase him from her mind. She took all his old clothes to a mission downtown and filled out a change-of-address card for him at the post office. She no longer ran to the window when she heard something that sounded like his footsteps; on the anniversary of the day he'd first kissed her she went to the Chinese take-out place around the corner and ordered everything he hated: shrimp with black bean sauce, spicy eggplant, mysterious flavored chicken.

On a Sunday early in March, when she had nearly managed to forget him, Rae got out of the shower and heard a knock at the door. She just stood there with a towel wrapped around her head. For a moment, right before she threw on her bathrobe and answered the door, she felt a surge of heat near her heart. She knew exactly who she wanted it to be out there in the courtyard, and after she opened the door and saw that it was only Jessup's partner, Hal, she was so disappointed it showed.

Hal had been out there for a while, trying to summon up the nerve to knock. He had brought her carnations which had been dipped in red dye, and the flowers made it impossible for Rae to turn him away. She made him some coffee, then went into the bathroom and got dressed. When she came back to the kitchen he was still stirring his coffee, and he seemed much more interested in the way Rae arranged the carnations than he did in having something to drink. She sat down across from him at the table and watched him carefully.

"Jessup didn't send you here, did he?" Rae asked. "Maybe he wanted you to see if I was all right or if I needed anything."

"Jessup?" Hal said, confused.

Rae put her elbows on the table and tried to smile. "I didn't think so," she said.

"I guess I just feel guilty," Hal said. "If he had told me about you I would have never asked him to come in on the ranch with me. To tell you the truth, I'm sorry I did ask him." Hal took a sip of his coffee and shook his head. "That god-damned Jessup. Whenever he runs out of something—like dishes or clean clothes—he acts so damned surprised, like there's an unlimited supply of everything. I'm telling you—no one can live with him."

"I did," Rae said.

"Well, you were in love with him," Hal said. He spooned more sugar into his coffee. Then, as if something had suddenly dawned on him, he said, "Don't tell me you still are?"

"If you're here because you think you broke us up, forget it," Rae said.

"I'd just like to help you out," Hal said.

He wasn't looking at her, so Rae could study him all she wanted. "Why?" she finally asked.

He seemed genuinely surprised by her question, and it took a while before he answered.

"Why shouldn't I?" he said.

"I don't know," Rae said.

"I could come visit you once in a while and take care of things," Hal said. "Maybe I just feel like doing something for you."

Rae promised him she'd think about it, and when there was a knock on her door the following Sunday, she didn't have any expectations. She knew exactly who it was. She let him carry the laundry downstairs and change the oil in the Oldsmobile, but it just made things worse. And when she walked him out to the pickup he and Jessup had bought, Rae felt a rush of desire. The truck was red, and Rae was certain that Jessup had been the one who'd chosen the color. She sounded sincere when she thanked Hal for all his help, but all she could think about was Jessup, sitting at the counter of the Dunkin Donuts in Barstow, watching that waitress, Paulette, from the corner of his eye.

Later, when she got into bed, Rae could tell she would have nightmares. She thought she would dream about the men in her life: Jessup would turn his back on her; Hal would knock at her window, waking her from a sound sleep; Richard would drive to the wrong hospital, leaving her waiting at the admitting desk, in labor and all alone. But that night Rae dreamed of Lila, and when she woke she was frightened the way she had been as a little girl, when she cried in her sleep and wanted her mother and no one else would do. Night after night Rae dreamed of Lila: she had a fever that could not be broken until Lila appeared; she was lost in a garden, and even though she could see Lila's house in the distance, every path led right back to the same locust grove. When she had been plagued by bad dreams as a child, Carolyn had taught her some tricks to chase them away. On the nights she felt she might have nightmares she was to wash her hair with lemon juice, and take some sewing or embroidery to bed, to work on just before she fell asleep. But now when she rinsed her hair the lemon juice always smelled bitter, and every time she picked up the embroidery needle she bought at the drugstore, she stuck her finger and drew blood.

After a few nights, the drops of blood that had fallen as Rae tried to work her embroidery formed the shape of a heart on her sheets, and she knew that if things kept on this way there would be only bad luck. But even when she willed herself not to have any dreams during the few hours each night that she slept, it wasn't enough. She did not expect Lila to agree to be at the baby's birth, but she might at least get her blessing. And so one evening, when she had cooked dinner but could not eat, Rae got into her car, and she drove without stopping to Three Sisters Street.

Richard's Volkswagen wasn't in the driveway, and that made Rae hesitate. But he was rarely there any more. Whenever he couldn't find a good excuse to work overtime he went and parked in the lot behind the liquor store. He didn't bother to go in and buy something to drink. He just parked and listened to the radio and avoided going home. When he did finally come home, Lila always knew. She froze the instant his car turned the corner, she could feel his weight as he came up the brick path to the door. It was not as difficult as she had thought it would be to live in the same house with someone and have nothing to do with him. If she and Richard met accidentally, in the hallway or the kitchen, Lila lowered her eyes and silently counted to a hundred, and by that time Richard had usually left the room. Every time Richard came into the house, and before he fell asleep on the couch, Lila made certain to keep the dresser drawer where her daughter slept closed. But as soon as she could she opened the drawer and picked up her baby, and sometimes, when she felt particularly brave, she took her outside and they sat together underneath the lemon tree.

The evening that Rae came to see her, Lila was sitting in the chair in her bedroom, rocking her daughter to sleep. She could feel someone walk up the brick path, and she knew it wasn't Richard. She got up and carefully put her daughter back in the drawer and covered her with a silk scarf that was so soft it slipped through your fingers. Then she put on her robe and went into the living room. She stood close to the wall, beside the drapes, and she lifted a fold of material so that she could look outside.

Rae's weight made her walk off-balance, and when she came up the porch steps she held on to the banister. Lately, she had developed a fear of falling, and she took each step gingerly, her left arm circling her belly protectively. Lila could almost see inside Rae to the baby she was carrying. Its eyes were closed, but it was moving its fingers, making a fist, then letting go. Already it had eyelashes, fingernails, a cap of soft down on its head. Beside this baby Lila's own child grew more ghostly, and Lila could tell, just thinking about Rae's baby sapped her child's strength: in the dresser drawer her daughter was right now struggling for breath.

When Rae rang the bell, Lila stood behind the drapes and

hid. Rae waited on the porch for longer than Lila had expected—nearly fifteen minutes. When she'd been there long enough to feel foolish, Rae turned and walked back to her parked car. Lila stood with her back against the wall; she wiped her eyes with the hem of the drapes. And later, when Lila summoned up the courage to pull back the drapes and look outside, there wasn't one single sign that anyone had come to see her, and no one who wasn't looking carefully would have noticed that there were at least a dozen new buds on the rosebushes at the front door, and that each and every one of them was blood red.

⋙

Hal and Rae had spent an entire morning shopping for a crib, going from one baby store to another. As the morning wore on, Rae began to feel more and more defeated. Everything was so expensive, so foreign. There were things she had never seen before—crib bumpers, walkers, infant seats with buckles and bells. All morning the baby had been pushing against her ribs, and when Hal asked her if she liked a particular crib, Rae turned on him.

"Why can't you just leave me alone?" she said before she stomped away. The pressure inside her grew worse then, and she wound up sitting on the floor, knees pulled up, hands shaking. She didn't know if she liked the crib or not because she didn't know what there was to like about it. In the end, she just pointed a finger at a wooden crib that didn't look any different from the rest and said she would take it.

As Hal loaded the crib into the rear of the pickup, Rae practiced her deep breathing in the parking lot. On the way home she was certain that if Hal said one word to her she would jump out of the moving truck. He wouldn't let her help him carry the crib across the courtyard, and once he had managed to get it inside they were both amazed by how much room it took up. They stood there watching it, hypnotized. Finally, Hal cleared his throat.

"That's some crib," he said appraisingly.

"I guess so," Rae said.

She sat down on the edge of the bed and ran one hand through her hair.

"I must be crazy," she said.

"I'll tell you what's crazy," Hal said. "We're making money. It's especially hard to believe because it was all Jessup's idea—we started advertising in *Variety* and in the *Times*. Go on and guess what *the* birthday present for kids in Beverly Hills is these days."

Rae looked up at him.

"Our horses," Hal said. "We deliver them wearing birthday hats."

Hal reached for his wallet and carefully peeled off ten hundred-dollar bills. He placed them at the foot of the bed.

"Don't do this," Rae warned him. "Don't you feel sorry for me."

"I'm not," Hal swore. "Listen, this is Jessup's money—only he doesn't know it."

"Really?" Rae said, interested.

"I'm in charge of the finances," Hal told her.

They smiled at each other then.

"I guess he owes me something," Rae agreed.

"I told you to get those bumpers for the crib," Hal said. "I told you they weren't too expensive."

"You know, you shouldn't be here," Rae said. "You should be out finding somebody of your own."

"That's okay," Hal said.

"I really mean it, Hal," Rae told him.

"I know you do," he nodded. "And I'm not expecting anything."

So Rae picked up the money he had given her, and she counted it twice. But she knew that you could easily say you weren't expecting anything, and still not quite believe you weren't really going to get it if you waited long enough.

That night they went out for an early dinner to celebrate the crib. The restaurant had once been a guest house on the edge of the Sisters' estate; they sat in the garden at a white wrought-iron table, and Rae insisted they order the most expensive items on the menu, since it was Jessup who was really paying. At first it was a joke, but by the time they had ordered dessert, Rae couldn't get Jessup off her mind. She actually ordered apple pie, which she hated, just because it was Jessup's favorite.

"Not that I'd take him back," she told Hal. "Imagine me having a baby with Jessup in the room watching. I'd have to worry about how awful I looked, and he'd be so horrible he'd probably ask me to jump off the bed and run out to get him a glass of ice water."

"You won't look awful," Hal said innocently. "You'll be beautiful."

"Oh, yeah?" Rae said coldly. "You're just the type of man who thinks a woman could be beautiful while she was up there on some hospital bed being tortured. I'll bet you want the woman you're with to be beautiful all the time—I'll bet that's why that girlfriend of yours left you."

Hal put down his fork. "Who said she left me?"

Hal wasn't the one she wanted to hurt, so there really was no point in this. "You know what?" Rae said tiredly. "I think I want to go home."

Hal looked so distraught as they walked through the parking lot, that Rae took his arm.

"I'll tell you how I knew," she said. "I was left, too, and it takes one to know one."

"I thought I was giving you a compliment," Hal said.

"I know you did," Rae said. "Don't pay any attention to me.

It's living with Jessup for so long—it's made me mean."

As they drove back on Sunset, Rae felt nervous. Everything was reminding her of Jessup—the sand on the floor of the truck, the shadows on the street. After a while she noticed that Hal was studying something in the rearview mirror. She leaned over and looked.

"Oh, shit," Rae said. "Is it him?"

Hal nodded and kept on driving. "I can't believe this fucking guy—he's got my car," he said.

For some reason, they both had the feeling they had done something wrong, and they spoke to each other in whispers.

"What are we going to do?" Rae said.

"What can we do?" Hal said, because by then they were stopped at a red light.

Jessup got out of Hal's Ford and slammed the door behind him. He left the Ford idling hard and came up and knocked on Rae's window. Rae looked at Hal and he leaned over and rolled her window down.

"What the hell is this supposed to be?" Jessup said.

"We went out to dinner," Hal said.

"Oh, really?" Jessup said. "How long has this been going on?"

"There's nothing going on," Hal said. He looked at Rae for a second, measuring what he was about to say. "But you know, while we're at it," he said to Jessup. "How about Paulette?"

"Paulette!" Jessup said. "Paulette is nothing."

"Come on, Jessup," Hal said. "Who do you think you're talking to—idiots?"

"I'll tell you what I'd really like to know," Jessup said. Rae wasn't looking at him, but she could tell by his tone that he was talking to her. "I'd like to know why you're too afraid to look at me."

Rae turned to him then, and as coolly as she could she said, "I'm looking at you now."

"Yeah?" Jessup said. "Well, take a good look."

As they stared at each other the light turned green; behind them someone sounded a horn. Without turning, Jessup raised his arm and signaled for the driver to go around them.

"Do you know what today is?" Jessup said to Rae.

The driver behind them leaned on his horn. Jessup jumped away from the pickup.

"Drive around us, you asshole," he called.

Hal leaned over toward Rae. "We don't have to sit here and take this from him," he said.

Jessup stuck his head in Rae's window again. The muscles in his jaw were tightening, the way they always did when he was upset.

"Today's my birthday, Rae," he said.

"Do you believe this?" Hal said. "Who does this guy think he is?"

"Do you really want me to spend my birthday alone?" Jessup asked Rae.

"What about Paulette?" Rae said before she could stop herself, and anyone could tell how interested she was no matter how cool she sounded. Next to her she could feel Hal sink down a little behind the steering wheel.

Jessup knew he had just had a small victory, and he grinned. "Come on," he said. "Let's go celebrate."

Rae swallowed hard, then turned to Hal. "I'm sorry," she said. "It's his birthday."

Jessup was walking around to the driver's door. He opened it and waited for Hal to get out.

"I appreciate everything you've done for me," Rae said to Hal.

"I don't need your appreciation," Hal said.

He got out, and Jessup stood aside so that Hal could walk back to the Ford. Then Jessup got into the truck. He pulled the door closed and took off. Rae leaned over to look in the rearview mirror and she could see Hal getting into his Ford, waving his hands at the line of cars waiting behind him.

"Well, I did it," Jessup said. He lit a cigarette and rolled down his window. "Just under the wire, before I turned thirty. I made it." He reached into his pocket, and for a moment the truck veered into the oncoming lane. "Take a look," Jessup said. He held up a billfold and smiled. "Thirty years old and I'm a success."

"Congratulations," Rae said.

"I told you I would be," Jessup said.

"I don't know," Rae said. "I just feel terrible about Hal."

"Let me tell you something about Hal," Jessup said. "He wants what anybody else has."

Rae gave Jessup a look.

"Or used to have," Jessup amended. "You know what I mean—whatever happens, we'll always be involved. It is my baby you're having, if I'm not mistaken."

"You're not mistaken," Rae said.

"There you go," Jessup nodded.

He pulled the car over when they passed a liquor store.

"Wait right here," he said, and he was gone before she could tell him not to.

Waiting there for him felt wrong. She had the feeling that this had all happened a hundred times before, only she'd been a different person.

Jessup jumped back into the pickup and put two bottles of Spanish champagne under his seat.

"What is that?" Rae said.

"That is champagne," Jessup said. "We're going back to the apartment to get drunk."

"I can't drink," Rae said. "I'm pregnant."

Jessup turned to her, annoyed. "It's my birthday," he said.

"I know," Rae said. "You keep reminding me."

"Yeah, well you sure didn't remember on your own."

Then Rae felt contrite—she had never forgotten his birthday before, but lately the only date she could remember was her baby's due date.

"All right," Rae said finally. "Let's go home."

They didn't talk for the rest of the ride. Once, Jessup caught Rae staring at him, and they both laughed, and it almost seemed like it was going to be all right. But as soon as Jessup had parked the car, Rae could tell it just wasn't the same as it used to be. She simply didn't trust him.

Jessup followed her across the courtyard, a champagne bottle in each hand. He was studying her as she unlocked the door and finally he said, "You sure do look pregnant."

Rae looked at him briefly, then pushed open the door.

When Jessup saw the crib, he put the champagne bottles down on the bureau, then walked over and ran his hand over the wooden bars. Rae had the strongest sense that he was about to say something important. But when he spoke it was only to tell her he was dying of thirst.

She went into the kitchen for glasses. Later she managed to act as if she was drinking by occasionally raising her glass to her lips. She was right to assume that Jessup wouldn't even notice that the only glass he kept refilling was his own.

"Why are you staying so far away from me?" Jessup asked her.

He was sitting on the edge of the bed. Rae was in the easy chair, watching him drink.

"I'm comfortable here," Rae shrugged.

"Like hell," Jessup said. "You're afraid of what might happen if you come a little closer."

Rae got up and went to sit next to him; balancing on the edge of the bed with nothing to support her strained her back. As he leaned toward her Rae thought about the first time he had ever kissed her. It was so cold that icicles had formed on all the streetlights. She really hadn't expected it; Jessup had been waiting for her outside the high school, and Rae left the girls she usually walked home with on the steps and ran to meet him. They walked along in silence, Jessup didn't even look at her, and Rae had to struggle to keep up with him on the slippery sidewalk. Then he'd turned on her, for no reason at all.

"Did you see the way they looked at me?" he said.

"Who?" Rae asked. They hadn't passed anyone on the street.

"Your friends," Jessup said. "That's who. You'd have to be blind not to notice."

"They didn't look at you," Rae said, although she expected they had, and that, by now, they had already dissected him right there on the steps of the school.

"Don't give me that crap," Jessup said.

"All right," Rae said. "They looked because they're jealous."

Jessup looked over at her.

"They are," Rae insisted.

"Bullshit," Jessup said, but she could tell he was buying it.

"I swear," Rae said, "they are."

"There's nothing to be jealous of," Jessup said then. "We're nothing to each other."

Rae looked down at the sidewalk.

"I'm warning you right now," Jessup said, "so you don't get hurt."

When he kissed her Rae knew that she was supposed to close her eyes, but she couldn't. She had to look at him to make certain it was really happening to her because she knew that when this first kiss was over, Jessup would back away and act as if nothing between them had changed.

This time, Rae was the one who backed away. Jessup looked at her, then reached down and pulled off his boots.

"What are you doing?" Rae said.

Jessup stood up and unbuttoned his shirt.

"What does it look like I'm doing?" he said.

"You really do think I'm stupid," Rae said.

"Go ahead," Jessup said. "Try and tell yourself you don't want me here."

"You should have gone out with Paulette," Rae said. "You would have had a much better birthday with her."

"Will you just forget about Paulette?" Jessup said. "In the first place she just got engaged to some cowboy."

Rae bent down and got Jessup's boots, then she walked across the room, opened the front door, and threw them out into the courtyard.

"Wait a minute!" Jessup said.

Rae stood at the open door and fanned herself to cool off.

"I told you this was going to happen to you," Jessup said. "I told you if you went ahead and got pregnant everything would change. You're not even thinking straight."

"You selfish bastard," Rae said. "If you think selling a few crummy horses means you're not a failure, you're wrong."

Jessup looked at her for a moment, then he buttoned his shirt and tucked it in. "Nobody talks to me like that," he said, and he walked right past her.

"Get out!" Rae said, even though she knew it sounded ridiculous—he already was standing in the courtyard. As she was about to slam the door behind him, Jessup grabbed it so it wouldn't budge.

"You had to go and do this on my birthday," he said. "You had to get back at me."

He spoke softly, almost in a whisper, but all the same Rae could tell that his voice was breaking. That was when she knew that he had come back because he needed her. On any other night it would have felt like a victory, but tonight she just felt sorry for him, and feeling that way about Jessup was the worst sort of betrayal there was. When she watched him walk across the courtyard he seemed hunched over, and Rae had the urge to run after him. But instead she closed the door and listened for his truck to start and drive away. She wondered if on that night in Boston when he told her he was leaving he had been holding his breath, desperate for her to beg to go with him. He had hidden it so well, all Rae had seen was endless courage, hot nights, a look that could make her do anything. But tonight Jessup was a thirty-year-old man who couldn't stay still long enough to last in one place. Someone who, when there was no one beside him in the passenger seat on the long ride out into the desert, wound up talking to himself for comfort. Someone who was totally exhausted when he got into the lower bunk bed in his trailer and found he still couldn't sleep.

Rae had been sure that she wouldn't be able to sleep either, but she was in bed and fast asleep long before Jessup reached the freeway. It wasn't that she didn't care any more—she did. But everything was different, in spite of what she felt. As she was falling asleep, Rae tried to picture Jessup's face and couldn't. Instead, she kept seeing the crib that was pushed up against the wall. With her eyes half closed the slats of the crib cast blue shadows across the room, and every time the headlights of a car out on the street flickered the shadows moved like water.

Sometime near dawn, Rae dreamed that she was with her mother at the house in Wellfleet. It was low tide, and you could hear the birds in the salt marsh beyond the house. They were out on the porch, and Carolyn was wearing a white summer dress, one she had owned years earlier, before Rae was born. They were facing the channel beside the marsh. It was an inlet, which whales sometimes mistook for deeper water; often, they got lost among the reeds and beached themselves, one after another. Now the channel was empty, and as smooth as glass. After a while, Rae realized that her mother was no longer beside her. When she found she was alone, Rae felt unusually calm. She leaned over the porch railing and listened to the birds, and when she looked again toward the reeds she saw that her mother's white dress was in the water, floating at the edge of the marsh, luminous as the moon.

In the morning, Rae woke up slowly. There was already the echo of traffic out on the boulevards, and a buzzing sound from one of the kitchen windows as a bee bounced against the screen. It wasn't until she got out of bed that Rae began to feel that something had changed: swinging her legs over the mattress was more difficult, walking across the room to get her robe was treacherous. Even when she looked at herself in the full-length mirror in the bathroom, it took a while before Rae realized that it was her own body that had changed. Before, all her weight had been high up, her belly pushed up toward her breasts. But sometime in the night everything had moved down—the baby had dropped, its head was down so far Rae could feel it resting against her pelvic bones. Rae let her bathrobe fall onto the tiled floor just so that she could look at herself. She stayed there so long that anyone would have thought she was terribly vain, but it was just that for the first time that she could remember she didn't wish for anything other than what she already had, and what she had was less than four weeks to go before her baby was born.

⋙

Lila and Richard had learned to be polite to each other, but their civility was so chilling it made their skins crawl. When they really tried they could actually manage to have a meal together in the same room. All they had to do was remember not to look at each other, not to ask each other for the simplest favors, not even to pass the salt, and under no circumstances could they even begin to think about what they had once had.

Nothing on earth could have made Lila turn to her husband,

nothing could force her to go to him now and admit that something frightening had begun to happen—she had begun to have visions. These were no orderly prophecies that appeared when beckoned, they came suddenly, at odd hours of the day and night, and they turned time into a wicked thing. There was no way to tell if something was about to happen, or if it had already come to pass. Lila never knew if she was really in her own kitchen, pouring juice into a glass, or if she was on the banks of a frozen bay, watching her first lover, Stephen, walk past the ice fishermen on his way home. In the afternoons, when she went out to water the geraniums, Lila saw her mother out on the patio with two other girls, all of them so young you could practically hear them counting the days until summer. When she dusted in the living room there was Rae, leaning over a bassinet to croon her restless baby to sleep. Each time she went into the bathroom and turned on the light she saw herself putting the stopper in the sink and running the cold water, before she reached for the straight-edged razor and studied her own submerged arm.

These visions brought blinding headaches and a peculiar chill that wouldn't go away. Now Lila knew why Hannie had always worn too many layers of clothing: black skirts, leather boots, sweaters, shawls. Time, Hannie had told her, grew more delicate as you got older, it was so tissue thin you could hold your hand up to the light and see how tapered the fingers had been at twenty-five, how the palms had been scratched by a fall into the brambles on the morning of your eighth birthday.

Sitting at the rear table, Lila had felt more and more uncomfortable as Hannie talked about getting old.

"There must be some way to stop it," she said.

It was a foolish remark, but Hannie didn't laugh. She nodded and bit a sugar cube in half, keeping one half between her thumb and forefinger, the other in her cheek to dissolve.

"There is a way," she told Lila. The fortune-teller's eyes were small, and a little too bright, so that people sometimes had to look away from her for no reason at all. "But I wouldn't wish it on you."

Lila got it into her head that Hannie knew some secret way to stay young, and already, at eighteen, she knew that certain men, like Stephen, couldn't tolerate a woman's growing old. Lila imagined that the secret was a lotion, a cream made of roses and diluted water and fruit, or a powder you dusted over each eyelid before you went to sleep. For days she pestered Hannie; she swore she wouldn't tell another soul. Hannie avoided answering; instead she told Lila the ingredients of the beauty treatments women in her village had sworn by: egg whites left on your face for one hour, cinnamon under your pillow, tea leaves mixed into your shampoo. But none of this was what Lila wanted, and she brought it up again and again, until Hannie finally gave in.

"When I was a child," Hannie told her, "there was a woman who was so beautiful that ravens used to come to her window just to see her. At night when she went inside the moon grew duller, the frogs who sat on her front porch never made bellowing noises like the ones by the river—they sat there silently, as though they were waiting for a glimpse of her feet underneath the crack of the door. Her husband adored her, her children refused to let go of her skirts because she smelled like lavender and sweet butter. She was so beautiful that no one was jealous of her, and others enjoyed her good fortune as if it were their own.

"But then something went wrong. She cried all day and all night, there were dark circles around her eyes and her skin looked like ashes in the chimney. This is what happened: She had found some gray hairs, and that had caused her to look even closer. When she borrowed a mirror from her mother-in-law she saw wrinkles that she had never noticed before, she saw that she had begun to grow old. She wrapped herself in a quilt and slept on the wooden floor, weeping in her sleep. Her children grew thin, her husband began to lose his hair. And then, one day, she suddenly seemed herself again, only now she smiled shyly, as though she had a secret. Everyone in the village watched carefully, everyone knew that something was about to happen, and sure enough, on their way to the schoolhouse one morning, the children found her body hanging from a pine tree. She had hung herself with a white silk scarf, the same scarf she had worn at her wedding. They buried her the very same day, and from then on she was talked about so much that everyone could still see her: all they had to do was close their eyes. In time her husband came out of mourning, her children recalled her tenderly, the men in the village talked about her each time they sat down by the river and got drunk. All the women in the village knew that she had managed to stay beautiful—she had simply paid a price she would have had to pay anyway, a little later on when her skin was all wrinkled and her hair so white you couldn't see her when she bent over in the snow. And all the young women envied her courage, but the old women looked at each other and knew her for the fool that she was."

Lila knew it was true—her daughter was the only one who didn't get lost in her confusion of time. The baby was always the same, quietly sitting on Lila's lap out in the garden, or waiting to be picked up from her bed in the dresser drawer. But the visions drained Lila's energy, and she went to her daughter less and less often. Sometimes she simply pulled a chair up beside the dresser and watched her daughter sleep. All day long she sat on a hardbacked chair, guarding her daughter, and when she went to sleep her dreams were murky so that in the morning she could never remember them.

Each day she was more on edge, and one evening in March, when the air was light and clean and the acacia tree in their neighbor's yard had begun to flower, Lila suddenly couldn't stand to have another dinner alone. She knew Richard wouldn't be back from the shop until sometime after eight, and so she took a tray out to the table on the patio. She was wearing corduroy slacks and one of Richard's wool sweaters; the evening wasn't very cool but she began to feel a chill. At first she thought it was the kind of coldness that accompanied a vision, but it was different, it was more like a steel knife that cut down her left side, from her fingertips to her chest. For some reason she couldn't smell the lemon tree, she couldn't hear jets when they passed overhead.

She was at the table, the tray of cottage cheese and fruit and iced tea right in front of her, when she began to feel paralyzed. She told herself that all she had to do was move and she'd be all right. But once she was back inside the house, it was worse. Her blood was ice. She went to the phone in the kitchen to call Richard at the shop, but she couldn't remember the number she had called a thousand times before. As she stood there Lila could swear that it was August, the air was so warm and still. She could hear someone down the hallway stir in bed. It was Janet Ross—she couldn't sleep so she got out of bed and went to the closet for her robe as the birds out on the lawn began to sing.

Lila reached up and dialed for the operator.

"I need to reach my husband," she said as soon as the operator answered.

"Can't you dial him directly?" the operator said.

"I can't," Lila said.

"Tell me his number," the operator said.

But that was just it—she couldn't remember.

Outside, the birds were making a terrible racket. Lila knew that any second Janet Ross would come to the nursery, so she crouched down, next to the crib. At first she thought her daughter was sleeping, but then she saw that the baby's eyes were open. Lila leaned her face against the wooden slats of the crib, and when her daughter exhaled, Lila swallowed it in. The taste was so sweet that she knew it was a last breath. As she crouched by the crib Lila heard her baby's heart stop. Just like that, on a morning when people all over East China were sleeping beside their husbands or wives, her daughter's heart stopped beating.

The curtains in the nursery were drawn, but anyone could tell it would be an ideal day, it had been that kind of summer. Eighty-two, and cooler in the shade. Eighty-two, and Lila was freezing. Her daughter's arms trembled slightly and rustled the crib sheet, and then, much too quickly, her body grew heavy as a stone, and pale as the sky in early morning. Lila cried out only once, but that one cry could break glass, it could break through time itself.

"Oh, please," Lila said. She was holding on to the phone receiver so tightly that her fingers were numb.

The operator recited Lila's number and asked for her address. But Lila couldn't answer, and by the time the operator had looked up the address herself, Lila had dropped the receiver on the floor. Everything was failing her now—her lungs, her eyes, her ears. She ran back out to the garden, desperate for air. Snails had begun to wind their way across the patio, but Lila couldn't see them; she stumbled and stepped on several and their shells broke beneath her feet. Her headache had taken over; it shattered into pieces that cut into her temples. She could feel herself falling, and although she had always expected herself to give in gracefully, she tried to hold on.

⋙

That evening was the last Lamaze class. They'd finished learning breathing techniques and tonight they were seeing a film. As soon as the lights were turned out and the credits came on the screen, Rae closed her eyes. Richard reached over and held her hand, but neither of them could stand to watch as the husband and wife on screen welcomed their infant son.

Later, as they walked out to their cars in the parking lot, Rae looked through her bag and couldn't find her keys. "Oh, shit," she said, and she sat down on the curb, disgusted.

Richard sat down next to her. "You don't really want me to be your labor coach, do you?" he said.

"Sure I do," Rae said, but she didn't look at him. She found her keys at the bottom of her bag and nervously swung them in a circle until the jangling made Richard put his hand on hers to stop it.

"Headache," he explained. "I can tell you'd rather have Lila."

"Well, she obviously wouldn't rather do it, so I appreciate the fact that you will."

"You could go talk to her," Richard said.

Rae looked over at him.

"She needs somebody and it sure isn't me," Richard said.

"I've already been to talk to her," Rae admitted. "She wouldn't open the door."

Richard got up and pulled Rae to her feet. It was just getting dark and the rest of the people in their Lamaze class were already on their way home to supper.

"I just want you to know I'm not insulted," Richard said.

"You've got nothing to be insulted about," Rae told him. But when he looked at her she had to laugh. "All right," Rae said, "maybe I would rather have another woman there with me."

But that wasn't the only reason, and she knew it. She still had the feeling that without Lila there she'd have nothing but bad luck. On her way home she drove past Three Sisters Street; she circled around and drove past again, and when she finally pulled over and parked she was surprised to find that her heart was beating fast.

When no one answered the door right away, Rae considered leaving. She leaned over to the window; with her face pressed against the glass she could see through the house to the kitchen—the back door was ajar. There was already the sound of a siren somewhere close by when Rae walked around to the garden, although the ambulance didn't arrive until Rae had covered Lila with her sweater and knelt down beside her. She screamed to the attendants when she heard them bang on the front door; they rushed the stretcher to the back of the house and found Rae kneeling over Lila, who was sprawled on the cold patio, unconscious. As the attendants lifted Lila they couldn't help but notice the gashes in the slate next to her, left by her fingernails when she tried so hard to hold on. And although it grew less noticeable with time, from that day onward the slate was scarred by fine lines, like the marks you find on wrists that never quite heal.

It wasn't until three days later that Lila was aware of anything, and then it was only a dream. She was in a place where the sunlight was blinding and tropical. The sky itself seemed white, and it took a while before she realized that it wasn't the sky at all but a thousand snowy egrets. The landscape was flat, and there were enormous trees that dripped moss into a bayou. In the water there were huge flowers, each one larger than the largest sunflower. And even while she was dreaming Lila knew that there was no place on earth where egrets fly straight toward the sun, nowhere where the water in a bayou is turquoise, where tropical flowers are as cold and as white as milk.

It occurred to Lila that she might be dying. She had always thought death would come for her in the form of a man dressed in black silk. He would be waiting in an alley on an icy night, lanterns would burn, and wolves would howl so horribly that the sound would send shivers down the spines of children as they tossed in their sleep. It seemed impossible for the end to happen here, in this tropical place. The only escape was to wake up, and she seemed to be stuck here, in this dream. When she did finally manage to wake up it was agonizingly slow. The bayou dried up and receded by inches, leaving behind a gray tiled floor that seemed to have ripples in it, perhaps because she looked at it through the curtain of an oxygen tent.

Richard had sat at her bedside for three days, waiting for her to die and blaming himself. At the end of the third day he seemed to have shrunk a little—he was wearing the same clothes, but they were all too loose for him now. Rae came to the hospital after work and relieved him so that he could go home and shower and sleep for a few hours on something other than a hardbacked chair. She had been there for nearly two hours when she heard the sound of something moving against the bedsheets—it was Lila, struggling to lift her arm under the weight of the IV. Rae leaned closer to the bed, and as soon as Lila opened her eyes Rae rang the buzzer on the wall.

"Don't call for the damned doctor," Lila said, but her voice wouldn't rise above a whisper and Rae couldn't hear her through the oxygen tent.

"She's awake," Rae called shrilly when the nurse responded through the intercom.

Lila tapped on the oxygen tent with one finger and Rae leaned toward her.

"Didn't you hear me?" Lila said. "Don't call the damned doctor."

"You don't know how worried we were," Rae said.

"Nobody has to worry about me," Lila said, but her voice betrayed her, and when Rae pressed her hand against the plastic tent, Lila didn't move her hand away.

While Lila was being examined, Rae went out to the hallway of the Intensive Care Unit and telephoned Richard. He was there in less than twenty minutes, and he told Rae it was all right for her to leave. Lila's doctors cornered him in the hallway. They advised him that even though Lila's heart attack had been mild, there was always the chance of a second, more brutal attack. Richard nodded when they told him her recovery might be slow; he really tried to listen, but all he wanted was to see her. Although when he finally went into her room he was suddenly shy, a twenty-year-old all over again. He stood near the door, ready to back out into the hallway.

"If you don't want me here, I'll understand," he told Lila. His voice sounded hoarse, even after he'd cleared his throat. "Maybe you don't want me to be your husband any more."

For the first time Lila realized that she was in pain. She pushed the oxygen tent away and signaled for him to come closer. Richard stood by the side of the bed.

"I've been going crazy," he said.

While Lila was unconscious Rae had brought her a potted blue hyacinth. In the overheated hospital room its scent was hypnotic—you could almost imagine yourself on the East China Highway during that one week in April when everything suddenly began to bloom.

"They're going to release you at the end of the week," Richard said. He still could not look anywhere but the floor. Yesterday he had forgotten to call his father, and when it was midnight in New York Jason Grey had phoned him. As soon as he'd heard his father's voice he'd started to weep, and ever since then he couldn't seem to control himself.

"I'm glad my doctor is talking to someone," Lila said. "He hasn't told me a thing."

"I don't want to lose you," Richard said.

When neither of them spoke they could hear the click of the IV as glucose dripped into Lila's vein. Lila tried to think about her daughter, left alone for days in the dresser drawer, but all she could see was that flat, white landscape of her dreams. It was so lonely there you could die of it, it made you want to turn and throw your arms around whoever it was you loved best.

Richard pulled up a chair and sat close to the bed.

"We can start over," he said.

Lila shook her head.

"Sure we can," Richard told her. "Even people who get divorced get back together sometimes, and we never even got divorced."

"Maybe we should," Lila said. "Maybe that's the answer."

Richard leaned toward her. "Is that what you want?" he asked. "A divorce?"

On the day he picked up that bucket of water he did it so easily, as if it was nothing more than a china cup. She knew she shouldn't have stood there for as long as she did, she shouldn't have looked at him twice.

"Why do you keep asking me such stupid questions?" Lila said.

Richard knew that it was now all right for him to lean over and take her hand. "I'll come and get you Friday," Richard said. "I'll close the shop and take you home."

The pillow under Lila's head was so soft it made her sleepy. As soon as Richard left she planned to close her eyes, she might even be able to sleep for an hour before they brought her dinner in on a tray. As she fell asleep she'd tell herself that she'd given in because he'd just badger her anyway until she agreed. But she had already begun to count the days until Friday, and really, after all these years together, she just couldn't imagine going home without him.

In the twenties, when the block was owned by the Three Sisters, pelicans nested on the roof and foxes came to sleep on the veranda at midday. The chaparral in the foothills was thick with manzanitas and wild morning glories. The aqueducts from Owens Valley had been completed, but you could still feel the desert every time you walked out your front door. Everyone was thirsty all the time—you could finish a pitcher of water and still have the urge for more, you just couldn't get enough to drink.

The Sisters regretted coming to California the instant they stepped off the train. The smell of citrus groves and the hollow clanking of oil riggings just made them more homesick. At night they dreamed of New Jersey and cried in their sleep. One sister had been persuaded to leave her fiancé behind, the other two had both passed thirty and they'd assumed they had nothing more to lose. But the odd afternoon light coming in through the windows was enough to frighten them so badly that they lost their voices from two until suppertime. Every day the real-estate boom grew closer to their estate; they could hear cottonwoods and eucalyptus being chopped down, and all night long, workmen hammered out the wood frames of new bungalows. In time the Sisters became fiercely protective of their property and they built an iron fence whose gate had only three keys. But they could never tolerate the luxury of their house, and the fact that the brother who had brought them out to California had designed it only made them more bitter. They fired the gardeners, drained the turquoise-colored cement fountain, sold the pair of screaming peacocks at auction. Most of the furniture was taken away in huge wagons, and the screening room was torn down before they had viewed even one of their brother's pictures. After a while their brother stopped inviting them to parties at his own house up in the hills. Instead he sent them handwritten notes once a month, and although he received polite replies he soon gave up altogether. In the end the Sisters rarely left the confines of their property.

Except for one. The youngest of the Sisters ran away and was married for a brief time. Years later she returned quite suddenly, and she lived on the estate long after the two older ones had died. Because no one in the family had left a will, the city claimed the estate and sold it off, parcel by parcel. But no developer seemed to want to touch the house itself—it stayed empty and intact until the Long Beach earthquake split the foundation and tumbled the turrets onto a grove of Hawaiian palms. In the neighborhood, people liked to say that the youngest sister had given birth to a child during her time away from the estate, a true heir who would one day return to claim the property. Then they would all have to move out of their houses and the block would once again be planted with eucalyptus and juniper trees and thick old rose bushes imported from New York and France. People actually seemed to look forward to this time when they'd be removed from their houses, either because it seemed so unlikely or because they were so tired of working in their fruitless backyards that they were willing to give it all up just to see somebody succeed.

For the most part people who owned houses on Three Sisters Street had the sense that their homes didn't really belong to them. Yet since Lila had come back from the hospital she felt more at home than she ever had before. The bungalow seemed simple and clean, and when the afternoon light came in through the windows it was so sharp it took your breath away. It was the nights that were difficult, because at night Lila could tell that she was losing her daughter. It was a case of neglect: she just didn't have the strength to will her daughter to life. Every night the baby was more transparent and her skin grew colder by the hour, even after she'd been covered with a towel to keep her warm. When it was very late, and everyone in the neighborhood had been asleep for hours, Lila could hear her baby struggling for breath. But there was nothing she could do. Richard wasn't sleeping on the couch any more, he was right there beside her, and because she was afraid of waking him all Lila could do was bite her lip and listen to her baby's chest rattling.

She knew that the kindest thing to do would be to let her daughter go. It seemed so simple and rational when she thought about it during the day. But at night she couldn't bring herself to give the baby up, and sometimes she took a terrible risk—she dragged herself out of bed and went to open the dresser drawer. But each time Lila held the baby the weight in her arms was lighter, and after a while she realized that her daughter could no longer open her eyes.

Richard insisted on treating Lila like an invalid and she didn't try to stop him. He'd changed his schedule and hired another mechanic so he had to go into the shop only in the afternoons. In the mornings he made certain Lila stayed in bed; he brought her tea and muffins and magazines. Her visions and headaches had never returned and her doctors insisted she was getting stronger, but after lunch, when she was alone in the house, Lila found herself listening to her own heart, waiting for an irregular beat. It was awful to want so much to be alive; it left you with no pride at all. When Rae phoned and said she could arrange to leave work early Lila found herself agreeing and let her come visit, although when Rae got there Lila wouldn't talk to her—the most she would tolerate was being read to from the L.A. *Times*. Rae would let herself in the front door with a key Richard had hidden under a terra-cotta flowerpot, then go to the kitchen and get one glass of milk and one glass of lemonade before going into Lila's room. Richard left a chair for her near the bed, and she kept her feet raised on the edge of the mattress. She usually began by reading the headlines, then the editorial page, the horoscopes, the TV listings for that night. Reading aloud reminded Rae of those nights when her mother would read her recipes listed in French cookery books as they dined on baked beans and hamburgers. Maybe that was why she felt homesick whenever she left Lila's house, and she looked for excuses to stay. If Lila fell asleep while she was reading, Rae went into the kitchen and finished reading the newspaper, and then, if there were no dishes in the sink to wash, she simply stood by the window and watched the light.

Even when Lila didn't fall asleep there were times when she didn't seem to notice Rae was there. But once, as Rae was reading the TV listings, Lila sat up straight and turned to her.

"I may be trapped in bed, but I don't have to listen to this garbage," Lila said. "Who in their right mind would read the plot summary of *Charlie's Angels*?"

"I think it's kind of interesting," Rae said. "The way they can reduce everything to one sentence. It's in my line of work—if I ever do anything more than file and answer the phone."

"Anything but TV listings," Lila said, and Rae felt as though they'd had some sort of breakthrough that afternoon. It was almost as if they'd had a real conversation.

The next day Rae brought a book of baby names instead of the *Times*.

"I can't seem to find a name I like," Rae explained.

"I'm sorry," Lila said, "this is not an appropriate thing to read to a sick woman."

But once Rae began, the litany of names was mesmerizing, and when she left off—at girls' names beginning with *M*—Lila felt disappointed. All through the weekend Lila looked forward to hearing the rest of the names, but on Tuesday Rae was late. At three thirty Lila actually got out of bed and went to the window to wait for her. For no reason at all she felt slighted, and as soon as she saw Rae's car pull up she got back into bed. When Rae came in with the tray of lemonade and milk, Lila pretended to be sleeping. Rae waited till four thirty, but Lila still refused to open her eyes, she closed them so tightly they hurt.

That night Rae began to have strange little spasms and her womb tightened until it was hard as a rock. Suddenly the birth of her baby seemed much too near, and by the time she called her doctor's service she was so hysterical that she lost her voice and had to croak out what her symptoms were. Her doctor insisted it was nothing for her to get alarmed about, only Braxton Hicks contractions—false labor. Still, the contractions changed something—it was no longer possible to imagine that this pregnancy would go on forever. She was really going to have this baby.

After that Rae couldn't concentrate on anything. At work she filed contracts into the wrong folders and disconnected everyone who tried to reach Freddy. One afternoon Freddy invited her along to a screening of a Canadian film—in it a woman named Eugenie was widowed after following her husband to a place that was so far north the snow was twelve feet deep; she fought off wolves with a shotgun, and loneliness with strong Indian tea. As she watched Rae was reminded of her own mother, Carolyn, and by the time the picture was over she was in tears.

"Give me a break," Freddy said when the lights came back on.

"Seriously?" Rae said as she wiped her eyes with the cuffs of her blouse. "You're not going to distribute it?"

"This is a picture for Canadians," Freddy told her. "In Toronto they think sitting around and waiting for spring is exciting."

Maybe it was because business was so bad, or because Rae felt the sort of daring that comes when you think you're about to lose your job anyway—Freddy had certainly never promised her a job to come back to after the baby was born—but when Rae went back up to the office she forged Freddy's signature and bought rights to *Eugenie.* When she drove to Three Sisters Street after work Rae was still flushed with the excitement of having done something rash. Not even Lila's flat-out refusal to let her read aloud from the book of names could dampen her spirits. But it didn't last long—on the way home Rae stopped at the Chinese take-out place, and while she waited for her order she had an overwhelming sense of disappointment. The only man she had ever loved would never be true, the labor coach she wanted wouldn't even discuss names for the baby, and the coach she had was so distracted he hadn't even talked to her in a week, he just left her notes taped to the refrigerator: *She's in a good mood today* or *Watch out—she woke up on the wrong side of bed for sure.* When she got back into the car the smell of eggrolls on the seat beside her made her feel queasy and even more distraught. Parking the Oldsmobile, all she could think about was the fact that her own mother was three thousand miles away, and she backed into a Mustang and had to leave a note wedged in behind one of the windshield wipers with the name of her insurance company.

She was still making a list of everything that had gone wrong since last summer as she crossed the courtyard, but halfway to her apartment she stopped cold. Just ahead of her, standing in the shadows, was the wild black Labrador she had seen in the courtyard before, just after the heat wave. Rae knew that the one thing she should not do was run. She stood there and held the brown paper bag of Chinese food to her chest. The air seemed cold, not like April at all, and even from this distance she could hear the dog growl. Anyone could see it was underfed; when it began to walk toward her, Rae could count its ribs.

"Good dog," Rae said.

Jessup had told her once that dogs always brought down deer by attacking their delicate legs. They had been driving along the Skyline Drive, to see the changing leaves, when they sighted a pack of dogs, running through the woods, after prey. Rae had been surprised that Jessup knew anything about deer, she'd doubted him until they heard the dogs yapping wildly, and then she'd begged him to step on the gas and get them out of there, fast.

This dog's tail was up, and she knew that wasn't a good sign. She could feel something sour in her mouth, and she wondered how a pregnant person could possibly be given rabies shots. Inside her the baby moved; when it turned on its side like that it was almost as if there was a wave trapped within her.

"I'm going to keep walking," Rae said to the dog. It was close enough so that she could feel the heat of its body. "I want you to stay," she told it.

Her legs were shaking, and maybe that was why it seemed to take such a long time to get to the front door. As soon as she heard the lock click she pushed the door open and ran inside. She stood there with her back to the door, shivering. Then she put the bag of Chinese food down on the bed and went to the kitchen window. The dog was still out there, in the exact place where she'd told it to stay. It looked around, confused; if it had come down from the canyons during the heat wave last summer it had spent the last months hiding, coming out at night to turn over garbage cans and search for water in bird-baths and gutters. But someone had once trained this dog well and it was compelled to obey Rae's command. It might have stood out in the courtyard all night if Rae hadn't filled a plate with fried rice and eggrolls and opened the door to call to it.

It was a female, and not quite as vicious as it had first seemed. It watched Rae, puzzled, but when she closed the front door, it ran to the food and devoured it. Rae sat in the easy chair and ate the rest of the food out of the containers; later, when she went into the kitchen to boil water for tea, she looked out the window and saw that the dog was still out there, curled up on her doorstep. That night, Rae took her embroidery into bed with her and she used a cross-stitch and red thread to make a border of hearts along the hem of a baby blanket. Through the locked front door she could hear the dog breathe in its sleep, long easy intakes of air that sounded like sighs. It was amazing how the sound of another creature's breathing could get into your dreams and bind you together. In the morning Rae set a bowl of milk outside her front door, and after a little while she found the courage to reach down and pat the stray dog as it drank.

The next morning she took the dog in for a rabies vaccination and bought it a collar and leash. She walked the dog three times a day. Her doctor agreed that it was good exercise, but she also suggested that it was time to start taking it easy, maybe time to stop working.

When Rae went to visit Lila, the dog climbed into the car and insisted on going with her. She left it tied to the garage door. Lila was crankier than usual, and after a while Rae gave up trying to read to her. At a quarter to five Rae went into the kitchen; she washed out some cups and cleaned the counter with a paper towel. When Lila heard the front door open she thought Rae had left, and she sat up in bed, frightened at being alone. But Rae had only gone out with a bowl of cold water for the dog. She came back and rinsed out the bowl, then stood in the doorway to Lila's room.

"Didn't you leave yet?" Lila said.

"Not yet," Rae said. "But I guess I won't be coming back any more."

Lila reached for the remote control and snapped on the TV.

"My doctor wants me to take it easy," Rae said. "It makes me wonder if there's something wrong with my baby," she blurted.

"Of course there isn't," Lila said. "They tell everybody to relax in the last weeks."

"Yeah," Rae said, unconvinced.

Outside the dog looked mournfully at the front door and then began to bark.

"Sounds like a big dog you've got," Lila said. She just couldn't bring herself to look at Rae.

"I'm scared," Rae said.

Even if Lila had tried there was no way for her to tell Rae just how much agony giving birth would be or how, in an instant, the pain would be so forgotten that it wouldn't even be like a dream, but more like a dream someone else had had. It was easier, of course, when you had someone there beside you to remind you how quickly it would all be over, how much you stood to gain: one child who reached out for you even before it opened its eyes.

Rae stood where she was in the doorway, and Lila knew that if she took one more step it would be impossible to turn her away. She wouldn't even want to. Rae held her car keys in her hand; the metal bit into her fingers until she couldn't stand it. Then she let go. She walked over to the bed, and together she and Lila listened to the dog outside, tied to the garage door, barking.

"I'm really, really scared," Rae whispered.

Lila leaned over and touched her hand. "Don't be scared," she said.

⋙

Each day Lila was able to get out of bed for a little while longer. Richard went back to work full time, and the doctors told Lila that her recovery was complete. But she still felt unsteady, as though bedrest had softened her bones. And she still couldn't bring herself to open the dresser drawer—it had been shut tight for nine days in a row—although sometimes she heard a rustling sound among her nightgowns.

Early one afternoon, when Lila went into the kitchen to make herself some tea, she looked out the window and noticed that all the birds in the yard had suddenly taken flight. For a moment the sky was filled with birds, and feathers fell to the ground in backyards and vacant lots all over Hollywood. When the birds disappeared the sky was still and gray. Everything was much too silent; Lila could hear a lemon as it fell from the tree and rolled across the patio.

Richard hadn't bothered to replace the teapot Lila had burnt when she first got back from New York, so she filled a saucepan and set it on the stove. As soon as Lila lit the flame the water in the pan appeared to be boiling. The water bubbled and swirled in a circle, first to the left, then to the right. Without thinking, Lila stuck her finger into the water to test it, and she would have been much less shocked to have burnt herself than she was when she discovered that the water was ice cold. It was then Lila knew that this was an earthquake. Tremors had begun to move up through the earth, through the foundation and the linoleum floor right through her bones. Lila held on to the countertop as the kitchen floor shifted. Dishes rolled out of cabinets, spices fell from their rack, glasses in the sink broke without being touched. A hot wind blew in through the open window, scorching the curtains, burning Lila's face. The lemon tree in the yard fell over, but it wasn't until it hit the ground that Lila realized the wrenching sound she had heard a moment earlier hadn't been thunder but roots being torn from the ground.

Richard was in a panic to get home; he left his mechanics to sweep up the broken glass, got into his car, and took off, leaving a hot trail of rubber behind him. It should have taken fifteen minutes to get home, but it was over an hour—the roads were jammed with traffic, and all over the freeways and side streets there were hundreds of frogs no one had even known existed until now when they fled from sewers and aqueducts. Richard pulled into the driveway so fast that he missed the asphalt and the tires tore up the lawn. He looked for her first in the bedroom. The mattress was tilted off the bed and the lamps had overturned and fallen to the floor. The house was so silent that Richard could hear his own pulse. He found that he could still feel some of the same fears he'd had as a boy, when the woods just behind the house seemed too dangerous and dark. As he looked into the empty bedroom, Richard had a sudden longing for his father. It seemed that everything he had ever done he'd done with his father in mind—not the old man back in East China, whose health and unpaid bills he worried about, but the man who'd seemed taller than everyone else. It was possible, Richard knew, to be away from home too long, to forget all the things you once knew by heart. He didn't want just his father, he wanted the boy he used to be, someone who could be comforted by the sound of his parents talking in the next room, someone who refused to come into the house for supper until after dusk because that was the hour when deer mysteriously appeared in the driveway.

He found Lila in the kitchen, and he felt as if he had never needed her quite as much. She was staring at her wind-burned hands, puzzled, and as soon as she saw him she lifted up her hands so that she seemed to be asking for help. Richard led her back to bed, then got some vinegar to cool off her burns.

"It's a good thing you weren't in bed," Richard said. "You would have wound up on the floor."

He got a handkerchief and Lila watched him fold it into quarters and pour out some vinegar. When he dabbed her skin the vinegar was so cool that she shuddered.

"I think I'd better start by cleaning up the kitchen," Richard said. He recapped the vinegar bottle and started to go, but Lila put her hand on his arm and stopped him. When he got into bed beside her Lila knew that it was possible to love two people best, and when he put his arms around her both of them could imagine that they were in the bedroom of his parents' house in East China, and that it was the time when orange lilies bloomed right outside the kitchen door, and without even trying to, they both fell in love all over again.

Later they learned that Los Angeles had felt only the outside circle of the earthquake. Its center was miles away, in the desert, and there the tremors were so strong they could lift a trailer right into the air and leave it lying on its side.

Rae was at work when the earthquake struck and immediately she thought: Jessup. It was her last day at the office, and Freddy had called her in after lunch. Rae assumed she was about to be fired. At least, she'd thought, he'd had the decency to wait long enough so that her hospital bills would be covered by the health insurance.

"Guess what?" Freddy said after she sat down on the couch and put up her feet on the coffee table. "Six theaters want to show something called *Eugenie*—which they tell me I own."

"Really?" Rae said innocently.

"I trusted you," Freddy said.

"I swear to God I don't know what made me do it," Rae told him.

She'd been so preoccupied, taking the dog for walks three times a day, getting the apartment ready, talking to Lila every morning on the phone for an hour, that she'd nearly forgotten she'd forged his name.

"It won best picture in Germany," Freddy told her.

"Eugenie?" Rae said.

"Lucky for you," Freddy said. "If luck's what it was."

Rae had to ask him to repeat himself when he told her he wanted her to come back after the baby, not as his secretary but as his assistant.

"Are you trying to squeeze more money out of me?" Freddy said.

"I'm not sure I heard you right," Rae said. "What did you say?"

"All right!" Freddy said. "You'll get a raise, but it won't be much at first."

He reached for a bottle of wine to celebrate with and was opening it when the tremors began. The steel girders in the building began to vibrate, the file cabinets all tilted to the right. Rae sat up straight: she imagined Jessup trapped in the trailer, pinned underneath furniture that couldn't be moved. Freddy held the wine bottle in the air and tried to dodge the spray of rosé. Afterward, they stared at each other.

"Did that just happen?" Freddy said.

They left the building together, by the rear stairway, and then, along with nearly everyone else in the city, they went home to see how much damage had been done. Rae could hear the dog howling inside her apartment as soon as she got out of her car, but when she unlocked her front door the dog was nowhere in sight. A framed print had fallen off the wall, and the glass had shattered and left shards in the bed; the blue-and-white dishes they had bought in Maryland had fallen out of the cupboards and cracked. Rae looked under the bed and in the front closet; she could still hear the howling, as if the sound had been trapped in the walls. The dog was in the bathroom, huddled in the tub. A long time ago, when they had lived in Florida, Rae had bought glass canisters of bath salts that had been so expensive she'd never been able to bring herself to use them. Now the bath salts were spilled in the tub, and the dog had left pawprints in the orange and blue crystals. Rae grabbed hold of the dog's new collar and helped it out of the tub. It sat obediently on the tiled floor, still shivering, as she toweled off the bath salts that clung to its fur. She had always begged Carolyn for a dog, but after lengthy discussions with Rae's father, the decision had always been no. It wasn't that Carolyn didn't like dogs, she did; on Saturday afternoons she and Rae often drove out to kennels in Concord to look at litters of golden retrievers and spaniels. But Rae and Carolyn both knew that in their house a dog was out of the question. One argument over fleas or chewed-up shoes would be enough to disrupt a peace as fragile as theirs.

Two weeks after they ran away to Maryland, Rae went out and got a puppy, but it turned out that Jessup hated dogs. They were all right if they served a purpose—a guard dog or a sheepdog was fine—but spending his paycheck to keep a poodle in dog chow was out of the question. It wasn't a poodle, just a mixed breed, but Rae didn't bother to correct Jessup. She stood out on the curb as he lifted the puppy into the back seat of the Oldsmobile, and while Jessup drove back out to the animal shelter, Rae threw out the plastic water dish and the five-pound bag of dog food she had bought that morning.

Now she was the one who wasn't so sure she wanted the responsibility of a dog, even one that was used to no attention at all. When the phone rang, Rae told the dog to stay in the bathroom, and she ran to answer, hoping that it was Jessup calling to tell her he was all right. But it was only Richard, checking up on her—Lila had told him that a change in the atmosphere could bring on an early labor. Rae assured him that she was fine. But all over the city things had started to go wrong. Everyone said it was the earthquake; it disrupted atoms in the air, bringing out the worst you had hidden inside. The newspapers were already reporting several knife fights—each time a suspect was picked up and questioned about how the fight had begun he always looked sheepish and didn't seem to know. The supermarket where Rae shopped was held up at gunpoint, and in a parking lot behind the drugstore a young girl was beaten and left unconscious just beyond the spot where the asphalt had buckled. There was still a trace of that hot wind, and everyone had the jitters—when you drank a glass of cold water you were likely to spill it.

Rae didn't bother to clean up the apartment, she sat on the bed, hoping that Jessup would phone. The phone did ring late in the evening, but it wasn't Jessup, it was Hal, phoning from the interstate on his way back to Montana. They had lost everything. Hal had been out in the barn, Jessup inside the trailer, taking a nap. Earthquake weather had just sort of sneaked up on everyone, even the buzzards and the hawks were taken by surprise and some of them were tossed nearly half a mile from their nests. The bunkbed had overturned on top of Jessup, and after he'd gotten out from under it, he'd kicked down the door to the trailer and climbed outside. Hal watched from the doorway of the barn as Jessup ran toward the corral, but it was too late. Anyone could have told him that. They'd never rebuilt it, and the wooden fence had split in two. Horses ran through the opening, the herd so close together it seemed like one animal. As the earth shifted, the sand moved like water, the wind was getting hotter all the time, and you could hear wind chimes in the distance, rattling like mad. Jessup had run over to the corral so fast that he had to bend over, low to the ground, just to catch his breath. By the time he stood back up, the horses were running toward the mountains, a trail of sand rising up behind them like a white wall.

Hal and Jessup had just stood there for a while, then Hal had gone into the trailer to see what he could salvage. As he picked through the mess Hal heard the engine of the pickup start, and when he came out, holding an armful of laundry, he saw Jessup driving away from the ranch at top speed. Hal filled the trunk of his car with everything he owned that hadn't been broken or ruined; then he drove into town. He'd managed to talk the sheriff into letting him go up in one of the helicopters searching for missing livestock.

From the air they could see cracks in the earth, and to Hal it seemed that those cracks were already filling with sand. In no time it would seem as if the earthquake had never even happened. There were a few cows and sheep up in the mountains, stumbling along the unfamiliar territory, and Hal found himself wondering if their horses had ever existed, that's how absolute their disappearance was, not one hoofprint, not one hair from a tail or a mane. There was no chance that the state emergency fund would reimburse them for the lost horses. Jessup had had his own ideas about tax evasion, so they'd listed their stock with the authorities as six horses rather than thirty. Hal was heading back home, and if he ever found anyone stupid enough to buy the land, he'd send Rae a check for half.

"And the thing that really gets me about Jessup," Hal told her, "is that he didn't see me standing behind him. He didn't even stop to find out whether or not I'd broken my neck. He just took off."

After she hung up the phone, Rae cleaned up the worst of the mess in the apartment. She had forgotten about dinner, so now she opened up two cans of tuna—one for herself, the other for the dog. She called to the dog sharply, but when it came into the kitchen she patted its head, and they ate dinner together and then went for a walk around the block. Outside you could hear buzz saws all over the city as road crews began to remove the fallen trees and telephone poles. In the distance there was the sound of sirens, and once the dog startled Rae by throwing back its head and howling along with an ambulance. They walked around the block slowly; the air turned foggy and thick now that the hot wind from the earthquake had settled down; the ground was steaming.

When they got back to the courtyard the dog turned toward the street and barked, and Rae looked behind her. For a moment she thought she saw a pickup truck, parked near the entrance to the apartment complex. The fog had grown so thick that Rae couldn't see any farther than the forgotten strand of Christmas lights stretched across the dark courtyard; tonight they were as disconcerting as fallen stars. The dog headed to the apartment, and Rae followed. Once they were inside, she double-locked the door.

The earth had already begun to settle, but that night everyone moved with caution getting into bed, as if anything might happen while you slept. The dog lay down beside the bed; it was so quiet that twice Rae reached down and touched its head, just to make certain she wasn't alone. She felt more a captive of her own body than ever—she longed to sleep on her stomach, her ribs and back ached. In the dark she could hear her own pulse, and it seemed too loud and too fast. Her pregnancy felt like a bottomless pool, and now that she had jumped and the water was almost over her head, she could not imagine why she had ever made this leap. Even though she now knew that Lila would be there with her in the labor room if she wanted her, something was missing. It wasn't just that Jessup had disappeared, it was the feeling that she was having this baby without having had any past of her own. Who would send presents, who would look for photographs of her as an infant so that she could compare and see if the baby took after her?

As she fell asleep Rae found herself trying to imagine Carolyn on the day of her own birth. She knew only this: It had taken two days for her to be born. For two days her father had sat in the waiting room, he had shaved in the visitor's washroom and ordered sandwiches delivered from a deli down the street. Down the hall, Carolyn had to be strapped into her bed. At the very end, when she couldn't stand it any more, they gave her Demerol, but it didn't last long enough, and when it wore off she begged them for more. For an hour they left her there, strapped to the bed, and when it came time for the baby to be delivered they told her about something called twilight sleep and then hooked an IV to her arm. After that the pain grew worse, too enormous to respond to, but she wasn't really there. She could hear herself screaming, yet she was detached, and although the nurse swore they had shown her the baby the moment she was born, Carolyn couldn't remember a thing about it, and when she was given her daughter to hold she held on tight, for fear it might be discovered that she hadn't really had a baby at all.

That night Rae had no dreams, as if she'd been given twilight sleep herself, and when she woke in the morning she realized that she'd been crying in her sleep. She had a cup of tea, then gave the dog two of the Pet Tabs she'd gotten at the vet. When they went out for a walk the air seemed back to normal, the flawless blue air of April. The dog carefully kept pace alongside Rae, but the one habit Rae hadn't been able to break it of was chasing birds, and it took off, behind some bushes, after a pair of jays. Rae clapped her hands and whistled, and as she waited for the dog to grow tired and trot back down the sidewalk she decided that she wasn't quite as prepared for the baby as she'd thought. The nightgowns and crib sheets were laundered twice and carefully folded, the hats threaded with ribbons were stacked in a neat pile, the medicine chest was stocked with Vaseline and cotton and rubbing alcohol. But there was still one more thing she needed, and she clipped the dog's leash on so that it wouldn't run off again, and went right back to her apartment. She got her car keys and her pocketbook, and then she went out and spent the rest of the day shopping for a pair of red shoes.

->>>

By the time Rae was ten days overdue, Richard and Lila had played a hundred games of gin rummy. They played at the kitchen table and they kept score. There was anticipation in everything they did, and each morning when Rae phoned to tell them still nothing had happened, they looked at each other and sighed. At night they both heard Rae's relaxation tape in their dreams—the sound of wind chimes, two flutes playing scales. Richard had taught Lila all of the breathing techniques, and he didn't hide his great relief that both of them would be there in the labor room with Rae. But secretly Lila wasn't certain that she'd go through with it.

Richard had decided to take care of the earthquake damage himself; instead of calling the tree service Lila had found in the phone book, he borrowed a saw from their next-door neighbor and began to cut the lemon tree into logs. He had already collected all the lemons from the ground, and each day Lila made a fresh pitcher of lemonade. When there were only three lemons left, Lila made one last pitcherful, and as she stirred in a cup of sugar she suddenly realized that if they had had a child together it would have been long gone, to a separate life, to a family of its own, and it would have been just the two of them in this house anyway. When she took Richard a glass of lemonade he switched off the buzz saw and drank the whole glass without pausing. All around them the air smelled sweet; if they saved the logs and rationed them carefully in the small fireplace in the living room they might be able to capture the scent of lemons all that next winter. They could hold hands in the dark and watch the wood burn from November to March, and each time it rained it would seem like April in their house.

Richard bent down and put his empty glass alongside the tree stump. When he stood up his back cracked. He couldn't use the saw for more than an hour without feeling it that night, and the job was taking him days longer than he'd planned.

"Maybe I should have hired a kid to do this," he said now. "Maybe it was a mistake not to call a service that would come and dynamite the stump." He surveyed his work and looked puzzled; the more logs he cut, the more wood there seemed to be still left to cut. "I should have been able to cut this all in one day," Richard said.

He seemed so fragile that Lila put her arms around him, and she stayed out there with him, sitting in the sun while he cut more wood. She thought of Hannie, who had been married less than a year when her husband had gone off with the other men in the village to buy grain, and had then disappeared. A sudden autumn storm had trapped the men in the woods; at night the people in the village could hear wolves howling, but there was nothing they could do. Later, four of the men were found in the woods, buried under new drifts of snow. All of the sixteen women who had become widows mourned their husbands together, but as she sat on a wooden crate in the ashes with the line of other women, Hannie had felt nothing at all—she was already pregnant but she barely knew her husband, she couldn't even remember what his favorite meal had been.

When Lila looked at Richard, she remembered everything about him. The way the bed creaked when he sat down and pulled off his shoes, the smell of blueberry pancakes, his favorite breakfast, on Sunday mornings. When she looked at him carefully she could see the boy he used to be, right there beneath his skin, and she had the urge to kiss him. Soon Richard finished cutting logs, and he came to sit next to her in a wrought-iron chair. Lila felt herself grow excited. When he looked at her that way she knew he was seeing her for who she really was.

That night they went to bed early, and they took off their clothes under the covers and laughed the way they used to when it was freezing cold in their bedroom in East China. When they made love they felt each other's bodies, but they also could feel the way they used to be, and the delight of knowing somebody so well was so staggering it made them weep and hold each other tight all night long.

On the morning when Rae was eleven days past her due date, Lila woke up with a lump in her throat. All that night she had dreamed of Hannie, and now she remembered the reason Hannie had come to New York in the first place: she had lost her son in the war. It had been the worst winter anyone could remember; the ice was thick enough to swallow you alive. Thousands had been left homeless and they wandered from village to village, stealing from root cellars and begging for food. When the mayor came to tell Hannie that her son had been killed, she couldn't contain her grief, her screams could be heard all over the village, and mothers held their hands over their children's ears. Hannie's son had been a soldier, but to her he was still a boy. Her neighbors built up the fire in her stove, but once they had gone out to bring her some soup, Hannie locked her door and wouldn't let them back in. She sat there by the stove, with a blanket around her, and as the night grew later, her grief grew as well. When her neighbors pounded on her door, Hannie ignored them. What good were they to her—they couldn't tell her what she wanted to know. She was obsessed with finding out the way her son died—if he had been in pain, if the end had been quick, if he had called out for her as he lay dying. After a while she convinced herself that he had—he had wanted his mother, and no one had come to him.

There was a storm that night, and the wind was fierce. Every now and then, Hannie heard a pounding on her door, but she didn't move to answer it. Her despair was blinding, it did away with time. When she called out to her son, she swore she could hear his childish voice answer and call her Mama. Finally, she fell asleep, and as she slept the drifts outside grew higher and the fire in the stove went out and a trail of smoke floated between the ceiling and the floor. When she woke up, Hannie opened the window and waved the smoke outside. Then she went to the door. It was jammed, and she had to push harder and harder. At last it fell away. The sunlight was so harsh that Hannie held one arm over her eyes to shield them, but of course she could see what had been against her door, and her blood drained away. It was a boy of ten, one of the many homeless, and he'd been frozen to the ground, his hands still reaching for the door. It had been his voice she'd heard all night, he'd been the one crying for his mother, and no one had come to him, no one had lifted him out of the ice to carry him home.

Hannie left her village the very next day, and during the two years it took her to reach New York, she decided to concentrate on the future. That's when she began to read tea leaves, at first for no money, and later for only a token.

When Lila had heard Hannie's story, she had not known how to react. It was too awful, condolences could never be enough. But Hannie had seemed so detached it was almost as if she had been telling a story about someone else. Hannie called for the waitress and ordered toast and jam, although when her order came she only spread butter on her bread very thinly, with the brittle motions of someone who knows she can't explain her grief any more than she can describe the moment when she knows she has held on to her grief for too long.

Lila knew that it was sometimes quite impossible to account for some very simple things: how your life can go on after you've lost your child, how the clear blue sky of an early morning can move you to tears, how a woman can stand by her own kitchen window and watch her husband go out to gather wood and not want anything more than that one moment—that instant when the man she loves sees her watching through the curtains, and turns to wave.

⋙

On the twelfth day after her due date Rae began to have chaotic cramps that came and went and a feeling that wire was being pulled taut all the way around, from her belly to her backbone. She drank herbal tea and read magazines. There was no point in alerting Richard and Lila because Rae thought it might be nothing more than back strain, something gone wrong with her spine. But the cramps grew stronger, and when they began to come at five-minute intervals Rae knew they were contractions. She phoned her doctor. She was ready to leave for the hospital then and there, but her doctor told her to call back when the contractions were two minutes apart.

Late in the day, when nothing had changed, Rae grew calmer. She got out the mop and washed the kitchen floor, then took the dog out and watched it chase birds in the courtyard. She did all this between contractions, which had begun to feel familiar, separate from childbirth, some flaw in her body she'd have to learn to live with. Then they changed. They were still coming five minutes apart, but they were hot, as if someone pressed a burning bar of iron into her flesh at regular intervals. She took a cold shower and let the water beat against her spine. But she was still so hot that she opened every window in the apartment, and as she leaned out the kitchen window, to gulp down some cool evening air, she saw that a pickup truck was parked at the curb.

Rae threw on a dress, then held the dog back by its collar until she could run out the door. All week she'd felt Jessup had been there, late at night, at hours when Rae didn't go out. Now she'd caught him. He was sitting behind the wheel, eating his dinner out of a McDonald's bag when Rae pounded on the passenger window. Jessup looked at her through the glass; he held his hamburger in the air and for a moment he seemed to be considering turning the key in the ignition and stepping on the gas as hard as he could. Rae knocked on the window again, and after he'd looked at her a little longer, Jessup leaned over and rolled it down. Rae held on to the base of the window and lifted herself up to get a better look.

"I knew you were sneaking around here," she said triumphantly.

"I'm not sneaking anywhere," Jessup said. "I just don't happen to have an address right now. That's all."

"So you've just been parking here," Rae said.

"That's right," Jessup told her.

"You just happened to pick my street out of all the streets in Southern California? How dare you park here and eat a god-damned hamburger? How dare you think you can do this to me?"

"All right!" Jessup said. "I happen to think I have a right to see my kid."

"Oh, really," Rae said.

"Are you going to let me see him or not?" Jessup said.

Rae was holding on to the edge of the window; she pulled herself up and held on tighter as she felt a contraction begin. For seven nights Jessup had been watching the apartment, but because he didn't want to be found out, he never saw more than what might happen in any apartment after midnight: a light switched on, a window opened, a shade lowered. Now, all he saw was Rae's face, her fingers, her narrow shoulders.

"It was a boy, wasn't it?" Jessup said.

She stepped away from the truck and let him see how huge she was. "It hasn't been born yet, but when it is I'll send you a telegram." She began to walk away. "If you have an address by then," she called over her shoulder.

When she heard the door of the truck open and slam shut, Rae began to walk faster. She could feel that this contraction was different; the wire around her was so hot and tight it was impossible to move.

"I want to talk to you," Jessup called.

Rae tried to keep walking but couldn't. She inhaled slowly and counted to five, then exhaled and counted again. By the time Jessup had run across the courtyard, she was doubled over.

"Are you okay?" Jessup said.

Rae took his hand and placed it on her belly so that he could feel the contraction.

"Jesus Christ," Jessup said, withdrawing his hand. "Rae."

Jessup leaned toward her so she could support herself on his arm until the contraction was over. Afterward, he tried to follow Rae into the apartment, but the dog stood in the doorway, barking.

"Get this dog away from me," Jessup said.

Rae looked through the drawer in the night table for an old watch with a second hand. Jessup tried to push the dog back with his foot, but each time he did its barks were worse than before.

"I'm going to have to kick the shit out of you," Jessup told the dog.

"Stop it!" Rae said.

Jessup and the dog looked over at her.

"I thought you were supposed to have already had this baby," Jessup said.

Rae went to the doorway and held the dog by its collar. She could feel the vibration of a growl low in its throat.

"That just shows how little you know," Rae said.

It wasn't just the dog's growl she was feeling, she could feel vibrations in the air.

"I need something to drink," Rae said. "Herbal tea."

Jessup looked at her confused. "You want me to make you tea?"

"I think you could manage it," Rae said. "They've trained chimpanzees to make tea—all you have to do is fill the kettle and turn on the burner."

Jessup went into the kitchen, and Rae could hear him rummaging through everything, making a mess.

"Mint," she called. "In the first cabinet."

After she sat down in the easy chair Rae realized she was still holding on to the dog's collar. The metal felt cool, like the chain-link fence that marked off Rae's parents' house from the next-door neighbors'. When Jessup came in with the tea, Rae waved him away. It had been a little more than two minutes between contractions, and this last one had gone on for nearly a minute. The blood had drained from Jessup's face, and all you had to do was look at him to see how scared he was.

"Let's go," Jessup said. "I'm taking you to the hospital."

"I have to time the next one," Rae said. She still couldn't let go of the dog. "I don't want to get to the hospital and have to turn around and come back home."

Jessup took the wristwatch and sat on the edge of the bed, facing Rae.

"You really have nerve," Rae said. "What makes you think I want you here?"

She could feel the next one beginning, low in her back, spreading out in a circle.

"Is it starting?" Jessup said. "Should I time it?"

Rae nodded and began to breathe deeply. She kept her eyes focused on the center of Jessup's forehead. As the contraction subsided she thought of how Jessup couldn't wait to be born, how they'd had to stop the elevator and deliver him right there. After twelve days of hesitation, Rae's baby suddenly seemed to take after its father. She could feel its urgency inside her, and she knew that the time had come. She let go of the dog's collar, and when the dog whined and rested its head on her knee, she gently pushed it away. And then Rae felt a pop, like the sensation you feel in your ears when a jet suddenly drops and the pressure changes.

"Something's happening," Rae whispered.

Jessup ran over to her, but before he could reach Rae her water broke. Her dress was drenched, and beneath the easy chair there was a pool of liquid.

"Oh, Jesus," Jessup said.

He knelt down beside her, stricken. It took Rae a moment to realize that he hadn't the faintest idea of what had just happened. As far as Jessup could tell she was dying, first water, then blood, then her bones might begin to dissolve.

In spite of herself, Rae smiled. "Don't be an idiot," she said. "This is supposed to happen. Get me a towel and the blue dress in the closet."

When she stood up to phone her doctor she was still dripping, amazed by how much fluid had actually been inside her. She left a message for her doctor that she would meet her at the hospital, then changed her dress.

"I want you to listen to me," Jessup said, but Rae couldn't. She held her hand up in the air to silence him and Jessup began to time her contraction. This time Rae imagined the moment when the horses escaped from the corral. The sound of their hoofbeats on the flat sand was deafening, the sand rose up like a twister, burning the horses' eyes, making them wilder and a hundred times more desperate to escape.

"That one lasted for a minute and a half," Jessup said.

Rae went into the kitchen and put out fresh water and dog food.

"Are you crazy?" Jessup said. He pulled his keys out of his pocket. "Let's go," he said.

"If you really want to help me you can take care of the dog."

"Shit," Jessup said under his breath.

"She needs to be walked three times a day."

The dog was lying near the bed, nose buried in its paws. It watched Rae carefully, following every move she made with its eyes. Jessup glared over at it.

"All right," he said. "All right, all right."

But just to make sure the dog wouldn't be locked up indefinitely if Jessup didn't live up to his word, Rae left the kitchen window open. That way the dog could escape if it wanted to: all it had to do was climb up on a kitchen chair and leap over the window ledge. The drop was only a few feet, and under the bamboo there were soft weeds and grass.

When the next contraction came, Rae leaned up against the refrigerator and rocked back and forth. All of a sudden she wanted Lila, she nearly got lost in between the waves of the contraction.

"We're leaving right now," Jessup said as soon as it was over.

Rae went to the telephone, but before she could dial, Jessup took the receiver out of her hands.

"Don't start up with me now," Rae warned him. "I swear to God I'm dangerous."

She grabbed at the phone, but Jessup wouldn't let go.

"I have to call my labor coaches," Rae yelled.

"Let me go with you," Jessup said.

They both held on to the receiver and stared at each other.

"Please," Jessup said.

She thought then of the one time she had gone to the apartment where Jessup had grown up. It was before she moved out to Newton; she'd been hanging around the front door of his building, hoping to see him, when his mother came home from work, carrying some groceries.

"I know you," she said to Rae, and she'd insisted Rae come up to the apartment. Inside, the hallways were dark, and they had to walk up four flights of stairs. The apartment itself was tiny, Jessup slept on a fold-out couch in the living room. Jessup's mother had sat Rae down at the kitchen table and made her a glass of chocolate milk. She was apologetic about everything—the lack of heat, the fact that she came home from work after six and didn't know where her son was—as if Rae were another adult, someone she had to impress.

"I'm so glad that Jessup has friends," his mother confided, and for a moment Rae didn't understand. Jessup never had any friends. Then it dawned on Rae that his mother meant her.

Jessup's mother put the groceries away, then slipped off her shoes and got herself a cup of coffee.

"He's told me all about you," she told Rae. "The girl with the red hair."

Rae was too shocked to speak; she gulped her chocolate milk as she listened to the details of his birth. When, at seven, Jessup still hadn't arrived, Rae told his mother that she had to go home. Jessup's mother walked her to the door, and as though by agreement they stopped to look at the couch that folded out to become Jessup's bed.

"He started walking when he was nine months old," Jessup's mother said proudly.

Rae's throat had begun to hurt. She knew that if Jessup found out she'd been there, he'd never be able to face her again.

"I meant to surprise him," she told his mother. "So maybe we'd better not tell him I was here."

Jessup's mother looked at Rae for a moment before she understood. "It will be our secret," she said, and Rae knew that she was talking about more than just this one visit.

"I know I've made some mistakes," Jessup was saying to her now.

"Several," Rae agreed.

"I know it," Jessup said. "I wanted things. I'm not going to lie to you—I still want them."

Rae held her hand in the air so that he would stop talking. This time her contraction lasted for nearly as long as the space between it and the last one.

"Are you all right?" Jessup asked when it was over.

Rae nodded and blew out air. She had expected it to hurt, but she'd never expected this.

"I want to tell you something, so you'll understand," Jessup said. "I always thought you'd leave me."

"This isn't fair," Rae said.

"I know," Jessup said.

He put his arms around her when the next contraction came, and counted the seconds.

"You can drive me to the hospital, but that's all," Rae told him. Jessup looked so grateful that she would have laughed out loud if she could have. She pointed to her overnight bag. He picked it up and stood in the doorway, waiting, until she waved him out.

"Go on," she told him. "I'll meet you in the truck."

When he left Rae could see him out the window as he crossed the courtyard; he was the exact same distance away as he'd been on those nights when Rae had looked out her bedroom window to see him out on the sidewalk. But she'd never noticed how frightened he looked from this distance, or that he had a nervous habit of rubbing his fingers together, as if he was worried that she might not appear.

Jessup threw the overnight case in the cab of the truck, started the engine, then got out and waited for her. It was dark by now, and the exhaust from the pickup was inky, the color of winter nights in Boston just before the snow begins. Rae went to her closet, steadied herself by holding on to the wall, then slipped on her red shoes. This child really was a lot like Jessup—it could hardly wait to be born. So she hurried—she bent down to stroke the dog's head, and before she went out to cross the courtyard, she phoned Richard and Lila to tell them she was ready at last.

They both heard the phone at the same time. Richard jumped up from the couch to answer it and, out in the garden, Lila knew it was time. That afternoon she had baked a cake—she had thought she was making it for dessert that night, but when Richard went to cut a piece, she stopped him. She'd been particularly careful with the ingredients: sweet butter, a cup of sugar, milk, a spoonful of lemon rind saved from their own tree. Lila wrapped the cake in waxed paper, knowing it was a gift for Rae. As she stored it in a metal tin she wondered if she would feel jealous when the call finally came, but now that it had she was actually relieved. It was a comfort to know what you did and did not have.

While Richard made arrangements to meet Rae at the hospital, Lila heard a rustling in the grass. She knew exactly what it was. A little girl with slate-gray eyes crawled across the patio, then lifted herself onto Lila's lap. Holding her was like trying to hold on to light, or water, or air. But when she reached up and put her arms around Lila's neck, Lila could feel the heat of her body, and no mother, in any nursery, could have loved her child more.

Inside the house, Richard hung up the phone and rushed to the bedroom to pack the few things they might need: a change of clothes, white washcloths, a good clock with a second hand. They had already begun to plan a trip to East China, and once they went back it would be nearly summer, the lilies would have already begun to send up green shoots. Richard planned to spend most of their visit helping his father work on the house. He'd be so busy with wallpaper and leaking pipes that he'd never notice when Lila took their rented car and disappeared for an afternoon. And even if he did notice, he'd know enough to let it pass. He and Jason would replace the gutters on the north side of the house and fix the rotten floor boards in the porch, while Lila drove out to a place where last winter's salt and ice had been so powerful they had cut through stone. A place where if you were standing in the right spot you could see the shadow of the moon in late afternoon, you could run your hand along a small headstone and imagine it was made out of memory and pearls and bones.

And so when the baby began to inch away, Lila didn't try to stop her. She bit her lip until she drew two drops of blood and watched as the baby lowered herself back onto the patio. Above them the sky grew darker. The baby moved along the flat stones, past the hedges, into the neighbor's yard. At this hour the potted gardenias next door smelled sweeter; the air was cool enough to make you shiver. Lila reached down and touched the warm slate, but when she went to look beyond the hedges there wasn't a sign of her child. Just another garden that had to be coaxed to grow, a row of thin tomato seedlings and a bent magnolia tree.

Richard was at the screen door watching her. She could feel his presence, and when she turned he called out that it was time. Lila motioned that she would meet him in the driveway, and when Richard went to start the car Lila went inside to get the cake tin from the kitchen counter. Into this cake Lila had baked three gifts: a cool hand to test for fevers, a kiss with the power to chase away nightmares, a heart that can tell when it's time to let go.

Outside, the car was idling and Richard had left the passenger door open. Everyone else on the block was already in bed. It was a still, blue night with no wind, a good night for sleeping, and the neighborhood was so quiet that if you listened very carefully you could hear the roses outside the front door unfolding. You could take one look at the sky and know it was the perfect time of night for a miracle.

GREYSTONE SECRETS

THE STRANGERS

GREYSTONE SECRETS

THE STRANGERS

MARGARET PETERSON HADDIX

ART BY ANNE LAMBELET

Katherine Tegen Books is an imprint of HarperCollins Publishers.

Greystone Secrets #1: The Strangers
 For information address HarperCollins Children's Books, a division of HarperCollins Publishers, 195 Broadway, New York, NY 10007.
www.harpercollinschildrens.com

Library of Congress Cataloging-in-Publication Data

Names: Haddix, Margaret Peterson.
Title: The strangers / Margaret Peterson Haddix.
Description: First edition. | New York, NY : Katherine Tegen Books, an imprint of HarperCollinsPublishers, [2019] | Series: The Greystone secrets ; #1 | Summary: Told from separate viewpoints, Chess, Emma, and Finn Greystone, ages twelve, ten, and eight, investigate why their mother went missing and uncover their ties to an alternate world.
Identifiers: LCCN 2018013963 | ISBN 9780062838377 (hardback) | ISBN 9780062892034 (signed edition)
Subjects: | CYAC: Missing persons—Fiction. | Brothers and sisters—Fiction. | Family life—Fiction. | Secrets—Fiction. | Supernatural—Fiction.
Classification: LCC PZ7.H1164 Str 2019 | DDC [Fic]—dc23 LC record available at https://lccn.loc.gov/2018013963

Typography by Aurora Parlagreco
20 21 22 23 PC/LSCH 10 9 8 7
❖
First Edition

For Meg

ONE

FINN

The three Greystone kids always raced each other home when they got off the school bus, and Finn always won.

It wasn't because he was the fastest.

Even he knew that his older brother and sister, Chess and Emma, let him win so he could make a grand entrance.

Today he burst into the house calling out, "Mom! We're home! It's time to come and adore us!"

"Adore" had been on his second-grade spelling list two weeks ago, and it had been a great discovery for him. So *that* was what it was called, the way he had felt his entire life.

Emma, who was in fourth grade, dropped her backpack

on the rug beside him and kicked off her red sneakers. They flipped up and landed on top of the backpack—someday, Finn vowed, he would get Emma to teach him that trick.

"Twenty-three," Emma said. There was no telling what she might have been counting. Finn hoped it was a prediction of how many chocolate chips would be in every cookie Mom was probably baking for them right now, for their after-school snack.

Finn sniffed. The house did not smell like cookies.

Oh well. Mom worked from home, designing websites, and sometimes she lost track of time. If today was more of a Goldfish-crackers-and-apple-slices kind of day, that was okay with Finn. He liked those, too.

"Mom!" he called again. "Your afternoon-break entertainment has arrived!"

"She's in the kitchen," Chess said, hanging his own backpack on the hook where it belonged. "Can't you hear?"

"That would mean Finn had to listen for once, instead of talking," Emma said, rubbing Finn's head fondly and making his messy brown hair even messier. Finn knew she didn't mean it as an insult. He was pretty sure Emma liked talking as much as he did.

Chess was the one everyone called "the quiet Greystone." He was in sixth grade and had grown four inches in the past year. Now Finn had to tilt his head way back just to see his brother's face. He also cupped his hand over his ear and pretended to be listening really, really hard. There was a low mumble coming from the kitchen—maybe a man's voice?

"Is Mom watching TV?" Chess asked. "She never does that during the day."

The kids all knew their mother's routine. She never listened to anything but classical music while she worked, because she said songs with words were too distracting. And when she really didn't want to be disturbed, she worked in a windowless room in the basement. The computer down there didn't even connect to the internet.

The three Greystone kids called that "the Boring Room."

Now Finn laughed at his older brother.

"Are you going to stand around asking stupid questions when you could get your answer just by walking into the kitchen?" Finn asked. "Let's go eat!"

He dashed toward the kitchen, dodging both Emma's backpack and the family's cat, Rocket, lying in the middle of the floor. He yelled, "Mom, can I cut up apples? It's my turn, isn't it?"

Mom was standing at the kitchen counter with her back to Finn, but she didn't turn around. She had both hands clenched onto the edge of the counter, as if she needed to hold on. Her cell phone lay facedown on the floor by her feet. Her laptop sat on the counter in front of her, but it was tilted up, so Finn couldn't see what was on the screen.

"Mom?" Finn tried again.

She still didn't turn around. It was like she didn't even hear him, like she was in a soundproof bubble.

This was not like Mom. She had never acted like this before.

Then she began to moan: "No, no, no, no, no. . . ."

TWO

EMMA

Emma had had a substitute teacher that day. The sub had dressed all in gray and had gray hair and a gray face and even a gray voice—somehow, Emma decided, that was possible. And the sub made the entire day so dreary and dull that Emma had started looking for and counting weird things about the day just to keep herself awake.

The thing was, if you started looking for weirdness, suddenly everything seemed that way. Wasn't it weird that the pattern of coats hanging up on the classroom hooks went blue-green-red, blue-green-red twice in a row? Wasn't it weird that the sub could have a gray voice? (Or was that just normal for her?)

By the time Emma got off the school bus and began racing toward the house, she'd counted twenty-one things she considered indisputably weird. To her way of thinking, that actually made the day pretty interesting, and she was excited to tell Mom about the new trick she'd discovered for surviving school.

Then she noticed that the porch light was still on, even though Mom usually turned it off when Emma and her brothers left for school.

And then, stepping into the house, Emma noticed that the living room curtains were still drawn tight across the windows, and so were the blinds on the bay window at the back of the house. This turned the living room's cheery yellow walls dim and shadowy; it made the whole house feel like a cave or a hideout.

Twenty-three weird things in one day. What if that was a normal amount, and Emma had just never noticed before?

She'd have to count again some other day—or, really, lots of other days—to know for sure.

Finn and Chess started yammering on about Mom and the kitchen and TV. Emma joined in and then rubbed Finn's head, because it felt good to do something normal again. Mussing Finn's hair was like petting a dog—you had to do it. Finn had thick, unruly hair with odd cowlicks that sprang up no matter how much Mom smoothed them down. Finn being Finn, he claimed this meant his hair had superpowers.

And . . . now Finn was racing off to the kitchen, shouting about apples.

Emma looked up at Chess, and they both shrugged and grinned and followed Finn.

But when they got to the kitchen, Mom wasn't hugging Finn and reaching out to hug Emma and Chess, too. Finn stood in the middle of the kitchen, staring at Mom. Mom stood at the counter with her back to the kids, all her attention focused on her laptop.

And the voice coming out of the laptop was saying, "The kidnapped children are in second and fourth and sixth grade."

THREE

CHESS

"Mom?" Chess said quietly.

His mother's shoulders shook. And then, as if she was fighting for control, her whole body went still.

Just like before, Chess thought.

Of the three Greystone kids, only Chess remembered the awful day their father died. Chess had been four; Emma, two; and Finn, only a baby. But even Chess's memories of that day were more like puzzle pieces he kept in a box in his mind, rather than one continuous video: Chess remembered the two sad-faced police officers at the door; he remembered the red Matchbox car he'd been holding in his hand when the door opened; he remembered the way Mom's shoulders shook before her back went ramrod straight, and she turned around to face Chess and Emma and Finn.

Now Mom was reaching for the top part of her laptop, as if she planned to shut it and hide whatever it said. Something made Chess stride quickly across the kitchen and grab her hand to stop her.

"Someone was kidnapped," he said. He caught a glimpse of a few words at the bottom of the computer screen. "Three kids in Arizona. Was it anyone you know?"

"No . . . ," Mom whispered.

Her dark eyes were wide and dazed. The color had drained from her face.

Shock, Chess thought. The school nurse had come in and taught a first-aid unit to the sixth graders earlier that year, and Chess was proud of himself for remembering the symptoms.

It was just a shame he couldn't remember any treatment.

Maybe he was feeling a little shocked himself. It was scary that anyone would kidnap anyone. But Arizona was a thousand miles away. And it wasn't like there would be some crime ring going around kidnapping kids from any family who had a second grader, a fourth grader, and a sixth grader.

"Mom, maybe you should sit down," Emma said.

Hmm. Maybe that was one of the treatments for shock.

Chess shot his sister a grateful look and took his mother's arm, ready to help ease her toward the kitchen table.

"Rocky, Emma, and Finn Gustano were last seen leaving their school, Los Perales Elementary, in Mesa," the voice coming out of the laptop speakers said.

Finn started cracking up.

"Isn't that funny?" he cried. "Two of those kids have the same first names as me and Emma! That's the third Finn I've ever known. Well, not that I actually know this one, but . . ." He slugged Chess in the arm. "Don't you feel bad that *you* don't have the same name as some kid who's famous now? And I bet when they find these kids, they'll get all the ice cream they want, and all the toys they want, and their parents probably won't make them do homework ever again!"

But what if nobody ever *finds these kids?* Chess thought.

He wasn't about to say that to Finn.

"Yeah, I've never met another kid named Rochester." Chess forced himself to fake a smile at Finn. "Or with the nickname 'Chess.' Oh well."

"Maybe you should *sue* Mom for giving you such a different name," Finn suggested.

"Or maybe I should sue for getting such a boring, ordinary name," Emma countered. "Did you know there are three other Emmas in fourth grade? And eight others in the rest of the school!"

But Chess tuned out his brother and sister. Because Mom lifted one hand and pointed toward the laptop screen. The way she held her hand was like a nightmare, like a Halloween ghost, like someone under a witch's spell in a fairy tale. It was like she could only point, not speak.

"We're repeating the information we have about the Gustano children," the voice coming from the laptop said. A photo of a friendly-looking, dark-haired boy appeared on the screen. "The oldest of the three kidnapped siblings, Rochester Charles Gustano, who goes by Rocky, just turned twelve last Tuesday. . . ."

Chess's hearing blanked out temporarily. His middle name was Charles, too. And his twelfth birthday had been last Tuesday.

How could there be another Rochester Charles, born the exact same day as him?

And how could that other kid have been kidnapped?

FOUR

FINN

Everybody was acting too serious. They'd all stopped talking. Even Emma. She'd taken the last two steps to join Mom and Chess at the counter, to stare silently at the laptop screen.

"Hello?" Finn said. "It's snack time—remember?"

Nobody answered.

"Remember how you're always telling me I have to quit right away when I'm playing computer games and you think it's time for me to do something else?" Finn tried again.

He walked over and reached his hand for the power button on the laptop. He wasn't *really* planning to switch it off—he'd heard too many lectures from Mom about not messing with her work. He just wanted to tease Mom a little, until she acted normal again.

Emma surprised him by grabbing his hand. At first it seemed like she was just trying to stop him from doing something dumb. Then it started feeling like she *needed* to hold his hand.

Finn stood on tiptoes and peered at the screen. He saw three pictures in a row, each with names and ages beneath. The kids in the pictures all had brown hair, just like Finn and Chess and Emma did, and they stared out at Finn with stiff school-picture-day smiles on their faces, as if they'd gotten the same warning Finn always got: "Remember, this is your official photo for the entire year, so no goofing off!" The youngest boy, the one Finn was already thinking of as Other-Finn, was perfectly snaggletoothed, with one adult front tooth partly grown in and one front tooth missing entirely.

Finn felt a little jealous. He'd lost both his front teeth two weeks after picture day last fall, and for some reason Mom wouldn't agree to let him have his picture retaken just because of that.

"But Mom, this is what I look like in second grade," he'd argued, sticking his tongue into the hole where his teeth used to be just for the sheer joy of it. "Don't you want to remember me this way forever?"

"Don't worry," Mom had said, laughing and pretending to try to catch his tongue before he yanked it back. "I'm not going to forget, regardless."

Finn dropped his gaze to see if Other-Finn was just a smidge older, and if that was the reason he'd been lucky enough to lose both his front teeth right before school picture day.

Finn Michael Gustano, it said below the picture. *Born 3/4/11.*

"He has the same middle name as me?" Finn said, stunned. "And wait—does three-four mean March fourth?"

"He has the same name as you," Chess said, sounding dazed. "And the same birthday."

"And that Emma is Emma Grace, just like me," Emma added. She kept her gaze aimed at the screen, as if she was too surprised to look away. "And her birthday is April fourteenth, too."

"That's crazy," Finn said. "Weird, weird, weird. Did they just steal our names and birthdays? Or—I know." He yanked his hand away from Emma, put his fists on his hips, and tried to look stern. "Mom, did you let that other family clone us?"

He wanted everybody to laugh. He *needed* everybody to laugh. And then Mom would shut the laptop and forget those other kids; she would bring out snacks and ask Finn and Emma and Chess about school. Just like usual.

But Mom did none of those things. Even when Finn went over and snuggled against her, she didn't move.

She just kept staring at the kids who'd been kidnapped.

FIVE

EMMA

"Finn, you're being silly," Emma said. "Clones would *look* like us, not have the same names and birthdays."

The girl on the computer screen had straight light brown hair while Emma's was darker and wavy. It was hard to tell from a tiny picture, but the other girl may have even had bluish-purple eyes, while Emma's were dark brown, almost black. Also: The other girl's chin was rounder, her cheeks were fuller, her gaze was a little too . . . peaceful. In every picture anyone had ever taken of Emma, she looked like she was trying to solve complicated math problems in her head.

Sometimes she was. Having your picture taken was *boring.*

Seeing the picture of someone with your exact same birthday and almost your exact same name who'd been kidnapped wasn't boring. It was the weirdest thing that had happened all day. But like all the other weirdness she'd catalogued that day, was it really all that stunning?

Emma was glad Finn's question had awakened her brain again.

"Statistics," Emma said. "Probability. There are billions of kids in the world. Probably millions of girls named Emma who have two brothers. Maybe thousands who have one brother named Finn, hundreds—or, well, at least *dozens*—who have a brother named Rochester. There's probably some formula you could do to figure out the chances that parents who like the name 'Emma' would like the other two names, too. And for the birthdays—there are only three hundred and sixty-five *possible* birthdays anybody could have. Three hundred and sixty-six, if you count leap day. So you just need three hundred and sixty-seven people in a room together to be sure that at least one pair has the same birthday."

"How many do you need to have *three* pairs of birthdays all the same?" Chess asked.

Emma was pretty sure there was a way to figure that out,

but her mind was attacking the harder problem: How would you calculate the chances that two sets of siblings would have the same names, in the same order? You'd have to know the number of all possible names, wouldn't you? Since people could just make up any name they wanted for their kids, was that even possible to put a number on?

Emma didn't like it when math failed her.

"The . . . kidnapping," Mom whispered. "The odds that anyone's children would be kidnapped are . . . are . . ."

"Tiny," Emma finished for her. "But this is like the chances of winning the lottery. There are overwhelming odds against anyone winning the lottery, so it's stupid to buy a ticket. But *somebody* is going to win. *Somebody* gets to be the one in a million. Or else it'd be zero-in-a-million chances. But it's *only* one person who has that good luck."

"Being kidnapped sounds like *bad* luck to me," Finn said, giggling. Then he furrowed his brow and pointed at the laptop screen. "Or are you saying those kids used up all the bad luck, so *we* never have to worry about being kidnapped? Thank you, Other-Finn and Other-Emma and Other-Rochester! Hope you get found soon!"

Mom seemed to shake herself and looked down at Finn as if she was seeing him—*really* seeing him—for the first time since he'd walked into the kitchen. Then she lifted her head, and her gaze darted first to Emma, then to Chess. She reached out and hugged all three kids, pulling them together so tightly that Emma could barely breathe.

"You *don't* have to worry about being kidnapped," she said in her usual firm voice. "I promise. I'll do everything I can to prevent that."

It would have been really reassuring, except that Mom's voice quivered at the very end.

And why would Mom think she'd need to prevent anything?

SIX

CHESS

Chess woke up in the middle of the night with aches in his legs. *Growing pains,* he thought. Mom had explained them to him a year ago, and then she'd helped him look them up online. Finn had asked, "What? It hurts to grow as tall as Chess? Maybe I'll just stay short!"

Finn was still so little he thought you could control things like that. Chess couldn't remember his own brain ever working that way, thinking he got to choose whatever he wanted. For as long as Chess could remember, he'd had to be the responsible oldest kid, the one who had to help Mom with Emma and Finn. The mini grown-up.

Was it just because Dad had died when all three of them were so young? Or did the other Rochester, the one who'd been kidnapped, feel that way, too?

Chess could picture the other Rochester—Rocky—crouched beside his younger brother and sister in some locked, windowless back of a van somewhere, or some locked, windowless basement. The younger kids would be crying. But Rocky would be telling them, *Everything's going to be all right. I'll take care of you.* Even if he was really thinking, *There's no way out! What are we going to do?*

Chess could picture it too well.

Those kids have probably already been rescued, he told himself. *They probably got balloons and welcome-home banners and toys and ice cream—just like Finn said—hours ago.*

But Chess had seen how Mom kept checking her phone under the table all through dinner, and even afterward, while everyone was doing homework. She also kept her laptop balanced on her knees when, as a special treat before bedtime, she let them watch the first half of *The Lego Batman Movie.* She *said* she was just typing up invoices to send out for her business, the kind of mindless work she could do while keeping one eye on animated Legos. But Chess was pretty sure she'd been checking news websites, too.

Mom would have told them if there'd been any news about the kids in Arizona being rescued.

Chess stretched his legs, then he slipped out of bed. Sometimes it helped to stand up. Sometimes it helped to walk.

He decided to go get a drink of water, but just as he put his hand on his doorknob, he heard another door open down the hall. Chess peeked out. The nightlight in the hallway cast eerie shadows, but he could tell that Mom's door was open, down at the opposite end of the hall. A moment later, he heard the creak of the third step down on the stairway.

So Mom's going downstairs, Chess thought.

Sometimes when she couldn't sleep, she got up and worked in the middle of the night. She always said, "That's the great thing about working for myself! I can work all night and sleep all day if I want to! I don't have a boss telling me what to do!" But Chess wondered if that happened more often when she was worried or upset.

Did she ever wake up in the middle of the night and try to remember everything she could about Dad, the way Chess did sometimes?

And was that maybe the reason she decided to get up and work instead?

Chess decided to follow her. He tiptoed down the hall and went down the stairs by twos—it was only the third and the ninth ones that squeaked, so his descent was totally silent. He didn't want to wake Emma or Finn. Sometimes when the younger kids weren't around, Mom would tell Chess things she wouldn't tell them.

But when Chess got down to the first floor, Mom was nowhere in sight. With all the curtains and blinds drawn, Chess had to navigate by the thin slats of moonlight that trickled in along the edges. Once he got to the kitchen, he also had the red glow of the digital clock on the stove.

It was 3:15 a.m. exactly when Chess noticed that the door to the basement was slightly ajar.

Seriously? Chess thought. *It's the middle of the night, and Mom still has to go down to the Boring Room to keep from being distracted?*

He started down the basement stairs but froze when he heard Mom talking.

"I thought you'd never call!" she was saying.

Who would call Mom in the middle of the night? Who would she *want* to talk to then?

Chess strained his ears, trying to listen for even the barest hum of a reply, but there was nothing. Maybe the person on the other end of the phone call was whispering.

"Do *not* tell me to calm down!" Mom said. "This is exactly what I was afraid of!"

The pause was shorter this time, then Mom exploded again.

"Oh, right, it's not my kids," she said. "Not *yet.* But it's *somebody's* kids. It's kids I can imagine really well, because I know exactly what an eight- and a ten- and a twelve-year-old are like. And I'll tell you, they're completely innocent. They're—"

The person on the other end of the phone call must have interrupted her. But maybe she interrupted him—or her—right back, because she didn't pause long enough to take a breath.

"It's not a coincidence, Joe," she said. She didn't even sound like Mom now. She sounded cold and mean and cutting. "You have to fix this. Or so help me, I will."

SEVEN

FINN

Finn could smell the French toast as soon as he woke up.

"Special breakfast?" he shouted. "It's a special breakfast day? Is school canceled? Is it a snow day? Or a holiday nobody told me about?"

He jumped out of bed and raced out into the hall. Emma was standing sleepily in her own doorway, sniffing the air.

"It's sixty-eight degrees out," she said. Finn was pretty sure she knew that because of a weather app, not from the smell of the air. But there was no telling with Emma.

"Okay, it's not a snow day," Finn admitted.

"Not a holiday, either," Emma said sadly. She leaned in

close and whispered, "It might be a bad-news special breakfast."

Finn remembered that the last time Mom had made French toast, it was because she'd gotten overwhelmed with her job and had to work an entire Saturday. That French toast was like an apology for not taking the kids to the park.

"There shouldn't be any such thing as bad-news special breakfast," Finn said. "It's going to make me stop liking maple syrup."

"You will *never* stop liking maple syrup," Emma said.

That was probably true. Finn was pretty sure he'd be able to drink it by the gallon, if Mom ever let him.

"*I* think it's going to be about good news," he said. "Maybe they found those kids in Arizona, and Mom's celebrating."

Finn expected Emma's face to light up at that idea, but she stayed serious.

"Finn, don't worry about those other kids," she said. "They—"

"Chess! Emma! Finn!" Mom called from downstairs. "Are you all up and moving?"

"I'll wake up Chess!" Finn shouted back. He realized Emma had yelled the same thing. They both took off running for Chess's room. Normally Chess was the first one up, so this was a treat, too.

As soon as he shoved past Chess's door, Finn launched himself toward the bed.

"Time! For! Breakfast!" he shouted as he landed. He bounced up and down with each word.

Beside him, Emma yelled, "Get up! Get up! Get up!"

Her bounces coordinated perfectly, too.

"We should be in the Olympics," Finn said, giggling. "Mom should sign us up for gymnastics. We'd win all sorts of medals."

He braced himself for Chess to push him and Emma off the bed. Maybe Chess would growl like a bear and pretend to be angry, and then they could have a mock wrestling match before breakfast.

But Chess just lay there. He blinked once, then twice. He had dark circles under his eyes, like he hadn't gotten enough sleep. But he'd had the whole night for sleeping.

"Chess?" Finn said, tugging on his brother's arm. "Talk to me, dude. Let me know you're in there!"

Finn saw Chess's face change, as if someone had flipped a switch. One moment, he looked groggy and sad—and just *wrong*, with those circles under his eyes. Finn might have even said Chess looked old, which was crazy.

The next moment, Chess had a goofy grin plastered on his face, but even that felt wrong.

"Arr, matey, who dares to disturb the pirate captain's

slumber?" Chess growled, which was from a book Finn had loved when he was little. Normally this would have been just as much fun as the bear growl and the wrestling match. But something was wrong with Chess this morning. He wasn't just pretending or acting; it was more like he was pretending to pretend and acting like he was acting. He had layers. Lots of them.

What if that had always been true about Chess, and Finn had just never noticed before? What if noticing was a sign that *Finn* was growing up?

Finn kind of wanted to tell Chess and Emma this. Maybe both of them would sling their arms around his shoulders and say, "Ah, grasshopper, let us initiate you into this stage of growing up. We're so proud of you! Neither of us figured out anything like that until we were nine!"

But Finn kind of didn't even want to think about it.

Mom poked her head into Chess's room just then. She put a stack of laundry on Chess's dresser.

"Come on, kiddos—get a move on!" she said. "As soon as you're all dressed, I have a special breakfast ready for you. . . ."

"It's because you have bad news, isn't it?" Finn blurted out. "We're having bad-news French toast. Like that day we couldn't go to the park."

For a moment it seemed like Mom had been wearing a

mask, and the mask slipped. It was almost like how Chess's face had changed, except in reverse. For just that one moment, it looked like Mom might start crying the way really little kids did, with a trembling lip and huge puddles of tears in each eye. But then Mom smiled and came over and ruffled his hair.

"You're onto me, huh?" she said. "I guess I'll have to save the French toast for good-news days from now on. Anyhow, it's not really bad news, just . . ."

"Spit it out," Emma demanded.

On a normal day, Mom probably would have scolded Emma for how sassy and disrespectful that sounded. But today Mom just gulped and smiled harder.

"I found out this morning that I have to go away for a few days," she said. "For work. I'm sorry."

"Oh, that's not *so* bad," Finn said. And maybe he was acting and wearing a mask a little bit, too. Mom didn't travel for her job very often, but when she did, Finn always felt strange the whole time. Even when he was at school and wouldn't have seen her, anyhow. "Tell you what, you *could* make French toast every day between now and then, to make it up to us."

Mom laughed, but it sounded especially fake. And sad.

"Finn, this is really last-minute," she said. "I have to leave today. How about if we have bad-news French toast today, and then a celebration special breakfast when I get back?"

"When will that be, Mom?" Chess asked.

Chess wasn't one of those kids who yelled at adults—neither were Finn or Emma. And Chess had actually spoken more quietly than usual, not louder. But Finn got a picture in his mind of Chess slashing a sword through the air and driving its point into the ground, like someone issuing a dare.

Finn glanced quickly back and forth between Mom and Chess. They both looked perfectly normal for a Tuesday morning. Chess's hair was mashed on one side and sticking out on the other. He was wearing his Lakeside Elementary Safety Patrol shirt over his pajama bottoms. Mom had on an old Ohio State University sweatshirt that had once belonged to their dad, along with old jeans with a rip in the knee that had happened because she'd worn them a lot, not because she bought them that way. Her hair, which was just as dark and curly as Emma's, was pulled back into a messy ponytail.

Still, Finn felt a little bit like he was watching strangers.

Mom started acting like she really needed to straighten one of the pictures on Chess's wall, above his bed.

"I'm not quite sure when I'll be back," she said as she reached for the frame. She kept her head turned away from the kids. "Things are a little up in the air. I . . . I may not even be able to call home every day."

Mom *had* turned into a stranger. She didn't leave things

up in the air. Whenever she went away, she left behind a list of what she was doing every day, and exactly where she would be, and how the kids or their babysitter could reach her every single minute, even if her cell phone broke.

Finn stopped feeling like he'd reached a new stage of growing up. No matter how much he tried to hold it back, his bottom lip started to tremble.

EIGHT

EMMA

Hello? Mom? Don't you see you're going to make Finn cry? Emma wanted to shout. *You do not do that to a second grader right before school!*

"So you'll have Mrs. Rabinsky stay with us while you're away?" Emma asked quickly. Mrs. Rabinsky was an old, grandmotherly type who made no secret of the fact that Finn was her favorite of the three kids. The idea of even just one afternoon and evening of Mrs. Rabinsky asking constantly, "What would you like for dinner, Finn?" and "Finn, could you tell us more about your day at school?" and "Do you want me to read you a bedtime story, Finn?" kind of turned

Emma's stomach. But she wasn't going to complain if it would cheer Finn up now.

"Actually, no," Mom said. She had her face turned to the side, but Emma could see that Mom was biting her lip. "I'm, um, still working out those arrangements, too. Like I said, this just came up. You know I'll cancel the trip if I can't be sure the three of you are all right."

"So why don't you just cancel the trip already?" Finn asked eagerly. "If it's not that important. If it's cancel-er-able."

Mom didn't laugh and tell him that "cancel-er-able" was not a word.

"Finn . . . ," she began.

"Two things can be important at the same time," Chess said tonelessly. "Mom's job and spending time with us, both."

Emma glanced over her shoulder at her older brother. Chess was just quoting an explanation Mom gave all the time. But did he actually think that was going to help, when he sounded so much like he was reading from a script?

Emma waggled her eyebrows warningly at Chess and mouthed at him, *Sound normal!*

The truth was, sometimes she, Chess, and Mom all acted like Mrs. Rabinsky. As if taking care of Finn and keeping him happy was the most important thing.

"*I* think Mom's going to have some big adventure,"

Emma announced. "And she'll bring back great stories. And presents."

This time, Mom did laugh. But it was an odd laugh, one that trailed off awkwardly.

"Emma, I'm just meeting with a client in Chicago who needs a lot of hand-holding," she said. "I don't think it will be much of an adventure. But I will bring presents. Okay?" She looked down at the clock on Chess's bedside table. "Now, seriously, everyone—move!"

They all scattered for a frenzy of clothes changing, face washing, and teeth brushing. Emma skipped combing her hair, because she wanted to be the first one down to the kitchen. She had a secret, and she hadn't quite decided yet if she wanted to tell Mom.

Last night after everyone had gone to bed, Emma had crept back out of her room and gone downstairs and slipped Mom's cell phone out of her purse. Disappointingly, Mom was one of those parents who thought kids should wait until middle school before getting phones of their own; she also didn't think looking at a screen right before bedtime was a good idea. So Emma had had to be sneaky. She'd typed in the password, which Mom probably didn't know Emma knew. And then, sitting alone in the dark, Emma had looked up everything she could about those kids in Arizona.

They'd actually been kidnapped on Friday. So three whole days had passed while three kids named Rochester, Emma, and Finn in Ohio had no idea that three other kids named Rochester, Emma, and Finn had been kidnapped in Arizona.

That was weird. It seemed like Chess, Emma, and Finn should have known instantly about everything that happened to their Arizona doubles. Like Emma should have felt a twinge in her side when she was sitting in social studies class and realized, *Oh no! The other Emma Grace is in danger!*

It felt like Chess, Emma, and Finn should have known all along that those other kids existed.

Emma found a site dedicated to missing children, and she tested herself looking at the page about the Emma from Arizona. *Why does this make me feel so weird? Would I feel this way if Emma Chang, Emma Pulaski, or Emma Jones from school were kidnapped?*

She would feel sad about *any* kidnapped kid. But she would feel even more sad if it was someone from her school, regardless of the kid's name. Just being from her school was enough of a link.

Emma had had the name Emma her entire life. She was used to sharing it with other girls.

She wasn't used to sharing it with another Emma who

also had an older brother named Rochester and a younger brother named Finn. Not when they also all had matching birthdays.

She tried to make herself feel better staring at all the details about Arizona Emma that were different: *Look! Arizona Emma is only four foot five, not four foot seven like me! And she weighs five pounds less, too!* When Emma clicked over to the other kids' information, she saw that the kidnapped boys' heights and weights were different from Chess's and Finn's, too. That made sense: Chess was taller than practically every other boy his age; Finn was one of the shortest kids in his class.

Emma zoomed in on the pictures of the two kidnapped brothers, which she hadn't looked at closely before. The younger boy's ears tilted slightly, making him look a little elfin, just like Finn. Other-Finn had the same mischievous gleam in his eye, too. Rocky Gustano held one eyebrow higher than the other, as if he hadn't expected the picture to be taken just then—Chess always looked surprised in pictures, too.

Both boys—and Other-Emma, too—had skin a shade or two darker than any of the Greystone kids'. But that could just be from living in Arizona, where there was more sunshine.

Or it could just be the way the pictures showed up on the

phone screen. If the Gustano and Greystone kids were standing side by side, maybe their skin tones would look identical. Maybe their hair and eye colors would, too.

None of those details are things I can count, Emma told herself. *But with things that are numbers, like height and weight, I could throw those into the equation if I wanted to calculate the odds of those kids having so much in common with us, and . . .*

It really bothered Emma that she couldn't calculate the odds, because of not knowing all the possible names in the world.

Because without that, she kept thinking, *This isn't random. There are too many similarities. We* are *connected to those Arizona kids. Somehow.*

That was what she wanted to tell Mom. Even if she had to confess that she'd used Mom's phone without permission.

But when Emma reached the kitchen, she found Finn already sitting at the table, digging French toast slices out of the dish where Mom had been keeping them warm. And Chess arrived right on her heels.

"Emma, your hair," Mom said. She pressed her hands against her own head and moved them outward, pantomiming an explosion.

That probably *was* what Emma's hair looked like. She hadn't actually checked the mirror.

"It's the humidity, isn't it?" Mom said sympathetically.

"Chess, you go ahead and start eating. Emma and I will go back upstairs and work on her hair together."

Perfect! Emma thought. She'd have Mom to herself.

But just then, Mom's phone pinged. Mom yanked it out of her purse and gave a relieved sigh.

"You don't have to go to Chicago after all?" Finn said hopefully. Syrup dripped from his forkful of French toast and rolled toward the dimple in his right cheek.

"No, sorry, I do," Mom said. She quickly typed something into her phone. "It's just, now I know who's taking care of you three while I'm away. She said yes. The perfect person."

"Who?" Chess said.

Emma saw Mom hesitate before she looked up from her phone. Mom glanced at the clock on the stove, then she put down the phone and pulled the ponytail rubber band out of her own hair. She scooped Emma's hair back and wrapped the rubber band around it.

"Sorry, Emma, I think we've got to go with the quick fix today," Mom said. She reached over and turned the water on in the sink, cupped her hand under the faucet, then slid that hand over Emma's hair, smoothing down all the stray locks. "There. Now go eat."

"*Who's* staying with us?" Emma repeated Chess's question

as she sat down and began filling her plate alongside him.

"Do you remember Ms. Morales, who was PTO president at Lakeside the year before last?" Mom said.

"Why would we?" Chess asked.

"You're making us stay with a *stranger*?" Finn wailed.

Mom looked back at her phone, but not before Emma caught a glimpse of Mom's face.

Is Mom . . . panicking? Emma wondered.

Emma felt like she was trying to solve some huge math problem that didn't involve numbers but people and events: The kidnapped kids in Arizona. Mom's unexpected business trip. And now this, the unknown babysitter. And Mom's panic.

None of it felt random.

Mom's trip is connected to the Arizona kids somehow, Emma thought. *And even though she doesn't want to, she's leaving us with some woman we don't even know because, because . . .*

Emma didn't know the answer to that part.

What if this was like the kind of huge math problems that Emma hadn't gotten around to studying yet?

The ones that didn't actually have any solutions?

NINE

CHESS

Chess should never have gone back to bed last night. He should have continued down the basement stairs and turned on the lights and said, *Mom, I heard you on the phone. What did you mean when you said, "This is exactly what I was afraid of"? And "Not* yet*"? Do you think Emma and Finn and I are in danger of being kidnapped, too? What's going on?*

He'd *almost* done that. He'd even touched his toes to the next step down.

But then he'd heard Mom sniffle. And it was definitely an "I'm about to cry" sniffle. And that made Chess freeze.

What if this has something to do with Dad?

That was the only reason Mom ever cried. After that day when the police officers came to the door, Chess remembered lots and lots of nights when he woke up and heard Mom crying. As a four-year-old, he'd go curl up beside her and try to wipe away her tears. And then one night she'd said, "Chess, this helps me, but I'm not sure it's good for you. Whenever you're sad, please come and tell me. You can cry on my shoulder anytime you want. But you really shouldn't have to comfort me all the time. You're only four!"

After that, Chess had started pretending he didn't hear her crying. He made himself stay in bed whenever he heard weeping. Not because he wanted to. But because he knew it made Mom sadder if he was sad, too.

All of that had happened eight years ago, but still, just that one sniffle last night had made Chess move his foot back from the stair below. It had made him decide, *I'll ask Mom about everything tomorrow. When she's not crying. First thing in the morning, when I get up before Emma and Finn.*

And then he'd accidentally slept later than Emma and Finn. And now Mom was leaving. And just as his job last night had been to keep from making Mom sadder, he knew that now she was counting on him to keep Emma and Finn from freaking out about having to stay with a stranger.

"Ms. Morales is the woman Finn always called Perfume Lady," Mom said, sounding desperate. "Remember? Because he said she smelled good?"

"Oh, right," Chess said, even though he didn't remember.

Finn and Emma had puzzled looks on their faces, too.

"So she'll make our house smell like perfume?" Finn asked doubtfully.

"No, the three of you are going to stay at her house," Mom said. They had never done that before with a babysitter. "You know, she has a daughter, too, and it wouldn't be fair to make them uproot their lives when they're doing a favor for us."

So there's some strange kid we have to get used to, too? Chess wanted to wail. It'd be fine for Emma and Finn. Finn got along with everybody, and Emma didn't care whether people liked her or not. But being around people he didn't know always made Chess feel like he had to be on his best behavior.

It wasn't like his *worst* behavior was ever that bad. But being on good behavior wasn't relaxing.

"Ms. Morales will pick you up after school," Mom said. "You know what that means, don't you?"

"We get to wear the same clothes and never brush our teeth the whole time you're away?" Finn asked, a gleam in his eye. "Because we're going to her house after that, not ours, and staying there until you get back?"

Finn's actually going to be okay with this, Chess thought in amazement. *He's acting like it'll be an adventure.*

Of course, Finn hadn't heard Mom in the basement last night saying, "This is exactly what I was afraid of."

"No, you don't get to re-wear clothes and have dirty teeth," Mom said briskly. "I'll pack suitcases for each of you and give them to Susanna." She glanced at the kitchen clock for probably the fifth time since Chess had stepped into the room.

"So what does it mean that Ms. Morales is picking us up after school?" Emma asked. Chess knew it was wrong, but he was glad that she sounded sulky. Maybe Emma and Chess together could get Mom to explain what was going on. They just needed to get Finn out of the kitchen so they could ask.

"It means you get to use the code word," Mom said. "Remember the code word?"

"Succotash!" Finn shouted. "I get to tell Ms. Morales I like succotash!"

"No, silly," Emma said. "Get it straight. *She* has to say succotash first. It wouldn't be much of a code if you told her what it was."

Mom had gone to some special parents' meeting a year or two ago about keeping kids safe, and she'd come home determined that the kids all know a code word any adult could say to them to prove that they were trustworthy.

Together, the three kids—mostly Emma and Finn—had decided that "succotash" was the best word to use.

"Because," Emma had explained, "nobody who's going to kidnap you would promise, 'Hey, little kid, would you like some succotash?' No kid's going to get kidnapped because they loved corn and lima beans too much!"

The family had turned it into a big joke that night. Finn had decided that succotash was the funniest word in the universe. And Emma and Finn had started taking turns pretending to be kidnappers. They'd even written fake ransom notes asking for millions of dollars and then, just to be silly, millions of dollars' worth of succotash.

"A kidnapper would have to be crazy to think we were rich enough to pay a ransom!" Emma had laughed.

It was true: The Greystones weren't rich.

But last night in the basement, Mom said, "Not yet," like she thought we were in danger of being kidnapped, Chess thought. *More danger because of those other kids with our names being kidnapped . . .*

His stomach roiled, and he put his forkful of French toast back on his plate.

Two years ago, even as Finn and Emma laughed and laughed, Mom had tried to explain that she wasn't *really* worried about kidnappers.

"It's just a precaution," she said. "Because what if my car breaks down sometime when I'm supposed to pick you up, and somebody else has to do it for me? I just want you to know who's trustworthy and who isn't. That's all."

Because Mom is really all we have, Chess thought. *Other kids have two parents, and sometimes even three or four. And they have grandparents and aunts and uncles and cousins, or even brothers or sisters who are already grown up.*

Except for Mom, the only relatives the Greystone kids had were each other.

The only ones who were still alive, anyway.

Now Chess really wasn't hungry. He pushed back from the table.

"Okay," Mom began. "So I've told you about Ms. Morales, and your suitcases, and the code word, and—"

"Are we taking Rocket with us?" Finn asked.

The family cat had just come strolling into the kitchen. He flicked his tail twice, as if to say, *What? Were you going to forget about me?*

"Oh, um, Susanna is allergic to cats," Mom said. She squinted her eyes and twisted her mouth, as if she was just now trying to figure out what to do about Rocket. "I guess I'll leave him with lots of food, and I'll tell Susanna to bring one of you over here every other day to clean his litter box."

Emma scooped Rocket into her arms, even though that meant that his tail got dangerously close to the pool of syrup on her plate.

"What if Rocket's lonely?" she moaned. "We should come *every* day, just to keep him company!"

"No," Mom said sharply. "That's asking too much of Susanna. She's already doing us a big favor—we don't want to inconvenience her any more than we have to."

Emma had her face buried in Rocket's gray fur, and Finn was watching syrup drip from his fork. So Chess was the only one who saw the way Mom's face quivered.

Then she caught Chess watching her, and her expression softened.

"I just want you to be considerate," she said. "I know you'll pick up after yourselves, and offer to help anytime you can, and . . ."

"Sounds like this is going to in'venience *us*," Finn said.

Mom turned her back on all three kids. Chess watched carefully to see if her shoulders started quaking. But she just stood still for a minute, and then she turned the water on in the sink.

"Oh—five minutes until the bus arrives," she called out over the sound of the rushing water. "Let's clean off the table and get a move on!"

Normally Mom would have helped. Normally she would

have noticed that Chess had barely eaten two bites and that Finn had licked all the syrup off his second piece of French toast but not actually bitten into it. Normally she would have noticed that a few unruly locks of Emma's hair were already slipping out of her ponytail rubber band and Emma had started absent-mindedly twirling one of them around her finger. In a few minutes, Emma's hair would probably look as messy as Albert Einstein's again—even as her brain was trying to solve quantum physics or the mysteries of time travel or some other mathematical or scientific conundrum.

Mom—look at us! Chess wanted to yell.

But he didn't, and she didn't turn around.

In no time at all, the three kids had cleared the table, loaded the dishwasher, and hurried to the front door to grab their backpacks.

At least Mom followed them to the door. She lifted the backpack strap over Finn's shoulder and then hugged each of them in turn.

"Have a good day at school," she said, her arms around first Finn, then Emma. "Be good for your teachers and Ms. Morales."

She could be any mother anywhere in the world, saying goodbye to her kids headed to school any day of the week.

But then she got to Chess. She wrapped her arms around his shoulders, engulfing him and his overstuffed backpack.

With her mouth near his right ear, she whispered, "And don't forget anything."

Chess pulled back.

"Wait—what?" he said confusedly. He peered into his mother's face. "Did you just say—"

But Mom was already turning his shoulders, aiming him toward the front door. Finn had opened it and was already leaping off the front porch, skipping all the steps; Emma was holding the door open for Chess.

Mom gave Chess a gentle shove.

"Go on," she said. "Don't . . . don't worry."

"Mom—" Emma began.

But Mom shook her head and reached for the door. To shut it.

"The three of you will be fine," Mom said. It sounded like she was trying to convince herself. "Absolutely fine. You have each other. Oh, look! There's the bus! Hurry!"

Chess looked down at his sister, and it felt like they were coming to understand the same thing at the same time: *Mom doesn't want us asking questions. Mom doesn't want to explain anything.*

Chess stumbled down the porch steps and blindly aimed his feet toward the driveway down to the bus. He kept his head down, as if he didn't trust his legs to move without him watching. Or maybe it was that he didn't trust his head not to swivel back toward Mom and the rest of his body to follow.

Once he reached the bus, he went to the very back seat—and only then did he turn around to look back toward the house and Mom.

Mom still stood in the doorway, her face frozen in an attempt at a smile. And she kept waving and waving and waving, as though she believed she'd never see Finn and Emma and Chess again.

TEN

FINN

Finn sat in a sea of empty desks. His class had already said the Pledge of Allegiance and listened to the morning announcements. (The most important one: Lunch was going to be pizza.) And still his friends Tyrell and Lucy hadn't shown up. Now he was supposed to be reading quietly while Mr. Habazz helped some other kids with math. Normally Finn loved any Commander Toad book (though he couldn't read them quietly, because he always laughed). But today he kept looking up from *Commander Toad and the Big Black Hole* to stare at the empty desks.

It made him think about Mom leaving, too. Was she still

at home, or had she driven to the airport already?

Why hadn't Finn asked what time she was leaving?

What if Finn suddenly got a stomachache? How would he know whether he was supposed to go home or to that strange woman's house?

Maybe Finn should get a stomachache, just so he could go home and spend every moment possible with Mom, until she had to leave.

If she hadn't left already.

His stomach did feel kind of funny.

"Finn, don't worry, I'm sure your friends will be here soon," Mr. Habazz said from across the room. "I got a message from the office that there's a late bus."

Just then, the speaker at the front of the room crackled, and Finn heard the school secretary say, "Pardon the interruption—bus thirty-two has just arrived. Teachers, please admit the late students to class."

Lucy, Tyrell, and three other kids came dashing into the classroom.

Tyrell raced to the front of the class and cried out, "Someone crashed into our bus!"

Lucy dropped her backpack and put her hands on her hips.

"Tyrell, you know it was just a bump, not a crash!" she said. "'Crash' sounds like somebody got hurt."

"But the police had to come!" another of Finn's friends, Spencer, added.

Mr. Habazz sighed.

"Okay, take five minutes," he said. "Tell the story. Then we'll get back to work, and you can save the rest of the conversation for recess, okay?"

"This green car came out of nowhere and hit us!" Tyrell said. "It was like the driver didn't even *see* us and, you know, that bus is as big as a house! And—bright yellow!"

"Who has a question for the bus thirty-two kids?" Mr. Habazz asked the rest of the class.

Mr. Habazz kept alternating between having the kids from the bus talk and letting the other kids ask questions. It made Finn a little sad that every answer made the crash sound less and less interesting. Even Tyrell had to admit, "No, I don't think there was a dent. But they wouldn't let us get off the bus to look. And we had to sit and wait *forever*."

At least five minutes passed without Finn thinking about his mom being away.

Finally, Mr. Habazz said, "Okay, bus thirty-two kids, time to sit down. Back to our normally scheduled programming. Silent reading or page ninety in the math book."

His heart wasn't quite in it, but Finn whispered to Tyrell, "At least *you* got to have an adventure this morning. I wish *my* bus had been in a crash. I mean, as long as nobody got hurt."

"Finn, we were saving the big news for you!" Tyrell said as he slid into his seat. "Lucy said maybe we shouldn't tell, but . . ."

"But what?" Finn asked.

"Tyrell, you know Finn's mother was not robbing that bank!" Lucy said, dropping a book onto her desk.

"Robbing . . . what?" Finn asked. "*My* mom? No way!"

"When that car hit us, we were right beside the bank," Tyrell said, talking fast the way he always did when he got excited. Which was pretty much . . . always. "You know, the one with the red sign? Anyhow, your mom came running out of the bank carrying a big bag, big enough that it was like she might have told the bank lady inside, 'Give me all your cash.' And then she got in her car and pulled out of the parking lot, and Finn, she even squealed her tires! Like she was making a quick getaway!"

Finn's mother did not ever squeal her tires. Much to his disappointment.

"You must have just seen someone who *looked* like my mom," Finn said.

"Nuh-uh, it was her," Tyrell said. "And that was your car, because it had the scratches on the side where you and Emma crashed your bikes into it. . . ."

Tyrell saw Finn's mom all the time. He knew Finn's mom's car, too. In fact, some of the scratches on it were probably from Tyrell's bike, not just Emma's and Finn's. Tyrell hung out at Finn's house so much that a neighbor had asked once if they were twins—even though Tyrell was black and Finn was white.

So Tyrell should have known that Finn's mom would never rob a bank.

"Nobody from the bank chased out after Finn's mom," Lucy said. "*Someone* would chase a bank robber. Probably she was just in a hurry."

"She—" Finn started to tell about how Mom was going on a business trip to Chicago. How she had been in a big hurry this morning.

But suddenly Tyrell grabbed Lucy's arm.

"Lucy!" he cried. "What if the *green car* was chasing Finn's mom? And that's why he didn't see the bus? Because she turned in front of us, and then . . . boom! We were in the way! Our bus stopped the green car from catching up with Finn's mom! What's it called when someone helps someone else with a crime? We're—"

"Accomplices?" Lucy asked.

"Oh, my beloved chatty kids! Finn, Tyrell, and Lucy!" Mr. Habazz called from across the room. "*Silent* reading, remember? Do you need to move to different seats so you're not so tempted to talk?"

"No, Mr. Habazz," the three of them chorused together.

Finn, Tyrell, and Lucy all bent their heads over their desks. Finn tried very hard to look like he was reading about Commander Toad standing at the edge of the black hole. But the words swam before his eyes.

"Don't listen to Tyrell's crazy stories," Lucy whispered. She had special skills when it came to not getting caught talking: She kept her eyes down and made it look like she was just moving her lips as she read. "*I* know your mom wouldn't rob a bank. Tyrell knows that, too. He's just having fun."

It's not fun today, Finn wanted to say. *Not when my mom's going away. And when kids with the same name as Chess and Emma and me got kidnapped. And . . .*

He didn't let himself think about anything else that might not be fun. But he still couldn't make himself read.

He just sat there staring at pictures of black holes.

ELEVEN

EMMA

When Ms. Morales came to pick up the three Greystone kids at the end of the school day, she was wearing a lot of makeup and hairspray. She also had on high heels, dramatically flared black pants, and a frilly blouse with swoopy sleeves. Emma thought that if it were wintertime, Ms. Morales could lie down on the ground in that outfit and make snow angels without even moving her arms.

"—and your mother tells me that your favorite food is succotash?" Ms. Morales was saying.

"Yes, ma'am," Chess said. Then his face turned bright

red. Emma wasn't sure if it was because he'd had to claim in public that he liked lima beans, or if he was afraid someone else in the school office would overhear their secret code word.

Or maybe it was just because he was twelve. Mom had explained once that sometimes when kids got into sixth or seventh grade, they started getting embarrassed easily. She'd explained that to Emma and Finn when Chess was away at a friend's house. Emma and Finn had thought this news was hilarious, and they'd both told Mom, "That is *never* going to happen to us."

Emma wasn't embarrassed, but it felt really weird to walk out the school door with Ms. Morales. Ms. Morales's clothes might as well have been shouting, "Hey! Everybody! Look at me!" Emma was more used to being around people whose clothes talked in a normal voice and didn't saying anything but, "Enh, look at me, don't look at me, who cares?"

Though Emma herself did have a Math Olympiad T-shirt she really loved. Was it also like shouting to walk around with the words "Math kids get pi" on your clothes?

"My SUV's over there," Ms. Morales said, pointing out into the parking lot. "There's been a tiny change of plans, because your mom ran out of time to drop your suitcases off at my house this morning. So we're going to swing by your house to get them. You can check on your cat while we're there and attend to the kitty litter, so we won't have to go back until the day after tomorrow."

"But Mom will be back by then, right?" Finn asked, stepping off the curb.

"Sorry, honey," Ms. Morales said, ruffling Finn's hair. "She still doesn't know when she gets to come home."

Finn stuck his lip out like he was sulking, which wasn't like him. But Emma liked Ms. Morales a little better, that she'd known to mess up Finn's hair.

"I can do the kitty litter," Chess said.

"That's nice of you to offer, but your mom said it was Emma's turn," Ms. Morales said.

Emma felt a little like her own mother had tattled on her.

But I didn't say I wouldn't *do the kitty litter!* she wanted to protest. *I was just . . . thinking about more interesting things!*

"Susanna!" one of the teachers on bus duty called over to Ms. Morales. "Great to see you back! We miss you at PTO!"

"Oh, believe me, I miss Natalie's elementary school days, too!" Ms. Morales called back. "Life was so much simpler then. . . ."

What did that mean?

Other teachers and parents kept calling out to Ms. Morales, but she kept shepherding the kids toward the parking lot, even as she stayed a few steps back from them. It almost felt to Emma as though Ms. Morales didn't want everybody to know the Greystone kids were with her.

Because we're *not wearing makeup and hairspray and swoopy clothes?* Emma wondered. Then she giggled, imagining what the three of them would look like with makeup and hair-spray and swoopy clothes.

"It's the white SUV at the far end of the lot," Ms. Morales said under her breath, like a spy. Or a gangster. "Go around and get in on the passenger side. *Not* the side that faces the school."

Okay, that was weird, Emma thought.

She looked toward Finn and Chess. Her eyes met Chess's; Chess instantly started patting Finn's back.

"Hey, Finn," Emma said. "Look how big that SUV is. And it's white. What do you bet the Morales family named it Moby Dick, like the whale? Moby for short? Won't it be fun to drive around in Moby?"

Finn turned back toward Ms. Morales.

"*Is* your car named Moby Dick?" he asked.

"Er—no," Ms. Morales said. She was looking around and barely even glanced at Finn. "I guess I never thought of naming it."

They reached the SUV then, and Emma huddled close to Finn as they circled around it.

"Don't worry," she whispered. "You still have Chess and

me with you. It's not like you'll be totally stuck with people who don't even name their cars."

Emma started to reach up for the handle of the front passenger door, but Chess shook his head.

"Someone's already sitting there," he whispered. "The daughter—Natalie?"

He opened the side door, and first Finn, then Emma, then Chess climbed in. As Emma settled into the middle seat, she peeked toward the front. All she could see of the girl sitting there was a waterfall of brown hair and the edge of a cell phone the girl was hunched over.

The girl didn't turn around or say hello.

Ms. Morales climbed into the driver's seat.

"Everybody, this is Natalie," Ms. Morales said. "Natalie, this is Chess, Emma, and Finn."

"Hi!" Finn shouted. "Nice to meet you!"

"Yeah," Emma said.

"Er, um," Chess said. His face turned red again.

Natalie *might* have made the kind of grunting noise prehistoric cave people made to one another before anyone invented language. But it was kind of hard to tell because Finn had been so loud.

Natalie's posture didn't change in the least. She didn't turn her head. Her fingers kept flying over the surface of the cell phone.

Ms. Morales sighed as she put her seat belt on.

"Natalie, wasn't it nice to see the elementary school again?" Ms. Morales said in one of those fake-cheerful voices grown-ups used all the time. "Where you have so many happy memories?"

Natalie might have grunted again, and this time the sound could have gotten lost in the noise of the engine starting up.

Something dinged.

"Oh, Natalie, could you check that text message?" Ms. Morales said as she turned the steering wheel far to the right, to back out of the parking space.

Emma found herself deeply curious about what Natalie would do next. Would she:

a) Grunt again, and maybe even make it audible this time?

b) Keep typing on her own cell phone and totally ignore her mom?

c) Actually reach into her mother's bright red purse and pull out Ms. Morales's phone and read the text message aloud? In a normal voice even?

Emma would have said there was no chance the answer was c. If she'd had a million dollars to bet on the odds of each answer, she would have put it all on a or b.

But after Natalie let out a loud sigh of her own—the

kind of sigh that said someone was in the greatest agony ever—she reached into the red purse on the floor between her and her mother. She slid her mother's cell phone through her curtain-like waterfall of hair, studied it silently, and then announced in a bored voice, "It's from those kids' mom."

Then she dropped the phone back into her mother's purse.

Emma was so busy deciding whether to count Natalie's bored tone as normal that she let it fall to Finn to cry, "What did Mom say? Is she going to call us? Is she coming home tonight?"

Ms. Morales switched the SUV from Reverse to Park and scooped up the phone. She glanced at the screen, then turned to face Finn and Emma and Chess.

"I'm so sorry," she said. "Your mom was texting to say that her meetings are going really, really late, and she's not even going to be able to call you this afternoon or evening. What would you like me to say back to her?"

Emma took a deep breath and grabbed Finn's hand. She squeezed it hard.

Don't let Finn cry, she thought. *Don't let Finn cry. Not in front of this awful girl Natalie.*

Was it possible that if Emma hadn't had Finn to think about, she might have needed to tell herself, *Don't let me cry. Don't let me cry. Not in front of Natalie*?

"Can we just type the answer ourselves?" Chess asked. Probably Ms. Morales and Natalie wouldn't be able to tell that his voice wobbled a little. Probably only Emma noticed, because she knew him so well.

Ms. Morales handed the phone back, and Emma peeked over Chess's shoulder.

Chess here, he wrote. **We're fine. We all had a good day at school and are with Ms. Morales now. Can you talk to us tomorrow morning? Do you know when you're coming home?**

"Tell her we love her!" Finn yelled, and Chess added that.

Emma stared at the phone screen. Three little bouncing dots appeared, which meant Mom was writing back.

Emma waited. In the driver's seat, Ms. Morales waited, too.

Natalie kept typing away on her own phone, as if nothing else mattered.

I hate not getting to talk directly! popped up on the screen. **Susanna, please pass this along to the kids: I promise, I will make it all up to you when I get home. Just think about all the fun we'll have then! I am trying to finish up as fast as I can, so I can come home as soon as possible. So I need to stop texting and get back to work. I love you all so, so much!**

Mom must have thought Chess gave the phone back to Ms. Morales right away, since she was writing to Susanna, not him. That was weird. Mom hadn't even answered Chess's questions.

This was not like Mom at all.

Chess started to hand the phone over to Ms. Morales, but Emma said, "Wait a minute." She took the phone from Chess's hand and tilted it to make it look like she was adding a message of her own. But really she was scrolling back through the text conversation, to see what Mom had told Ms. Morales earlier in the day.

Maybe Mom had actually told Ms. Morales how long she was going to be gone, and it was just such a horrifyingly long time that no one wanted to break the news to the kids.

Well, Emma would rather know.

But Emma reached the top of the text conversation between Mom and Ms. Morales, and the *only* texts from Mom were the ones she'd just sent this afternoon, about how she didn't have time to call.

What did that mean?

Maybe Ms. Morales is just one of those people who deletes text messages right after she reads them, Emma told herself. *Or maybe she has a work phone and a personal cell phone, and all the other messages were on that other phone.*

Or maybe there was something really weird going on.

We aren't being kidnapped! Emma told herself. *Not like the kids in Arizona! Ms. Morales knew the code word! Mom* arranged *for her to pick us up! She told us so!*

But none of those thoughts were comforting.

After Emma gave the phone back and Ms. Morales turned back around to drive, Emma slipped her other hand into Chess's. Now she was clinging to Finn on her left and Chess on her right.

Whatever was going to happen, at least they could deal with it together.

TWELVE

CHESS

Ms. Morales's daughter, Natalie, was a Lip Gloss Girl.

Chess hadn't recognized her until he heard her voice. He still hadn't seen her face, and he hadn't figured out until she spoke that she didn't have the same last name as her mom, and her *real* name was Natalie Mayhew.

Natalie Mayhew and the other Lip Gloss Girls had kind of run the whole school last year, before they moved on to middle school.

There'd been a moment last spring when Chess was out at recess, pretending to be part of a baseball game—but not pretending very hard, because nobody was actually going to hit the ball that far into the outfield. And Natalie and three other Lip Gloss Girls had walked over to him, and one of them had said, "You know, you're kind of cute."

And then Natalie had added in a scornful voice, "For a fifth grader, anyway."

What was Chess supposed to say to that?

Chess didn't say anything, and the four girls had walked away, all of them with hair rippling down their backs like they were princesses in some Disney movie.

For weeks after that, Chess had tried to figure out what he should have said. Would "Thanks!" have sounded conceited? Would "You're really pretty, too" have sounded like he was a jerk? If he'd tried to say anything, could he have gotten the words out without snorting or belching or stammering or doing something else that made him seem like a total dork?

It was probably a good thing that he'd just stayed silent.

But Chess had wondered if that moment was something he could have talked about with his dad, if his dad had still been alive. Dad probably would have been able to give him all sorts of advice about how to talk to girls.

Of course, Chess could have just asked his mom. But . . . it wasn't the same.

Now Chess was sitting in the SUV with Natalie Mayhew, and his little sister was holding his hand. And, over on the other side of Emma, Finn was holding *her* hand, so the three of them probably looked like really, really little kids going off to preschool or something like that.

Chess felt his face go hot again. He was not going to let go of Emma's hand just because Natalie Mayhew was sitting in the front seat and could turn around at any minute and see him.

She probably wasn't going to turn around, anyhow.

She probably didn't even remember talking to him last spring.

She was a *middle school* girl now, and she'd probably forgotten about everything that happened in elementary school.

Before Chess knew it, Ms. Morales was pulling up in front of the Greystones' house.

"You can park in the driveway," Finn volunteered. "Mom won't mind. And Rocket stays in the house, so it's not like he'd come out and make you sick. Because of your allergy."

"That's okay," Ms. Morales said. "I'm already parked. I'll just stay here and take care of some work email. Natalie can go in with you and help you carry out your suitcases."

Natalie Mayhew is going to come into my *house?* Chess wanted to scream.

"Ooo—let's see if she obeys this time," Emma whispered

in his ear. "Can Natalie put down her phone that long? What's your prediction?"

Chess watched Natalie. She seemed to be texting one-handed as she shoved her door open. She slid out the door in one smooth move and began walking up the driveway. As far as Chess could tell, she didn't take her eyes off the phone screen once. She also didn't stop texting.

"Never mind," Emma whispered to Chess.

Chess followed Natalie, Finn, and Emma toward the house. He was a little afraid Finn would suggest, *Hey! Let's race like we always do!* And then probably Natalie would laugh at the way Chess ran. But even Finn seemed weighted down, his steps sluggish.

Even the cowlicks in Finn's hair seemed to droop.

When they got to the door, Chess pulled out the key and turned it in the lock. The house already had a closed-up feeling to it, as if it had been empty for days, not just a matter of hours. Three suitcases sat by the door: Chess's was an ordinary blue, Finn's had a giant Pokémon logo, and Emma's was bright red and covered in stickers.

"Really, I can carry my own suitcase," Finn said, and his voice echoed a little. "Natalie doesn't have to help."

"Mom would have made me come in here anyway," Natalie muttered without looking up from her phone. She leaned back against the wall by the door.

"Why?" Emma asked, as if this was something that deeply fascinated her.

"Don't worry about it," Natalie said. "Just take care of your cat. Or dog. Whatever it is."

"Weren't you *listening*?" Finn said. He sounded offended. "Rocket's a cat!"

"Yeah, yeah," Natalie said. She kept her head bent over the phone. But Chess could have sworn he saw her eyes dart right to left, her gaze shooting past the phone.

Maybe she really was looking around their house. She just didn't want them to know she was looking around the house.

Chess wanted to share this observation with Emma, but he couldn't do that with Natalie standing right there.

"I'll help you with the kitty litter," he offered to Emma. "Finn, why don't you go pet Rocket and keep him company for a few minutes?"

"I'll have to find him first!" Finn said. He bent down and looked under the couch.

"He's probably on the window seat in Mom's room," Emma said. "That's where he goes when no one's home."

Chess was a little worried that Finn would say, *How do you know where Rocket goes when no one's home? If nobody's home, nobody's here to see him!* And then Emma and Finn could get into one of those "If a tree falls in a forest, and nobody hears it, does it still make a sound?" discussions. And Natalie Mayhew would just stand there rolling her eyes.

But Finn said, "Okay," and raced toward the stairs.

Oddly, Natalie followed him.

Chess wanted to call out to her, *Hey, who said you were allowed to go upstairs? Who even invited you into our house?* But that would have been rude. It would have made it seem like he didn't trust Natalie.

Was there any reason not to trust Natalie?

Mom trusts Ms. Morales. Mom knew Ms. Morales had a daughter. So . . .

"Are you going to help me or not?" Emma asked, backward-walking toward the kitchen and the door down to the basement.

"Oh, er—yes," Chess said.

He and Emma were partway down the basement stairs—past the step where he'd stood in darkness the night before, listening to his mother's phone call—before he figured out what he wanted to say to his sister.

"Do you remember Natalie from last year, when she went to our school?" he asked.

"No," Emma said.

Chess guessed there was a big difference between him being just one year younger than Natalie and Emma being three years younger.

"Natalie was part of this group of girls . . . they all wore lip gloss," he began.

"Really?" Emma said, as if he'd just said something like *Cheetahs can run up to seventy-five miles per hour* or *Bats are the only mammals that can fly.* "Girls wear makeup in sixth grade? Do girls in your class do that this year?"

"Um . . . some do," Chess said. "I guess. But it's not the same as . . ."

Why was he having so much trouble explaining this to Emma?

Emma got ahead of him again, jumping past the last three steps. Now she was almost where Mom had stood the night before.

Maybe Chess should tell Emma what he'd heard Mom say on the phone, instead of trying to explain about Natalie.

But what if that just scares her?

It was scary that Mom had said, "You have to fix this. Or so help me, I will" to some strange person—Joe?—at three a.m. And then just four hours later she was announcing an unexpected business trip.

It was scary that her last words to Chess had been "Don't forget anything."

But telling Emma about all that wouldn't make it any less scary.

Mom's the one I need to talk to, Chess decided. *She'll call tomorrow morning, I bet. I'll just have to take the phone somewhere private, away from Emma and Finn. And away from Ms. Morales and Natalie. And then I'll get Mom to explain.*

Chess needed to hear Mom say, "Everything's under control. Don't worry." Maybe he even needed to hear her say, "The police have found those kids in Arizona and they're perfectly safe. They're back with their parents, and the kidnappers will be in prison for the rest of their lives. And, really, it was just a false alarm, me thinking those kids had anything to do with us."

"Can you hold the bag for me?" Emma asked.

She crouched down beside the litter pan, the scoop in one hand, a plastic grocery store bag in the other. Chess walked over and took the bag from her.

"Natalie's a teenager," Emma said as she dug the scoop into the litter. "Mom told Finn and me that sometimes kids start acting weird about the time they turn thirteen. Or even just twelve. Like you."

She dropped the clumps of litter into the bag and jokingly flicked the empty scoop at him.

"*I* don't act weird," Chess said.

"Oh yeah?" Emma challenged, taking the bag from him

and tying the handles together so it wouldn't leak. "Then why are you just standing there all moony, talking about Natalie? Why is it different if *she* wears lip gloss than if girls in your class wear lip gloss?"

"I'm not—" Chess began.

But just then he heard Finn shout from upstairs:

"Chess! Emma! Get up here now!"

THIRTEEN

FINN

Finn had really wanted to pet Rocket. It could have made everything at least a little better.

Finn hadn't even had a chance to tell Chess or Emma about Tyrell saying Mom was a bank robber. Mom would never do that, and even if she had, wouldn't the police have already caught her? Wouldn't they have come for Chess, Emma, and Finn, too? Finn was pretty sure that was how things worked.

Still, Finn wouldn't have minded snuggling with Rocket and whispering into his furry ear, *Tyrell says Mom robbed a bank, and Mom went to Chicago, and Chess and Emma and I have to stay with some lady we don't know, and, oh yeah, some kids with our names were kidnapped, so . . . purr, Rocket, purr! I need to hear you purr!*

Finn looked in his and Emma's and Chess's rooms, but Rocket was nowhere in sight. He saved Mom's room for last, because he thought looking there would make him miss her even more. But Emma was right—Rocket *loved* sleeping on Mom's cushioned window seat, especially on sunny afternoons.

Finn walked into Mom's room, and the blinds were drawn, so there wasn't any sunny spot on the blue cushion by the window. The whole room was dim.

Someone flicked on the light behind him. It was that girl, Natalie. He hadn't even heard her come upstairs.

"You go walking around in the dark, you'll run into something and get hurt," she said. "Then my mom will get mad at me for not protecting you."

"I can walk around my own house without getting hurt," Finn said. He waited, because he was pretty sure she was going to say, *Oh yeah?* And then he'd have to say, *Yeah, what's it to you?* Something about Natalie made Finn want to argue with her. And Finn didn't even like to argue.

But Natalie just gave a half snort and tilted back against the wall. She kept her head down, looking at her phone, and her long brown hair slid forward, hiding her face.

Good, Finn thought. *I don't want her watching me pet Rocket.*

He didn't want her in Mom's room, either, but he decided to ignore that and focus on finding Rocket.

Rocket wasn't under Mom's bed.

Rocket wasn't curled up in the chair where Mom piled clothes sometimes when even she was too lazy to put things away.

Rocket wasn't perched on the top of Mom's dresser, where sometimes he acted like he was a lion or a tiger out in the jungle waiting to pounce on his prey.

"Is that your cat's tail under the dresser?" Natalie asked in a bored voice.

"Huh?" Finn said, looking down. "Oh. Yeah."

Rocket's striped gray-and-black tail curled out from behind the dresser. Finn bent down and saw that Rocket was lying upside down, his paw swiping up toward a cord plugged into the wall behind the dresser.

"Rocket! Don't play with electrical cords," Finn said, reaching for the cat.

But Rocket seemed to think Finn was playing, too, and batted his paw at Finn instead. The cord caught on Rocket's claw and whipped toward Finn.

"Is that—? Oh no!" Finn said. "Mom forgot her phone charger! How's she going to call and text us when her phone dies?"

"I bet she has a backup charger," Natalie said, sounding more bored than ever. "Or she can buy one."

"No, she—" Finn was not going to explain to Natalie that this was Mom's special charger, with a sticker on it from each kid: Finn's was a grinning cat; Emma's, a pink robot; and Chess's, a tiny zigzag like a Harry Potter scar. "We have to mail it to her! Overnight!"

Finn unplugged the charger and tugged on the other end of the cord, which went under the back of the dresser.

The cord did not come snaking out. It seemed to be caught inside the dresser.

Finn switched to yanking on the bottom drawer. If he could move that out of the way, he could see where the cord went.

The drawer slipped out and sagged toward the floor. This drawer held Mom's sweaters, neatly folded and stacked. Finn tilted sideways, his eyes even with the top of the drawer, so he could see the cord winding down from the back of the drawer and into the middle pile of sweaters. He shoved the top sweater away—and there, hidden beneath it, still attached to the cord, was something that almost made Finn's heart stop.

It was Mom's phone. She'd left it behind, too.

FOURTEEN

EMMA

Emma took the stairs three at a time, right alongside Chess.

"We're coming, Finn!" she yelled. "What's wrong?"

Emma and Chess were only at the top of the basement stairs; all she could hear from Finn was, "Because Mom . . . Mom . . ."

Emma raced through the kitchen and then sprinted through the living room to the next flight of stairs. Rocket came galloping toward them from the opposite direction, streaking down the stairs and then around the corner toward the basement.

"That's not good," Emma muttered.

"Cats spook easy," Chess said. "And Rocket—"

Emma stopped listening and lunged for the stairs. She saw Finn and Natalie in the doorway to Mom's room. They appeared to be playing tug-of-war with Natalie's phone—had Finn tried to take it away from her?

That didn't seem like Finn.

Then Finn turned the phone to the side and Emma caught a glimpse of the case: hard plastic with a crookedly drawn heart and the words "We love you, Mommy."

The phone they were fighting over wasn't Natalie's.

"You've got Mom's phone?" Emma said, screeching to a halt when she reached the landing. "So Mom's home?"

"*No,*" Finn said. "She left her phone in her *drawer.* Where she *never* leaves it. So who put it there? And who just texted us pretending to be her?"

"I tried to tell him," Natalie said breathlessly. "She's probably texting from her laptop or an iPad or something like that. Some other device. *You* tell him. Maybe he'll believe you. He tried to bite me."

"That wasn't my teeth, that was the cat's claw," Finn said with great dignity. "You shouldn't have tried to grab the phone away from Rocket and me. Emma? Chess? What's going on?"

Natalie made a sweeping gesture with her arm, the kind

that clearly said, *Be my guest. You talk sense into him.*

"I . . . I guess Mom could text from her laptop," Emma said, trying to remember if she'd ever seen Mom do that. It *seemed* possible. "But—"

"Mom would never leave her phone behind on purpose," Chess said firmly from behind Emma. "She wouldn't forget it, either."

Emma wanted to cheer, *Go, Chess!* He might have been acting kind of moony and weird about Natalie down in the basement, but now it was almost like he'd sprung in front of Finn, put out his arms protectively, and shouted, *Don't you make fun of my brother! He knows what he's talking about!*

And Chess wasn't just talking about Mom's phone. He was talking about the crooked heart and the "We love you, Mommy" on the case, too.

Mom wouldn't forget that, either.

"Something's wrong," Emma said. She reached out and grabbed Finn by the shoulders, pulling him closer. She kept both arms around him, with her face nestled against his messy hair. So now it was all the Greystone kids together facing off against Natalie. Three against one.

Natalie held up her hands in an "I surrender" pose. But, oddly, she didn't lean back against the wall or mutter "Never mind" or let her hair hide her face while she did nothing but text. She peered directly at the three Greystone kids, with a look in her brown eyes that might have even been kindness. Or . . .

Pity? Emma thought.

"Look," Natalie said softly, her hands still up in the air. "Usually when my mom tells some friend—or acquaintance—that she'll babysit her kids for a few days, no questions asked, it's because . . . well, you know. Sometimes parents fight. And sometimes a woman needs to go away, while things cool down. So she can work things out. And . . . cell phones have GPS, and sometimes even when you think you've disabled it, well . . . Haven't you heard your parents fighting? Don't you see—"

"Our dad is dead," Chess said flatly.

"It happened *eight* years ago," Emma said.

"Oh, sorry," Natalie said, and Emma liked that she didn't make it all fake and dramatic, *I feel so bad for you! What a terrible thing!* It was more like Natalie was sorry, but she was distracted from that by trying to figure everything out with this new information.

That was how Emma liked to deal with information, too.

"Then I guess in your mom's case," Natalie went on, "it'd be a boyfriend who—"

"Mom doesn't have a boyfriend," Emma said.

"Are you sure?" Natalie asked, and it was almost like she was taunting Emma and apologizing, all at once. "Maybe she just hasn't wanted to introduce you to him yet. Maybe she goes out at night after you're asleep, and—"

"Mom doesn't go anywhere at night but the Boring Room!" Finn roared.

"The what?" Natalie asked.

"Her office," Chess said tonelessly. "In the basement."

Natalie took a step back.

"Okay, look," she said. "Do any of you know your mom's code, to unlock the phone? I think maybe there's a way to see what other devices the texting is linked to, and then at least the little guy will see that she really did send those texts, and there's nothing wrong. Or . . ." Natalie winced and finished in a hurried mumble, "At least, there's nothing wrong that she isn't trying to fix."

"I don't know any code," Finn said.

Emma looked back to find Chess shaking his head silently.

"Emma?" Natalie said.

Emma didn't say anything.

Finn whimpered.

"All right! All right! I know the code!" Emma admitted.

She glared at Natalie. "But you do *not* get to watch me type it in. And you don't type anything on Mom's phone we can't see. I don't want you changing anything. And you *just* look at the texting."

"Sure," Natalie said.

Finn slipped the phone into Emma's hand. Emma could have sworn she felt the crooked heart against her palm, even though it was just a Sharpie drawing on plastic and perfectly flat.

Mom loves us, Emma told herself. *Mom would never go off without us—or her phone, to link to us—without a good reason. Either Natalie's right, or something weird happened and* Mom's *in danger, or . . .*

Emma couldn't think about the rest of that sentence. She kept one hand on Finn's shoulder and used the other to tilt the phone out of everyone else's sight and type in Mom's passcode: 111360. The reason Emma remembered it so well was because she knew where it came from. One time she and Mom had been talking about numbers, and Mom had said that they were symbolic. Three ones in a row, she said, always reminded her of Chess and Emma and Finn, not just the number 111.

"But the three of you together add up to a way bigger number," she'd said.

"Like three hundred sixty?" Emma had answered. "That's two squared times three squared times ten. And there are three hundred sixty degrees in a circle. And the line that makes a circle goes on and on and on, without any end."

Emma had been in kindergarten or first grade then, and Mom had laughed.

"Oh, Emma," she'd said. "What all are you going to do in this world, my little mathematician?"

The way she'd said it had made Emma feel proud. And a little possessive. Later, when she noticed that Mom had started using 111360 as her cell phone passcode, Emma wanted to keep the information to herself. She was the middle child, stuck between adorable Finn and responsible Chess—sometimes she just needed something to be all hers.

The keypad vanished from the screen, revealing the menu page. Emma held the phone out so Natalie could see the screen. Natalie squinted at the texting symbol at the top.

"Your mom uses an encrypted texting service?" Natalie said. "*That's* interesting. What did you say she does?"

"*We* didn't tell you," Emma said.

"But she's a graphic designer," Chess added, just as Finn said, "She makes websites."

Emma tried to decide if she should glare at her two brothers. But she was too busy watching Natalie's fingers fly across the screen.

"Huh," Natalie said. She bent closer and started to lift the phone higher. Emma pulled it back down.

"You don't see anything we don't see," Emma reminded her.

"Are you sure you want to . . . ? Oh!" Natalie jerked back, knocking the phone to the side.

Chess's hand shot out, steadying it again.

"Mom sent another text?" he asked. "Or—lots of them?"

Now it was Chess lifting the phone higher. Emma had to stand on tiptoes to see the screen, which was suddenly full of one green bubble of words after another. Emma read only, **Tell the kids I can't believe this! My schedule today is just as crazy today as yesterday but . . .** before Natalie was scrolling farther down, through bubble after bubble after bubble.

"Technically, she hasn't sent these yet," Natalie said. She sounded apologetic again. "It's like she's got some auto-service set up, so these are set to go out at certain times. Tomorrow morning, tomorrow afternoon, then . . ."

Emma caught only bits and pieces of each text: **. . . so, so sorry . . . Believe me, this is not what I want . . . don't want to interrupt at school . . . wish so much I could be home with . . . really do wish I could call . . .**

Then the words on the screen stopped moving, and Natalie slapped her hand over the last bubble of text. Emma could see only the date above that bubble: It was for Tuesday, May 12. Exactly one week away.

"Let. Us. See," Finn said.

Natalie started shaking her head, her long hair whipping out like snakes.

"No," she said, and now her voice turned pleading. "You don't want to read this. Maybe you'll never have to. It's actually to my mom. And it's the kind of thing that—"

Emma and Chess and Finn together ripped the phone out of Natalie's grasp.

And then Emma saw the last words on the screen:

Please tell the kids this was the last thing I wanted to happen. But I have to stay away for good, to protect them. That's the only way to keep them safe. Tell them, you'll always have each other. But also tell them never to look for me. I'm mailing you a letter to give to them today. It will explain everything—when they're ready.

FIFTEEN

CHESS

“Mom would never do that to us,” Chess said.

“Unless she had to,” Emma said. “Mom always says she would do anything to protect us.”

Chess hated how Emma could be so brutally logical, even at a time like this.

Even if she sounded like she was about to cry.

Chess put his arm around Emma’s shoulder, so now all three Greystones were linked: Chess holding on to Emma, Emma holding on to Finn.

But it’s not the same without Mom, Chess thought.

How could she possibly be gone for good? How could anybody not cry, if that was true?

Chess felt too frozen to do anything. But Finn sniffed. Then he whirled around and buried his face in the hollow between Chess's shirt and Emma's sleeve. He *was* crying.

Natalie reached out like she wanted to pat Finn on the back, but Emma glared and clutched Finn closer. It was possible that Chess's face had shaped itself into a glare, too. He seemed to have lost control of his expression.

Natalie drew her hand back.

"Parents are so awful!" she snarled. "I hate my mom, too. And my dad. But even they never—"

"*Our* mom isn't awful," Finn mumbled into Chess's shirt and Emma's sleeve. "She loves us."

"Finn's right," Emma said fiercely. "Mom probably needs *our* help. We need to see that letter. Now, not next week."

"We can't get it out of the mail," Chess said. "We don't even know where and when she's putting it *in* the mail. But if she typed it on her computer . . ."

Natalie raised an eyebrow at Chess, like he was supposed to understand something the younger kids wouldn't. Maybe she was trying to say, *What if you really* don't *want to see that letter? What if it's too awful to read?*

Chess shook his head at Natalie. If he hadn't minded

Finn and Emma overhearing, he would have said out loud, *My father* died *when I was four. You think I'm scared of a* letter?

No, he probably wouldn't actually say that. But he could think it.

Whether it was true or not.

"If she left her phone here, maybe she left one of her computers, too," Emma said. "The one she doesn't use for work. And maybe the letter's on that. Or we can use that computer to get to the cloud, where she might have saved it."

"*I'm* going to go find it," Finn announced, and Chess knew without looking that Finn would have his lip stuck out and his face set, a vision of obstinacy.

But then Chess did glance down at his brother, thinking it would help his own resolve. And Finn had tear tracks down his cheeks, along with a bubble of snot threatening to balloon out of one of his nostrils. His whole face trembled.

Finn looked like he *wanted* to act stubborn, but he'd gotten stuck on forlorn.

"Finn, why don't you look around up here," Chess suggested. "I'll check on the first floor, and Emma can try the basement. She needs to go back down there to throw away the kitty litter she scooped, anyway."

It felt good to be making plans—taking charge—even though his voice shook. And Emma shot him a glance that Chess knew meant, *Why do you have to be so bossy?* Still, Emma started down the stairs, and Chess quickly followed her.

Because if he hadn't, he would have had to meet Natalie's gaze again. And she might have even asked the question Chess was trying very hard not to think about. Chess hoped it *never* occurred to Finn or Emma.

Natalie's mom had agreed to take care of the Greystone kids for a night or two. Or maybe three. But if Mom wasn't coming back—or even if she only got delayed—what would happen to the Greystone kids then? Where would they go? Who would take care of them?

This is crazy, Chess told himself. *A misunderstanding. A mistake. Of course Mom's coming back. That will happen regardless. Whether we find her spare computer or not. Whether we do anything or not.*

Still, as soon as he got down to the living room, Chess began looking under pillows, pulling out drawers.

Because there had to be something he could do.

He had to prove that none of this was true.

SIXTEEN

FINN

"You can go help Chess or Emma," Finn told Natalie as he opened Mom's closet. "I've got this."

Finn hoped she couldn't tell that what he really wanted was for her to leave so he could bury his face in Mom's clothes. Maybe he could pull them down from the hangers and just curl up in a nest of Mom's shirts until she came back. They'd still smell like her as long as nobody washed them, right? Finn sniffed a sleeve, and there it was: Mom's unique odor, a mix of vanilla and Spring Breeze laundry detergent, with maybe some cinnamon and grass stain lurking underneath.

And apples. Mom's clothes also smelled like apples.

"I . . . ," Natalie began, and Finn forced himself to turn around and look at her. She stood in the doorway, half in, half out of the room. "I want to help. And Chess and Emma don't trust me."

If they don't trust you, why would I? Finn wanted to say.

Most of the time, Finn said what he wanted to say as soon as he thought it.

But he'd never before thought it was possible that he'd never see his mother again. So right now he didn't trust his own brain. Or his own mouth.

I will see Mom again, he told himself. *I will. I will. I will. Soon.*

He was like that train in the book for little kids, chugging out, "I think I can. I think I can. I think I can. I can!"

He liked feeling like there wasn't room in his brain for any other thoughts besides that.

He ignored Natalie and began pushing clothes from one side of the closet to the other, even though he didn't really believe he would find a laptop behind or underneath them. He just liked the way moving the clothes set off more puffs of Mom smell.

He heard the doorbell downstairs and then Ms. Morales's powerful voice calling, "Natalie? Finn, Emma, and, uh, Chess? What's going on? This was supposed to be a quick stop, remember?"

Good thing Chess is downstairs, Finn thought. *He'll explain everything, and then Ms. Morales will understand why we have to stay here longer.*

Ms. Morales was a grown-up. A mom. Once she heard about the messages on Mom's phone, she'd probably say, "Why didn't you show me that right away? Of course that's a mistake. In fact, your mom just called, and she's on her way home right now. You won't have to spend the night at my house, after all!"

But Finn *didn't* hear the rumble of Chess's voice downstairs answering Ms. Morales. Instead, he heard Natalie's footsteps, headed out toward the landing.

"Mom, go back to the car before you start sneezing all over the place!" Natalie yelled. She was standing at the top of the stairs. "The kids needed a few things their mom didn't pack, so we're getting everything together. Just five more minutes, okay?"

"Are you *sure* everything's all right?" Ms. Morales asked.

"Of course," Natalie said. "Now, go away before your whole face swells up!"

"*Just* five more minutes," Ms. Morales said. Then she sneezed. "I'll be waiting in the car. Hurry!"

Natalie came back into Mom's room.

"You didn't tell her about the text messages?" Finn asked. "Wouldn't she—?"

"Help" was the word Finn wanted. No, that wasn't strong enough. He wanted Ms. Morales to solve everything. He wanted her to undo the text messages, make it so they'd never existed in Mom's phone, and so Finn, Emma, and Chess—and Natalie—had never seen them. He wanted Ms. Morales to fly to Chicago and back in the next five minutes and bring Mom home, just like that.

Sometimes it almost seemed like Mom had superpowers, taking care of everything Finn and Emma and Chess needed. Weren't all moms like that?

Natalie snorted.

"You do *not* want my mom to know about that text message," she said. "She'd make everything worse. Believe me. *She's* the one you can't trust."

Mom's far, far away, Finn thought. *I can't trust Natalie. She says I can't trust her mom, either. All I have is Emma and Chess.*

It was the most grown-up thing Finn had ever done, that he kept standing there peering into Mom's closet.

When all he really wanted to do was run downstairs, grab hold of Emma and Chess, and never let go.

SEVENTEEN

EMMA

Math, Emma thought as she descended the basement stairs. *Square roots. Prime numbers. Pi.*

Those were the most comforting things Emma could think of. They were constants. Two was always the square root of four. One, three, five, seven, and eleven were always prime. Pi was always 3.14, with an endless string of other numbers behind it.

Mom had always been a constant in Emma's life, too.

Yeah, well, she's still somewhere, Emma told herself. *She hasn't ceased to exist. And even if she* thinks *there's some reason she can't come home, we can find her and prove to her that she can.*

Emma picked up the plastic bag of dirty kitty litter and put it in the wastebasket by the bottom of the stairs, even though the kids were really supposed to put all litter bags directly into the trash can outside.

Mom will be so grateful when we rescue her, she's not going to get mad about a little kitty litter, Emma thought.

She regarded the main part of the basement: the one saggy couch that had been retired from the living room upstairs after Finn spilled grape Kool-Aid on it. The foosball table that could convert into a mini Ping-Pong table or a mini pool table. The bucket of Nerf balls. The Koosh dartboard. The tub of Legos. She remembered Finn's friend Tyrell asking once, "Isn't this your family room? Where's the TV?"

And Finn had said indignantly, "It's our *rec* room. Don't you think we'd *wreck* a TV if it was down here?"

That was when Mom explained that, really, "rec room" stood for "recreation room," and that a TV would distract her when she was working in the Boring Room, Mom's little closed-off office at the far side of the basement.

Why was a TV distracting when Finn and Tyrell screaming at the top of their lungs wasn't?

Emma stepped past the couch and the foosball table and went straight to the door to the Boring Room.

It was locked.

Sure, Mom, Emma thought. *Because of course that's going to keep Chess, Finn, and me out.*

She walked over to the couch and bent down to lift the little flap of fabric that covered the couch's legs. She felt around the couch's middle leg. From the front, that leg looked like a solid block of wood. But it had a notch carved into the back of it. Emma pulled a little metal key out of the notch.

Mom knows Chess, Finn, and I all know about this hiding place, doesn't she? Emma thought, sitting back up. They'd played hide-and-seek games with Mom where the hidden thing was a coin or a Polly Pocket—hadn't Mom herself sometimes hidden the coin or the doll in the couch leg for the kids to find? It was hard to remember, because those games seemed so long ago—maybe even before Emma started school.

But if Mom wasn't hiding this key from Chess, Finn, and me, then who was she hiding it from? Emma wondered.

Just that thought made Emma want to start reciting reliable things to herself again: *Fibonacci numbers. Multiplication tables. The Pythagorean theorem.*

"Hey, Emma! Come on up!" Chess shouted from the top of the stairs. "I found Mom's computer! And Finn and Natalie found the one she lets us use. So she must have taken the one from down there with her!"

Oh, good, Emma thought. *I don't even have to look in the Boring Room.*

This wasn't scientific or logical, but Emma was a little afraid of the Boring Room. Outside of the Boring Room, Mom was so *Mom*: always there instantly when one of the kids scraped a knee or wanted to show off a bike trick or was just exploding with a brilliant new idea. But if Mom was in the Boring Room, she kept the door shut. If one of the kids knocked, there was sometimes a long pause before Mom answered, "Yes? Do you need something?" And even if Mom answered immediately, Emma had discovered that it was possible to count to a hundred sometimes—sometimes even more—before Mom inched the door open, stepped out, carefully shut it behind her, and finally peered down at Emma with her usual amount of concern.

It was like the Boring Room made Mom *not-Mom*.

Those text messages on Mom's phone were really *not-Mom-ish,* Emma thought.

Just the text messages about Mom not calling them were not-Mom-ish. The one about Mom not coming back made it seem like she'd been swallowed up by someplace like the Boring Room, and she'd completely become the person she was in the Boring Room, not the person she was everywhere else in the world. And . . .

You're being silly, Emma told herself. *Not logical. Not like yourself, either.*

She sat still for a moment, holding the key, and then she forced herself to walk over to the Boring Room door. It was like she had something to prove. If she could face the Boring Room, then she (and Chess and Finn) could figure out where Mom was and go rescue her.

Emma put the key into the lock and turned it. She heard the click that meant the lock had given way. Quickly, before she lost her nerve, she shoved the door open and reached for the light switch on the wall. The dim glow overhead revealed a room with blank walls, mostly empty bookshelves, and a desk and a chair that were so unremarkable that Emma could almost believe they came from a store called Amazingly Boring Office Furniture for the Home. That was a joke Mom had made once, and remembering that made Emma's eyes go a little misty.

Never mind that, Emma told herself. *Does anything in here look any different than usual?*

It was hard to tell, because when was the last time Emma actually looked into this room? She had vague memories of being a little kid playing with Finn out in the rec room while Mom sat at the desk in the Boring Room with the door open—maybe that was so long ago that Mom had needed to keep an eye on them all the time, even while she worked.

Emma could call up a fuzzy image in her mind from those days: Mom's eyes barely visible over the top of her laptop. . . .

Oh, duh, Emma thought. *Of course. The laptop's missing. It always sat right in the middle of the desk, and now it's not there.*

Maybe Emma's mind wasn't working very well right now. Maybe she was expecting too much, to think that her brain could work at all with the words of Mom's text message for next week still burned into her eyeballs: *I have to stay away for good, to protect . . .*

Emma reached for the light switch to turn it off again. But just shifting her position that much put her at a different angle; now she could see the edge of a piece of paper sticking out of the top of Mom's drawer.

A clue? Emma thought. And she wanted so strongly to believe that, that she left the light on and circled around to the other side of the desk. She pulled out the drawer, and the paper got stuck, smashed into accordion-style pleats. Emma gently eased the paper out, flipped it over, and smoothed it out.

The paper was a fuzzy copy of the back of Mom's phone, a reproduction of the crooked heart drawn on it. But it was *only* the heart; the words "We love you, Mommy" didn't show up.

Emma wanted to cry all over again. Nothing made sense.

Why would Mom have made a copy of that drawing when she always had her phone—with the original drawing on the case—right with her?

Except Mom didn't have the phone with her now.

She doesn't have this copy of that drawing, either.

Emma started to shove the picture back into the drawer. But then Emma saw what had been hidden in the drawer beneath the paper: Mom's work computer. The one she always used in the Boring Room.

So Mom went on a business trip and she didn't take her business computer with her? Or—any computer? Emma thought. *She left every single one of her computers at home?*

It wasn't exactly foolproof logic, but Emma was pretty sure she could make a deduction: Mom wasn't on a business trip at all.

EIGHTEEN

CHESS

The sun was still shining brightly when Chess stepped outside. That surprised him. It felt like the whole world should have gone dark while they were inside the house, like the sun should never come out again.

This was a feeling Chess remembered from when Dad died.

Mom isn't dead, Chess told himself. *I'm sure she's fine. And we have all her computers now. So we're going to find her. And everything will be okay.*

Still, Chess felt like his feet got ahead of him as he climbed down the porch stairs. His suitcase pulled him off balance, and his legs just didn't feel sturdy. It didn't help that Finn kept trying to walk so close beside him that the two of them might as well have been glued together.

It also didn't help that he could see how pale and drawn Emma's and Finn's faces were, or how they were weaving and stumbling just as badly as Chess.

"Don't say anything about any of this to my mom," Natalie hissed to Chess, Emma, and Finn as she turned to lock the front door. Evidently she'd taken the key from Chess while he wasn't paying attention. Evidently now she was slipping the key back into his hand.

Chess felt like there could be all sorts of things happening that he might have missed.

"Why shouldn't we tell your mom?" Emma asked Natalie.

Chess was aware enough to see Natalie bite her lip.

"Mom will go crazy," Natalie said. "She'll call social services and the police and the FBI and the TV news."

"Don't we want the police and the FBI helping us?" Finn asked, so innocently he practically chirped the words. "Don't we want grown-ups who know what they're doing finding Mom?"

Natalie shot a glance at Chess over Finn's head.

"Your mom said she wrote a letter that's *just for you*," Natalie said. "Don't you want to see that for yourself before anybody else sticks their nose in your business?"

Chess didn't know why Natalie kept looking at him like that. He kind of wanted to say, *Can't you tell I'm not really* that *much older than Emma and Finn? Can't you tell that when I saw that text message from Mom, I went back to being a four-year-old again?*

Chess, Emma, and Finn tripped down the driveway toward Ms. Morales's SUV. Somehow Natalie got ahead of them. She guided them into putting their suitcases into the back of the car. Then she yanked open both doors on the passenger side, one for her and one for the other three kids.

"That was stupid, Mom," Natalie complained as she slipped into the front seat. "Why didn't *you* pick up the suitcases before you picked up the kids? The bags were right beside the front door—you wouldn't have sneezed too much. And now these kids are homesick and missing their mommy, and it's all your fault!"

Chess helped Finn up into the SUV, into the middle row of seats again. Chess and Emma followed, as Ms. Morales answered Natalie, "For your information, young lady, I was *working* right up until I had to pick *you* up from school. Would you have preferred taking the bus?"

"No! Why would you even say that?" Natalie snarled back. "You don't understand *anything*! I've got all this homework to do, and I just had to spend a whole hour helping that little boy find his lovey so he could sleep tonight. . . ."

Chess noticed that Finn was clutching a teddy bear that was missing an ear and an eye because he and his friend Tyrell liked to use it as a football. It wasn't Finn's "lovey."

"Natalie told me to bring this," Finn whispered in Chess's ear. "As a prop."

"If you spent less time texting, you'd have plenty of time to do your homework," Ms. Morales told Natalie, even as she started the car and pulled away from the curb. "Anyway, you weren't there an *hour.* It was barely twenty minutes."

"Right, and you still thought you had to come in and hurry us up?" Natalie moaned. "Mom, you are *so* embarrassing!"

And then, while Ms. Morales was peering right and left, preparing to turn onto the next street, Natalie spun around and winked at Chess, Emma, and Finn.

Oh, Chess thought. *Is she fighting with her mom on purpose? To distract attention from Finn's teary face and from the fact that all three of us are just numb and clumsy and stupid right now?*

Ms. Morales made the turn, and then Chess could see her eyes peering back at them in the rearview mirror.

"Kids, I'm sorry that my daughter is being so rude," she said. "I promise, we'll make this a fun night for you. We'll order pizza, and you can have any kind you want. And, well,

Natalie says *she's* outgrown it, but we still have a trampoline in our backyard, and . . ."

Chess's ears buzzed; he felt too dizzy to listen well. He kind of grunted when Ms. Morales paused and it seemed like she needed an answer, but he had no idea what he was agreeing to. Or disagreeing with. A grunt could mean anything.

And Mom's text messages? Could those mean something different than what we think, too?

He needed to see her phone again, to force himself to read the horrible words again. Maybe he'd just imagined them. Maybe he'd find an *April Fools!* or a *Psych! Got you!* or a *Hahaha! Just kidding!* right below.

But they'd stuffed Mom's phone and charger and all the computers into the suitcases, and Chess would have had to take his seat belt off and climb over the back row to reach them.

He knew that wouldn't go over very well with Ms. Morales. He didn't know if Natalie was right that they shouldn't tell Ms. Morales what they'd found. But he felt overwhelmed at the thought of saying anything. Even *uh-huh* or *hunh-uh* seemed beyond him now.

How well do Ms. Morales and Mom even know each other, if none of us remember Mom talking about her? Chess wondered. *What if Ms. Morales just decides that Mom is a bad person?*

He didn't quite understand what Natalie meant when she talked about Ms. Morales calling social services, but he could see why it would be a problem to call the police. What if *they* thought Mom was a bad person for leaving her kids behind and saying she was never coming back? What if they tracked her down just to arrest her?

Some time must have passed—fifteen minutes? Twenty?—and then Ms. Morales aimed the SUV into a long driveway that wound up a hill. The house at the top of that hill was easily three or four times the size of the Greystones' house, and Chess got a lump in his throat thinking about how Mom always called their house "a cozy Cape Cod." She had a way of saying those words that made Chess feel a little sorry for anyone who *didn't* live there.

"Is that your house, Natalie?" Finn asked, gaping at the mansion ahead of them. "It's enormous!"

Maybe he'd been chattering away all along—Finn talked whether he was happy, sad, worried, or (sometimes) even sound asleep.

"Yeah, Mom got the house in the divorce," Natalie said bitterly.

"Natalie!" Ms. Morales scolded. "Stop being so difficult! You don't have to tell the whole world everything!"

Beside Chess, Emma let out a sound that could have been a snort or a nervous giggle.

Oh. It was kind of funny—or ironic, anyway—that Natalie was getting in trouble for telling too much, when really she and the Greystones was keeping a gigantic secret.

They took the suitcases inside, and Ms. Morales pointed out where everyone would sleep. Chess couldn't keep the rooms straight—maybe Ms. Morales and Natalie had so many bedrooms that they could each use a different room every night of the week if they wanted.

"I'll give the kids a tour of the rest of the house while you're ordering the pizza," Natalie told her mother. Then, as she shepherded them down a hallway, she said in a softer voice, "Mom likes to eat dinner early and go to bed early. Because she gets up at five a.m. to exercise. So we'll meet at ten p.m. in her office, where she won't be able to hear us." She made her voice loud again, loud enough to carry down the hall to her mother. "And this is Mom's office!"

Chess thought time would drag until they could finally meet and pull out the computers. But evidently weird things happened when you were feeling completely numb and stupid. Ms. Morales made them play on the trampoline, and then they ate and did homework, and then she made them play Wii for a while, and then she made them play a long, boring game of Monopoly right before bedtime. And during all those times, Chess would just be sitting there thinking about Mom, and suddenly realize half an hour had gone by.

Finally they'd all brushed their teeth and Ms. Morales had tucked the younger two into bed and said to Chess, "Are you like Natalie, saying you're too old for a bedtime story?" and he shot out a panicked "Yes!"—and she left him alone.

And then it was time to creep back down the stairs, clutching the laptop that had been shoved into his suitcase. He was joined in the dark hallway by Emma and Finn, each bearing laptops of their own. Emma also held Mom's phone.

"Don't giggle," Chess whispered, because normally both of them would have. But now they looked up at him, their faces shrouded in shadows, and he could tell that tonight neither of them found anything amusing. Chess switched his whispered instructions to, "Don't worry. We're going to find out everything."

They tiptoed down to Ms. Morales's office. Natalie stood in the shadowy doorway and waved them in.

"Everybody's here?" she asked. "And you've got everything? Good. Now I can shut the door and turn on the light."

The four of them stood blinking in the sudden brightness. Chess's eyes took forever to adjust.

"Are you *sure* your mom won't hear us in here?" Emma asked, pushing a stray lock of hair behind her ear. She'd lost her ponytail rubber band on the trampoline, and her hair had puffed out again like so much dandelion fuzz. Chess was torn between wanting to smooth her hair down himself and wanting to snarl at Natalie, *Don't you dare say anything about Emma's hair being a mess! She's in fourth grade! Fourth graders don't have to care about stuff like that!*

But Natalie was moving briskly toward her mother's desk, a piece of furniture so vast and shiny that it seemed like it might have its own gravitational pull.

"I'm sure," she told Emma. "This room is soundproofed."

"Soundproofed? Why?" Finn asked, his eyes wide. "What does your mom *do*? I mean, besides making big pictures of her own face."

He pointed behind the desk, and Chess noticed a whole pile of signs leaned against the wall. They all held the words "For sale!" or "Sold!" along with Ms. Morales's picture.

"She's a Realtor," Natalie said, as if that was completely unimportant. "She sells houses. At least, that's the job we can talk about."

"Does she have another job you can't talk about?" Emma asked. "Can you tell *us*?"

Natalie tilted her head to the side, which made her hair stream down like silk.

"We told you everything *our* mom does," Finn said.

"Okay," Natalie agreed. "On the side, Mom's a private investigator. That's what she calls it. *I* call it a professional snoop. My grandmother called it being a busybody. Mom spies on men who are—" She glanced at Finn. "Let's just say they're not very good husbands. Mom gives the wives proof, so they have the upper hand in the divorce."

Chess thought about what Natalie had assumed about his mom—that she had a bad boyfriend, and that that was why she'd had to go away.

Mom didn't have a boyfriend. Chess would have known.

But she was talking on the phone to some man last night, he remembered. *Joe?*

Mom had not sounded like she was talking to a boyfriend. More like . . . a coworker? An employee? A boss?

Mom didn't have any coworkers, or employees or bosses, either. And she never used such a surly tone with clients. She was always nice to them.

She was always nice to everyone.

Chess saw that Emma was peering at the screen of Mom's phone.

"Can I—?" he whispered.

She handed it over, and Chess opened the call history. If he could find out who Mom had talked to last night, that would be a huge clue.

But the call history was empty.

So were Mom's contacts.

So were all her emails and text messages—except for the automatic ones she'd set up for Ms. Morales.

Natalie had stopped talking and was watching Chess

stare at his mom's phone. Chess gave the phone back to Emma.

"Let's talk about *our* mom," he said, and he didn't care that now *he* sounded rude. He slid the HP laptop he'd been carrying onto the desk. "This is the computer that Mom uses the most often. She doesn't usually let us use it to do homework or play games, so it's probably the one she'd write a letter on, if she didn't want us to see that letter until . . ." He had to gulp. "Until next week."

"Okay, you should start with that one," Natalie agreed.

"This is the computer Mom lets us use for homework and stuff," Emma said, putting the battered Dell laptop beside his and opening the screen.

"And this one's from the Boring Room," Finn said, adding the third laptop.

They powered up all three of the computers. Chess felt a gurgle of tension in his stomach like before a huge test, only much, much worse.

"How about if I look through your mom's phone while you three—" Natalie began.

"You stay away from Mom's phone!" Emma said, hugging it to her chest.

Didn't she know there was nothing on the phone worth seeing?

Chess didn't say anything.

"Okay, okay," Natalie murmured. Still, she hovered behind the three Greystones. It made Chess even more nervous.

Finn elbowed Chess.

"Do you know Mom's password for this laptop?" he asked. "Or Emma, do you?"

"No," Chess and Emma said together.

"Then I can't see anything," Finn said dejectedly. His shoulders slumped, and he looked like he might start crying again.

"Next time we go back to your house, we can look for your mom's password," Natalie said in the fake cheerful voice people used with toddlers. "Maybe she has it written down somewhere."

He's eight, *not three!* Chess wanted to yell at her. *Stop being so . . . so . . .*

"Patronizing" was the word he was looking for. But maybe he also meant *stop being so helpful.* Natalie was acting like this was her problem, too. And it wasn't. Now that she'd shown them the soundproof room, why didn't she just go back upstairs with her mom?

"Here, Finn," Chess said, stepping back. "Why don't you stand between Emma and me, and you can go back and forth between looking at both of these computers with us. You might see something we miss."

He shut down the laptop from the Boring Room and

maneuvered Finn between him and Emma. Oddly, Emma didn't move to the side to make room. She stood frozen, staring at her laptop screen.

Chess followed her gaze. She'd reached the desktop, with the background picture of all three kids at Halloween last year: Finn as a clown, Emma as a ninja, and Chess as a skeleton. Finn and Emma were totally cracking up, but Chess's face was hidden behind his mask. Though, actually, the image of all three kids was largely hidden, because they had so many files and games and shortcut links strewn about the desktop. It would be hard to find anything in that mess.

Then Chess saw that Emma had the cursor hovering over a file marked "FOR THE KIDS."

"Was this here before?" Emma asked.

"I never saw it," Finn said, but his voice was so hushed and scared he sounded like someone else.

Chess just shook his head.

Emma clicked the mouse. Chess started to object—did he want to warn his brother and sister that maybe he should read the file first; maybe he should protect them from whatever it was going to say?

A box appeared. Emma hadn't opened the *file*. She was only checking its properties.

"Mom saved this at four a.m.," Emma whispered. "Just this morning."

"So open it!" Natalie cried behind them.

Emma looked back over her shoulder.

"I—I'm afraid," she admitted.

Emma, afraid? Emma was *fearless.* Emma could face down math problems that made Chess's head hurt. And one time when she was only a third grader, Chess had seen her wade into a pile of sixth graders who were fighting, and she'd screamed, "Don't hit the little guy!" And then the kid who was being bullied just walked away.

But this was scarier than that. Chess himself felt like he'd forgotten how to breathe.

"We open it together," he suggested. "All three of us."

He put his hand over Emma's, and Finn put his hand on top.

Chess thought maybe it was actually Finn who had the courage to push down.

The file opened, and Chess blinked the words on the screen into focus:

Dearest Chess, Emma, and Finn,

I love you so much, and that is why I had to do this. I'm sure you have questions, and this letter will tell you everything you need to know. Only the three of you will be able to read it.

Eagerly Chess moved on to the next paragraph. But it was all gibberish.

He raked his finger down the touchpad, scrolling through the rest of the letter—page after page of more gibberish.

After the first three sentences, nothing in the rest of the letter made any sense.

NINETEEN

FINN

Finn stopped trying to read at the start of the second paragraph.

Those must be all third-grade words, he thought. *At* least *third grade. Good thing Emma and Chess are older than me and will know what they mean.*

But Emma and Chess were squinting harder and harder and harder.

“Is it . . . code?” Emma finally asked. “Or a cipher? I forget which is which—one is where each individual letter or number or symbol stands for a different letter, and one is where the whole word is replaced by a different word, which you can only figure out if you have the key to the code. Or the cipher. Whichever."

Finn could tell that Emma was doing what he did sometimes, where she was so upset she was just talking and talking and talking to keep herself from thinking about how upset she was.

If Emma was rambling on like that, she didn't understand either.

"Chess?" Finn whispered, tugging on his brother's arm.

"Mom wanted us to know about this," Chess said. He swayed a little. "But . . . I guess . . . she must not have wanted us to know *yet*. Not right away."

"And she thinks a little thing like a code is going to hold us back?" Emma asked indignantly.

That sounded more like the real Emma.

"Yeah!" Finn said. He reached up and patted Emma's head, and that gave him confidence again. There was a brilliant brain underneath all Emma's bushy hair. "Even I know *something* about codes. We talked about this at school. You always look for the *e*'s."

"You mean, you look for the most common symbol or letter in the code, and you can assume that that symbol stands for *e*, because *e* is the most common letter in English,"

Emma corrected. "And then you can work through the other common letters—*s*? *t*? *r*? We could always look it up, the use of all letters in order."

Finn was pretty sure that Emma was a genius. Maybe Chess was, too.

For all Finn knew, Natalie also might have an IQ that was as huge as her house.

He felt better already.

"So what do you think that first word is?" he asked, pointing at the screen.

"Um, Finn, this might take a while," Chess said faintly.

He stared at the screen. Emma stared at the screen. Finn looked back to see what Natalie was doing.

She was staring at her phone.

"I bet there are codebreaker apps," Natalie said, her fingers flying across the surface of her phone. "We could plug in that whole letter to some special site, and then—"

"Do we really want Mom's letter floating around out there on the internet?" Chess asked. Then he looked back at Natalie, too, and it was like the big kids were talking without even using words.

Usually Finn hated feeling left out and too young, but now he wanted to cheer, *Hurray! The three of you are going to take care of everything! You're even better than grown-ups!*

Natalie stopped typing on her phone.

"Oh, maybe not," she said. "I guess we would need to know what that letter says before we know if it's safe to use the internet to solve it."

"That doesn't make any sense!" Finn said, and he hoped the other three would laugh.

They didn't.

Emma and Chess went back to staring at the computer screen. Natalie shoved in beside them, which knocked Finn away, putting him at the wrong angle even to see the screen.

"I want to help, too," Finn said, pushing against Emma, which knocked her against Natalie.

"Hey!" Natalie said. "I'm trying to focus here!"

Chess looked down at Finn with a very Chess-like expression. Only Mom and Chess had ever looked at Finn that way: as though they really saw him, and understood that even though Finn could be loud and noisy and silly, he wasn't *just* loud and noisy and silly. In fact, Finn was sure that he had a quiet, still, serious part inside himself somewhere. Maybe *only* Mom and Chess could see it.

And now, with Mom gone . . .

"Finn, maybe we should take turns working on this code," Chess said. "Emma and I will start, and you and Natalie can look at Mom's work computer. See if there's anything strange on there."

"But that's just 'voices and stuff like that," Finn complained.

"Voices?" Natalie asked.

"*In*voices," Chess corrected. "The bills she sends to her clients. Mom said she was going to Chicago. Maybe you can find out which clients she has in Chicago."

"Oh, that's a good idea." Natalie was using her fake voice again, the one that made Finn feel like she thought he was stupid.

"That's not as important as the letter!" Finn protested. "You're just trying to . . ."

Shove me away. Get rid of me.

That was what Finn wanted to say. But then Emma reached down and squeezed his hand twice, before giving him a nudge in the side as she looked up at Natalie with narrowed eyes.

And Finn understood.

Emma and Chess aren't trying to get rid of me, Finn thought. *They're trying to get rid of* Natalie.

Finn felt like a genius himself.

"Oh, all right," he said resignedly, as if he were still a little angry.

Natalie squeezed her lips together, like she was angry, too. But she moved over beside Finn and clicked the touchpad a few times.

"Your mom has ten customers in Illinois," she said as a

grid appeared on the screen. "What do you bet all those cities on that list are suburbs of Chicago? I think I've heard of Evanston before. But . . . Buffalo Grove? Northbrook? Elmhurst? Wheaton?"

"How am I supposed to know?" Finn asked. "I've never been to Chicago!"

Natalie let the cursor hover over the list of cities. A moment passed. Natalie wasn't even looking at the list now: She had her neck craned to look back at the code on the computer screen in front of Emma and Chess.

"Maybe we should look at the websites Mom made for all those clients," Finn said. "You'll have to help me. Mom never lets me use this computer by myself because she's scared I'll mess something up."

Was that too obvious?

Natalie sighed and clicked on a link at the far right side of the grid. A website came up advertising a landscaping company. Finn scrolled through pictures of perfect yards, the kind grown-ups had when they didn't have kids. None of them looked like very good places to play.

Natalie gazed back at Emma and Chess's computer again.

"That's the logo my mom uses on all her websites," Finn said, pointing to a tiny purple butterfly at the bottom of the page. "She likes butterflies because . . . because . . . what's the reason, Emma?"

"Rebirth," Emma said absently. She didn't take her eyes off her own computer screen. "Metamorphosis. Second chances."

"Yeah," Finn said. "She says it's not just because they're pretty."

"Huh," Natalie said.

What did Finn have to do to get Natalie's attention?

He clicked out of that website and tried one for a bakery.

"Oh, look," he said. "Don't these pictures make you want a doughnut? What kind do you think they are, Natalie? Maple bacon? That's *my* favorite."

If someone wanted to distract Finn, food was always a good topic. Maybe Natalie was the same way.

But Natalie barely flicked her eyes toward the doughnut pictures before turning back toward Emma and Chess's computer.

"And, see, here's my mom's butterfly logo again," Finn said, reaching the bottom of the bakery homepage. "She made this one a little more blue, and . . ."

And it wasn't at all the same butterfly logo as on the landscaper's page. But Mom had done both of these websites, hadn't she? Had she changed her logo and not even told the kids?

It was hardly the same as going off on a business trip and then setting up an automatic text to arrive a week later saying she was never coming back. That was just . . . unbelievable, in connection with Mom. But usually she was so predictable that even changing her logo seemed strange.

Finn clicked back to the landscaper's site. He zoomed in on both butterfly images.

It wasn't just the color that was different—so were the number and pattern of the dots. And the shape of the wings.

Finn made copies of both of the butterfly logos and pasted them into a new document.

He began opening other websites, one after the other, whether they were for businesses in Illinois or not. He copied and pasted every new butterfly logo he found into his own document.

Finally, when the variations just started repeating again and again and again, he stopped. He went back to the screen holding every single version he'd found: seven different kinds of butterflies, each one a different color. He zoomed in as close as he could on each butterfly without making everything go blurry.

The dots on the butterflies' wings weren't just in different places on each logo. They also contained patterns of their own, intricately drawn lines and angles.

Why go to the bother of drawing lines and angles inside

a dot, if those patterns weren't going to show up unless you enlarged the dot again and again and again?

Suddenly Finn knew why. He tugged on Emma's arm.

"Everyone, *look*!" he shouted. "I think this is a code, too!"

TWENTY

EMMA

Emma was stuck.

She was used to knowing answers instantly. She got in trouble for that sometimes in math class when the teacher would say, "Emma, honey, you have to show your work." And Emma would say, "The work was, I looked at the problem, and I knew the answer. How am I supposed to show that?"

Sometimes teachers told her she shouldn't say that in front of the other kids.

But the endless stream of letters and symbols and numbers in Mom's letter made no sense to Emma at all.

Not being able to understand made her feel itchy and weird and not like herself.

Or maybe she was already feeling itchy and weird and not like herself, because of Mom being away and saying she wasn't coming back.

Maybe Emma had felt itchy and weird and not like herself ever since . . . ever since she'd come home from school the day before and found out that kids with her and her brothers' names and ages had been kidnapped.

What if Mom *was actually kidnapped?* Emma wondered. *What if this is actually a ransom note, and we're never going to be able to rescue Mom because we're never going to be able to figure it out?*

It was a relief when Emma realized Finn was tugging and tugging and tugging on her arm, and shouting, "Would you *listen*? You have to look at this! I think it's a code, too! And there's not as much to it, so maybe it's easier to figure out!"

Of course Finn didn't know anything about codes. Emma had gone through a phase last fall where she'd checked out a lot of books from the library about codes and codebreaking, and she hadn't been able to get Finn or Chess to show any interest at all in writing secret messages back and forth in lemon juice, or substituting numbers for letters, or even using a mask decoder, which was the simplest thing of all. No one she knew at school was interested, either. So it had fallen to Mom to be the one Emma wrote notes to, saying things like, "H KNUD XNT." And when Mom wrote back, "J MPWF ZPV, UPP," Emma had been delighted, knowing they were both saying "I love you," using the same kind of code, just going in a different direction through the alphabet.

Oh oh oh.

Something amazing occurred to Emma. It was nowhere near as wonderful as figuring out Mom's letter would be, but now she felt all tingly, as well as itchy and weird.

Did I start checking out those code books on my own? Or was Mom the first one who picked up a code book and handed it to me and said, "I think you would like this"?

It was hard to remember exactly. Mom took Emma and Chess and Finn to the library a lot, and Emma always checked out a huge stack of books. Sometimes she chose her own books; sometimes Mom or Emma's favorite librarian, Mrs. Quinn, slipped them into her hands saying, "What about this one?" Sometimes it was even Chess or Finn asking that question.

But it *seemed* like maybe Mom had given Emma the first code book; it seemed like Mom might have said something like, "Sometimes kids who like math also like codes."

Had Mom been *preparing* Emma? Even way back last fall, had Mom been worried that some danger was coming, and she wanted Emma to be ready for it by learning about codes?

Emma didn't just feel tingly now. She felt like her heart was about to pound its way out of her chest.

She looked at the array of butterflies Finn had lined up on his computer screen. He enlarged one set of wings after another, showing the pattern hidden inside each dot.

"How can butterfly drawings be a code?" Natalie asked.

Something jiggled in Emma's brain. Something she'd read in one of the books about code.

"The guy who started Boy Scouts!" she shouted. "*He* did butterfly codes! When he was a spy!"

Natalie looked at her like she was crazy.

"Why would he do that?" Finn asked.

"Tell us about it," Chess said quietly.

"I don't actually remember his name," Emma admitted.

Chess reached for Mom's phone and typed in "Boy Scout founder spy butterflies."

"Lord Baden-Powell?" Chess said.

"I guess," Emma said with a shrug. "Anyhow, there was a war going on, or there was about to be a war starting, in, oh, *somewhere*—"

"Dalmatia?" Chess asked.

"Wherever that is," Emma said. "Anyhow, this lord guy pretended he was just a butterfly collector roaming around drawing pictures of the butterflies he found. But he was *actually* hiding spy drawings inside the butterfly pictures.

Drawings of all the military fortifications along the coast. So he could help his country's military know what to expect."

"You think Mom's helping the military?" Finn asked, going back to alternately zooming in and out on Mom's butterfly logos, growing and shrinking the dots and wings. "You think these are drawings of *forts*?"

"Only if the forts are built out of sticks." Natalie snickered. "How do you know you even have them in the right order? It's like there's every color of the rainbow there."

Emma felt tingly all over again.

"Natalie! You're brilliant!" Emma said, actually throwing her arms around the older girl's waist as though she were a friend, not a total stranger. "I bet it *is* a rainbow! Let's see, ROY G. BIV, red, orange, yellow . . ."

Emma took control of the touchpad on the computer Finn had been using. She moved the butterflies around, starting with the red one and finishing with the purple one—the one that might just as easily be called violet.

Chess patted Emma on the back, which felt like he was complimenting her. Finn squealed, "Those are the right colors!"

"So does your mom like rainbows, too?" Natalie asked, making a mocking face.

"It's like an inside joke for her and me," Emma said.

She was glad that neither Chess nor Finn said, "What are

you talking about?" Maybe they didn't even remember how disgusted Emma had been by some of the girls in third grade last year, who went around talking about rainbows and unicorns and butterflies and magic. And one night, when Emma was complaining at the dinner table, Mom had said very quietly, "Emma, it's possible to like rainbows and unicorns and butterflies and magic *and* math. Personally, I'd love it if the world were full of all of those things."

After that, "rainbows and butterflies" had become sort of code between Emma and Mom. It meant that Emma shouldn't get mad at other kids who didn't like math, and she shouldn't let anyone act like there was something wrong with her because she did.

Huh, code again, Emma thought.

"I still don't get it," Natalie said. "So you put the butterflies in rainbow-color order. So what?"

"So maybe, if we put all the dots together now . . . ," Emma began.

She enlarged all the dots from the butterfly wings one by one, until each dot joined with the one above, below, or beside it. Just as Emma hoped, the mysterious lines inside each dot joined, too.

"It makes a rectangle!" Finn shouted. "With . . . other shapes inside!"

"Is it . . . a map?" Natalie asked. "But what's it a map of?"

Emma jerked to attention. Her brain was working quickly again.

"Mom's office," she said. "The Boring Room." She pointed at one shape after the other. "See? There's the desk. There's the bookshelves along the walls."

"But what's that star over here?" Chess asked. "Is this a treasure map? Where *X* marks the spot? You were just down there—what's against the back wall of the Boring Room?"

Emma couldn't remember anything there but an empty bookshelf.

"I don't know if it's a *treasure* or not," she said slowly. "But I'm pretty sure that's where we're supposed to look."

TWENTY-ONE

CHESS

Chess reached for the doorknob of the Boring Room.

It was the next afternoon, and the three Greystone kids had convinced Ms. Morales that they *had* to stop by their house again to visit Rocket. Chess had been worthless all day at school—twice, his teachers had called on him and he'd had so little idea what they'd asked him that he wasn't sure if they were talking about language arts or social studies, math or science. Ever since about ten thirty last night, he'd been longing for this moment.

And dreading it, too. He had to force himself to carry through every action: *Now wrap your hand around the doorknob.*

Turn your wrist to the right. Push the door forward. . . .

"Is it terrible that I didn't lock the door of the Boring Room again last night?" Emma burst out behind him. She and Finn were crowded so close beside him that Chess's elbows knocked against them.

"Why didn't you lock it?" Natalie asked. At least she was a few steps back.

"I didn't think!" Emma wailed. It took a lot to make Emma wail. "I had too much else to think about! Why would Mom keep the Boring Room locked, anyhow? Why would it matter? And we *did* lock the front door of the house yesterday when we left, and that was still locked when we got here today, and there aren't any windows broken, so we know nobody would have come in here, so . . ."

Chess flashed his sister a warning look, hoping she'd get the message: *Don't talk about scary stuff like people maybe breaking into our house. Not around Finn. Don't scare Finn.*

Or did Chess really want to say, *Don't scare me?*

"Let's just see what's in this room," Natalie said. And Chess still felt weird about her being a Lip Gloss Girl (or a former Lip Gloss Girl?) and being in his house and even talking to him. But he liked how steady her voice stayed. He liked that she was older than him and knew things he didn't.

It made him feel a little bit less like that other Rochester—Rocky—in Arizona, who was probably still having to stay brave for his little brother and sister. Unless they'd been found already.

Chess hoped they'd been found already.

The door creaked open. Chess reached in and turned on the light.

"Somebody did come in and steal everything!" Natalie cried, peering around.

"No, no—this is what the room looked like yesterday," Emma said. "Just the same."

"Mom keeps the Boring Room empty on purpose," Finn added fiercely. "If she had pictures and, I don't know, toys, it'd be too interesting, and she wouldn't get any work done."

"Oh," Natalie said.

But just that one word made Chess see the Boring Room differently. It *was* kind of weird how the room looked so abandoned, like someone had moved out everything but the heavy furniture. The room held nothing but the desk, an office chair, and three bookcases. Chess couldn't remember the Boring Room ever looking any different. But why did Mom bother having three bookcases in here for just—Chess looked around—two books?

Chess crossed the room and looked at the two books leaning forlornly against each other: an ancient-looking dictionary and a binder labeled "Computer Manual."

"Couldn't she just look that up online?" Natalie said,

right at Chess's elbow. The sound of her voice made him jump.

"Mom doesn't use the internet down here," Finn said, spitting out each word like a bullet. "That would keep the Boring Room from being boring! Why can't you understand that?"

"Didn't you say she designs websites?" Natalie asked. "Wouldn't she always need the internet?"

Chess froze. He'd never thought of that. But it was true: He couldn't think of many parts of Mom's job that didn't require the internet. Once or twice when their internet was down, Mom had had to go work at the library or Starbucks to have Wi-Fi.

Chess couldn't look at Natalie. It felt like she was saying Mom was a liar. No—it was worse than that. It felt like she was saying Mom lied about *everything*. Even little things, like the picture Mom had given Chess of his dad as a kid, telling him, "See this? You look exactly like your father did when he was your age. Same straight nose, same strong jawline, same handsome eyes. . . . This picture proves it."

It felt like, if Natalie saw that picture, she'd say, "It's so fuzzy! That could be anyone! You probably don't look anything like your dad. You just want to believe the stuff your mom says. Why can't you think for yourself, like I do?"

But Natalie would never see that picture, because it was

tucked away in a shoebox on the very top shelf of Chess's closet.

It wasn't actually a little thing.

Was thinking all this making Chess act strange? Desperately, Chess looked toward Emma for help.

Emma didn't even seem to be listening. She was peering intently at a paper they'd printed out the night before in Ms. Morales's office: the map of the Boring Room that came from putting together the butterfly spots.

"The spot with the *X* has to mean something," she muttered, drifting across the room. "And that spot is right about . . . here."

Her fingers brushed the wall above one of the empty bookcases.

"It's just a blank wall!" Finn said.

"The map is only two-dimensional," Emma said. "So the actual spot could be anywhere from the ceiling to the floor."

"I'll check the floor then," Finn said, rushing over to crouch beside Emma.

"I guess the ceiling's mine," Chess managed to mumble.

He brushed past Natalie, still without looking at her. To his surprise, she reached out and patted his shoulder, which made him feel slightly better and a lot weirder, all at once.

The ceiling of the Boring Room was lower than anywhere else in the house. But even standing on tiptoes, Chess still couldn't reach the top part of the wall. He pulled the desk chair over, positioning it a little off to the right from where Emma had pointed.

"Careful," Natalie said as he stepped up onto the chair.

What was wrong with Chess? He really wanted to snarl back at her, *What's it to you? Why do you care?* And maybe also, *Do you care?*

He kept his mouth shut and concentrated on reaching his hand toward the ceiling. Then he felt silly brushing his hand against the clearly empty wall.

"If there was anything to find here, wouldn't we see it?" he complained.

"Not necessarily," Emma said. "Maybe we need a magnifying glass. Maybe we need a microscope. Maybe we need to douse the wall with lemon juice or some other *reagent*."

Chess was not going to ask his little sister in front of Natalie what a reagent was. He hoped that Finn would do it for him. Or that Emma would just explain without waiting for anyone to ask.

But Natalie spoke next. "Um, guys, I'm not sure how long we have for searching before Mom gets suspicious and starts looking for us. If you think we need a magnifying glass or . . . something else . . . we should get it now."

Apparently Natalie didn't know what a reagent was either. And maybe she was embarrassed about asking, too?

"I don't know what we need," Emma said impatiently. "Not yet. Can't you call your mom and tell her we need more time with Rocket? Like, hours? Tell her he's really sad and missed us, and he needs us a lot!"

"Mom won't leave us alone in here very long," Natalie said. "Not when she thinks . . ." She glanced at Finn and fell silent.

Not when she thinks there's an angry boyfriend that Mom ran away from, Chess thought. *Not when she thinks there's danger.*

"I'm not finding *anything,*" Finn complained.

Chess looked down. Finn was running his hands again and again in wide circles over the floor and the lowest portion of the bookshelf. Emma had started searching along the next two shelves of the bookshelf, and Natalie was feeling along the wall immediately above the shelves. When Natalie moved her hand over to the left, Chess stepped one foot onto the top of the bookshelf so he could reach farther.

But just as Chess sometimes forgot how tall he'd gotten lately, he also sometimes forgot how big his feet were. The rubbery front part of his sneaker jabbed too hard against the wall and bent like clown shoes. He had to dig his toes into the crack between the wall and the bookshelf to keep his balance.

And then the bookshelf shifted beneath his foot. It began to swing back away from the wall.

"Watch out!" Chess yelled at Natalie, Emma, and Finn.

Natalie jumped back, and Chess instantly wished she hadn't. Now there didn't seem to be any way to keep the bookcase from falling over on Emma and Finn.

"Catch it!" Chess yelled at Natalie, even as he himself fell backward against the chair, which also rolled backward. He scrambled to the edge of the seat and held out his hands, hoping he could at least stop the bookcase from hitting his brother and sister quite so hard.

The result was that he fell to the floor, so he was also in the path of the falling bookcase.

But the bookcase didn't move the way he expected; it didn't topple straight out from the wall. It moved at a slant, one side swinging out wide while the other tilted toward the corner of the room. Nothing made sense: The side that Chess had stepped on wasn't even the side that had separated the most from the wall.

Or—had it actually separated? Had the wall somehow come with it?

Tangled up on the floor, Chess couldn't make sense of anything.

But as soon as the bookcase stopped moving, Finn popped up and poked his head around the side of the bookcase.

"There aren't any books on this bookcase because it's not *really* a bookcase!" he cried. "It's a secret door!"

TWENTY-TWO

FINN

"Where's it go?" Emma asked breathlessly. "What do you see back there?"

"Um," Finn said. "It's too dark to see."

The darkness was awful. It was the thick kind that made Finn think of spiders and snakes. He wasn't afraid of creepy-crawly things, but the space that had opened up behind the secret door had damp air like he'd encountered in other people's basements—the kind that were full of centipedes and millipedes and pill bugs. The air had a strange smell to it, too—maybe the space behind the bookcase was full of *dead* centipedes and millipedes and pill bugs. Maybe dead rats and mice, too.

Maybe even dead humans? Finn thought. And then he decided he had to stop scaring himself.

"Where's the nearest flashlight?" Natalie asked.

"I'll find one," Finn volunteered, scrambling back from the edge of the bookcase.

It was a relief to be away from the darkness, away from the scary air. Emma and Chess were still jumbled up on the floor, their faces stunned and confused.

"Did you *look* for a light switch?" Emma asked.

"How can I look when there's nothing to see but darkness?" Finn asked, stepping past her.

"You use your hands," Emma said. "Look with your fingers."

"Why don't you?" Finn asked.

Emma being Emma, she actually stood up and walked over to the opening behind the bookcase. She ducked down and stepped into the darkness.

"Emma!" Finn screeched.

Emma turned around, but only to reach up and feel around on the other side of the wall.

What if something bites you? Finn wanted to shout at her. *What if there's a mousetrap back there, or, or . . .*

"Here it is," Emma said.

She must have hit a switch, because suddenly light glowed around her.

"Oh, good," Finn said. "I didn't know where the flashlights were, anyway."

Chess and Natalie were already rushing toward the opening. Both of them had to hunch over and touch their hands to the floor to duck through the secret doorway—it was really more like a half doorway. At least Finn only had to bob his head to the side and then back up again as he scrambled after them.

He stepped into the secret room and joined the others in looking around and around.

Despite the smell, the room he stood in now was clean and neat with no evidence of bugs, dead or otherwise. The walls were lined with shelves, and unlike the shelves in the Boring Room, these shelves were packed. Finn saw cartons of Campbell's soup and ramen noodles, and bundles of water bottles and peanut butter jars. He saw row after row of canned peas and tuna fish and pear slices, applesauce and mandarin oranges and corn.

"It's just a pantry?" Finn said in dismay. "We have something as cool as a secret room hidden under our house, and Mom just uses it to store food?"

"And old shoes?" Emma asked, pointing at a stack of shoeboxes Finn hadn't noticed.

Maybe they were full of spare *new* shoes—Finn saw that the picture on the side of the nearest shoebox was of the very same sneakers he wore on his feet.

"What if there aren't shoes inside?" Chess asked. He lifted the lid of the one of the boxes and said, "Ooooh . . ."

Finn rushed over beside his brother and peered into the box. Everything inside it was green.

"Money?" he said disbelievingly. "It's full of money?"

"Is every box like that?" Emma asked, lifting another off the shelf.

"Oh no," Finn said. "Oh no, oh no, oh no." Each "no" came out sounding more and more like he was crying.

"What's wrong?" Emma asked, grabbing another shoebox. "It looks like we're rich!"

"No," Finn wailed. He could barely get the words out. Or breathe. "It looks like Mom really did rob that bank!"

TWENTY-THREE

EMMA

“What are you talking about?” Emma asked.

“Tyrell and Lucy—yesterday—their bus was late because there was an accident, and they said they saw Mom running out of a bank carrying a big bag like she’d robbed it, and—”

“Mom would never rob a bank,” Chess said decisively, like he was slamming a door. “Not *our* mom.”

Yesterday we thought Mom would never go away and leave us behind forever, either, Emma thought. And for a moment, Emma was lost. She was so lost, it didn’t seem like there was a single math fact that could save her.

Then Natalie said, "I'm pretty sure Chess is right. Your mom didn't rob a bank."

Emma, Finn, and Chess all whirled toward the older girl, who was rifling through one shoebox full of money after another.

"How do you know that?" Emma challenged.

"Because," Natalie said, "it looks like every single one of these bills is either a one or a five. If someone robs a bank, they take twenties, at least. Probably even fifties or hundreds."

"Why?" Finn asked with a forlorn sniff.

Emma knew the answer to this one.

"Bulk," she said. "You steal a million dollars in ones, you have to carry one million strips of paper. If you steal it in hundreds, that's still a thousand—no, ten thousand—bills, but that's a *lot* less than having to lug around a million one-dollar bills."

Oh yeah, she thought. *Knowing math* did *help.*

Having Natalie around had helped, too.

Natalie was still calmly scanning through shoebox after shoebox.

"If these people you're talking about—Tyrell? Lucy?—saw your mom carrying a big bag out of a bank, it was probably because she had a lot of ones and fives," Natalie said. "Not because it was a lot of money altogether."

"But why would Mom want all this money here?" Chess asked. "Or all this food and water?" He tilted his head back, looking up at the shelves that stretched toward the ceiling. "Our whole family wouldn't eat this much food in a year!"

"Was your mom a Doomsday prepper?" Natalie asked. "Did she talk all the time about how society was going to fall apart, and how it would be everybody for themselves, and the only people who would survive were the ones who prepared ahead of time?"

"No," Emma, Chess, and Finn said, almost as one.

"Yeah, I guess that's stupid," Natalie said. "Because if she were a Doomsday prepper, she wouldn't want cash. She'd have gold bars, or silver, or something like that. Things you could barter with. I'm pretty sure the Doomsday preppers think paper money will be worthless when society collapses. Okay, then, this is just a panic room."

"A what?" Finn said. "How do you *know* this stuff?"

"Don't you guys ever go online?" Natalie asked. "Or watch TV?"

"Mom let us watch *The Lego Batman Movie* the other night," Finn began. "And—"

"Just tell us what a panic room is," Emma said through gritted teeth. She hated not knowing things.

"Okay," Natalie said, shrugging in a way that made her

hair ripple down her back. "Panic rooms are what rich people have in their houses, where they can go and be safe and lock themselves in if someone breaks in. Or if someone is trying to kidnap them."

"But we're not rich!" Finn protested. "Unless you count having shoeboxes full of one-dollar bills."

"*I* wouldn't count that," Natalie said.

Emma wanted to add, *And nobody would want to kidnap us!* But her memory nagged at her: She'd thought the same thing before, after the kids in Arizona with the same names and ages as Emma, Finn, and Chess *had* been kidnapped. They probably hadn't expected it, either.

Emma gazed around again at the well-stocked shelves.

But Mom expected something. *She was preparing for* some *threat or danger. . . .*

Emma remembered what Mom had said the day they'd learned about the kidnappings in Arizona: "You don't have to worry about being kidnapped. I promise. I'll do everything I can to prevent that."

Had Mom set up this whole room after that? Had she gotten all the money and all the food and water the next day, before leaving?

And did she dig out a whole other part of our basement and build these walls and shelves in that time, too? Emma wondered. *That's so not logical! It'd be impossible!*

Anyhow, why would she have done all that work and then . . . just left? Without even telling the kids what she'd done?

"So I wonder . . . ," Natalie began.

"What?" Chess asked.

"I don't know if your mom's a Doomsday prepper or if this is just a panic room, for some reason," Natalie said. "I don't even know your mom. But either way, I think there'd be more hiding places, even inside the panic room. Like, maybe for other secret things that are more valuable than food or one-dollar bills? Or . . . weapons? Those Doomsday preppers always have lots of guns."

"Let's look!" Finn said enthusiastically.

Guns? Emma thought. *What would we do if we found guns?*

"Maybe there's something hidden behind these shelves," Natalie said, tugging on the wood frame of one that held boxes of granola bars. "Chess, what did you do to get the bookshelf back in your Mom's office to move?"

"I'm not sure," Chess admitted with a gulp.

His face looked pale, as if he was just as distressed as Emma at the idea of guns.

"I'll go look," Emma said.

She ducked back out of the secret room and peered down at the empty bookcase/door, which still hung completely open. To her surprise, Chess followed her.

"Chess, you didn't know Mom had this secret room down here, did you?" Emma asked.

"What? *No,*" he said. He held up his right hand. "Scout's honor."

Emma believed him.

"So when you opened the door . . ."

"I was just standing on the top of the bookcase," Chess said. He peeked toward the secret room, then back at Emma. "Well, I kind of kicked the wall, too, but that was by mistake."

He brushed his fingers against a scuff mark on the wall.

"And then?" Emma said. "Is that when the shelf moved?"

"Yes," Chess said. "Er, no, first I tried to dig my toes in to keep from falling. And that's when the shelf moved and I did fall."

"Then maybe it's something right where the bookshelf and the wall meet," Emma suggested. She felt along the back of the shelf. "Oh!"

Emma's finger brushed a tiny button that looked like nothing more than a small defect in the wood. The shelf began to move back toward the wall.

"Stop! Stop! Stop!" Emma screamed. She jammed her body between the shelf and the wall.

Chess tugged on her arm, trying to pull her away.

"What are you doing?" he yelled. "You'll get hurt!"

"No! Finn and Natalie will get trapped!" Emma yelled back at him, keeping her shoulder wedged in place.

The bookshelf-door ground to a halt as soon as it touched her arm. It sagged a little, half-open, half-shut.

"Did we break it?" Chess asked.

"I—I don't know," Emma whispered.

Then Natalie and Finn were there, peeking out from the secret room.

"What's all the shouting about?" Natalie asked irritably.

"We found the button that makes the bookshelf move," Emma told her. She looked at the awkward way the shelf tilted. "But now maybe it's stuck."

"Worry about that later," Natalie said, tossing her hair over her shoulder. "Come see what we found."

"It's a lever!" Finn said excitedly. "We can all try it together." He scrunched up his face. "Do you think we're really going to find guns? Remember how Mom always said she wanted to protect us from guns?"

Emma didn't answer. She didn't admit how shaken she still was by the thought of Finn and Natalie being trapped in the secret room. What if the button had stopped working after that, and Emma and Chess couldn't get Natalie and Finn out?

We would have told Natalie's mom, Emma thought. *She would have figured out how to rescue them. And they would have had plenty of food and water. And money.*

But what if there wasn't enough air in the secret room when the door was shut? What if the lights automatically turned off?

Stop it! Emma told herself.

She turned back toward the bookcase door, to reassure herself that it was still open and there was nothing to worry about. Their cat, Rocket—whom they'd totally ignored, ever since arriving at the house—was just poking his head curiously into the doorway.

"Scat!" Emma yelled at him. "You be safe!"

Rocket turned tail and ran away. Chess looked curiously down at Emma.

"Are you okay?" he muttered.

"Sure," Emma said.

And then Natalie was showing them the lever.

"At first Finn and I thought it was just part of the top of this shelf, but it sticks out a little," she said.

"And even though it's the same color as the wood, it's actually metal," Finn added.

"And if you pull it—?" Chess asked.

"Let's see," Natalie said.

She reached up and eased the handle down. At first nothing happened. But then the floor jerked—forward a little, back a little, then steadily forward. It made Emma think of a merry-go-round starting up.

"The whole room moves?" Finn crowed delightedly. "Even the walls?"

Emma felt dizzy. The room *was* rotating, faster and faster and faster. It was like a merry-go-round where you didn't even have a horse to hang on to.

Emma grabbed the side of one of the shelves. The lights blinked off and on and off again.

"Where's it taking us?" she shrieked.

"I thought . . . I thought it would just open a secret compartment!" Natalie cried.

"Hold on!" Chess commanded. He grabbed Finn's arm and Emma's shoulder. Emma reached one hand back and clutched his hand.

And then the spinning stopped.

"What *was* that?" Finn asked.

Nobody answered him. Emma glanced back over her shoulder, back toward the opening where she'd seen Rocket's face just a few moments ago. But now there wasn't an opening anymore, just row after row of solid shelves blocking the way out.

"The door's gone!" she cried. "The door's gone, and now we're *all* trapped!"

TWENTY-FOUR

CHESS

“Emma, Emma, Emma,” Chess said, patting his sister’s shoulder. “It’s not gone. It just moved. Or—we moved, so it looks like it’s in a different place.”

He pointed off to the left, where a thin sliver of light spread across the floor like an arrow pointing toward a crack in the wall. He was still getting oriented himself. The overhead lights had gone out and come back on and flickered again, and now they were on only dimly, like emergency lights leading out of a burning building or a crashed airplane.

Okay, maybe those aren’t the best comparisons to make. . . .

The floor beneath them gave a shudder, as if it were considering starting up again.

"Let's get out of here!" Emma cried, running toward the sliver of light and the opening. "Rocket! Rocket, are *you* okay?"

"Emma . . . ," Chess began.

But Finn and Natalie ran after her, as if they were just as spooked.

Chess dashed for the door as well, because Emma had infected him with a sudden fear: What if the door closed and he got stuck in the secret room all by himself?

But what if the door closes after we're out and we never get it back open again? he thought. *What if there's some secret in the hidden room that we need so we can figure out how to find Mom?*

Just before he stepped out, he bent down and grabbed a can of green beans from the nearest shelf. He wedged the can against the doorframe, so even if the door tried to shut on its own, the can would keep it propped open.

Then he slammed headfirst into Natalie's back.

"Oh, sorry," Chess mumbled. "I wasn't looking where I was . . ."

Natalie surprised him by clutching his arm.

"Didn't we leave the light on in your mom's office?" she asked.

Finn and Emma grabbed on to Chess as well. Chess

blinked, trying to make out the familiar furniture of the Boring Room: the desk, the chair, the bookshelves. His eyes adjusted a little to the strangely dim light, but he couldn't get them to see anything but blank floor and empty walls.

"L-light switch," Emma said, daring to step away and stride toward the opposite wall.

She hit the wall, and Chess braced for the bright overhead light of the Boring Room to come back on.

A lightbulb flickered and sizzled then steadied, but only sent out a low-wattage glow.

Chess looked down at swirls on the floor—swirls of dust on an otherwise empty concrete floor.

"This isn't your mom's office!" Natalie cried. "We ended up in somebody else's house!"

TWENTY-FIVE

FINN

"Ian? Mr. and Mrs. Han? Mrs. Childers?" Finn started calling out the names of all the closest neighbors he could think of.

"Shh," Emma said, grabbing his arm warningly. "We don't know *whose* house we're in."

"Right," Finn said in what he thought was a very reasonable tone. "So we should make as much noise as possible, so someone will come down and tell us. Also, so no one thinks we're sneaking around doing something wrong. Like stealing stuff. The Hans live on one side of us and Mrs. Childers lives on the other, so whichever way that room spun us around, we—"

"Finn," Chess said sharply. He walked over to the doorway that led out from the little room they were in, into what Finn guessed had to be the room beyond. Chess opened the door a crack, then looked back at the others. "Do either the Hans or Mrs. Childers have a totally empty basement?"

"No, silly," Finn said, laughing. "Ian Han has more toys than we do in his basement. And Mrs. Childers . . . remember that time she paid us to move her Christmas ornaments down into her basement? Well, she wanted to pay us, but Mom said it was enough that she fed us Christmas cookies. Even though they were kind of stale. And . . ."

Emma pushed past Finn and Chess, and shoved the door leading into the next room completely open. Finn saw a space like the wide-open part of the Greystones' basement, with tiny half windows at the top letting in murky light.

The light shone down on nothing but a bare concrete floor.

"This basement doesn't even have carpet," Emma said. "Don't the Hans and Mrs. Childers have carpet?"

Natalie turned side to side, facing first one direction, then another. She pointed, and her lips moved silently. Then she looked up at everyone else.

"The main part of your basement was on the side that faced the street," she said. "So if we're not in the house to the left or the right, on the same street as you . . . what do you know about the house *behind* yours, on the next street over? Behind your backyard, I mean?"

"There's not a house right behind ours," Chess said. "There's a bunch of trees."

"If it weren't for all those trees, it'd be a great place to play football," Finn said. "*That's* how much space there is before you get to the next street over."

Emma walked out into the main part of the basement and squinted up at the tiny windows.

"Nothing but bushes," she muttered. "At least, that's all we can see from here." She whirled back toward the others. "It felt to me like we were just spinning, but what if the secret room is on some sort of track? Like . . . a trolley? Could it have carried us all the way to the street behind ours?"

"I guess," Chess said. But he had his whole face smooshed up into a squint, like he was really saying *None of this makes any sense.*

"I'll find out where we are," Natalie said, yanking her phone from her back pocket. Her thumbs flew, then she looked up, squinting just as hard as Chess. "That's weird. I don't have service down here."

"Then let's go upstairs!" Finn raced for the stairs. He

glanced back to see that nobody else was following him. He paused on the bottom step. "What are you waiting for?"

"Finn . . . ," Chess began. He pointed back toward the door they'd come through. "Maybe we should just go back to our house. Through the secret room. We probably still have time to pet Rocket a little before Ms. Morales gets worried about us."

"What if we go back through the secret room and it spins again, and we end up somewhere else?" Emma asked. "Or . . . we get stuck?"

"Why can't I get my phone to work?" Natalie grumbled. She waved it in the air and held it up toward the nearest window, as if that would make a difference.

Something surprising occurred to Finn.

"Are you all scared?" he asked. "Just because you don't know where the spinning room took us? Does it scare you that much when you don't know stuff?" He jumped up to the next higher step. "You should all remember what it's like to be a second grader. There's *lots* of stuff I don't know or understand, and I'm fine!"

That wasn't entirely true—if he thought about Mom being gone, he didn't feel fine at all. But he was fine with the spinning room. He was fine with being in a strange house.

As far as he was concerned, the mystery of it all was a great way to keep his mind off missing Mom.

"Here," he said. "I'll make it easy for you. Catch me!"

He dashed up the rest of the stairs and burst through the door at the top crying out, "Hello? I'm lost! Whoever lives here, can you tell me where we are?"

As soon as he was through the door, Finn poked his head around the corner and looked around.

"You all are worrying about nothing!" he called back over his shoulder. "This whole house is empty! We're not bothering anyone!"

It *was* a little creepy to see the expanse of bare floor before him. And why wasn't there more light? Instinctively, Finn gazed toward the place where he'd see the nearest window if he'd come up the basement stairs in his own house.

Oh. There was a window, but it was boarded up, covered with plywood. The only reason any light crept into the house at all was because the plywood was cracked.

Natalie shoved her way up the stairs behind Finn.

"What's with the windows?" she asked. "Nobody would be able to sell a house with the windows boarded up. Who does that?"

"None of our neighbors," Finn said. "No one on our street."

"So *is* this house on the street behind yours?" Natalie asked.

"Let's see," Finn said. He crossed the room before him,

which seemed to be about the same size and shape as his family's living room. He reached for the doorknob of the front door. It was stiff and hard to turn, so by the time he managed to wrench it open, not just Natalie but even Chess and Emma were clustered right beside him.

The door opened in, so everybody had to step back.

Finn saw a crumbling porch first; then a weedy, overgrown yard; and then the tall fences blocking off the houses on either side. The fences soared so high that probably even Chess couldn't see over them.

They also had rusty, spiky wires lining the top of them.

"Do you recognize where we are now?" Natalie asked, turning from Finn to Emma to Chess. "Does anything look familiar?"

Chess's face had turned stark white. Emma's eyes had grown so big it seemed like they'd taken over her face.

It fell to Finn once again to do all the talking.

"I've never been here before in my life! None of us have!"

TWENTY-SIX

EMMA

Logic, Emma told herself. *Sense. Facts. Think about those, and you won't panic. We can't be that far from home.*

But even the air seemed to be conspiring against her, making her think otherwise. The weather had been clear and sunny when she and the others had stepped into their own house just—what? Ten or fifteen minutes ago? But the threat of a storm had apparently blown in, just in that short amount of time. The sky now was full of low, ominous clouds, and the air felt murky and thick. It was the kind of air that made it hard for people to breathe if they had asthma. Emma had

had a problem with that when she was little; she was just lucky that she'd outgrown it.

Was it coming back now?

Stay logical, Emma reminded herself again. *Stay calm.*

She made herself take a deep breath of the nasty air.

"This *could* be the street behind ours, and it's just changed a lot since the last time we were over here," she said, trying to force the doubt out of her voice. "We don't come this way very often because none of us have friends in this direction, and we always go the other way to get out of the neighborhood. And, you know, there are all those trees in the way, so we never really see what's happening on this street. . . ."

"Oh," Natalie said. "That makes sense. I'll just look at the GPS location on my phone, and . . ." She peered intently down at her phone, then back up. "Ugh! It's still not working!"

"Maybe if we walk out to the street, we'll see something familiar," Emma suggested, stepping out onto the porch. Finn and Natalie—who was holding the phone up in the air again—followed close behind.

"I think we should go back," Chess said. He remained right on the threshold, the door open behind him.

Emma's stomach clenched at the thought of going back through the strange house, back through the secret room—and maybe even back through another round of spinning.

She *really* wanted to see something familiar and figure out where they were.

And then we can walk back to our house through our own backyard. And tonight back at Ms. Morales's house, we'll figure out the code behind Mom's letter, and we'll know how to rescue her that way, and we'll never have to go into that secret room again. At least, not without her being with us, telling us how to work it. . . .

Emma reached back and tugged on Chess's elbow, throwing him off balance.

"Come on, Chess," she said. "Where's your spirit of adventure?" This was something Mom said sometimes; it was amazing that Emma could speak the words without starting to cry. "I just want to look and see if we can find any street signs. Nothing's going to happen if we walk down this driveway for a minute!"

Chess toppled forward, barely missing stepping on Natalie's heels.

Maybe Chess's long, gangly arms caught the edge of the door somehow; maybe there was a breeze that Emma hadn't noticed. But as soon as Chess was out of the way, the door swung shut behind him with a loud bang.

Chess jumped, knocking his shoulder against the scarred wooden door.

"Oops," Emma said.

Chess reached back and twisted the doorknob. It didn't budge.

"We better hope we see something familiar," he muttered. "Because this door's locked now. We *can't* get back to the secret room!"

TWENTY-SEVEN

CHESS

“I’m sorry,” Emma said.

Chess shook his head, unable to choke out any words.

Why is this so hard? he wanted to scream. *I just want Mom to be home and everything to be normal. I don’t want to have to think about secret rooms or letters written in code or the fact that we were down to having only one parent, and now she’s gone, too. I just want to be an ordinary sixth grader, with an ordinary life. . . .*

He might as well wish that Dad was still alive.

“If we stick together, everything will be fine,” Natalie said, as if she could tell he was about to lose it. But even she had a tense look around her eyes, like she was fighting against squeezing them shut and pretending none of this had happened. "Maybe if we go out to the street, my phone will work. Sometimes there are dead zones in certain houses. Mom says she sees that all the time when she's selling houses, and sometimes the buyers even ask for lower prices because of that. . . ."

"*I* wouldn't buy a house where a phone wouldn't work!" Finn agreed.

Don't let Finn see how upset I am, Chess thought. *Don't let Finn see how scared I am. Don't let Finn see how confused I am, how I don't understand anything. . . .*

"Lead the way," Chess said to Natalie. He waved his arm out to the side as if he were just being a gentleman, letting her and the others go first.

Really, he just wanted to walk behind Finn and Emma so they couldn't see his face and Chess wouldn't have to stiffen it into a confident, cheerful, unconcerned mask. He wasn't sure he was capable of doing that right now.

Natalie stepped down from the crumbling concrete porch, followed by Finn and Emma together, with Chess bringing up the rear. A short sidewalk led over to the black-topped driveway, and both the sidewalk and the blacktop were just as crumbly as the porch, with large patches of rocks and dirt showing through.

"What a mess," Natalie said. She covered her mouth for

a moment, as if she'd said something wrong. "I mean, your house is nice, and the other houses on your street are, too, and if this is just one street away, it's not fair that the people who own this house let things get so run-down. That makes it so you wouldn't get as much money if you sold your house."

"We're not selling our house," Emma said.

Oh no . . . If Mom really doesn't come back, would we have *to sell our house?* Chess wondered. *Would we have to be adopted by some family we don't even know? Would we maybe even be split up, me and Finn and Emma all going separate places?*

Chess's stomach twisted, as if someone had grabbed it and tried to squeeze it down to nothing.

"Mom would never let anyone sell our house!" Finn agreed with a little laugh, as if the whole idea was ridiculous. "Mom . . ."

From behind, Chess saw the exact moment Finn's shoulders sagged, as if a terrifying idea had just hit him: What could Mom do to prevent someone from selling the house if she wasn't even there? If she never came back?

"Hey, Finn," Chess said too loudly. "How long do you think it took to build those huge fences on either side of this house? Do you think they used different-colored boards on purpose? Would you do that, if we decided to build a fence around our house?"

"I don't like fences," Finn said sulkily. "They make it so you can't *see*."

Chess caught up to Finn and put his arm around his brother's shoulder. Ahead of them, Natalie stepped past the corner of the nearest fence. She pulled Emma alongside her and asked, "See anything familiar now?"

"Umm . . . ," Emma began, turning her head right to left to right again, looking up and down the street.

Natalie dipped her head toward her phone screen once more.

"Searching, searching, searching . . . ," she muttered.

Chess shepherded Finn out past the fence as well. Chess could have sworn every street in their neighborhood had sidewalks, but there wasn't one here. He stepped directly from the crumbling blacktopped driveway out into the street. He immediately tightened his grip on Finn's shoulder and looked both ways for cars.

"Watch out!" he warned Natalie, who was still peering at her phone.

She looked up, but Chess's caution was unnecessary. There weren't any cars. The only movement on the street was a group of five boys headed toward them.

Chess squinted, hoping he'd recognize someone from school. Maybe one of them would even be able to tell Chess the name of this street and how to get back home. But these boys all looked older, maybe even high-school age. One or two of them had the beginnings of beards. They all wore matching dark blue and orange, as if they were all on the same elite sports team. They also all moved with the same intimidating swagger. It reminded Chess of certain boys he tried to avoid at school, the ones who went around in packs, challenging other kids to fight.

Only, these boys had a lot more muscles. They looked like they actually *could* fight. Not just threaten to.

"Don't say anything to those boys," he whispered to Finn. "Just . . ." What did Chess know about dealing with menacing older boys? Nothing. He gulped. "Just let them walk on by."

But the boy at the front—the tallest and most muscular—was looking their way. Even at a distance, Chess could see amazement flow over the boy's expression.

"Natalie?" the boy called. "Natalie *Mayhew*?"

"Is that someone you know?" Chess hissed at her.

Natalie squinted toward the older boys.

"I don't *think* so," she whispered back. Then she raised her voice and called back to the boy, "Uh, hi . . ."

The boys came closer.

"It *is* Natalie," the guy in the front called out excitedly. Was he the leader? As if on command, all five boys stopped a few paces away. The four behind the leader slouched, seeming not so much menacing now as idling, waiting for their next command.

"Yeah, it's me," Natalie said, shrugging. "So what?"

Chess felt oddly proud of her. Of course. She'd been a Lip Gloss Girl; she'd practically run the whole elementary school. She could hold her own even against a group of stupid high school boys.

"So what are you doing in *this* neighborhood?" the leader asked.

Natalie glanced down at Emma and Finn. Somehow her gaze also took in Chess, making him feel both smaller and younger.

"Babysitting," she said scornfully.

Chess slid from feeling a little younger than Natalie to feeling like he was practically a baby.

"*You* babysit?" the leader asked, narrowing his eyes at Natalie. "You?"

Natalie fixed such a withering gaze on the leader that he seemed to shrink an inch or two.

"My mother's making me," she said. "Do you *know* my mom?"

"Yes, yes, of course," the boy immediately behind the leader began babbling.

The leader shot him an annoyed glance, and the other boy shut up.

"I thought maybe you were helping scope out the neighborhood," the leader told Natalie. He stood taller, puffing out his muscular chest even more. "Because, you know. This is where the criminal was found. You heard the news, right?"

"What news?" Emma dared to pipe up.

Chess was torn between being proud of her courage and wanting to beg the leader, *Please don't hurt my little sister. Please. She doesn't know any better. She doesn't even see that you're a bunch of bullies, and you probably run this whole street, and . . .*

But the leader perked up, like he was excited about getting to tell.

"I don't know how you could have missed it," he said. "I thought *everybody* knew. There are signs up about the criminal on practically every corner. They caught her yesterday. You know she'd been on the run and in hiding for eight years? But the government set a trap. They spread the news that her children had been kidnapped—or maybe they really did kidnap her children. I don't know. Anyhow, she showed up, thinking she could rescue her kids and—boom! I heard there was a SWAT squad waiting over there, and there, and there. . . ."

He pointed up and down the street, toward one tall fence or hedgerow after another.

"And there's going to be a public trial and sentencing this

weekend. On Saturday," the leader continued. "Of course everybody'll go."

Chess's whole body felt tingly and strange. Maybe he was about to faint.

Kidnapped children, he thought.

Had the *government* kidnapped those kids in Arizona who had the same names and birthdays as Chess, Emma, and Finn? Or had the government *pretended* to?

And was Mom connected somehow?

Eight years . . . eight years ago was when Dad died. . . .

"What did . . . did . . . ," he started to stammer out, because he needed to know what the criminal had done, what made her a criminal. He wanted to know her name, too, because he thought that might prove that Mom *wasn't* involved, that this really didn't have anything to do with her.

He didn't want it to have anything to do with the kidnapped kids from Arizona, either.

But before Chess could say another word, he heard a furious shout behind him.

"Natalie Maria Mayhew! Just *what* do you think you're doing?"

TWENTY-EIGHT

FINN

Finn swiveled his head toward the loud voice. A figure loomed in the doorway of the house they'd just left. The *open* doorway.

"Ms. Morales!" he cried, running back toward her. "You found us! And—you unlocked the door!"

Out of the corner of his eye, he saw the boys they'd been talking to take off running, as if they were terrified of Natalie's mother. Or, maybe, of any adult.

A grown-up! A mom! She'll fix everything, Finn thought. *All she had to do was show up, to get rid of those scary boys!*

But Ms. Morales's face was like a storm cloud.

"Natalie! I asked you to explain—"

"Stop it, Mom!" Natalie yelled back. "Why do you always think everything is my fault?"

"Because I left you in charge," Ms. Morales said. "You were supposed to *only* go into one house, the Greystones', and visit a cat for five or ten minutes, and let me know *immediately* if there was any problem. And then you don't answer your phone, and nobody answers the door when I go in after *half an hour,* and I find you've led the kids through some secret tunnel, and *trespassed* in an empty house, and Lord only knows who it belongs to, and—*achoo!*"

She stopped seeming quite so fierce when her first sneeze was followed by six more.

"Rocket!" Finn burst out, because he saw the cat rubbing against Ms. Morales's ankles and her high-heeled shoes.

"Get him—*achoo!*—away from me!" Ms. Morales commanded.

Finn stepped back into the empty house and scooped up Rocket. He held the cat off to the side, away from Ms. Morales.

"I will, I will," Finn promised. "But listen, nothing about that empty house was Natalie's fault. We—"

"I saw four sets of footprints in the dust," Ms. Morales huffed. "Of varying sizes. Don't try to lie and pretend you weren't here."

"No, I mean, yes, we were," Finn said. "But it was *my* fault. I'm the one who led everyone else through the empty house."

"And I'm the one who didn't want to go back through the, uh, tunnel," Emma admitted, right behind him.

"And I opened the door to the tunnel," Chess said, stepping up onto the porch with Emma.

Only Natalie was still out by the street, peering off into the distance.

"Natalie, if you go chasing after those boys, so help me, I'll—" Ms. Morales began.

"I'm coming, I'm coming," Natalie grumbled, turning back toward the house.

Ms. Morales looked down at the cat in Finn's arms. Rocket waved his paws, struggling to be put down.

"Your cat might run away if we take an outdoor route back to your house, right?" Ms. Morales asked Finn, her voice a little gentler than it had been when she was yelling at Natalie.

"Maybe," Finn said. "Mom says cats think for themselves. They do whatever they want."

Ms. Morales sniffed.

"All right, quick," she said. "Everyone back in this house and we'll go back through the basement tunnel. But don't touch *anything*. You didn't damage anything already, did you?"

"What's there to damage?" Natalie asked, catching up to the others.

Ms. Morales didn't answer. But as soon as everyone was back in the house, she slammed the door *hard*.

They all made a silent procession back toward the basement stairs, except for Ms. Morales sneezing twice more, and complaining, mostly just to herself, "How could anybody sell a house like this, with that *stench* everywhere?"

Finn realized that the bad smell he'd noticed in the secret room wasn't just there; it was in this house and out in the yard, too. He'd just kind of gotten used to it.

It's like something dead and rotting mixed with lots of dirty stuff and . . .

The words that came into his head were "and with something evil," but Finn didn't like those words. Not when Mom was away and Ms. Morales was mad at Natalie.

"You were really smart to find us," he said to Ms. Morales, because sometimes when Mom was mad, it cheered her up to hear a compliment. "We really didn't know *where* we'd ended up."

"Thank the cat, not me," Ms. Morales said stiffly. "I followed him."

They all climbed back down the stairs and went into the little room that was shut off from the rest of the basement the same way the Boring Room was in the Greystones' basement.

"Did the, um, tunnel spin when you went through it?" Emma asked Ms. Morales.

"Spin? Of course not," Ms. Morales said. "But I could barely see anything. I had to use the flashlight on my phone. See?"

She switched it back on as they ducked back into the secret room. Or the panic room. Or the tunnel. Finn wasn't sure what to call it now. Behind them, Chess switched off the light in the empty basement. Somehow the lights that had been on before in the secret room were gone now, so Ms. Morales's phone flashlight was the only glow around them. Finn stepped a little closer to her.

"At least your phone works," Natalie said sulkily. "Mine completely blanked out. Honest—I didn't hear you call. Not once."

"Really, Natalie? Really?" Ms. Morales said. "Try your flashlight—I bet your phone's working now."

A light sprang on behind Finn.

"Uh-huh," Ms. Morales said.

"You never believe anything I tell you!" Natalie accused. "Even when I'm telling the truth!"

"So you're admitting that sometimes you lie?" Ms. Morales said. "How am I supposed to know the difference?"

Finn wasn't used to being around kids fighting with their parents. Or, really, anybody fighting.

"Rocket doesn't like hearing people yell," he said, and it was weird how injured his voice sounded.

"Sorry, Finn," Ms. Morales said. She patted his shoulder and made her voice soft and gentle. "What would you like for dinner tonight? Mac and cheese, maybe?"

But Finn saw the look Ms. Morales shot Natalie. Even in the dim glow of the phone flashlights, he saw the looks Emma and Chess exchanged.

It felt like everyone was keeping secrets from him.

TWENTY-NINE

EMMA

This doesn't make sense, Emma thought, silently trudging behind Finn and Ms. Morales.

The secret room that had spun them around and somehow joined the Greystones' basement with the mysterious house really did feel more like a tunnel now. Emma started counting her steps as soon as they entered the tunnel—right after Chess pulled the door to the empty house's basement shut tight behind them. She made it up to thirty-two. Then she lost count because she started distractedly thinking, *Surely we didn't walk thirty-two steps before. Surely there wasn't that much distance between our basement and the empty house. Surely the secret room didn't spin us that far forward, when I didn't even feel like we were moving forward at all. . . .*

It wasn't like Emma to lose count of anything. But there was almost a haze in the air, as if the overcast, about-to-storm sensation from outside had seeped down into the tunnel as well. It felt like it had seeped into her mind, too.

Why did it seem like there weren't even shelves lining the walls anymore?

Science, math, facts, logic, Emma told herself.

Fact: Walking in the narrow glow from a flashlight—or even two flashlights—had the effect of making everything outside that glow seem eerie. Walking with a flashlight worked that way anywhere. If nothing else, it made everything outside the flashlight glow hard to see.

Fact: Emma, Chess, Finn, and Natalie hadn't exactly explored the secret room thoroughly before Natalie hit the lever, the room spun, and then they fled into the empty house. So there might be huge sections of the secret room that they hadn't seen. Some of those sections might not have had shelves. Maybe there'd been . . . a bend in the room. An entire corner they hadn't even seen.

So why weren't they turning any corners now?

They reached the half doorway that led back into the Boring Room. As Finn, Ms. Morales, and Natalie ducked under and stepped through, Emma caught a glimpse of

Mom's desk. It was all Emma could do not to run over and throw her arms around the desk, because it was finally something familiar, something she recognized.

The desk was there. Mom wasn't.

Emma didn't hug the desk.

Mom, we're going to figure all this out and find you, Emma thought, as if she really believed she could communicate with her mother telepathically. *We are. Don't worry.*

Emma caught up to Natalie. Ms. Morales and Finn were already out of the room, headed for the basement stairs. Chess was still a few steps behind.

"Ten o'clock tonight?" Emma whispered to Natalie. "Same place?"

Natalie gave a sharp nod.

"Absolutely," she said. She narrowed her eyes. "We've got a *lot* more to look up and figure out."

THIRTY

CHESS

"Would you mind helping your brother and sister do their homework?" Ms. Morales asked Chess as soon as they got back to her house. "Natalie and I need to have a little talk."

"Uh, sure," Chess said.

Finn and Emma did not need his help with homework. Sometimes when Chess was stuck on a math problem, Emma helped *him*.

But Finn, Emma, and Chess all plopped their backpacks down beside the huge table in the kitchen and began taking out folders and books. Ms. Morales held on to Natalie's arm and steered her past them toward her office.

"Seriously, Mom?" Chess heard Natalie grumble. "Are you sure you don't want to put me in handcuffs, too?"

Behind Ms. Morales's back, Emma gave Natalie a thumbs-up and made a zipper motion across her lips. As soon as Natalie and Ms. Morales were in the office and Ms. Morales shut the door, Emma scampered after them.

"That office is soundproof, remember?" Chess called softly. "It's not going to work to press your ear against the door. Besides, you'll get caught."

Emma's shoulders sagged and she stopped following.

"But I want to know *everything*!" she complained, slouching back toward the table. "Can we really trust Natalie? Did Mom tell Ms. Morales anything she's not telling us? Has Ms. Morales heard anything new from Mom besides those stupid automatic texts?"

"*I* trust Natalie," Finn announced, his pencil hovering over a worksheet. "And Ms. Morales, too. They're nice."

Finn would probably think a murderer was nice.

Or was it that even a murderer would be nice to Finn?

Chess patted the back pocket of his jeans.

"Natalie . . . gave me something," he said slowly. He wasn't sure what to do. "In the car. She said it was . . . in case her mom is so mad she sends Natalie to her dad's and Natalie doesn't get a chance to say goodbye. Or to see us again at all. But I think maybe . . . maybe . . ."

"Just tell us what you're talking about!" Emma demanded. She put her hands on her hips and whipped her hair over her shoulder sort of like Natalie always did.

Chess dug out a pair of wireless earbuds and held them up for Finn and Emma to see.

"Natalie wants you to listen to music?" Finn asked.

"No," Chess said. He pushed his hand a little deeper into his pocket and pulled out the other object Natalie had given him: a phone. "She says her mom keeps burner phones around just, well, just in case someone needs them. So she gave me one. She said she'd set hers to call me if there's something she wants us to overhear. And with these earbuds . . ."

"The earbuds mean she'll call you and we can listen *secretly*! Without Ms. Morales knowing!" Emma's eyes lit up. "Ooo, *I* like Natalie, too! I like the way her brain works!"

But is Natalie really trying to help us—or just trying to get back at her mom? Chess wondered. *Is it really a good idea for us to hear whatever Ms. Morales is going to tell Natalie?*

Still, he handed one of the earbuds to Emma. He stuck the other in his own ear.

"None for me?" Finn said, making a pouty face.

"Sorry, Finny," Chess said. "There are only two. Anyhow—"

"I know, I know," Finn said. "I'm too young. It might scare me. Don't you know I'm brave? Don't you know I want to help get Mom back as much as you and Emma do?"

It hurt the way he said that—as if he'd already grown up too much. Already Finn had changed from the eager, bouncy, silly boy he'd been two days ago. Even his face seemed less rounded and babyish, his cheekbones more noticeable than his dimples.

You're imagining things, Chess told himself. He wanted to tell Finn, *Don't think I'm babying you. I'm not even sure* I'm *old enough to deal with all this.*

But he just said "Sorry" and ruffled his brother's hair. Then he held a finger to his lips, because the phone in his hand began vibrating. He hit the button to answer, and he heard a burst of sound from the earbud. At first, it was just an indistinct noise, but he twisted the earbud slightly in his ear, and then he could make out words.

"But I didn't do anything wrong!" Natalie was protesting to her mother. Her phone was probably buried in her pocket but set on the speaker function—that was why everything sounded so muffled.

Chess double-checked to make sure he had the phone in his own hand set to mute any noise he, Emma, or Finn might make.

"Natalie, you *know* every woman I help is someone in a dangerous situation," Ms. Morales said. "That means we need to be extra cautious about . . ."

Chess hoped Emma was listening closely to hear what they needed to be extra cautious about, because he blanked out for a moment.

So even Ms. Morales realizes Mom is in danger?

Then he remembered what Natalie had said the day before, thinking that Mom was running away from a dangerous boyfriend. That was probably all Ms. Morales meant. Chess knew she was wrong about that danger.

". . . I trusted you to help these kids, to be aware of issues they wouldn't understand, and this is what you do? Sneak away to a dangerous area to meet up with a bunch of older boys?" Ms. Morales was asking.

"Mom, I did not walk through that other house just to go meet those boys!" Natalie said, and even through the earbud, Chess could tell she was gritting her teeth. "I wasn't looking for them! They said hi, I said hi—it was a one-minute conversation! I don't even know them!"

Chess noticed that she didn't tell her mom that the boys had known *her*. That they'd called her by name.

"And you had little kids watching you—were you *trying* to show the Greystone kids that it's okay to talk to strangers?" Ms. Morales asked.

"Mom, it wasn't like that!" Natalie protested. "We were lost! My phone wouldn't work! We—"

"And it never once occurred to you to just turn around

and walk *back* through the tunnel to the Greystones' house?" Ms. Morales asked, her voice rising with incredulity.

"Mom, that tunnel wasn't . . . the secret room wasn't . . . Did *you* know Mrs. Greystone had that secret place—whatever it was—attached to the basement of her house? At first I thought it was just a panic room, but . . . didn't it seem really, really weird to you?" Natalie asked.

"People have panic rooms all the time," Ms. Morales said stiffly. "There are houses I've driven by for years, and I didn't know they had panic rooms until the owners listed the house to sell."

"And those panic rooms you've seen—are they like the one the Greystones have?" Natalie asked, her voice rising. "Are they connected to a completely different house on a completely different street?"

"Well, no . . . not that I've ever seen before," Ms. Morales admitted.

"How well do you even know Mrs. Greystone?" Natalie challenged, and Chess felt that something had changed. Now it was Natalie interrogating Ms. Morales, not Ms. Morales interrogating Natalie.

Good for you, Natalie! Chess thought, even as he listened more intently.

"How well do I know . . . Mrs. Greystone was in PTO with me for years," Ms. Morales said. "She was always quiet, but she was one of those people who, if she volunteered to do something, she did it. On time, and the right way. And she didn't complain about it, or ask a million questions that were so annoying I started wishing I'd just taken care of everything myself."

Chess felt a little proud of his mom.

"And that was enough to make you volunteer to take care of her kids for who knows how long?" Natalie challenged. "Didn't you ever think that she might be tangled up in something really strange and awful, and—"

"Yes, I *did* think she might be tangled up in something really strange and awful," Ms. Morales countered. "And that's why I offered to help. Because I don't think it's something that's her fault at all. I pray you never learn this directly for yourself, Little Miss Superior, but lots of times people—especially women—get caught up in awful situations they didn't cause, that they need help getting out of. Think about it. Why would I help someone who doesn't need it?"

"Mom, I put up with you inviting all sorts of people into our house. People you trust just because they're women and children," Natalie said. "There was the kid who broke my laptop, the one who stole my favorite jeans—"

"That you might have lost yourself," Ms. Morales interrupted.

Natalie just kept talking.

"And, you know, that woman who cried all the time."

"She had good reason to cry," Ms. Morales said, her voice tense.

"Don't you think the Greystone kids are different than the others we've had here?" Natalie asked. "Not as . . . scared all the time, maybe?"

Chess thought about the careful way Ms. Morales had shepherded the three of them through the school parking lot, as if she was hiding them from some unknown danger. As if they were supposed to understand. He *hadn't* been scared then.

But he was now.

"Some people hide things better than others," Ms. Morales said. "I wouldn't have pegged Kate Greystone as the type to get involved with a dangerous man, either. But there was always something about Kate. Something . . . mysterious. And sad. She never talked about her husband or her past."

"See, Mom? Not everyone goes around telling anyone who will listen what a scumbag their husband used to be," Natalie said. "You should learn from that, and—"

"Natalie, Kate Greystone isn't divorced," Ms. Morales said. "Her husband died. Years ago. Before they moved here."

Moved? The word caught oddly in Chess's brain. Everything had changed after Dad died. There'd been a period of time when it felt like the sun burned out, like nothing Chess ate had any flavor, like he spent weeks doing nothing but lying on his bed, staring up at his ceiling. One morning he'd awakened, and the ceiling he opened his eyes to was different: smooth and white and peaceful, instead of swirled and shadowed and cobwebbed. And he got up, and he remembered going to find Mom and hearing her explanation: "Do you like our new house? I didn't want to disturb you kids any more than I had to, so I brought you here while you were sleeping. Do you like your new furniture? Everything is new. It's a new start. I promise you, we'll be happy here. Everything will be better."

Had Chess been too busy thinking *Nothing could be better without Dad* to ask any questions? Or to listen to anything else Mom said that day?

Chess's mind worked strangely thinking about anything from the time surrounding Dad's death. Maybe it was just because he'd only been four; maybe it was because Mom never talked about certain memories. Maybe he'd been too sad to remember everything.

But Chess was pretty sure they'd just moved from one house to another, not from one town to another.

So why did Ms. Morales make it sound like we moved from an entirely different place?

Now that he thought about it, wasn't it weird that Mom

had moved them in the middle of the night? Without warning them ahead of time?

Or had Mom warned them, and Chess just didn't remember?

"Don't forget anything," Mom had told him just a few days ago—practically the last words she'd spoken to him before she vanished.

But what if he'd already forgotten something important?

What if he hadn't remembered what he was supposed to from the very beginning?

THIRTY-ONE

FINN

"Finally," Finn exploded as soon as he stepped out into the hall. It was 10 p.m. exactly—Finn had watched the numbers change on the digital clock in his room.

"Shh," Chess said, falling into step with him and looking around nervously. Then he crouched beside Finn. "Listen, Finn, it's really late for you to still be up, and this is the second night in a row. . . . Maybe you should just go back to bed and get some sleep. Emma and I can tell you everything we find out in the morning."

"Except you wouldn't tell me *everything*, if you thought it was going to scare me," Finn said. He could feel his lower lip start to jut out, like he was just a sulky little kid. He forced himself to keep his lip in, stand up straighter, and stare Chess right in the eye. "I want to help, too. I . . . I have to."

Chess's face was shadowed; it wasn't possible to see how he was going to answer.

"Finn comes with us," Emma said, stepping between her brothers. "We don't leave him behind."

And then she ruined everything by adding, "Even if he falls asleep in one of those chairs down in the office, he stays with us."

I won't fall asleep, Finn told himself. *I'll never sleep again, if that's what it takes for me to help find Mom.*

But he couldn't help himself: He let out a jaw-cracking yawn.

He hoped it was too dark in the hall for Emma or Chess to notice.

The three of them tiptoed along, with Natalie joining them right at the top of the stairs. She held two laptops under her arm.

"Extras," she whispered. "So we'll all have something to work on."

Natalie isn't saying I should just go to sleep! Finn thought, and he climbed down the stairs walking alongside her.

But when they got to the office, the other three kids went right to work, and Finn wasn't sure what he should do.

He stood in front of one of Natalie's laptops—he wasn't tall enough to reach it if he sat down—and he stared at the Google drawing of the day, which seemed to be a bunch of men and women staring at a computer. It was probably something about computer history that Finn didn't know about, but he wasn't going to ask the others.

Mom would just tell me, he thought. *If Mom were here, she would have known I didn't know, and I wouldn't have to ask, and . . .*

Finn couldn't let himself think about how everything would be better if Mom was there.

He sneaked a peek at the computer Emma was working on: She had Mom's letter full of gibberish up on the screen and she was muttering to herself, "Substitution code? Is the key maybe part of the code? Would it be numerical, since Mom would *know* I'd look for a number pattern?"

"Hey, Emma," Finn said. "Why don't you email me Mom's letter, and then I can work on it over here? Maybe I'll see some clue to help you."

It took Emma a million years to turn her head toward Finn. Sometimes she got like that when she was thinking hard.

"Hmm?" she said slowly. "Oh, um, Mom put some sort of coding on this letter so we *can't* email it anywhere. Or copy it. Or print it out. I already tried to email it to myself, to have a backup copy, and it wouldn't work. *Maybe* I could do some extra research to figure out how to unlock all that, but . . .”

But Emma thought it was more important to work on solving the code herself.

And maybe she was right. Finn didn’t know much about codes.

Finn turned toward Natalie, who had called up a picture of the Greystones’ house on her computer. She tugged on Chess’s arm.

“This is your address, right?” she asked.

You could have asked me! Finn wanted to shout at her. Instead, he just said quickly, before Chess could answer, “It is. Why?”

“I’m looking around the area on Google Street View to figure out exactly where we ended up today,” Natalie said.

“How does that help us find Mom?” Finn demanded.

“Well, if we find out who owns the empty house that’s connected to yours by that tunnel, then maybe we’ll know who might have, uh . . .”

Finn saw Chess put his hand over his mouth. Was Chess signaling Natalie to be quiet, so she didn’t scare Finn?

Finn had to prove he was brave enough to hear anything.

“You think our mom was kidnapped?” Finn asked, trying so, so hard to keep his voice from wavering on the last word. “Maybe by someone from that other house? Or by the 'criminal' those boys were talking about?"

"I don't know what to think," Natalie said, spreading her hands wide, as if to show how much she didn't know. "I can't find anything about some fugitive criminal being caught, or about any kidnappings around here. I thought it might help to find the address of that house we were in, but there's no house on any street near yours that matches what it looked like."

"That doesn't make sense," Finn protested. "Do you know about Google Earth? Where it's like you're looking down from above? Just look for the fences that were around that house!"

Natalie ran her finger over the touchpad, making the view on the screen race up and down the Greystones' street. All the houses there looked exactly like they should: totally familiar.

"I don't know, Finn, maybe the Google pictures of the other street were taken so long ago, those fences weren't built yet," Natalie said.

"But those fences looked really old," Finn said, remembering the mismatched, faded wood. "Like, even older than *me*!"

"Yeah . . . ," Natalie said absently, switching to a broader view of the neighborhood.

Finn glanced toward Chess again, hoping his older

brother noticed how Finn had had that whole conversation with Natalie without falling apart at the thought of Mom being kidnapped.

But Chess still had his hand over his mouth.

Then Finn saw what Chess had written in the search box on his computer: "Andrew Greystone obituary."

Finn's stomach twisted.

"You're looking up something about our dad?" Finn asked Chess, and this time he had no control of his voice. "Why? What's an oh, obit . . . uh . . ."

"Obituary?" Natalie finished for him, snapping her head toward Chess's computer. "You mean the news story from when he died? Let's see."

But Chess had already X-ed out of that screen.

"Never mind. It was just . . . something I wondered about," Chess said. He seemed to be breathing hard.

"You mean, you're looking for who all is listed as survivors? So maybe you can find relatives you haven't met who might have more info about your mom?" Natalie asked. "That's smart."

"Uh . . . something like that," Chess muttered. "But it doesn't matter. I can't find anything. I guess maybe eight years was too long ago."

"Try looking up some other relative," Natalie suggested.

"Maybe one who died after your dad?"

"All our other relatives died before Chess was even born," Finn said, and his voice came out too loud this time, as if, even though they were in a soundproof room, he was trying to wake Ms. Morales.

He really wouldn't mind if she did wake up, and came down and took care of him.

But the other kids would be mad.

Natalie and Chess kept talking about dead people. Finn stared at his own blank computer screen, the picture of the unknown computer programmers seeming to taunt him about everything he didn't know, everything he was useless at helping the other kids find out.

I might as well be asleep, he thought. *Or, no—I might as well be kidnapped myself, like those kids in Arizona who started this whole mess. . . .*

He knew it wasn't fair to blame the kids in Arizona for their own kidnappings—and it wasn't like that was even connected to Mom's business trip or her weird texts. But hearing the news of their kidnappings had been the start of everything weird; it had marked the first day that Finn felt strange about anything.

I bet those kids were rescued a long time ago, and we didn't even bother looking it up, he thought. *If I found out that they're home safe, and back with their parents . . . well, that would be like proof that we're going to find Mom again, too, and everything's going to be okay.*

Painstakingly—because he hadn't really learned how to type yet—he keyed in "Rochester, Emma, and Finn" and added the words "kidnapped" and "news."

The first headline that came up said, "Gustano Parents Beg for Kidnapped Children's Safe Return."

Okay, that did not make Finn feel better.

He reached for the laptop, ready to close out the whole screen and pretend he'd never seen it. But maybe he was too tired to operate a computer properly. His finger dragged across the touchpad, bringing to life a video that took over his whole screen. Instinctively, he slammed the lid of the laptop down, shutting off his view.

But that didn't shut down the sound.

"Please, we just want our children back," a woman's voice cried out.

Finn froze. On either side of him, Emma and Chess snapped their heads toward Finn's computer.

"Is that *Mom*?" Emma said.

"How do you have a recording of Mom's voice?" Chess asked.

Emma reached past Finn and lifted the laptop lid again.

And there on the screen was Mom's face.

THIRTY-TWO

EMMA

"Does Mom have an identical twin she never told us about?" Emma asked.

She was so glad her brain supplied that explanation, because otherwise, she would have had to believe she was hallucinating. The woman in the video on the computer screen looked and sounded so much like Mom. It was hard to believe it wasn't Mom—a version of Mom, anyway, who had gotten her hair cut a lot shorter, so it curled around her ears like a pixie cap, and who'd been out in the sun a lot more, so her skin was tanner, maybe even a little leathery.

A version of Mom, maybe, who lived in Arizona.

"You say that woman looks like your mom? She's identical, even?" Natalie asked. She squinted at the computer screen in front of Finn, her eyes scanning the words at the bottom of the news report. "But . . . she's the mother of some kids who were kidnapped way out in Arizona?"

"Kids who have the same names and birthdays as us," Finn informed her. He turned to face Emma. "If you think this is Mom's twin . . . does that mean we have *cousins* with the exact same names as us? Can that happen?"

"And Mom never told us any of this?" Chess asked. His voice came out sounding wild, like even calm, easygoing Chess was on the verge of panic. "That day when we saw the news about those kids being kidnapped—wouldn't she have *said* we were related? That she knew them?"

"There's a lot Mom never told us," Emma said. And this was another fact. But it wasn't a comforting one.

"I don't understand anything!!" Finn complained. The corners of his mouth trembled, and his eyes filled.

Quickly Emma slid her arm around Finn's shoulders.

"We'll figure this out, Finny," she said. "We'll figure this out, and we'll rescue Mom, and, and those other kids will be found, and . . ."

Chess wrapped his long arms around both Finn and Emma. But he didn't say anything else.

Natalie took a step toward the three Greystones, then looked at all of their faces and took a step back.

"Mothers!" she said.

"Our mother had a logical reason for whatever she did, whatever secrets she kept," Emma said. "I'm sure of it. And she left us a letter to explain. . . ."

"In a code you can't figure out," Natalie said scornfully.

Emma couldn't look at Finn to see if his eyes were still swimming with tears, or if the tears had started rolling down his cheeks. Because if she looked, it might make her eyes flood with tears, too.

Really, there wasn't anything Emma could look at right now.

She squeezed her eyes shut.

"Maybe . . . maybe you and your family are like, I don't know, *royalty* from some other country," Natalie said. Her voice was soft now, like someone telling a fairy tale. "And your mom and her twin sister went into hiding, to keep you safe. In totally different states. But they gave you and your cousins royal names to keep the connection alive—that's why they're the same. And . . ."

Maybe Natalie meant her little fantasy story to be comforting. Maybe she thought Emma had gone through one of those little-girl phases where she wanted to be a princess, like all the other girls when Emma was in kindergarten. Maybe Natalie thought Chess and Finn had secretly seen themselves as knights and noblemen.

First of all, Emma wanted to say, *I dressed up as a scientist in a lab coat for Halloween in kindergarten, when the other girls were wearing princess crowns. And secondly—do you think there's any ending to that story that doesn't put Mom and Finn and Chess and me in danger, too?*

Emma couldn't say that in front of Finn.

Maybe she wasn't capable of saying it aloud, regardless.

"What does the kidnapped kids' dad look like?" Chess asked. "Did you find any pictures or video of him?"

Curiosity was enough to make Emma open her eyes again.

Chess thought about their dad a lot more than she did. Emma knew that. For her, their dad was like the unknown in a math problem that you didn't have to solve for. She didn't know that much about algebra yet, but it seemed that sometimes there were *x*'s and *y*'s both in a problem, and you only needed to find the value for one of them. She didn't have a single memory of Dad from when he was alive, and he was gone now, and nothing would bring him back. And Emma had Mom and Chess and Finn, and that was all she needed.

Except, she didn't have Mom anymore, either.

And apparently the Arizona kids' dad was still alive,

since she'd seen the word "parents" at the bottom of the computer screen.

Chess began fast-forwarding through the video of the Mom-twin. (The Mom-clone? The Mom-double? The Mom-who-wasn't-Mom?) Emma hadn't really wanted to listen to any more of what sounded so much like Mom's voice, weighted down so heavily with worry and fear. But the sped-up video made the resemblance seem even clearer: That was exactly how Mom tilted her head when she was upset. That was exactly the way Mom's face developed twin worry lines on her forehead—and then the worry lines erased—when she was trying to sound more optimistic and cheerful than she actually felt.

Maybe Emma hadn't fully understood before that there were times when Mom was only *pretending* to look and act and sound optimistic and cheerful?

The camera angle shifted in the video, zooming out, then zooming in again on a dark-haired man standing next to the Mom-who-wasn't-Mom. The tagline below said, "Arthur Gustano, father."

"He's not as tall as Daddy was," Chess murmured, and Emma wondered if he knew that he'd said "Daddy," not "Dad."

"*You* were a lot smaller eight years ago," Natalie said, almost apologetically. "So it's not really—"

"That man is only a little taller than his wife," Chess said. "And our dad was a lot taller than Mom. I know that. From pictures I've looked at . . . recently."

"Yes, but you don't actually *know* that that woman is the same height as your mom," Natalie said. "I mean, okay, sure, you say she looks and sounds like your mom, but even if they're twins—or just sisters—then—"

"Shut up," Finn said.

And this was crazy. Finn never told people to shut up. He never sounded that fierce and hurt and angry.

He turned his head side to side, peering back and forth between Emma and Chess, like they were the only other ones in the room.

"Is that what our daddy looked like or not?" Finn asked, his voice trembling.

"Chess?" Emma said, even though she'd seen plenty of pictures of their father before and should have been able to answer.

"No," Chess said decisively. "I mean, brown hair, brown eyes—yeah, that's the same. Or similar. But this guy's nose is bigger and his face is blockier, and his hair's straighter. And *listen*. His voice isn't anywhere near deep enough."

Chess even remembers what our dad sounded like? Emma thought, and she felt a stab of something that might have been jealousy.

The man on the screen inclined his head toward his wife.

"Nobody who hasn't gone through this could imagine what a nightmare this is," he said. "How could anybody be so cruel? Our children are innocent! They—"

Some heartless news reporter in the crowd in front of the man called out, "But is there any reason you can think of that someone would be trying to get revenge on you and your wife? Any reason that—"

"There is no reason for any of this," Mr. Gustano snarled. "Are you asking if my wife and I have ever done anything that would lead to our kids being taken? *No.* We are ordinary, law-abiding American citizens. We're *blameless*. Our kids are blameless. But nobody could deserve this horror. My kids should be in school right now, drawing pictures in art class and playing tag on the playground and . . . and . . . not . . ." He looked straight at the camera. "Please, if you can hear this, if you have any humanity in your hearts at all, don't harm my children. Just let them go. Let them come home."

He buried his face in his wife's shoulder. She stared out at the reporters, then it felt like she was staring out at Emma, Chess, Finn, Natalie, and anyone else who might be watching. And her steady gaze was so much like Mom's that Emma got chills.

"That is all we have to say," the Mom-twin snapped, then gently guided her husband out of the camera's range.

Emma shoved the laptop sideways, toward Natalie.

"Natalie, you have to find out everything you can about those kidnapped kids and their parents," she said. "Finn, Chess, and me—we can't watch anymore. It's too hard. And we need all three of our brains for figuring out Mom's code."

"Even mine?" Finn asked. He sniffled. "You really think I can help—"

"Help solve this?" Emma asked. "Finn, I *know* we can do this together. Because we have to. There isn't any other choice."

THIRTY-THREE

CHESS

Emma sounds like Mom, too, Chess thought. *She sounds exactly like Mom when she's telling all of us what to do.*

A memory tugged at Chess's brain, one that was so painful and from so long ago that he could only reassemble bits and pieces of it. Maybe it wasn't even real. Or maybe he just wanted to convince himself it hadn't happened. He could remember lying on the floor—playing with his red toy car again, maybe. Only, was it *after* they'd gotten the news that Dad had died? This wasn't part of his usual memories about Dad's death. Maybe it was a few days later. Maybe he'd stopped playing. Maybe he'd been screaming and pounding his fists on the floor. Or just lying still, too sad to move. And then Mom was there, picking him up. And he'd cried to her, "I want Daddy back! Make him not dead!"

And Mom had murmured, "Oh, Chessie, I want that, too. But we don't have that choice. It's not possible." She'd smoothed back his hair and hugged him close and whispered, "Other choices, though . . ."

The next thing that had happened was that Mom laughed. It had startled Chess, and somehow, even though he was only four, he'd understood that the laugh wasn't a happy one. But he'd been too young to understand what a laugh like that could mean instead, and that had frightened him.

He hadn't understood Mom's next words, either: "What am I talking about? I *have* to do this. There isn't any other choice."

There isn't any other choice. He heard the words the way Mom had said them eight years ago, and the way Emma said them now, and the tone was exactly the same. Both of their voices were full of determination—determination fighting with fear. With the determination winning.

It was that similarity that had jarred loose Chess's memory.

"We're all like Mom," Chess said dazedly. "All three of us. We're *all* . . . well, not Mom-twins, but . . . mini-Moms, anyway."

Emma, Finn, and Natalie all snapped their heads toward Chess. All three of them looked puzzled, and Chess realized their conversation had moved on while he'd been stuck in the past, stuck hearing echoes of Mom's voice in his head. He flushed, realizing how dumb he sounded. He expected Finn to protest, *What are you talking about? I'm not like Mom! I'm not a girl!*

But Finn, for once in his life, wasn't rushing to talk. He just looked up at Chess, so trustingly, as if he thought Chess had figured out something big, and he was waiting for Chess to explain.

Ohhhh . . . Maybe I did just figure out something big, Chess thought.

"Mom says we're the only ones who will be able to read her letter," he said, pointing to the computer screen Emma had been poring over before they'd heard the voice like Mom's. He stretched out his arm so his fingers brushed five words in particular in the few lines that were understandable: *Only the three of you . . .*

"Because you're the ones she's mailing that letter to," Natalie said with an annoyed flip of her hair over her shoulder. "She's only sending it to you three, so—"

"No," Chess said. Somehow he found that he didn't care anymore that Natalie had been a Lip Gloss Girl in charge of everything at school, and nobody ever challenged her.

"That's not what this means. She wants us to be the only ones to know what's in this letter, and so she put it in a code that only we can read. Because we're the only ones who would know the key."

"You mean, it's going to be something with math," Finn said glumly. "Because Emma's a math genius. Mom knows Emma can solve any math puzzle. I can't help, after all."

"No," Chess said again. Would he have to disagree with everyone until he got them to understand? He saw Emma recoil, and he tried again. "I mean, yes, Emma's a math genius, but so are other people. If it's just some tricky math answer, we could send it to the head of, I don't know, MIT, and *he* could solve this."

"Or *she*," Emma said. "Do you actually know if the head of MIT is a man or a woman?"

"I don't," Chess admitted. "There are lots of things I don't know. But ever since . . . since Mom left, all three of us have been saying things like, 'Oh, Mom would never do that,' and, 'We know Mom loves us. She . . .'" The words stuck in his throat, but he forced them out. "'She would never abandon us unless she thought she had to.'"

"You're saying we're all experts about Mom," Emma said, finally catching on. "And you think that's what's going to matter, solving this code."

Chess saw Natalie start to open her mouth, and just from

the way she twisted her face, he knew she was going to say something like, *But you didn't know she was going to vanish!* Or, *You didn't know she had a look-alike twin in Arizona! (If that's even a twin. You don't know for sure.)* Or, *You didn't know she had a room that spins and a secret tunnel under your house! You're not very good experts!* And Chess was going to need to stop her from saying any of that.

But before Natalie or Chess could speak, Finn said, "I know Mom smells like apples. Some guy—or woman—from MIT wouldn't know *that*."

And the way he said it—Chess's heart squeezed. Finn could just as easily have said that Mom smelled like sweat and grass and gasoline when she came in from mowing the yard, or like pumpkin pie when it was Thanksgiving, or like rosemary-mint shampoo when she'd just washed her hair. But all that would have been true of lots of moms.

Their mom did smell like apples. Even when she hadn't been around apples. It was just how she was.

Chess saw Natalie shut her mouth. He stopped watching her and turned back to Emma.

"I didn't always pay much attention when you kept talking about codes all the time last winter," Chess said. "But wasn't there one kind where you had to know a quote from the Bible or a line of poetry or some other phrase, and that's how you could figure out the solution to the code?"

"You think that's the kind of code Mom used," Emma said. Her eyes lit up. "And you think that the key to this code is some phrase that Mom says all the time, that only the three of us would know."

"Yes." Chess felt triumphant, almost as if they'd already solved the code and found Mom.

"Then you don't actually need me at all," Natalie said, bitterness in her voice. "Because I wouldn't know any of that. Don't mind me—I'll just be over here listening to parents sobbing about their kidnapped kids."

And you think that's a tougher job than listening to Emma, Finn, and me talking about our missing mom? Chess wanted to shout at her. *Or than* being *us, trying to remember everything we can about Mom, when we already miss her so much?*

But something weird happened. Natalie caught Chess's eye, and it was almost like she understood what he wanted to shout.

"Sorry," she muttered.

Chess felt a little dizzy. He wasn't used to having anyone understand him except Mom, Emma, and Finn.

"I'll start saying stuff Mom says," Finn said excitedly. "Is someone going to write it all down? She says, 'I think Captain Underpants is really funny, too.' She says, 'Sure, go ahead and jump on the bed. You only get to be a kid once.' She says . . ."

"Finn, Mom does *not* say you're allowed to jump on the bed!" Emma corrected. "She just pretends not to notice. But that thing about only being a kid once . . . that's a good one. I'll try it as the decoder." She reached for a piece of paper from Ms. Morales's desk and started writing. "What else can you think of? '*Everybody* should know how to clean a toilet,' maybe? Or, 'It's okay to mess up. Nobody's perfect'?"

Chess caught Natalie still watching him. He realized he'd winced at every Mom-phrase Finn or Emma quoted.

"I'm really sorry," Natalie repeated. "Sorry that you think you have to, to *dwell* on everything like this. And that . . ."

"We're going to find our mom!" Chess interrupted before she could finish. "It's going to work! It is! All right?"

And somehow, even though he hadn't meant to, this time he really did shout at her.

THIRTY-FOUR

FINN

Finn woke up in a different place than where he'd fallen asleep. Again.

It was his third morning at Ms. Morales and Natalie's house, and the past two nights, no matter how much he'd tried to stay awake and help the older kids solve the code, each night Emma had started going on and on about matching up letters, and, "No, no, *this* is how you test for whether that's the right phrase. . . ."

And the next thing Finn knew, he was waking up in the bedroom Ms. Morales had assigned him, rather than the office, where he'd fallen asleep. Probably Chess had carried him up to bed each night, and Chess was so tall and strong and nice that he probably hadn't even asked Emma or Natalie to help.

Finn stretched, his left hand clunking against the wall that he kept forgetting was there, because his bed back home sat in the middle of the room, not off in a little alcove like this one.

And this bed had a comforter covered in weird red flowers, which would be about the last comforter design in the world that Finn would have chosen. But he wasn't going to complain about that to anyone, not when there was so much else going wrong.

Like Mom being away. And not calling us. And . . .

Finn's eyes flooded, and he balled up his fists and pressed them against his eyelids until the tears went away. He wasn't used to having to stop his brain from thinking about whatever it wanted to think about. But over the past few days, he'd learned that he couldn't think about Mom during school or around Ms. Morales. He couldn't think about the kids in Arizona either. Why had the kids in that family vanished, when in Finn's family . . .

Finn scrambled up out of bed to distract himself, so he wouldn't have to dig his fists into his own eyes again. *Take off your pajamas, put on your clothes, don't think about how Mom always has you pick out a shirt the night before, and Ms. Morales didn't. . . . Don't think about how Chess, Emma, and I have been working on solving Mom's code for two nights straight, and we're still stuck. . . .*

Finn wasn't sure he buttoned and zipped everything properly, but he left his pajamas in a heap on the floor and raced out of the room like he was scared his own thoughts would chase him. He wanted to find Chess or Emma, but when he passed their rooms, he could see that his brother and sister were still motionless lumps in their beds.

Natalie, then . . .

Natalie had to get up earlier, because middle school started before elementary school.

Her room was totally empty, but he could hear someone walking down the stairs.

I'll sneak up on her and then jump out and surprise her, Finn told himself. *That's a normal thing for me to do.*

It was weird how he thought about his every action now, too. Before Mom went away, he'd just done whatever he wanted, mostly without thinking. But now he always had to ask himself, *Am I acting like myself?*

The alternative to acting normal was jumping up and down and screaming, *I want my mommy back! Mommy, come and get me! Now!*

He couldn't do that, because what if he did, and it *still* didn't bring Mom back?

Finn made himself concentrate on tiptoeing silently down the hallway, then down the stairs behind Natalie.

None of the stairs in the Morales house gave off a friendly little *squeeeak* like the stairs back home. So Natalie didn't hear him. She didn't turn around.

I could be a spy, Finn thought. *I'm good at this. Mom would be proud.*

That last part made him gulp hard, and not exactly silently. But Natalie didn't seem to notice because she was stepping into the kitchen, where a coffee maker gurgled, and Ms. Morales had a TV turned on low, some announcer talking about stocks or bonds—boring grown-up stuff.

"Did you sleep well?" Finn heard Ms. Morales say in a fake, hearty voice, and Natalie snapped back, "Does it matter? Would you let me go back to bed if I didn't?"

Finn decided he wasn't ready to talk to Natalie and Ms. Morales yet this morning. He'd keep being a spy.

He pressed his back against the wall separating the kitchen from the dining room, and stood still. On the other side of the wall, Ms. Morales sighed.

"I know you still love me," she told Natalie. "Someday when you get past being thirteen years old, and you're not so angry about the divorce, you're going to thank me for just smiling back at you when you're like this."

Natalie made a sound that was halfway between a snort and a harrumph.

"And . . ." Maybe Ms. Morales was leaning in closer toward her daughter, because Finn had a harder time hearing. "I do need your help, Natalie. I still don't know when Kate Greystone's coming back, and she's so vague in all her texts—when she even answers my texts. I'm starting to get worried. I told her to take as much time as she needed, but . . ."

"What do you want me to do about it?" Natalie snarled.

"You're not allergic to cats," Ms. Morales said. "You don't have to take Benadryl for days and *still* be all foggy-headed after being around a cat for five minutes. That means—"

"That maybe I got *something* good from Dad's side of the family?" Natalie asked.

Maybe Ms. Morales made a face at Natalie. Her voice got a little louder, but other than that, Ms. Morales kept talking as if Natalie hadn't said anything.

"That *means* that you can take care of the Greystones' cat for me this afternoon," Ms. Morales said. "If we're going to have those kids stay with us for more than just a few days—and it looks like we are—I don't think it's a good idea for them to keep going back to their house so often and getting upset all over again. I'll pick you up after school, you can take care of the cat, then we'll get the kids when their school day ends, and we'll tell them, I don't know, maybe that their mom wanted me to take them to—what's that place that's like Chuck E. Cheese's, except for older kids? Dave and Buster's? That should keep their minds off missing their mother for another night."

"Oh, so you want me to clean up cat poop and lie to a bunch of little kids," Natalie said. "Great, Mom. Thanks."

"It's only a white lie," Ms. Morales protested. "I'm sure Kate does want me to keep her kids happy while—"

"What about the tunnel under that house?" Natalie demanded. "Aren't you afraid I'll sneak through it again to meet boys? The ones I don't even know, but—"

"Natalie, I'm *trusting* you. I'm giving you another chance to act responsibly." Finn could practically hear the frown in Ms. Morales's voice. "Because I know you *are* capable of being trustworthy and responsible."

"Thanks for the vote of confidence." There was a thud that might have been Natalie slamming the refrigerator door.

"I do want you to stay out of that tunnel," Ms. Morales said, and her voice was hesitant now. Maybe even scared. "You're right—it does worry me. I tried to find out about the design of that house—I looked for building permits filed at the courthouse and everything. But there's nothing. It doesn't make sense. I think I'm missing something."

Finn held his breath. If he'd been Natalie, he would have spilled everything right there. He would have opened his mouth, and the whole story of the automatic text messages and the coded letter and the website butterflies and the secret lever in the panic room would have tumbled out, whether he wanted it to or not. Even now, even though Ms. Morales wasn't *his* mom, he was tempted to round the corner into the kitchen and tell all.

But Natalie was just yelling at her mom.

"Yeah, Mom, you're missing a *heart*, because of how you treated Dad. And me. You always treat me like you think I'm going to make the same mistakes you made and ruin my life like you did and . . ."

Natalie came dashing out of the kitchen and smashed directly into Finn.

And then Ms. Morales was there, too, right behind Natalie, bending down to take Finn by the shoulders and say in the fakest, heartiest voice of all, "Oh, Finn, we didn't hear you get up. Did you just come downstairs?"

Her eyes begged him to say yes, and Natalie's gaze was as intense as lasers. Finn was pretty sure Natalie was trying to say, *No matter what you heard, don't tell Mom anything! Lie if you have to!*

"I just got here," Finn mumbled obediently. Then,

because he thought anybody could have told he was lying, he added a normal-Finn line, "Is it breakfast time yet?"

"Almost!" Ms. Morales said, her voice flooded with fake cheer. "Just give me a few more minutes!"

"Hey, Finn," Natalie said too loudly. "Why don't you come outside and wait for the bus with me? Then when the bus comes, you can go back inside, and Mom will have your breakfast ready."

"Th-that's a good idea," Ms. Morales said, as if she was stunned that Natalie had suggested it.

"Okay," Finn said.

Natalie slid a yogurt container, a granola bar, and a water bottle into her backpack and hoisted it to her shoulder. Finn trailed after her, out the front door.

As soon as the door shut behind them, Natalie asked, "You heard everything, didn't you?"

"Yep."

Natalie reached down and unbuttoned and rebuttoned two buttons of Finn's shirt. Evidently he had done it wrong.

"Mom's not really that much of a monster," she said apologetically. "It's just, she's the one who asked for the divorce, and that just . . . just . . ."

"I don't think your mom's a monster," Finn said. "At least you *have* your mom."

Emma or Chess would have immediately hugged him and said, "We will, too! Soon! We're going to get our mom back!" Natalie just kind of froze.

And somehow, this morning, Finn liked that better.

"I didn't think you took the bus," he said as they started walking down the long, long sidewalk toward the street. "I thought your mom drove you."

"She does, except when we have other kids staying here," Natalie said. "Which . . . probably makes me selfish that I get mad about that."

"Sorry," Finn said.

Natalie laughed. "You could make it up to me by telling Mom you're craving carne asada. She also always serves really boring meals when we have kids here, and that bugs me, too."

"Is that food?" Finn asked. "I bet I would crave it, if I knew what it was! I like food!"

And then Natalie really did hug him. A little bit.

"I don't mind having *you* around," she said. Finn didn't know if she meant that about just him, or about Emma and Chess, too. He decided not to ask.

"Nothing happened after I fell asleep last night, did it?" he asked. Which was a stupid question, because he'd made Emma and Chess promise to wake him up the instant they solved the code. In the bright sunlight, with Natalie, it was possible to ask a little more. "Or . . . maybe . . . did someone find those kids in Arizona?"

Somehow it seemed like if the kids in Arizona were found, it would be a sign that he and Chess and Emma would get their mom back, too.

"No . . . ," Natalie said. She kicked at the mulch that lined the sidewalk. "But, Finn . . ."

"What?" Finn said. She wouldn't look at him. "You know something! Tell me!"

Natalie's face twisted and untwisted, like she was trying to decide.

"Okay," she said. "I haven't said anything to Emma or Chess, because they're all 'We've got to solve the code! That's all we can think about!' And they're already upset. You know I've been using earbuds, so none of you have to hear . . . what I'm working on."

Finn knew what she wasn't saying: *So you don't have to hear the voice that sounds like your mother's but isn't.*

"But I have been looking at everything I can about the kids in Arizona and their parents," Natalie went on. "And—did you see that the mother's name in Arizona is also Kate? Just like your mom's. For some reason, it wasn't in the original news coverage. But that woman in Arizona looks almost exactly like your mom *and* has the same first name."

"No," Finn said. His mind couldn't take that in. He

wasn't going to ask if that other mom had the same birthday, too, just like her kids had the same birthdays as Chess, Emma, and Finn. He couldn't. His voice turned accusing. "Are you sure you read it right? Or heard it right?"

He tried to think if he'd seen or heard the Arizona mother's name before, either on his mother's laptop that first day while she stood in their kitchen, or on the laptop he used in Ms. Morales's office two nights ago. He'd been too distracted both times.

"Finn, I'm sure," Natalie said. "And . . . I used facial recognition software that Mom has on her computer. Emma helped me get a photo from your mom's phone and I took a screenshot of the other woman. And that software thinks your mom and the Arizona mom are the same person exactly."

Finn absorbed that. Wouldn't facial recognition software think identical twins were the same person?

But why would identical twins both be named Kate?

He thought of a better question.

"Which one?" Finn asked. His voice cracked. "I mean, does the computer think my mom is Kate Gustano, or that the Arizona mom is . . . is Kate Greystone?"

He could barely even say his mother's name.

"I'm not sure," Natalie said, squinting at him thoughtfully. "That software doesn't give an identity by name, it just says they're the same person. But maybe if I can find a better program, like what police use, then . . ."

"My mom's not a criminal!" Finn protested.

"That's not what I'm saying." Natalie patted his shoulder. "I just . . . I have a theory. But you and your brother and sister aren't going to like it."

"Try me," Finn said. He puffed out his chest a little, hoping that made him seem older and better prepared for whatever Natalie was going to say.

"Well, sometimes grown-ups who say they're just traveling a lot for their jobs actually have . . . two different families, in two different places," Natalie said. "They lie. I mean, usually it's fathers who do this, not moms, and if the birthdays aren't lies, too, then either you or those kids in Arizona are adopted—and now that I'm saying this out loud, it sounds kind of crazy, but—"

"Natalie, my mom travels for her job maybe once or twice a year!" Finn exploded. "Just one or two days at a time! She's almost *always* with us, except . . ." He couldn't say it, but surely Natalie understood that he meant, *Except now.* "My mom doesn't have another family! She doesn't lie! She isn't a criminal! You can stop thinking about any theories that make her a bad person!"

"Okay," Natalie said softly.

And then she hugged him again, almost exactly like

Chess or Emma would. As soon as she let go, Finn turned around, to face away from the street. If the bus came now, he wouldn't want anyone on it to see how close he was to tears. But now he was facing the house. Something moved in the huge picture window in the front—it was Ms. Morales stepping off to the side, behind the drapes.

She'd been watching them. And it was funny: When Mom watched out their front window while Finn, Emma, and Chess were waiting for their bus, it always made him feel safe and secure. Loved. Protected.

Having Ms. Morales watch him and Natalie now—and dart behind the drapes so he didn't see her—just scared him more.

What was Ms. Morales afraid of?

What if it was something that even a grown-up couldn't protect him from?

THIRTY-FIVE

EMMA

"Ten thousand failures," Emma muttered.

"Huh?" Chess said, swiveling in his chair beside her. They were back in Ms. Morales's office for their third night in a row of trying to solve Mom's code with her own words. "You think we've already tried that many possibilities?"

"No, I'm trying to remember a Thomas Edison quote." Emma tapped her pencil against her jaw. "Something about how he didn't fail ten thousand times, he just found ten thousand ways that didn't work. Or took ten thousand steps to success, or something like that."

"Oh," Chess said.

He didn't look any more encouraged than Emma felt. Back *before*—that was how Emma had started thinking about everything in her life up to the last moment she'd seen her mother—Emma had loved reading and hearing and thinking about inventors and scientists and mathematicians who'd overcome all sorts of obstacles on their way to some brilliant new breakthrough. The obstacles made their stories even more exciting.

She'd never known how exhausting all that failure was.

How discouraging.

And, really, Edison had tried so hard just because he wanted to beat other inventors, and be more famous. It wasn't *his* mother's life on the line.

I don't know that my mother's life is on the line, either, Emma reminded herself. Even exhausted and discouraged and scared, she wasn't going to start treating something like a fact if she wasn't sure.

But this *felt* like a life-and-death issue.

Mom loves us so much, she wouldn't go off and leave us like this if it weren't incredibly, terribly important, Emma told herself.

If this wasn't life and death, it was really, really close.

That was why Emma had been working on her mother's code as close to around the clock as she could. She'd carried notebooks full of notations to school with her, and worked on the code every time the teacher looked away. She'd worked through recess and lunch.

"New project, Emma?" her math teacher, Mrs. Gunderson, had asked fondly as Emma walked to gym class scratching off letters and symbols in her notebook. "Is this going to be the one that wins the Nobel Prize?"

Emma liked Mrs. Gunderson—she liked anyone who liked math. But it was amazing how close Emma had come to breaking down into tears at that moment. She wanted to shout back at Mrs. G.: *This isn't some cutesy little-kid-pretending-to-be-a-mathematician project! This isn't the kind of thing I used to do! This is REAL!*

Would Mrs. G. have used that tone with Katherine Johnson at NASA when Katherine Johnson was calculating how to get John Glenn up into space and back down again without crashing?

Would Mrs. G. have smiled so patronizingly at the Enigma codebreakers during World War II who were trying to figure out how to stop Nazi subs from sinking Allied ships?

Even way back in the 1940s, those codebreakers had had early versions of computers to help them. Emma was pretty sure there was a way to set up a secret computer program to test various keys to Mom's code, but it seemed like it would take too long to figure that out.

Or to make completely sure it was private and secure. Mom always made a big deal about that.

"'Anytime you put something online, you have to ask yourself if you want the whole world to see it,'" Emma said aloud, quoting Mom. "That's another saying we should test."

"Are you sure it isn't, '*Whenever* you put something online . . .'?" Chess asked.

And that was the problem with Mom's sayings. They weren't *exact*. Sometimes Mom had said "Anytime," and sometimes she'd said "Whenever." That meant Emma needed to try both versions, writing out the complete phrase, and then listing, *a, b, c, d, e* . . . etc. above each letter.

And what if the key to the code was actually "Every time you put something online . . . "?

Maybe Emma was wrong about everything. Maybe Chess was, too, and they weren't even trying the right approach.

Emma's pencil snapped against her paper, sending the tip spinning into the air.

"Maybe you should take a break," Natalie said from across the room, where she had twin earbud cords snaking out of her hair down to her laptop. She also had Finn curled up beside her, with his head drooping against her arm—he'd fallen asleep an hour ago.

"No," Emma said stubbornly. "We have to solve this."

"Well then, at least take some time to look at the books I brought from your mom's office," Natalie tried again. "Maybe that will help."

"No, thanks," Chess said, and Emma was glad that he spoke for both of them. She would have left off the *thanks.*

It bugged Emma that Natalie had been at the Greystones' house without Chess, Emma, and Finn. Ms. Morales had had Natalie take care of Rocket because, Ms. Morales said, that gave them more time to have fun with their special Friday-night treat: a trip to Dave & Buster's.

Emma hadn't had fun at Dave & Buster's. Ms. Morales had insisted she leave her notebooks in the car, so Emma had been reduced to writing potential code keys on napkins and awards tickets, and stuffing them in her pocket.

Surprisingly, this had also proved that she was better at Skee-Ball when she didn't look while throwing the ball than when she did.

But all afternoon, anytime Ms. Morales was out of earshot, Natalie had made a big deal about how she'd smuggled out the two books from the Boring Room bookshelves: the dictionary and the old computer manual. It was like Natalie thought *she* had to be the one who provided a way to solve Mom's code.

"I thought they might be important," Natalie had said. "I looked up codes online, and there's one type where you can use a dictionary or some other book."

"Right—if the person who made the code gives you a page number and another number that tells you how far down on the page the key word is," Emma retorted, almost as if they were arguing. "Mom didn't leave us any numbers!"

Now Emma did at least reach across the desk and absent-mindedly rifle her finger across the pages of the dictionary. Just because it was Mom's. Then she moved her hand to trace the crooked-heart picture on the back of Mom's phone.

"What you should have brought us was the heart picture from inside Mom's desk," Emma told Natalie. "*That* might have been a clue."

"You said it was just a copy of the picture on Mom's phone," Chess reminded her. "Do you think the *original* picture is a clue? Finn drew it on Mom's phone case three years ago! How could it be a clue?"

"I don't know!" Emma snapped back at him. "Doesn't it feel like we don't know anything?"

Chess stared back at Emma. His eyes looked watery, as if he might be on the verge of crying.

Or maybe it was just that Emma was seeing him through watery eyes.

"We're all tired," Natalie said, in a surprisingly gentle tone. "I don't think we're going to figure out anything else tonight. Tomorrow's Saturday. Why don't we all just go to bed, and then tomorrow morning—"

"No!" Emma and Chess said together, both of them shouting at Natalie.

Natalie jerked her head back at the force of their words. That must have yanked her earbud cord out of her laptop, because suddenly Mom's voice surrounded them: "—I'm sure they're taking care of each other. Ever since they were born, I've told my kids, 'You'll always have each other.' I'm an only child myself, so—"

Natalie scrambled to plug the metal tip of her earbud cord back into its port, and the Mom voice went silent.

"Sorry!" she cried. "I'm so sorry! There's a new interview with the Gustano parents out tonight, and I was listening to that, and . . . I guess this destroys our theory about your mother and Mrs. Gustano being twins, right? I mean, if she was telling the truth about being an only child, and—"

"Play it again," Emma said.

"Emma, we don't have to torture ourselves," Chess said. "We can let Natalie—"

"Play it again!" Emma insisted.

Natalie fumbled with the laptop.

"I'm not sure I'm rewinding to the right place, but—"

Mom's voice sounded again: "—since they were born I've told my kids, 'You'll always have each other . . .'"

Emma flipped over Mom's phone and, fingers flying, punched in the code and opened the texting app.

"Mom told us the code key from the very beginning!" Emma cried. "We've had it all along!"

"What are you talking about?" Natalie asked.

Emma pointed at a clump of words on the screen of Mom's phone. Natalie was too far away to see, but Chess leaned in close, then away.

"Emma, it hurts to look at that text message, Mom saying she'll never see us again, ever," he began, choking on his own words. "Do you really think . . ."

Emma tapped the sentence that began *Tell them . . . ,* and Chess went silent. Meanwhile, Emma was counting.

". . . twenty-four, twenty-five, TWENTY-SIX! It's perfect! With the apostrophe and the period, 'You'll always have each other" has exactly twenty-six characters, just like the alphabet, and that is something Mom says all the time, and if she'd only wanted to remind us of that, she would have said, 'Tell them *they'll* always have each other,' so this has to be it! It has to!"

"Try it," Chess said.

Dimly, Emma was aware that Natalie eased Finn's head onto the arm of the couch and left him behind to come over and watch Emma writing down letters. Dimly, Emma heard Natalie ask Chess as he stood up and leaned in to watch, too, "Do you think this will explain the Gustano kidnappings, too, or just your mother going away?"

Dimly, Emma heard Chess mutter, "Let's see if it works at all, first."

It will work, Emma told herself. *This time I know it!*

"You'll always have each other" wasn't a perfect code key, because some letters duplicated—there were four *a*'s, three *l*'s, and three *e*'s, and so that meant anytime Emma encountered one of those in the coded message, she had to write down a variety of choices, and then go back and figure out which was correct from the context. She decided to focus on just one sentence at a time.

"Yes!" she screamed. "It makes sense! It's real words!"

"Let us see!" Natalie demanded.

Emma kind of wanted to show only Chess first, but she was too excited to care. She slid her arm back, revealing the deciphered words in a sea of cross-outs and false starts.

Only then did the meaning of the sentence before her start to sink in:

How much do you know about alternate worlds?

THIRTY-SIX

CHESS

"Alternate . . . worlds?" Chess repeated numbly.

Natalie was typing on her phone.

"I got the definition," she said. "They're parallel universes. Places that could be almost completely identical to our world, or very, very different. And there's something about how they go along with theories of quantum mechanics, blah, blah, blah . . . an infinite variety of worlds existing alongside ours, but—"

"We know what alternate worlds are!" Emma exploded.

She was breathing hard, her eyes wild, her cheeks flushed, her hair held back only by a pencil she'd stuck behind her ear two hours ago and clearly forgotten about. She looked feverish, or maybe even delirious.

For himself, Chess only felt dizzy and confused. He knew what the word "alternate" meant. He knew what "worlds" were. Together, the two words were harder to grasp.

"Maybe if we . . . translate more of the code . . . ?" he began.

"Good idea," Natalie said.

Emma opened her mouth, shut it, and picked up her pencil again. She held one finger beside the computer screen, inching the fingernail forward to touch every letter.

"So that becomes a *w*, then an *e*, then . . . ," she muttered.

Chess knew he should offer to help his sister; maybe he should suggest they take turns with alternating words?

Oh, alternating. Alternate . . .

Chess felt dizzy again. His thoughts weren't making sense. He kept his mouth shut.

Emma dropped her pencil and held up the paper she'd been writing on.

"Mom's next sentence is 'We all came from an alternate world, and I had to go back,'" she announced. "Could that be right?"

She sounded like she doubted her own ability to read.

"'Two parallel universes might start with only one difference separating them,'" Natalie read from her phone. "'Some scientists theorize that a new universe might split off every time anyone makes a decision, creating a separate world for each possible choice. Then the differences multiply. Or they might be erased. So if you walk into an ice-cream shop, there might be one universe created where you pick chocolate ice cream, one where you choose vanilla, one where you choose strawberry. . . .'"

"Nobody ever chooses vanilla or strawberry!" Emma protested, as if that actually mattered.

Maybe not in this universe, Chess wanted to joke. He was seized by an awful desire to laugh. He wanted Emma to shout out, *Ha, ha! This was just a joke! Did you think I was serious? Mom's coded messages actually says . . .*

He couldn't think what he wanted Mom's coded message to say. He didn't even know what was possible.

Were alternate worlds possible?

"Why are we talking about ice cream?" Chess asked. "Mom did not leave us because of ice cream!"

"We don't know that!" Emma said, waving her hands helplessly at Chess. "Any little decision could change anything!" She blinked, dazed, as if struggling to go back to being her usual, logical self. "Like ice cream . . . This isn't about Mom, but here's how it could be a big deal. Say you pick vanilla instead of chocolate, and so the scooper guy has to go back to the walk-in freezer that much sooner to get a new tub of vanilla, and that's where he is when a robber comes in with a gun, and so he isn't shot and killed. . . . Or maybe it's the other way around, and he *doesn't* go back for the next tub of chocolate ice cream as quickly, and so he's still at the counter when a robber comes in, and that's why he dies . . . just because of ice cream! So now there are two different worlds created from that one little decision, one where the scooper guy is alive, and one where he's dead. And, I don't know, maybe he was supposed to become president someday, but because he's dead in the one world, that means —"

"Can we stop using examples where people die?" Chess asked quietly.

Natalie looked up from her phone. Her gaze felt too sharp, too focused.

"We already know the difference between this world and, um, the other one," she said, as if that was supposed to make everything better. But then she bit her lip. "Part of it, anyway."

Chess could only stare at her. Even Emma stopped raving about ice cream.

"It's your mom," Natalie said. "Your mom and that woman in Arizona."

Emma clenched the arms of her chair so tightly that it seemed like she might leave dents.

"Explain," she whispered.

"Well, I don't know if this is what split the worlds, or just a, a consequence," Natalie said. "But . . . what if your mom and that Arizona mom are different versions of the same person?"

Chess recoiled. Mom was not a "version" of anyone. She was fully herself, totally unique. She was *Mom*.

Chess waited for Emma to start shouting about that—he *wanted* her to start shouting at Natalie. But Emma just gulped and held on to the chair even tighter. Now the color seemed to have drained from her face.

"Your mom and that Arizona mom look almost exactly alike," Natalie said. "They sound alike. They use some of the same expressions—'You'll always have each other'? And . . . they're both named Kate."

Chess hadn't known that part, but at this point, he didn't even care.

"So maybe, before the worlds split, your mom and the other woman were totally, one hundred percent the same person," Natalie said. "But the worlds did split—somehow. I'm a little fuzzy on how that could have happened. Maybe it's like . . . I don't know. Copying a picture on your phone, and editing the two versions differently?"

"Maybe the worlds split before Mom or that other woman were even born," Emma interrupted. Her breathing was more ragged than ever. "So they were always separate.

Did you ever think of that? Our mom is not just a copy!"

Chess wanted to cheer Emma on. But he felt too paralyzed to speak.

"Okay, okay," Natalie said, her hands out as if she were backing away from a dangerous animal. "You're right. We don't know *when* the worlds split. Maybe that's in the rest of the letter. But we *do* know there are two worlds, and two Kates. And one world's Kate marries a man named Arthur Gustano in Arizona. And the other marries a man named . . . what was your dad's name?"

Neither Emma nor Chess told her it was Andrew. Natalie kept talking anyway.

"Each woman still ends up having kids named Rochester, Emma, and Finn, on the exact same dates," she added. "So . . . is that the only really big difference between the two worlds? Who your mom married? And then did that lead to all the other differences? What state they lived in, and . . . ?"

And the fact that those other kids got kidnapped, and we didn't, Chess thought. *That's different, too.*

He couldn't quite follow what Natalie was saying. But he couldn't forget about the kidnappings.

What if that was *why* Mom wanted them to be in this world, instead of wherever they'd started out?

How could she have known ahead of time that the kidnappings were coming?

Chess sat down, because he was afraid he might fall over instead.

"It isn't possible to travel between two different alternate worlds!" Emma shouted. "All of this is just . . . hypothetical! Alternate worlds are just hypothetical!"

"Maybe they figured it out in the other world?" Natalie said. "Maybe you three and your mother were the first to make this kind of trip?"

Emma pressed her hands over her ears, like she was trying to shut out Natalie's words.

"This is not what I expected," she muttered. "It doesn't . . . I can't . . ."

Emma's brain must have been spinning as badly as Chess's. His thoughts were completely out of control.

"You have to translate the rest," Natalie said.

She sounded calm. Or at least, calm*er*. Natalie mostly just seemed excited to have finally solved the mystery. It wasn't her mom who was missing, in a completely different world. So of course Natalie could act like this was just a matter of deciphering code.

Natalie seemed to notice that neither Emma nor Chess were reaching for a pencil.

"I'll do it," she said.

Chess and Emma both watched dazedly as Natalie tilted

the computer screen so she could see the coded message better.

"*A*'s and *e*'s and *l*'s are tricky, because they could be lots of different letters," Emma explained weakly, pointing to her own scribblings.

"Got it," Natalie said.

She snatched up a pencil. Chess blinked, then felt amazed that he was capable of that much movement.

"We said we'd wake up Finn as soon as we solved the code," Chess told Emma. "As soon as we had an answer."

"Do we really have an answer yet?" Emma asked. "Do *you* understand this well enough to explain it to Finn?"

No, Chess thought.

He made no move toward his little brother. He just sat there watching Natalie scrawl letters onto paper. Emma unfroze a little, starting to point out to Natalie, "If that *h* translates into a *t*, that makes that word 'this.' And that word's got to be 'old' . . ."

Chess couldn't have begun to translate any code right now. His brain still felt like an echo chamber: *Alternate worlds. Mom says we're from an alternate world. So Emma, Finn, Mom, and I don't belong here at all?*

It was true that he'd always felt different from the other kids at school. But he'd always thought that was because he was the only kid he knew whose father was dead. The only kid he knew who'd had to comfort his crying mother when he was only four, and sad himself.

The only kid he knew who'd had to become a father figure for his little brother and sister, when he was barely older than them himself.

Chess glanced over at Finn, draped across Ms. Morales's office couch and still soundly asleep. One arm dangled off the edge of the couch, and his mouth was open; that made it look like he was both reaching for and calling out to Chess.

"I think we still have to wake Finn," Chess said, finally answering Emma's question out loud.

He got up and stumbled toward the couch. He slid his arms under Finn's neck and knees and lifted.

"Finny?" he said softly, cradling his brother against his chest. "Finn? We've got good news. . . ."

He didn't actually know yet if it was good or not. It didn't feel that way.

"Mmm," Finn murmured, which could have been the start of saying *Mom* . . . or just a protest at being disturbed.

Chess carried Finn back to where Emma and Natalie were working. Finn snuggled his face against Chess's neck, as if he thought this was just a new place to sleep. His legs dangled awkwardly. Chess was tall for his age and Finn was small for his, but it still wasn't comfortable for a twelve-year-old to carry an eight-year-old.

"Finn?" Chess said. "You need to wake up and—"

"What? Did we mess up somewhere?" Natalie cried, stabbing her pencil against the paper. "None of this is making any sense now!"

"That would be an *a*, that would be a *b*—oh no!" Emma clutched her head, smashing her hair down. "You're right, Natalie. It looks like Mom changed the code for the next section! We can't read the rest! Not without figuring out another key!"

"But you got some of it?" Chess asked hopefully.

"This," Natalie said, handing him a page full of scratch-outs and crooked letters. Natalie's calligraphy-like printing mixed together with Emma's mad-scientist-style scrawl; even the pretty lettering got messier and messier, the farther he looked down the page.

Chess shifted the weight of Finn's drowsy body to the side and hesitantly began: "'I don't . . .'" He got stuck on the next word, because it had too many scratch-outs and erasures. Emma snatched the paper from his hand.

"Here, I'll read it," she said, her voice harsh. Chess didn't think she was really mad at him, though. "Mom wrote:

"'I don't know how old you are, reading this. I see you

as eight and ten and twelve, but maybe I made this code too hard, and you are older now. Maybe even much older. So it is hard to know how to explain.

"'The world the four of us came from was a dangerous place. Your father and I were part of a group trying to make it better by exposing the lies of the people in power. But powerful people like to stay in power, and the truly evil ones will do anything to keep control. Our leaders made it illegal to criticize them—or even to reveal the truth about what they were doing. We thought we could do our work in secret, and eventually the truth would win. But then they killed your father, and—'"

"Wait—what? 'Killed'?" Chess interrupted. His legs collapsed beneath him. Still clutching Finn, he almost missed the chair. "*Killed*? Dad's car wreck wasn't an accident? And Mom never told me?"

His ears rang; his vision seemed to go in and out.

"Chess, you were—what?—*four* when it happened?" Natalie asked gently.

Chess tightened his arms around Finn, who was still soundly asleep. He resisted the impulse to cover Finn's ears, so he wouldn't hear. And Finn was eight.

"But . . . now," he managed to say. "Now I'm twelve, and Mom—"

"And Mom is telling you now," Emma said. Her gaze was so steady.

So much like Mom's.

Weakly, Chess lifted his hand, motioning for Emma to continue.

She cleared her throat, and read on in a husky voice:

"'. . . killed your father, and I knew I had to leave. To save the three of you. But I couldn't just abandon everyone else I cared about, everything I knew, everything I could help with. So I made a bargain . . . a dangerous one. I kept up my work from here. But I thought the three of you would be safe. I didn't think anyone could follow me to this world.

"'But some of our enemies did. Just now.

"'I'd always known I should never attempt to find my doppelgänger here in this world. I tried very hard to make sure that our paths never crossed. That was part of the reason I worked so hard to keep my own name and face and identity out of any public records. If you looked up the records for our house, it wouldn't even say that I'm the one who owns it.'"

Chess looked over at Natalie, whose face flushed. Evidently she'd known that already. What else had she tried to look up about Mom, only to find . . . nothing?

Emma was still reading Mom's words:

"'I tried to keep you kids' identity private, too. That's why I always signed the forms saying your names or pictures couldn't be used on the school website; that was why I was always so careful about what I let you do online. I tried to keep all of us as invisible as possible. Just in case.

"'It never occurred to me that my secrecy would endanger my doppelgänger. But I covered my tracks too well. So when the bad people came, they found her and her family, not me. They thought she *was* me. After all, our fingerprints matched, other details matched—I'm sure they thought the details that didn't fit were just part of my attempts to hide. Those kids in Arizona were kidnapped because of me, because the bad people thought those kids were the three of you. The bad people must have thought that was the only way to lure me back.

"'I know it's a trap. But I can't leave those innocent kids in danger, because of me. I can't leave those other parents grieving. I think I know a way to rescue the kids without endangering myself. I have to try.

"'I've always kept a supply of food and money—all in small bills that wouldn't be traced—to share with people suffering back in the other world.'" Emma glanced up. "That's—"

"What we saw in the panic room," Natalie finished for her.

"Go on," Chess urged, because he couldn't care about canned food and dollar bills when he felt such dread rising inside him. The word "killed" still echoed in his ears.

And if that's what they did to Dad, then Mom . . . Mom . . .

Emma peered back to the paper in her hand. Chess noticed that her hand was shaking.

"Let's see, '. . . suffering . . . ,' oh, yes. 'Cash is important in that world, because so much is done in secret. I thought if I had a lot more money, I could hire some of the people I'd helped, to turn around and help me rescue the Gustano kids. I had to cash out your college savings—'"

"That's what Finn's friend saw her carrying out of that bank!" Natalie exclaimed. "Hear that, Finn? Your mom didn't rob a bank!"

Finn barely grunted in his sleep. Emma glared at Natalie.

"We already knew that," Emma practically snarled. "*We* never thought she was a robber."

Chess didn't care about banks or money, either.

"That's not the end, is it?" he asked. He had to steady himself by holding on to Ms. Morales's desk.

"She goes on to say, 'I'm really sorry about the college accounts. I'll figure out how to build them up again when I get back,'" Emma said. Her eyes flickered; she was reading ahead. "But, Chess—"

"She says she's coming back!" Chess blurted, and to his

own ears, he sounded as young as Finn. He fought to regain control. "That's all that matters."

"Oh, Chess," Emma said. Her face had gone mournful and still, like stone.

Chess waited, unable to speak. Finally Emma lowered her head and read in a choked voice:

"'If I've been gone long enough for you to get this letter and decode and read this, that means I was wrong, and I failed completely. I'm so sorry. You must never try to follow me, because . . .'" Emma gulped, and finished in a whisper.

"'Because it's too late.'"

THIRTY-SEVEN

FINN

Finn heard the word "never." He heard the words "too late." They slipped into a dream he'd been having about playing Trouble and Jenga and other games with Mom. Part of the time they were playing in their regular house, and part of the time they were playing in the abandoned house he'd found after going through the secret tunnel with Chess, Emma, and Natalie.

And then Finn was waking up, lifting his head from where it bobbed against Chess's shoulder.

Maybe Chess had jerked back suddenly, and that had jolted Finn awake.

"What's too late?" he mumbled sleepily.

He opened his eyes to see Chess, Emma, and Natalie staring back at him in alarm.

"Never mind," Chess said, pressing Finn's head back toward his own shoulder. "Don't worry about it. Shh, shh, shh . . . go back to sleep."

Being told to go to sleep always made Finn wider awake.

He kept his head up and shoved Chess's hand away. He saw Emma slide a piece of paper behind her back.

"What's that?" he asked. He started squirming his way out of Chess's grasp to reach for the paper. "Emma! Did you solve the code? And you were going to surprise me? That's great! You're a genius!"

"Finn, it's . . . complicated," Emma said. She kept the paper away from him.

"We're still trying to understand it ourselves," Chess said. "It may not be something you need to . . . know. Yet."

Was anything more annoying than big kids and adults telling little kids they weren't old enough to know something?

"But it's something about Mom, right?" Finn said. He told himself it was because he'd just awakened that he sounded so whiny and, well, little. Babyish.

"It's scary," Natalie said, as if that settled it. "You don't want to know. We'll take care of things. Emma, Chess, and me. We promise."

Finn slid down to stand on his own two feet. He leaned away from Chess, to gaze toward the laptop and the papers on the desk behind Emma and Natalie.

"What are al-ter-nate worlds?" he asked, because those were the words he could see.

Emma sagged back against the side of the desk.

"We have to tell him that much," she said. "It's not fair otherwise. Finn, they're places like our world, with a few differences. Or, there could be lots of differences, but they all start with one different decision, and . . ."

For such a smart person, Emma never explained things very well. Or maybe Finn's problem was that he'd been asleep a moment ago, and his brain wasn't fully awake yet. He blinked, still not entirely sure he was really with Chess, Emma, and Natalie in Natalie's mom's office, rather than with Mom at home. Or in the boarded-up, abandoned house from his dream.

That dream . . . I was in both our house and that other house in the dream, but it was almost like . . .

It was almost like the two houses had been the same. In the dream, Finn sat in the same places to push down the bubble over the Trouble dice; the rays of the sun hit at the same angle over Mom's shoulder as she pulled out the wooden Jenga blocks.

"Oh!" Finn shouted, so loudly that Chess winced. Chess had started to bend down, so Finn's mouth was right by Chess's ear. Finn tried to speak a little more softly, going on, but his voice still rose in excitement. "You mean like how our house is built just like the house we found when we walked through the tunnel, only we live in our house, so it's got furniture and everything, but nobody lives in that other house, so it's empty? Is that how you mean two places can be the same but different?"

"Finn, that other house was just—" Chess began, but Natalie interrupted.

"Guys—he's right! He's exactly right!" she said. "I just realized—I think that other house did have the same floor plan as yours, at least, what we saw of it. The windows were boarded up, but they were in the same locations, the basement stairs came out at the exact same spot on the first floor, the kitchen was in the same place—believe me, my mom has dragged me through enough empty houses she's trying to sell. I *know* houses. But . . ." She stopped looking so excited. "Lots of neighborhoods have cookie-cutter houses, because it's cheaper for builders to just use the same design over and over again. It doesn't mean anything."

"How many of those houses are connected by a secret

tunnel?" Emma challenged. "One that you reach by going into a panic room and flipping a switch and making it spin? Where you feel disoriented the whole time you're in the tunnel? This has to be *why* that tunnel didn't make sense, and we couldn't find that house on any online map. Finn, you just solved everything! When we went to that other house, we were in an alternate world! And we just have to go back to find Mom and rescue her!"

THIRTY-EIGHT

EMMA

Emma grabbed Finn by the shoulders and started jumping up and down, like kids on the playground whose team had just scored a goal or a touchdown or a home run.

"I did?" Finn said. "We do?"

He didn't even sound awake yet, but he joined her in jumping and dancing around. His hair flopped up and down, side to side—even his hair was dancing.

Emma reached out, ready to pull Chess and Natalie into the celebration, too. But Chess pulled back.

"Emma, Mom said *not* to find her. She says it's too late," Chess moaned. "We did all this work for nothing. Mom sent us that letter for nothing. Or just so we didn't always wonder, I guess."

Emma stopped dancing. But only for a moment. Then she started jumping again.

"We got the letter early, remember?" she asked.

Now all the other kids stared at her.

"Mom was sending us that letter in the *mail*," Emma argued. "Maybe she even gave it to somebody and said, 'Don't mail this until next week,' so it wouldn't get to us very fast. She didn't know Finn and Rocket were going to find her phone in the dresser drawer that very first day, which made us search her computers right away. I bet she just left this letter on her laptop as a backup, in case the letter got lost in the mail. She knew we would search and search and search."

Especially me, Emma thought. *Mom knew I would never give up.*

She glanced at the coded portion of the letter they hadn't translated yet, the part that required finding a different key to break the code. Had Mom made that code even harder? Was that her way of making them wait until they were older to know what it said?

Maybe that wouldn't ever matter. If—no, *when*—they got Mom back, they could just ask her directly.

"We're smarter—and luckier—than Mom thought, so we *can* go and rescue her," Emma told Chess.

Chess was still shaking his head.

"It's dangerous," he said. "Mom wants us to be safe. And we really don't know. . . . We don't know anything about the alternate world, if that was the alternate world, except that Mom says it's a dangerous place. And all we saw was that empty house and the tall fences and . . . and those boys Ms. Morales got so upset about. . . ."

"And the boys said there was a criminal who'd been trapped and captured because of some kidnapped kids!" Emma said. Everything was falling into place in her mind. "Just like Mom said the bad people from the alternate world used the kids from Arizona as a 'lure,' and she had to rescue them. Chess—that criminal who was captured in the alternate world—what if that's actually *Mom*? Not that she's really a criminal, but if they have bad laws . . . The people from the alternate world think the Gustano kids are hers. And . . ." Now the ideas in Emma's brain were working like a tidal wave, everything flowing together and growing by the minute. "And those boys told us the 'criminal' was going to be tried and sentenced on Saturday! We *know* she'll be safe until then. But after that . . ."

"Saturday's tomorrow," Finn said solemnly, as if he was the only one who could have figured that out.

Chess's expression was still so doubtful, it seemed he didn't even trust the days of the week.

"But we don't even know where or what time on Saturday," he argued. "Or—"

"But can't we find out?" Natalie asked. Emma whirled to look in the older girl's direction. Natalie had one eyebrow cocked, and the beginnings of a smile on her face. "Those boys said there were signs with information about the criminal on practically every street corner."

Emma reached out and hugged Natalie.

"You're right! You're right!" Emma said. "So we get your mom to take us back to our house and we go through the tunnel and we walk around to look for a sign. And that will tell us where to find Mom. It's simple!"

THIRTY-NINE

CHESS

It wasn't simple.

Chess fell asleep Friday night feeling like he had a weight pressing down on his heart, and he woke up Saturday morning feeling like the weight had done nothing but grow overnight.

Mom wants me to keep Emma and Finn safe, he thought.

But how could they *not* try to rescue Mom, if there was any chance that was possible?

Chess slipped out of bed and tiptoed into Emma's room. She was still sound asleep in the dim morning light—four late nights in a row had taken their toll. He thought he'd have to quietly rummage through her suitcase to find what he wanted, but one ray of sunlight came in through the blinds and showed him exactly what he was looking for: Emma had Mom's cell phone clutched in her hand, pressed against her cheek.

It looked like she'd fallen asleep trying to call for help.

Chess blinked, and another image slipped into his head: Emma at two or three, clutching her "lovey." Other little kids might have had a blanket or a stuffed animal as their lovey, but Emma had carried around a piece of paper like it was her favorite thing ever. And of course *her* favorite "lovey" paper had been covered in numbers.

Numbers written in Dad's firm script.

Chess froze, even as he held his hand out toward Emma. He hadn't thought about Emma's paper lovey in years. It didn't seem fair that he could remember that so well, when so many of his other memories felt so slippery. He shook his head, trying to clear it. Dad was dead, and Mom was in danger, and what was Chess supposed to do now?

Chess reached down and gently tugged Mom's cell phone out of Emma's grasp. Emma stretched out her fingers, still reaching for what she'd lost, and she let out a soft, distressed, "Unhf . . ."

But she didn't open her eyes.

I'll bring it back, Chess wanted to tell her. *Just give me a minute.*

Chess tiptoed back into his own room.

As soon as he was inside the doorway, he typed the unlock code into the phone. He'd watched Emma do it enough times now that he knew it, too.

"Okay, Joe," he whispered, as if he could talk to the unknown person he'd heard his mother argue with on the phone in the middle of the night, right before she went away. "It'd be really great if you tried to call back. Right. Now."

The phone stayed silent and dead in his hands. He opened Mom's call history, and it was just as empty as before. He checked her texts—avoiding the row of fake ones she'd set to send out automatically—and her email. Unless the message from the pediatrician's office about Finn's eight-year-old checkup had a hidden meaning, the phone contained nothing new, nothing helpful.

Why had Chess thought that it might, just because another eight hours had passed since the last time he'd looked?

"Think we should wake up Finn and Emma and start Operation Let's Trick Mom?" Natalie's voice from the hallway made Chess jump.

"Natalie . . . Maybe . . . Those two get grumpy when they don't get enough sleep," Chess said. And even though he'd been at Natalie's house for days now—and talking to her and everything—his voice this morning came out sounding like he was still that flustered fifth grader who didn't know what to say when a sixth-grade girl said he was cute.

Or maybe he just sounded like he wanted to believe the only thing his little brother and sister needed protection against was not getting enough sleep.

"Do you think . . . ?" he began to ask Natalie. But he couldn't even figure out how he wanted to finish his sentence.

"That your mom's going to call you on that phone and tell you everything's going to be okay?" Natalie finished for him. "From a totally other dimension—or alternate world, or whatever it's called? *No.*"

Without even thinking about it, Chess tightened his grip on his mother's phone. The rigid edges cut into his hand.

"Maybe we should tell *your* mother what we found out," he said.

"About your mom being in an *alternate world*?" Natalie's voice cracked with incredulity. "She'd never believe us. She'd ground me for lying and, I don't know, have the three of you committed to a mental institution. She didn't even believe me when I told her I didn't know those boys on the other street Wednesday afternoon. When they literally weren't even from the same *universe* as me. We didn't talk about this last night, but don't you think those boys acted like they knew the Natalie Mayhew from their world? Do you think the other Natalie Mayhew is just like me or not? Am *I* one of the differences in that world?"

It kind of freaked Chess out to hear her talking about the alternate world like it was a fact. And—like it was something fun to speculate about.

"You—You're older than us," Chess stammered. "You've got to see. . . . This isn't just a game."

"No, it's about getting your mom back," Natalie said, her voice ringing with certainty. "And maybe those kid-napped kids, too. I *hope* we can rescue those kidnapped kids, too. This'll probably be the most important thing any of us do in our entire lives. We'll be heroes!"

Her eyes glowed, and her face was flushed with excitement. Maybe it wasn't a game to her, but it wasn't something she was afraid of, either.

Maybe that was because she wasn't a coward like Chess.

Or is it just because her parents are only divorced, not dead and in danger like mine? Chess wondered.

He let out a sigh that did nothing to relieve the pressure he felt on his lungs and heart.

"You wake up Finn," he said. "I'll get Emma."

"Operation Let's Trick Mom, here we come!" Natalie drummed her fingers against the wall, ending with a dramatic thump. "Mom doesn't have a clue what's about to happen."

"Neither do we," Chess whispered.

But Natalie was already gone, racing for Finn's room.

FORTY

FINN

Maybe I should be an actor when I grow up, Finn thought as he buckled his seat belt in Ms. Morales's SUV. *I am really good at this.*

Over breakfast, he'd made himself start thinking about how much he missed his mom. And then, even though Ms. Morales had gone out special that morning and gotten the exact kind of bagels and cream cheese Finn loved best, big globs of tears had started to form in his eyes. Then his lips began to quiver, and he'd pushed his plate away, claiming, "I'm not hungry." (When, duh, anyone who knew Finn would know that he was always hungry. Especially when he was really happy, because this was the day they were getting Mom back!)

And then Ms. Morales had started fussing over him—"Oh, do you want me to fix you eggs instead? Or something else?" And Finn had let loose with a loud wail: "I just want my mommy!"

He'd started listing all the things he missed about her, finally getting down to the smell of her clothes. And even though Chess missed his cue to say, "Yeah, sometimes when Mom's away, the only thing that makes Finn feel better is sitting in her closet, breathing in that smell," Natalie picked up on it, and pretended that she'd noticed Finn getting calmer in Mom's closet, and wasn't it better to try that than to have to listen to a hysterical eight-year-old over breakfast?

Maybe Finn and Natalie would be famous actors together someday.

After they got Mom back.

So now Ms. Morales was driving all four of the kids back to the Greystones' house. And even though Natalie was pretending to argue with her mom about going along ("Don't you know I have homework to do before I go over to Dad's this afternoon? Don't you know I have a life of my own, even if you keep trying to ruin it all the time?"), every time her mother looked away, Natalie kept turning around and winking and waggling her eyebrows at Finn, Emma, and Chess.

Finn sniffled and reached for Emma's hand, just in case Ms. Morales looked in her rearview mirror. Chess put his arm around Finn's shoulder. And maybe Chess was kind of good at acting himself, because the one-armed hug felt exactly like it did when Chess was really trying to comfort Finn.

Soon they were pulling up in front of the Greystone house. Ms. Morales turned to face Finn.

"You can sit in your Mom's closet for a little while," she said. "While Chess gets the poster board he needs for his science project and Emma gets the next book she wants in that series she's reading. Harry Potter, wasn't it?" These were excuses Chess and Emma had added for needing to go along to the house with Finn. Ms. Morales kind of had an odd gleam in her eye—maybe they'd piled it on a little thick? Was she getting suspicious?

Finn gulped in air, ready to distract her.

"I miss—"

"Yes, yes, we know," Ms. Morales said quickly. "You didn't let me finish. What I was going to say was, when you come back out, why don't you bring some shirt with you that smells especially like your mom? So you don't have to come back here the next time you want to, uh, sniff it?"

Like Natalie made me bring that teddy bear to act like it was my "lovey," that first day? Finn thought. *Ms. Morales is going to think I'm a total baby!*

Finn could live with that, if it got Mom back.

"O—kay," he said, making sure he paused in the middle of the word to sniffle again. And then he drew out the *aaay* part as if he was leading into more tears.

Chess, Emma, and Natalie all helped him out of the SUV, making it look like it took three of them just to make sure he could walk upright.

They got to the front door, and Finn was *really* happy about being just a few steps away from no longer having to walk all stooped-over and sad. As soon as they were in the house, he could run just as fast and excitedly down to the basement as he wanted. But then, just as Chess started pulling out his key, Natalie took an abrupt step back, almost falling off the front porch.

"Oh no," she said. "Ohhh no."

"What's wrong?" Finn asked. He glanced over his shoulder. "Your mom's staring at her phone right now. You don't have to keep acting mad."

Natalie didn't exactly look mad anymore. She stared at the doorframe looking more like she'd just seen a ghost. Was she still acting or not?

She brushed a finger against the crack between the door and its frame.

"It was right here . . . ," she murmured. "I'm sure of it."

"What are you talking about?" Chess asked.

Natalie teetered on the edge of the porch.

"Somebody's been here," she said. "Since yesterday. Somebody's been in your house."

FORTY-ONE

EMMA

“Explain,” Emma said. “How do you know that?”

She was not going to freak out about anything until she had all the facts. And then . . .

Well, get all the facts, and then see what you want to do.

“I left a piece of tape on the door,” Natalie said. “I got the idea from what the chaperones did on our Cedar Point trip the last day of sixth grade—they put tape over everyone’s hotel room door, so they’d know if anyone tried to sneak out. Or, at least, they *told* us that’s what they did.”

Emma almost got distracted thinking about how weird life must be in sixth grade. Almost.

"You tried to tape someone *in* our house?" Finn asked. "You thought a piece of Scotch tape would trap them there?"

"No," Natalie said. "I put the tape there after I came out, when I knew the house was empty. Just so I could see if someone came in or out while we were away. Like . . . if someone came back through the tunnel and out your front door."

Now that they knew the tunnel led to an alternate world, that idea was scarier than ever.

"Was it windy last night?" Emma asked. "Or stormy? Maybe the tape just blew away."

She hadn't been paying attention to the weather; all she'd been able to think about last night was Mom's code and the alternate world. She was so focused, she wasn't even sure what the weather was like *now*. (She glanced over her shoulder. The sun was out.)

Finn, Chess, and Natalie all made doubtful faces, as if none of them had been paying attention to the weather either.

"So there," Emma said. "Not seeing the tape—that doesn't prove someone was here. If the tape had still been there, still stuck to the door, that could have proved that no one opened the front door after you. But the proof doesn't work in both directions."

"I . . . guess," Natalie said, as if the words were being dragged out of her.

Chess opened the door, and they all stepped through. But Emma didn't race down to the basement the way she'd been planning. She stepped cautiously, looking around constantly. Would she notice anything amiss if someone had been there searching the house? The middle drawer of the coffee table stuck out just a little—maybe an eighth of an inch—but for all Emma knew, maybe it had been like that before.

"I, um, put tape over the door in the basement, too," Natalie said. "The one that leads to your Mom's office. What you all call the Boring Room."

"Well, let's go look at *that*," Finn said, with only a little of his usual bounce.

It took a lot out of him, pretending to cry for the past half hour, Emma told herself. *That's the only thing that's wrong.*

All four of them trooped down the stairs. Chess reached over and turned on the basement light.

"Meowr?"

It was only Rocket standing and stretching on the basement couch, but Emma jumped. She was pretty sure the others did, too.

Finn recovered first.

"You'd tell us if anybody sneaked into the house, right, Rocket?" Finn asked, bending down to pet the cat. "You're a good guard cat, aren't you, boy?"

Natalie walked toward the Boring Room door.

"None of us locked that door after we came back from the alternate world, did we?" Emma asked. She'd been too spooked to think about it herself. And besides, she hadn't wanted Ms. Morales to know about the key and its secret hiding place in the couch leg.

Nobody answered Emma. Nobody said anything as they watched Natalie run her hand across the top of the frame around the door leading to the Boring Room.

"This tape's gone, too," she said.

"There's no wind in the basement," Finn said, unnecessarily.

"But maybe it just fell," Emma argued. "Maybe it didn't stick very well, and then Rocket started playing with it—you know how he's always carrying ponytail rubber bands away when Mom or I drop them on the floor?"

"It was good tape," Natalie said. "I stuck it on there *hard*. And now it's completely gone. Like someone saw it and took it. *Not* your cat."

Emma still wanted to argue: *But this isn't* absolute *proof, is it? You can't be one hundred percent sure! There's a—what's it called?—margin of error, right?*

"We have to tell your mom," Chess said heavily, turning to Natalie. He sounded like an old man, maybe someone speaking with his dying breath.

Natalie lifted her chin defiantly, mimicking the same kind of head toss she constantly gave her mom.

"She wouldn't let us back into the house then," she said. "Not until the cops have examined every inch of the house. You think cops are going to believe anything we tell them about an alternate world?"

"What if the cops keep us out of the house for hours and then we really are too late going to rescue Mom?" Finn asked, in the same sorrowful, little-kid voice he'd been using all morning with Ms. Morales. Only this time, it was entirely real.

"Here's what we do," Emma said, surprised she could find her own voice. "We go into the alternate world, we find a sign on the nearest street corner that gives the information about Mom, and *then* we bring it back and show it to Ms. Morales. And tell her everything."

She saw Chess hesitate. And then she saw his shoulders slump—not as if she'd won the argument, but as if they'd both lost.

"Okay," he said. "We'll do that."

Natalie opened the door to the Boring Room, and they repeated the procedure from their last trip through the tunnel. Chess pressed the button hidden at the back of the bookcase—just with his finger this time, not his shoe. The doorway to the panic room/secret passageway/tunnel to the alternate world opened up, and Emma reached in to turn on the light.

"Should we leave the door open or shut?" Natalie asked.

No one answered. But no one pulled the door shut behind them, either.

"The lever was above the peanut butter shelf, right?" Finn asked.

It was like they were all trying to be brave, all trying to prove that they weren't worried about what was going to happen next.

"We should pay attention to everything," Emma suggested. "Count the number of times the panic room spins, or how many turns the tunnel takes, if it's nothing but a tunnel now, not a place that spins like it was the first time we went through here, and—"

And the room was already spinning. Emma had to grab a shelf to hold on once again, but this time she made sure she was facing the exact spot where the door back out to the Boring Room had been.

Watch for the door, she told herself. *Count how many times it passes.*

The spinning made her eyelids want to close, but Emma reached up with her free hand and held her right eye open.

Surely we've made a complete rotation—why haven't I seen the door yet?

A moment later, she thought, *Did we maybe pass it, and I forgot to count? So let's just say it's been one, uh . . .*

Emma couldn't quite remember what number came after one.

The room spun faster.

Are we going forward? Sideways? Backward?

Emma thought those words, and then wasn't entirely sure what they meant.

And then the spinning stopped, and Emma was facing a door once more. They'd left the door back into the Boring Room wide open, with the lights on bright. And this door was open just a crack and barely lit. Did that prove anything?

Emma sensed rather than fully saw the others starting to unfreeze and let go of the shelves they'd been holding on to.

So there are *shelves at this end of the tunnel now?* Emma wondered. *Even though they weren't here when we came back going the other direction with Ms. Morales? And* she *never felt the room or the tunnel spin at all, in either direction. . . .*

Emma wanted so badly to figure out how the tunnel worked. Maybe the spinning *opened* the tunnel, and then the section of the room with shelves snapped back to being part of the Greystones' house again? And maybe the tunnel stayed open if . . .

"Everybody okay?" Chess asked, in such a grim voice

that Emma could tell he was thinking, *Mom isn't. She's in danger.*

Emma forgot about figuring out the tunnel and took a wobbly step toward the door.

"It *smells* as bad as before," Finn said, wrinkling up his nose. "Maybe worse."

"Burning rubber?" Natalie said, sniffing the air. "Dead mice? Formaldehyde?"

"Everything horrible, all at once," Chess said, as if he were ending the discussion. "Let's get this over with."

He went through the door first, stepping out into darkness. After he switched on the light, the others followed, and Natalie started to shut the door behind them.

"No!" Emma exclaimed. "Last time Chess put a can in the doorway to prop it open. We have to do everything the same!"

The others watched her grab a can of peaches from a shelf and wedge it into the doorway. Nobody said anything.

Do I feel so terrible now just because I'm worried about Mom and I don't really understand the alternate world? Emma asked herself. *Or is there something about this place that really messes with your mind?*

Maybe it was just the trip through the spinning room that had thrown her off. If that really had been a journey between alternate dimensions, no wonder she felt disoriented.

Emma rubbed her forehead and shoved her hair back from her face.

One, she told herself. *Two, three, four, five, six, seven . . .*

At least she could remember how to count now.

I should have stayed up all night and figured out how to translate the rest of Mom's code, she told herself. *That probably explains everything we want to know.*

All they had to do was grab a poster and go back to Ms. Morales. Maybe if Ms. Morales decided to call the cops, there'd be cops who could help with the code. Maybe they'd figure it out in a matter of minutes. Emma was only a little girl—why had she thought she could do anything?

Stop that! she told herself. *What's wrong with you?*

She grabbed Finn's hand, then Chess's.

"Come on!" she said.

She saw Natalie put her hand on Finn's shoulder.

All four of them walked through the empty basement and up the stairs in a clump, almost like a single creature—an amoeba, maybe. The first floor of the house was still empty, the windows still boarded up.

"It is like our house," Finn whispered, peering around, his eyes wide. "Our house without us, and without Mom and without Rocket, and really, really sad. . . ."

They burst out of the house, and Emma wanted to gulp in fresh air. But the air outside smelled just as bad, only bad in a different way.

More like burning rubber, less like rotting dead mice? she thought.

Still, it was a smell that beckoned Emma forward, as if a smell could whisper, *Come see. You have to find the source, to destroy it. So you don't have to live with this forever. You have to look now. . . .*

"We should prop this door open, too," Chess said firmly, and Emma saw that he'd carried a can of corn up from the basement.

"Good thinking," Natalie said.

Were her teeth chattering? Was Natalie that scared?

"Check your phone," Emma suggested.

Natalie barely glanced at the screen.

"No signal," she whispered.

Chess left the can in the door, and they all inched forward: off the porch, down the driveway. . . .

"Do you feel like . . . like we're going through patches of fog?" Emma asked. "Only it's patches of feelings? Hope, fear, hope, fear . . . And it goes along with how strong the smell is?"

"Yes!" Natalie said.

"I thought I was the only one feeling that!" Finn said. "I

thought I was going crazy!"

"Shh," Chess said. He pointed. They'd reached the end of the driveway and the edge of the tall, faded, multicolor fence. And out in the street, people were walking by in clumps.

"Is that . . . Mrs. Childers?" Emma whispered. The white-haired woman, who'd been their friendly, chatty next-door neighbor for as long as Emma could remember, walked by without even looking at them. Though maybe it wasn't her after all—her face seemed to have extra lines and wrinkles, as if she'd started frowning and squinting all the time. She was a lot thinner, too. And she was wearing a shirt that was bright orange and navy blue, the same colors as the jackets of the teenaged boys they'd seen before.

Did the high school change its school colors, and nobody told me? Emma wondered.

The Mrs. Childers they knew wouldn't have bothered dressing in a sports team's colors any more than Emma would.

How different could people be in this world?

"I don't think anybody is going to know us here," Chess whispered back. "If anybody remembers us, it would be from when we were really little kids, and we didn't look the same. . . ."

"Except for Natalie," Finn chimed in.

Natalie flipped the hood of her sweatshirt over her head,

hiding her hair and the top part of her face.

"Maybe we should get away from standing in front of this house," Natalie said. "Just in case."

Without even discussing a direction, they all turned and started following Mrs. Childers and the other clusters of people. None of the people around them were talking. Many of them were wearing the same shades of orange and blue as Mrs. Childers, but their grim expressions made it seem more like they were headed to a funeral than to a sporting event.

Is there anyone in the crowd who doesn't *look afraid?* Emma wondered. Even the littlest children—also mostly dressed in orange or blue—cowered against their parents' shoulders. One toddler actually seemed to be trembling with fear. *No, wait, now everybody looks angry. And . . . now it's back to fear again. . . .*

Was it possible for lots of people to have their feelings controlled all at once? Maybe by a smell?

But who's doing it? Emma wondered. *And why?*

"There's a sign on that pole, up on the corner," Chess murmured. "But I can't see. . . ." He took two long strides forward, breaking off from the others.

Emma stretched out her legs to catch up with him. Beside her, Finn and Natalie did the same. Finn was almost running.

"It's—" Finn began, and Emma clapped her hand over

his mouth so he couldn't give them away.

It was Mom's face on the sign.

Good, Emma told herself. *That's what we wanted. Now grab the sign and run back to the house, back through the tunnel or the spinning room, whatever takes us back to Ms. Morales. . . . That's all you have to do!*

But it was so terrible to see her beloved mother's face under the dark, nasty words "CRIMINAL CAUGHT!" It was indisputably Mom—and her name, "Kate Greystone," appeared directly below, along with the words "Enemy of the People." But this was a picture of her mother Emma had never seen before. Maybe it had just been taken, after she was captured—or maybe it was altered. Everything strong about Mom's face looked defiant and ugly. Everything hopeful looked mocking.

She still looked like Mom, but she also looked like a criminal. Or an enemy.

Emma dropped her gaze, forcing herself to read the rest of the sign:

PUBLIC TRIAL AND SENTENCING

ALL MUST ATTEND

SATURDAY, MAY 9

10 A.M.

PUBLIC HALL

Emma's eyes darted back to the time: 10 a.m.

"Natalie!" she whispered. "Check your phone! What time is it?"

Natalie didn't move fast enough. Emma reached over and yanked the phone out of Natalie's sweatshirt pocket. She hit the button to light up the screen.

The clock numerals glowed in white: 9:45.

"We don't have time to go back to Ms. Morales!" Emma gasped. "We have to go rescue Mom *now*!"

FORTY-TWO

CHESS

“Cover for me,” Chess said, reaching for the sign on the pole. “Don’t let anyone see.”

Emma grabbed his arm.

“Didn’t you hear me?” she demanded. “There isn’t time for that plan! That sign doesn’t matter now!”

Even with Emma tugging on him, Chess kept moving his arm forward.

“Here’s what we do,” he said. His voice came out sounding deceptively calm and steady. “You and Finn take this sign back to Ms. Morales. Tell her everything. Natalie and I will go rescue Mom.”

The plan seemed so clear and perfect in his brain. Finn and Emma would be safe this way. They'd be with grown-ups. Maybe even cops. But as Chess yanked on the paper sign, he also turned to glance at Emma.

And she couldn't have looked more betrayed and hurt if Chess had balled up his fist and smashed it into her face, full force.

"You don't think we can help," she whispered.

"You'd still be helping," Chess said. He held out the sign to her. "Just in a different way. By getting Ms. Morales to help."

"No," Finn said. He crossed his arms over his chest.

"Right," Emma said, mimicking his stance. "I say no, too. You can't make us go back, Chess."

Had they been taking lessons all week from how Natalie treated her mother?

"Don't you understand?" he began.

What was he going to tell them? *Dad died in this horrible place. He was* murdered. *Do you want that to happen to us? We're just a bunch of kids; what can we do to rescue Mom? Don't you see how even Natalie is terrified, too? Did you see how she had her phone primed to call 911 the whole time we were walking through our own house, in case someone was still there, and jumped out at us? And now there's no way to call 911? And maybe the police here are the bad guys, if they arrested Mom?*

"We understand that we have to rescue Mom," Emma said. "Don't you wish you could have done something to rescue Dad before he died?"

She understood enough. She'd found the one thing to say that would change Chess's mind.

"I—" Chess began. He looked down at the poster in his hand. It didn't seem real. There wasn't enough time. Why hadn't they figured out a way to come last night, as soon as they knew about the alternate world?

Because we didn't want to believe any of this was real . . .

To the others, he settled for saying, "We don't even know where this 'Public Hall' is!"

"I think we can just follow everyone else," Natalie said. "'All Must Attend.'"

She was reading from the sign.

Chess stuffed it into the pocket of his windbreaker—his dark green windbreaker, which looked out of place in the midst of so many people wearing navy blue and orange. At least Natalie's sweatshirt was black, which sort of blended in. But Emma's T-shirt was maroon, and Finn's was a bright yellow. They might as well be wearing signs that spelled it out: "We don't belong here."

Or maybe, "Arrest us, too."

"Fine," he told Natalie, biting off the word in a way that made her wince. He tried to soften his voice, but it came out more like a bark. "Let's walk fast."

He couldn't understand what Emma had meant about going through the patches of feeling—fear, hope, fear, hope, fear. . . . For him, as they moved forward in a group—trying not to be too conspicuous about passing other groups ahead of them—he felt more like he was on a constant downward slide into despair.

We don't even have a plan, he thought. *We can't have a plan because we don't know where Mom is being held or how many guards are around her. We don't know anything about this public hall or how a trial and sentencing works here. And maybe I don't understand anything about alternate worlds. I thought there were supposed to be similarities beyond the design of one house and people with the same names being in both worlds. Nothing looks familiar around us—nothing!*

This last part, Chess realized, wasn't entirely true. The houses they passed were all fenced off or hidden behind towering hedges, so he could barely see any of them. But when they turned a corner, he saw a small pond off to the right. It was the same size and shape as the retaining pond in his own neighborhood. But the pond back home had lilac and forsythia behind it, with picnic tables, a small playground, and a winding bike path off to the side.

This pond looked muddy and dark, surrounded by nothing but sparse blades of dying grass. Any picnic tables or playground equipment that might have once stood nearby had been swallowed up in dense, thorny-looking bushes and trees.

Why is it different? Chess wondered. *What happened here?*

Had Mom seen all this when she sneaked back to this world to try to rescue the three other kids named Rochester, Emma, and Finn? Had she understood what the alternate world was like? Had it been this bad back when Chess's family had lived here?

Chess remembered that the boys who'd recognized Natalie had said "the criminal" was captured by SWAT teams right on the same street as the abandoned house. No matter how much Mom knew or understood, her plan had failed before she even got off the first block.

So what hope is there for us kids? he wondered.

He kept walking forward anyhow.

After they'd gone six or eight blocks, the scenery changed even more: The street opened out into a wide boulevard with imposing buildings on either side. Maybe as the neighborhood Chess knew was falling apart, this part of the town had turned fancy, more like a big city. These buildings were steel and glass and hard to tell apart; they all held enormous banners that swept from their lowest to highest windows. The banners were orange and blue, and maybe they were just for some holiday that existed in the alternate world but not in the world Chess knew. Maybe they were supposed to be festive, like the decorations people put out for July Fourth, Halloween, or Christmas. But these banners were too stiff and formal to seem cheery. They made Chess think more of military flags, as if some invading army had taken over and wanted everyone to know.

Chess wanted so badly to get away from this strange, unfamiliar street. But so many people surrounded them now that he and the others could no longer dart ahead as a pack, slipping beyond the rest of the crowd. He felt Emma slide her hand into his; when he glanced over his shoulder, he saw that she was also holding on to Finn's hand, and Finn was holding on to Natalie's.

"You lead," Emma whispered, and Chess nodded. They had to thread their way through the crowd single file now, and holding on to one another was the only way to keep from being separated.

If we get out of here alive, I'll have to thank Natalie for being at the end, and making sure Finn doesn't get pulled away and swallowed up by the crowd, Chess thought.

Maybe it counted as hopeful that he could even think *If we get out of here alive. . . .*

Soon the crowd grew so thick that Chess could no longer see where they were going. If he craned his neck, he could squint up at the murky sky. Otherwise, he couldn't see past the steel-and-glass buildings with their blue-and-orange banners, or the blue-and-orange clothes of most of the people around him. So he was surprised when he slid his foot forward and clunked it against a marble step. Then there was another one.

"Stairs!" he called back to Emma, Finn, and Natalie. "Be careful going up the stairs!"

Others beside him were talking now, too. An excited buzz rose all around him.

"—heard she wanted to kill us all—"

"—see her get what she deserves—"

"—people like that should be punished as severely as—"

Chess felt sick to his stomach. Were they talking about Mom? His mother, who wouldn't even kill a spider in the house? He wanted to put his hands over Emma's and Finn's ears, so at least they didn't have to hear. But he could only keep trudging forward and up the stairs, partly carried along by the crowd, partly pulling the others along.

The stairs ended in a long, flat surface, and then the crowd bottlenecked through a pair of narrow doorways. The doors and doorframes were marble, too, and ornately carved. As they squeezed through, Chess's face pressed painfully against the stone head of a creature that might have been a demon or just a man caught in the worst agony of his life. But on the other side of the doorway, suddenly there was space. Chess saw a giant pit-like auditorium filling before him.

Okay, we've come this far. Now just find Mom. . . .

After coming in from outside, he would have expected to need time for his eyes to adjust to the dim interior of the Public Hall, or whatever this huge, ornate building actually was. But he had the opposite problem: The glare at the front of the vast, open room was almost too intense to look at. Blinking and squinting helped him realize: The searing light came from a giant screen at the front of the room. It was probably the equivalent of two or three stories high, and maybe the width of a city block.

A dark shadow blocked the middle of the screen—was it a chair? With someone in it?

Suddenly the glow of the screen changed. Now there was a spotlight on the chair, and the overpoweringly bright blankness of the screen was replaced with a magnified image of the stage before it. The camera angle zoomed in and panned from the floor up, showing the bolts holding the chair in place, then blue-jeans-covered legs shackled to the rungs of the chair, then two wrists held together by handcuffs.

It was all wrong: the bolts, the shackles, the handcuffs, even the solitary placement of the chair. Those were all things for criminals, for prisoners, for people who couldn't be trusted.

It was all wrong, because Mom was the one sitting in that chair. Chess knew long before the camera reached her face. Maybe he'd even known when the chair was just a dark shadow, a dark blot in the overwhelming glow.

In spite of everything, Chess felt almost proud that Mom could sit so calmly—imposingly, even—in that cage of a chair. She kept her shoulders back, her head high, her expression firm and clear. This was her "Nobody can hurt me" pose. Chess had seen her look exactly like that in the days and weeks and months after Dad died, every time she left the house.

But he knew better than anyone that it had only been an act eight years ago. And surely it was only an act now.

The resolution on the screen was so precise that he saw Mom's chin tremble, ever so slightly. She only lost control for an instant, but it was enough to make the crowd jeer and cry out, "Coward!" "Traitor!" "Destroy her!"

Nobody silenced them. Nobody said, "She's innocent until proven guilty, remember?"

Chess sniffed, the foul smell of the alternate world filling his nostrils once again. He could feel the anger of the crowd growing around him like something physical—a beast devouring everyone. He felt a surge of anger himself. What could Mom say or do to defend herself against that mob? What could anyone do to help her?

The full meaning of the glowing screen and the chair on the stage finally sank in.

"We're already too late!" he turned to hiss at Emma. "If we try to rescue Mom now, every single person in this room will see us!"

FORTY-THREE

FINN

The big kids have a plan, Finn told himself. *The big kids have a plan. They know what they're doing. We're getting Mom back.*

Those words kept him moving forward, even as the crowd pressed in around him, constantly threatening the grip he had on Emma's hand in front of him and Natalie's hand behind him. He almost broke the link when Emma stepped through the doorway with all the terrifying carvings, and someone smashed Finn's hand against the stone head of some evil beast—a wolf, maybe? But then Natalie shoved him from behind and aimed her elbow right into some man's belly to make a space for both of them.

They were inside the building now, and Finn had never felt so small before in his life. The pillars that lined the walls around them soared high over his head, with more carved marble creatures staring down at him from the heights. The statues threw horrible distorted shadows onto the ceiling, because all the light in the room came from the front.

And then the floor before him sloped downward, and he could see the source of the light:

It was Mom.

Well, that wasn't exactly right. It was the *image* of Mom. She herself hadn't grown to thirty feet tall, or whatever the actual size was of the glowing screen before him. But there was her radiant face, bigger than life, framed by her familiar brown curls. Finn was so used to that face he had every detail memorized: the dancing eyes, the hint of freckles across the nose, the wide mouth that always seemed ready to smile at Finn's antics. Even when she looked serious—as she did now—her face held the *possibility* of joy and laughter.

Finn hadn't entirely understood what the sign had meant about a "trial and sentencing," or why anyone would call his mother a criminal. There hadn't been time to ask. But surely anyone seeing Mom's face right now would understand that she hadn't done anything wrong.

The crowd around them began to yell, and Natalie crouched beside him.

"Don't listen to them," she whispered. Her voice trembled. He had to tune out everything else to hear her. "And don't look at how your mom's trapped, with the handcuffs and all. I'm sure . . . I mean, she'll have a defense attorney, of course, and . . ."

"She's wearing handcuffs?" Finn asked. He stood on tiptoes, trying to see. Even though Natalie had told him not to.

"It's not showing on the screen right now anyhow," Natalie murmured. "But in person . . ."

And then Finn saw that there wasn't just the *image* of Mom, up there at the front, but she was actually *sitting* there. He felt a little mad at being tricked.

"Can't we get closer, to see her better?" he asked Natalie. He cupped his hands between his mouth and her ear, to block anyone else from hearing. "Or will that ruin the plan?"

He saw Chess and Emma conferring in whispers ahead of him. Probably in a moment they'd turn around and tell Finn and Natalie what to do.

But before that could happen, a man's voice boomed out from overhead, louder than any of the crowd's screams.

"Order! Order! The trial will commence. *The People versus Kate Greystone*."

The crowd immediately went silent. Finn reached forward to clutch Emma's hand again.

Up on the stage, a raised platform slid out, along with

two large wooden structures. Finn had seen a cartoon version of a trial once—maybe for Bugs Bunny?—and that was enough for him to realize that these were seats for a judge and a jury. And maybe witnesses, too—didn't trials have witnesses?

The chair Mom was in slid back and locked into place behind one wall of the wooden structure. Maybe she was the first witness? But now Finn could no longer see her in person, only on the giant screen.

Then four guards marched out on the stage. The one in the fanciest uniform stepped to the front, and his face appeared on the giant screen, instead of Mom's.

Finn felt like he'd lost her all over again.

"The protocol will be different than previously announced," the guard said, somehow sounding stiff and formal and angry all at once. "The defendant has decided to confess. That will happen first."

Confess? Finn thought. Wouldn't that mean Mom *admitted* she'd done something wrong?

Around him, the crowd gasped and buzzed. The man held up his hand for silence.

"Let us begin," he said.

And then Mom's face was on the giant screen again. She leaned forward to grasp a microphone someone had put on a stand beside her; she had to reach with both hands, since they were bound together at the wrists. The handcuffs clanked.

Finn tugged on Emma's arm, and then Chess's, too. His brother and sister had to know how to stop this. They had to stop it *now.*

But when Emma and Chess glanced back, their faces were anguished, their matching dark eyes full of matching despair.

Emma and Chess don't have a plan, Finn realized. *They don't know what to do any more than I do.*

Finn turned to Natalie, still crouched beside him. She had her head down, defeated.

None of the big kids know what to do, Finn thought. *We're all exactly the same.*

Up on the screen, Mom opened her mouth and began speaking into the microphone.

"I am guilty of everything I have been accused of," she said in a strong, firm voice that was completely hers, completely the way she always sounded. "I committed all of those murders." Her voice filled the entire room. She paused only to stare more directly at the camera. "I even killed my own husband."

Chess and Emma slumped in front of Finn, staggering as if they'd been hit. Natalie buried her face in her hands.

Maybe they weren't all the same. Finn didn't stagger or slump or drop his head. He straightened his spine and lifted his chin. Because suddenly he knew exactly what to do, exactly how to help Mom.

He opened his mouth, too.

"None of that is true!" he screamed. "Someone's making her say that! She's just doing it to . . . to . . ." Ideas clicked together in his brain. "To save those kids! Somehow!"

He stepped forward, ready to run down to the stage and grab the microphone from Mom's hand and keep screaming, keep explaining until the whole crowd rose up and agreed, "Oh, you're right. We're sorry. We're sorry about those kids being kidnapped, too."

But before he could take another step, someone grabbed him from behind.

FORTY-FOUR

EMMA

Oh, Finn, Emma thought, one horror flowing over another. He'd said what she was thinking, but he'd said it *out loud*. When they were already standing in this dangerous place, surrounded by people who looked mad enough to kill.

For a moment, she was too paralyzed to do anything. Then she saw the angry faces of the crowd turning toward Finn. Now it looked like they wanted to kill *him*. She spun around and hissed, "Stop talking! Stop talking and *run*!"

How could Finn *not* see how much danger they were in? Hadn't he heard the terrible things the crowd had screamed? *Traitor . . . Killer . . .* Couldn't he see how much these people despised Mom without even knowing her? How the people at the front had started banging their hands against the clear Plexiglas wall separating them from the stage, as if that was the only thing keeping them from running up and attacking her?

How could Finn be so brave—and so stupid?

But Finn was no longer right behind her. She whipped her head left to right, and there was Chess still frozen beside her, all the color drained from his face, and Natalie scrambling up from the floor, her hands pressed over her mouth in horror. But Finn, Finn, Finn . . .

Finn was nowhere in sight.

An arm thrust out from the crowd and drew Emma in; an old lady in an orange cap put her face to Emma's ear and whispered, "If you run, you look guilty. Move with the crowd. Blend in. It's the only way to hide."

Emma yanked her head back. She would have started screaming as loudly as Finn—screaming his name, probably—except that in that moment the old lady moved her dark blue coat to the side, giving Emma a quick glimpse of Finn's brown hair and startled face, hidden behind her.

Emma pressed her finger to her lips. She let her eyes beg Finn: *Stay quiet, stay quiet, oh, please, you can't make a sound. I think this woman is helping us. . . .*

An instant later, the glare of a spotlight cut through the

crowd, reaching the exact spot where Finn had stood only seconds earlier. The crowd as a whole darted away from the light, leaving an empty space on the floor. Emma and Finn and the old lady moved back, too. Panicked cries rose around them: "It wasn't me!" "It wasn't my kid!" "Whoever it was ran away!"

Emma saw Chess and Natalie on the other side of the empty space, at the edge of the circle of light. They seemed to have unfrozen enough to call out with the others around them, "It wasn't me!" Chess's voice cracked. Natalie seemed about to cry.

The booming voice from the man on the stage called out, "Five-minute recess while the guards deal with a disturbance in the crowd. They need to make another arrest."

Mom's face disappeared from the giant screen, replaced by the blank, blinding light again. And that made Emma's eyes flood with tears, too. Emma *needed* Mom so much right now. Even if Mom was up there saying the most un-Mom-like things ever.

She didn't kill Dad, Emma told herself. *She didn't kill anyone. I know it. . . .*

It was like knowing that two plus two equaled four, like knowing how to breathe.

But how could Mom even speak those words? How could she think saying that would save anyone? How could anyone believe her?

Emma didn't have time to think it all through, because a dozen guards came shoving their way through the crowd. The shoving was unnecessary; all the clumps of people in blue and orange fell over themselves to get out of the way. A young woman with dreadlocks sagged against the man beside her; Emma wondered if she'd fainted in fear.

Emma took a shaky breath, fighting against terror herself. How had the mood of the crowd changed so quickly? Was just the sight of the guards enough to horrify everyone?

The acrid odor around them seemed worse than ever.

Maybe, maybe . . . maybe I don't *actually know how to breathe anymore? Maybe it doesn't work the same here? Or breathing in makes me smell the odor more, and* that's *making me more and more afraid?*

She held her breath, and somehow that steadied her. She could concentrate on locking her muscles, keeping herself from trembling. But as soon as she inhaled again, she felt lost.

Or maybe this time it was because the guards were so close now. They were so muscular, so stern in their dark blue uniforms. They thronged into the circle of light, just inches from Emma and the old lady—and from Finn hiding behind the old lady's coat.

"Who was yelling?" the guards demanded again and again as they stared out into the crowd. "Who dared disturb the trial?"

The crowd's panicky cries of "It wasn't me!" were replaced by mumbles: "I didn't see. . . ." "I didn't hear. . . ." "I was watching the screen. . . ." "That was behind me. . . ."

Could it be true that nobody saw Finn except the old lady? Emma wondered. *Or . . . is the crowd trying to save him, too?*

Did the crowd care about Finn, or were they only trying to stay out of trouble themselves?

Or were they all just too scared to think straight?

When the guards weren't looking directly at her, Emma tried to scan the faces around her, too. They were young and old, fat and thin, dark skinned and pale, surrounded by thick curls or bald scalps. . . . But all of the faces were twisted in terror, and that made them all look alike.

The old lady dug a bony elbow into Emma's side.

"Look down," she commanded, in a whisper so soft that Emma might have just been reading her lips. "Don't let them see your face."

But how could Emma see the guards and the crowd without letting them see her?

How could she see if it was time to grab Finn and run?

Emma compromised, bending her neck only partway. She peeked out through her eyelashes and the random strands of hair that slid down over her face.

She saw a man's dark shoe on the other side of the circle nudge something round and metallic toward the clump of guards. Was it a magnet? A bullet? A miniature *bomb*?

Emma's teachers were always telling her she had a scientific mind, but science only helped when you had enough data to come up with a good hypothesis. All Emma could see was a piece of metal rolling out into the bright light. The guards blocked her view, so she couldn't even see who had kicked it.

Are there light-activated bombs? she wondered. *Heat-activated bombs? Remote-control bombs?*

She shouldn't think about bombs. Or any other dangers besides the guards.

The round metal thing clunked against one of the guard's shoes and fell over on its side. Through her lowered lashes, Emma saw the guard bend down and pick up the piece of metal. Still crouched low, he held it up to the light. Then he stood and carried it over to another guard, the one whose uniform held the most medals and the fanciest braided orange trim. Was he the guard leader?

Emma held her breath again. She forgot the old lady's advice and lifted her head to watch.

The guard leader held the metal in one hand and tilted his head to the side to speak into his collar.

"Looks like it was an electronic voice we heard," he said. "The perp who set this up could be anywhere in the crowd by now. We'll reroll the security footage, do the facial rec—we'll have this arrest by the end of the sentencing."

Emma felt the old lady behind her stiffen at the words "facial rec."

Rec, Emma thought numbly. *Recognition.*

She couldn't understand everything the guard had said, but she'd caught enough. The guards thought they were looking for someone who'd set out an electronic device; they thought Finn's voice had only been a recording.

But there was security video of the crowd. And when the guards looked at it, they'd see Finn. They'd know he was the one who shouted. They'd come back for him.

The spotlight dimmed, then disappeared. The guards began marching away, shoving a few more people for no reason, as if the guards were just overgrown playground bullies.

Emma leaned back against the old lady who'd rescued her and Finn.

"Thank you," Emma breathed. "You saved us. Can you . . ."

She had a whole list of ideas to ask for. *Can you help us save our mother? Can you get us out of here safely? Can you tell us what to do?*

But the old lady was pulling away.

"You didn't see me," she murmured. "I wasn't here."

The old lady nudged past Finn and melted back into the crowd. Emma had never really gotten a good look at the woman—her main impression was of pruny lips and the orange cap that shadowed the rest of the old lady's face. So that's what Emma looked for.

No one anywhere near Emma was wearing an orange cap now.

Did the old lady take it off so I wouldn't *find her?* Emma wondered. *Or is she just hiding from the guards?*

"Emma, please . . ."

It was Finn, grabbing her around the shoulders and holding on tight. If he'd been too fearless before, he seemed terrified now. His eyes were wide and swimming with unshed tears. His lower lip trembled.

"It's okay," Emma lied, patting his back. "We're fine. Just stay quiet. We'll get back together with Chess and Natalie and maybe, maybe . . ."

She scanned the crowd. How could she explain that she was searching for a man she'd seen nothing of, except for a dark shoe? A man who may not have even known what he was doing when he kicked a little electronic device toward the guards? How had that become her only hope?

Maybe Emma didn't know anything about shoe fashions, and it'd been a woman instead.

Most of the men across from them were wearing dark shoes.

So were the women.

The crowd pressed forward, jostling Emma. Everyone seemed to want to get away from the spot where the guards had found the device. Chess raced over and grabbed Finn, and his arms were long enough to wrap around Emma at the same time. Natalie put her hand on Finn's head and Emma's both.

The others silently turned to the front. Even though the screen stayed blank and there was no movement on the stage, it seemed like the trial could resume any minute. Still, Emma kept facing backward. She gave up on trying to identify shoes and raised her gaze, studying all the people crammed in behind her. She was hoping for a wink or a nod or maybe a simple hand signal—something to tell her who she could trust. The man who'd kicked the electronic device had done nothing but buy a little time for Finn, but maybe he'd done it on purpose. Maybe Shoe Man—Shoe Person?—was braver than the old lady. Maybe he'd be willing to help more. Wouldn't he give her some sign of that?

The people behind her shifted restlessly: squinting, frowning, biting their lips, crossing their arms. . . . Maybe someone in the crowd behind her *was* trying to signal her, and she just couldn't tell. Why hadn't she learned sign language? Or semaphore codes? Or whatever people used in this alternate world?

Why hadn't Mom taught Emma, Chess, and Finn

everything they needed to know about the alternate world from the very beginning?

People were starting to stare at Emma for being different, for not turning around and looking back toward the huge screen at the front of the auditorium like everyone else. One tall, scowling man with thick glasses even tilted his head and made a shooing motion with his hand, as if her steady gaze was making him angry, and he just wanted her to go away.

No. He wasn't shooing her away. He was showing her something in his hand, but keeping his hand cupped so no one else would see it, too.

The thing in his hand was a paper.

A paper unfolded to reveal a crookedly drawn red heart.

FORTY-FIVE

CHESS

Chess was already having trouble standing up. He wasn't sure if he was holding on to his brother and sister more for their sake or his own. So when Emma began tugging on his arm and pulling him back, he almost fell over.

"We can't—" he began.

It was too hard to say the rest. Not to mention dangerous. *We can't stand out. We can't save Mom. Or the Gustano kids. Or ourselves.*

The only thing they'd achieved, coming to the alternate world, was to doom more people.

It made his heart ache to think of the people he'd

personally endangered by not sending them back: Finn. Emma.

And Natalie, who wasn't even related, who didn't have the same reason they all did for wanting to save Mom.

Emma pulling on him was just another reminder of how badly he'd failed.

"We have to follow someone!" Emma whispered, yanking on his arm harder and harder. "Someone who can help!"

It was odd: Emma didn't look or act like *she* thought they were doomed. She was practically jumping up and down. A moment ago she'd been as slumped over as Chess and Finn and Natalie. But now her eyes shone and her cheeks were rosy; it was possible to believe that if she touched his arm again, he'd get an electric shock.

"Okay, okay, shh," Chess whispered, more to calm her down than because he believed there was any hope.

The four of them silently began skulking through the crowd, with Emma leading the way. The people around them were milling about and muttering, clearly impatient for the trial to start again, so Chess hoped the kids' movements wouldn't stand out too much. Emma seemed to be following a man a few paces ahead of them in a dark blue jacket—not that that was unusual, since so many in the crowd were wearing dark blue or orange. This man was tall like Chess remembered his father being; he had dark hair and dark skin, and in his dark-colored clothes he could step into the shadows and hide a lot better than the Greystones or Natalie could. Even his horn-rimmed glasses seemed like a disguise.

When they got to the edge of the crowd, Chess thought maybe Emma had lost the man completely. Then he saw the man's hand reach out from behind one of the pillars with one finger curled back, summoning the kids forward.

Chess grabbed Emma by the shoulders.

"What are you doing?" he asked. "This is like every 'Stranger Danger' lecture ever! What—"

"We can trust him," Emma said. "I'm sure of it!"

"Why?" Natalie challenged.

Emma's answer was to speed over to the man and whisper in his ear. He pulled something out of his pocket and held it out. Even in the dark space behind the pillar there was enough light for Chess to see the heart on the paper.

"Hey, I drew that!" Finn said. "Well, not that exact one, I guess, but the heart just like it on Mom's phone. . . ." He spoke softly—for Finn, anyway—but he still glanced over his shoulder as if terrified the guards would come again.

Chess squared his shoulders and tried to look taller and more confident than he really was. He stared straight into the man's eyes, past the man's thick glasses.

"Where'd you get that?" he demanded.

The man seemed to cower back into the shadows even more. His eyes darted about.

"Someone mailed it to me years ago. Your . . . mother. That is, if I'm right about who you are." The man spoke slowly, as if he wasn't all that confident either. His gaze came to rest on Natalie's face. "Though, I thought there were only three of you. . . ."

"Natalie's just helping," Finn volunteered, and Chess despaired again. Hadn't Finn learned his lesson? Would he ever *not* talk too much?

Natalie took the heart drawing from the man's hand.

"You expect us to believe that Mrs. . . . uh, that *some woman* sent you this heart picture her kid drew?" she asked skeptically. "When you don't even recognize the kid?"

The man held his hands up, a gesture of innocence.

"Hear me out!" he begged. "It's true! We needed a symbol we could show, in case we ever had to meet and . . . and it wasn't safe to identify ourselves otherwise. I didn't even know what Ka—er, what the woman I was talking to—really looked like until today. It wasn't safe. But this heart . . ." His finger brushed the paper. His voice turned husky. "It's a good symbol. Everything we've done was for you and other kids like you. For our hopes for the future. *Your* future."

Chess wanted to weep. He wanted to scream, *Don't you*

see there's no hope now? Couldn't you have shown up and saved her sooner?

"So you do know who we are," he said, biting off the words. "We don't have to tell you. But we don't know you. Be fair. Tell us *your* name."

The man's face spasmed between sorrow and fear. He jerked his head around, and muttered as if he was only talking to himself, "I swept this area for any listening device. I rerouted the security camera on this pillar. It really should be safe. . . ." He clenched his teeth, looked back at Chess, and said, "Your mother knows me as Joe."

Chess had never been a violent kid. When other boys wanted to fight on the playground, he always walked away. But rage swelled within him now. He slammed the palms of his hands as hard as he could against Joe's chest. He didn't worry for an instant about Joe hitting back. He didn't even worry about guards hearing him. All he wanted to do was accuse Joe:

"It's your fault she's here!"

FORTY-SIX

FINN

Finn watched his calm, sane, *perfect* brother go crazy.

The big man—Joe—wrapped his arms around Chess, more like he was hugging him than trying to fight back.

Strangely, Emma was doing the same thing, as if she were on Joe's side, not Chess's.

"Don't breathe," Emma commanded, putting her hand over Chess's mouth and nose. "Don't inhale at all."

"What?" Finn said. "Emma, that's backward. When people are upset, you're supposed to tell them to take *deep* breaths. You say, 'Breathe in. Breathe out. . . .'"

"Not here," Emma said. "There's something wrong with

this air. Something that makes people more upset. It's worse every time the smell's worse."

"Really?" Finn said.

Chess stopped struggling. Joe pulled away from Chess to stare at Emma.

"You may be right," he whispered. "That explains . . ." He clutched his hands against his head. "What other horrors did they come up with while I was away that I don't know about? What *else* am I missing?"

"It's just a theory," Emma said modestly.

Natalie put her hands on her hips.

"Let's back up," she said. She narrowed her eyes at Chess. "*You* know this Joe guy?"

"I heard my mom on the phone with him," Chess said. His shoulders slumped. He exhaled a little, took a shallow breath—a mere sip of air—and admitted, "Or *somebody* she called Joe. It was the night before she left, and she said, 'If you don't fix this, I will.' I think she was talking about rescuing the Gustano kids."

Out of the corner of his eye, Finn saw Mom's image on the screen behind them again. He wanted to gaze and gaze at her. But he didn't want to hear if she told any more lies.

"Order!" the bossy man's voice came again from the front of the room. "We are about to resume."

Finn turned his back to the screen and glared at Joe.

"So she wouldn't even be up there if it hadn't been for you?" Finn asked forlornly. "She'd still be safe at home with us?"

Joe began shaking his head no. But the way the corners of his lips turned down, it was more like he was saying yes.

"I—I have kids, too," he said. "Kids *I* was trying to protect. And I didn't think her plan would work, to come back here. I didn't know what to do."

"But you're here now," Natalie offered.

Joe bowed his head.

"And I still don't know what to do," he whispered. "There's no way to rescue the four of you, the Gustano kids, and your mom—and get all of us out of here alive. This has gone too far."

Behind Finn, the public address system crackled, and then he heard his mother's voice boom out throughout the entire auditorium: "I killed everyone who disagreed with me. . . ." Finn put his hands over his ears. But he could still hear.

"What good does *that* do?" Emma asked, pointing back toward the screen. She had tears in her eyes. "How are those lies supposed to help anyone?"

Joe lifted his head and let out a bitter laugh.

"Oh, *she's* not saying any of that. This world—they have technology that doesn't exist in the other world. The leaders can take the image of anyone and make it look like they're saying anything. And no matter how much you analyze the video, you can't tell what's real and what isn't."

"But she's sitting right there—" Finn pointed behind him, though he couldn't look himself. His eyes were too blurry with his own tears.

"People can only see the screen," Chess muttered. "Not her. And they think they see what she's really saying and doing."

"It's like a magic trick," Emma said. "An *evil* magic trick. All about distraction."

"Yes." Joe put his hands on Finn's shoulders. "They're making it look like she's saying everything live, right now, speaking into a microphone this very minute. But that's a fake tape they prepared ahead of time. The leaders can destroy anyone they want that way, by controlling what people see and hear, so they only get lies. That's what we were fighting against, your parents and I. And our allies. We were gathering proof of the *leaders'* crimes—proof that couldn't be denied for once. We thought, in the safety of the other world, we'd have time and space to put it all together. But . . . then the leaders found the other world, too."

"This place sucks," Natalie said, and now it sounded like *she* wanted to punch somebody.

Was Finn the only one who still didn't understand?

"But *I* told people the truth!" he said. "They heard *me*! Why didn't that work?"

Once again he felt the horror of the moment after the old lady grabbed him. She'd whispered, "Hide, before they kill you!" And he'd peeked out from behind her coat, and people were looking back with murderous expressions.

Finn had never seen anyone look like that before. Certainly not looking at *him* that way.

But if it helped Mom, I'd do it again, he thought.

Wouldn't he? Couldn't he be that brave?

Joe shook his head. It seemed like all he ever did was shake his head.

"Only a few people heard you before the guards came. It was just lucky I was standing nearby. One little boy's feeble voice against an entire totalitarian government—it's not going to work. You'd need the entire auditorium hearing you all at once. And even then . . ."

"That one old lady did help us," Emma offered. She cupped her chin in her hand, as if that helped her think. "*She* didn't show us a heart picture. So she wasn't someone working with you and Mom, right?"

"Not that I know of," Joe said, spreading his hands helplessly. "We've had to operate in such secrecy—it hasn't been safe for anyone to know more than one or two contacts."

"So there could be lots of people here who are secretly

on our side!" Finn said excitedly. He thumped Emma on the back, as if they'd figured out something together. "They just need to know it's safe to unite! All we need to do is give Mom a microphone—a real microphone. And she could say from the stage what's true and what isn't. And then—"

"Huh," Joe said, tapping a finger against his cheek. Was that like Emma cupping her chin? Was Joe taking Finn's idea seriously?

"You had that little electronic device that made the guards think Finn's voice was a recording," Emma added excitedly. Her eyes shone. Finn *loved* seeing his sister this way. He could tell her mind was racing. "Do you have a microphone hidden in that coat, too? Could we drop it down from over the stage? Or, I don't know, there's got to be some way to make this work!"

Finn looked from Emma to Chess to Natalie to Joe. Chess and Natalie looked like they were thinking hard, too.

But by the time Finn's gaze reached Joe's face again, Joe was already slumped back against the pillar. Giving up.

"I'm sorry," he said. "There's no endgame in that plan. No escape hatch. See that clear wall keeping the crowd back from the stage?" He pointed. "We couldn't get past that to rescue your mom if the idea didn't work instantly. And there are guards by every door. We'd endanger ourselves even more. The guards would just take the microphone away from your mom before she got two words out."

Chess slouched. Emma hung her head. Finn blinked hard, trying to make sure that no tears began rolling down his cheeks.

But Natalie bolted suddenly upright, staring past Finn's ear. She grabbed Finn's arm and Emma's shoulder, and spun them around. Then she yanked Chess forward, too.

"Guys, guys, guys!" she hissed. "Do you see what I see? Or am I only imagining it, because . . ." She laughed, a strange noise that came out sounding strangled. "Because it's what I want most?"

Natalie pointed at the screen. Finn had been trying so hard to block out everything the booming voice of his mother was saying behind him. He'd actually kind of succeeded. And he'd kept himself from staring adoringly at her face the whole time.

But Mom's face had disappeared from the screen, replaced by another woman's. This woman had long, flowing hair and a ruffled collar. She had a firm chin, a determined gaze, a proud tilt to her head. She looked like she could take care of anything.

"Don't you see?" It was hard to tell if Natalie was laughing or crying. "It's *my* mom! *She* came to save us!"

FORTY-SEVEN

EMMA

“No, it’s not,” Emma said. This felt like the cruelest thing she’d ever done, killing Natalie’s hope. “That’s *this* world’s version of your mother.”

Natalie squinted at Emma. The corners of her mouth trembled.

“No! It has to be . . .”

“Your mother was wearing a neon green exercise shirt when she dropped us off at our house this morning,” Emma said. Logic had never felt so mean. “She wouldn’t have gone home and changed before following us. That woman is wearing a *robe* under that ruffle. Why would your mom do that?”

"And she's sitting in front of a sign that says 'Judge Susanna Morales,'" Chess added quietly. "Your mom isn't a judge."

Natalie let out a wail and turned to the side, hiding her face.

"Natalie's mom is nice in our world," Finn said. "So wouldn't this world's Ms. Morales be nice, too? If she's a judge here, won't she say, 'Order in the court!' and let Mom go?"

Now Emma needed to use logic to be cruel to *Finn*. She needed to remind him that he couldn't count on anyone or anything being the same in this world as back home. This world's Mrs. Childers hadn't been friendly like their familiar neighbor back home; this world's version of their house wasn't happy and welcoming like theirs was. . . . Whatever original difference had split one world from another had also led to one ripple of other changes after another.

How could Finn understand this, when Emma was struggling herself?

Before Emma could say anything, Joe bolted out of the shadows. He shoved Chess, Emma, and Finn to the side, and grabbed Natalie by the shoulders. He whirled her around, so he could stare her directly in the face.

"You're *Susanna Morales's* daughter?" he asked. "Who's your father? Is it . . . is it . . . ?"

"R-Roger Mayhew," Natalie stammered. She jerked away from him. "Let go of me!"

Joe was leaning in like he wanted to hug her, but he took a respectful step back. His expression, which had been so hangdog a moment ago, now glowed with joy.

"So you three crossed into this world with Natalie Mayhew," he muttered. "Natalie *Mayhew*. Genetically indistinguishable from Susanna Morales and Roger Mayhew's daughter in this world. Either your mom's a genius, or you kids are, or . . . or we are the luckiest people ever!"

"What do you mean?" Emma asked.

Joe waved his arms, like he was dying to hug *someone*. He settled on Finn, scooping up the little boy in his arms so joyfully that Finn's legs swung side to side.

"This changes everything," Joe whispered, holding Finn tight. "Now Finn's idea will work!"

FORTY-EIGHT

CHESS

"I don't understand," Chess whispered. But nobody was listening.

Natalie stood beside him, her eyes narrowed thoughtfully, her head tilted so far to the right that her hair seemed several inches longer on one side than the other.

"I'm someone important here?" she whispered. "Or my family is? Is that why those boys the other day were so scared of my mom?"

She gazed off toward the huge image of her mother—no, this world's Susanna Morales, the *judge*—up on the screen, pounding a gavel and looking severe.

Meanwhile, Chess's mother—his *real* mother, the only one he had in either world—was in handcuffs and shackles. And she'd just finished confessing to murders Chess knew she didn't commit. Because she couldn't have. He *knew* that, even if certainty about everything else had abandoned him.

Chess looked down.

On the floor by Chess's feet, Finn and Emma bent protectively over Joe, hiding whatever he was assembling out of tiny bits of plastic and wire.

"Ooo, Emma, this is like when you built that mechanical insect for me," Finn squeal-whispered. "After all this is over, you two should go into business together. Mr. Gadget and Kid Gadget!"

How could Finn flip from fear to excitement so fast?

He trusts Joe, Chess thought. *He believes we really are going to be able to save Mom. And ourselves. And—the Gustanos?*

Chess crouched down. Now he was at eye level with Joe, Emma, and Finn.

"Tell us exactly what you're doing," he asked Joe. "So we know our part. And so . . ."

So if anything goes wrong, the rest of us can still save Mom.

Chess didn't want to say that in front of the younger kids. Or even Natalie. He didn't want anyone else thinking about possible problems.

Joe's eyes met Chess's over the top of the man's glasses.

Chess clenched his jaw and kept his gaze steady. Wouldn't that make him look older and more trustworthy himself? Joe raised an eyebrow at Chess, a shadowy motion in the near-darkness behind the pillar. But this was like the looks Mom sometimes gave Chess over the top of Emma's and Finn's heads, the looks that said, *I know you are almost an adult, and so you are old enough to know things that I can't tell Emma and Finn. You understand, don't you? You trust me, right?* But this was different, because Joe wasn't Mom. He'd been a stranger until a few moments ago. Regardless of any heart drawing, he was a stranger still.

Chess wanted so badly to trust Joe anyhow. It *felt* like Joe wasn't just looking at him adult-to-near-adult. It felt like his gaze and his raised eyebrow were more . . .

Man-to-man.

"Are you building a drone?" Emma demanded, before Joe had a chance to answer Chess. "Do you think you can *fly* a microphone up to Mom? Won't the whole auditorium see that? You need to tell us your plan so we can double-check everything, make sure it's foolproof."

"I do want this to be foolproof," Joe murmured as he twisted a tiny screw into whatever he was building on the floor. He shifted his gaze from Chess to Emma, and it felt like he was answering both of them. "And I wouldn't be surprised if you could build this without me, given enough time. But there *isn't* time to explain. Just be ready to run."

"Where to?" Finn asked.

"Safety," Joe said.

Yes, Chess thought. *Get Finn to safety. And Emma. And Natalie. And Mom.*

He had to trust Joe. He didn't see any other choice.

FORTY-NINE

FINN

"Now," Joe said.

Finn had to hold himself back from jumping up and down with excitement. The five of them had wormed their way up to the front of the auditorium. Now they were right by the see-through wall that separated the crowd from the stage. Toward the center of the auditorium, the people beside the clear wall were pressed in close, pinned together by the pressure of the crowd behind them. But Joe, the Greystones, and Natalie were off to the side, away from the bulk of the crowd. They were beside a door in the clear wall. The *only* door.

"You really think Natalie's going to be able to open that because of her *genes*?" Finn asked. He wanted someone to congratulate him for remembering the science word.

Instead, Joe tugged gently on his shoulders.

"Stand back," Joe said. "An alarm might go off if the wrong person touches it. They might have set up that level of security."

He meant that the Greystones were the wrong people. But so was Joe, so Finn couldn't get offended.

All the others seemed to be holding their breath. But Finn couldn't tell if that was because they thought the air was dangerous or because they were scared.

Natalie reached one shaking hand to the knob of the door. She wrapped her hand around the knob.

Nothing happened. No alarms sounded.

Natalie let out a huff of air.

"Slowly, slowly," Joe coached her.

Natalie turned the knob and pushed forward, as gently as breathing. The door opened a crack.

"Yes!" Emma whispered.

Chess's pale, terrified-looking face turned even paler.

"Good girl," Joe said to Natalie. He glanced quickly over his shoulder. "And . . . nobody's watching."

He slipped his hand down onto the side of his leg. To anybody farther away than Finn, it would have looked like a man merely shifting positions. Joe didn't even look down. He peered off toward the giant screen behind the stage, just like Natalie, Chess, and Emma were doing. Just like everyone else in the auditorium.

But Finn couldn't resist watching a tiny crawling thing slither out of Joe's hand and down his pant leg. It moved like a lizard or a snake.

Joe hadn't built a drone that could *fly* a microphone up to Mom, in plain sight of the whole auditorium. He'd built one that could creep along the floor and up the side of her chair, unseen.

Joe tucked his other hand into his coat pocket, where Finn had seen him hide a remote. The drone lizard scampered through the doorway and up the first step toward the stage.

"It's working!" Finn couldn't help whispering.

"Shh," Emma warned him.

But she grinned, too.

Chess put a hand on Finn's head and one on Emma's shoulder. It felt like that was Chess's way of grinning, too.

Natalie hesitated by the door.

"Should I shut it now?" she asked. "Or open it wider?"

"Just wait," Joe whispered.

He still seemed to be peering intently toward the giant screen at the front of the room. But Finn knew Joe was really watching the screen embedded in his own glasses. That was how he could see the progress of the lizard drone as it moved the rest of the way up the stairs and onto a part of the stage completely cloaked in darkness.

Up on the screen, the too-serious, too-grim version of Ms. Morales—the judge—was using a lot of big, unfamiliar words.

"Some would contend that this confession would obviate the need for a lengthy trial," she said in a cold, heartless voice that made Finn miss the real Ms. Morales. Even when she was yelling at Natalie, Finn had never heard the real Ms. Morales sound so cruel. "But we are a society that believes in justice and—"

Joe snorted, blocking out her next words.

"This isn't justice," he muttered.

But behind him, the crowd cheered, as if they believed every word Evil–Ms. Morales spoke.

No, not just that—it was like they *adored* every word Evil–Ms. Morales spoke. Like they worshipped her.

"It's at the base of the chair now," Joe whispered, and Finn shivered with anticipation.

If the crowd could worship the evil judge, just wait until they heard Mom.

Finn watched Joe's face: His eye twitched, he winced, then the corner of his mouth moved just a little higher.

"It's in her hand now," Joe said. "Success!"

Finn resisted the urge to grab Joe's glasses so he could see Mom's face when she looked down at the lizard drone. It'd probably be like her face on Christmas morning, or on Mother's Day when Finn made her *two* cards. She'd glow.

Because the drone lizard didn't just carry a miniature microphone. It also held a tiny paper with a message: another of Finn's crooked hearts with the smallest of words written below, "Kids=safe."

"Won't that make her think the Gustano kids are all safe *now*?" Finn had asked anxiously as he watched Joe write the words. "Won't that kind of . . . trick her?"

"Kiddo, there's not room on this page for future tense or conditional verbs or nuance," Joe had said. "We can't write out that Natalie's our secret weapon or that we're going to grab the Gustano kids next. What if the guards intercept this? Or . . . Judge Morales?"

Now Finn glanced toward Natalie, who stood with her hands pressed against the clear wall. How awful it must be for her to have a good mom *and* an evil one.

Or, at least, an evil one who looked like her real mom.

"Shouldn't Mom start talking already?" Emma whispered anxiously.

"Give her a minute to figure out what we sent her," Joe muttered.

Finn's heart started beating too fast. He hated waiting.

Then a boom sounded overhead—the exact kind of feedback boom a cheap, quickly built microphone would make when it was switched on.

Evil–Ms. Morales's frowning face remained on the screen, but another voice spoke over hers: "This entire trial is a fake!"

Mom! Finn exulted. *Go, Mom!*

"Your leaders are lying to you!" Mom's voice was steady and strong and perfect. It was everything Finn wanted. "I never—"

There was another boom, cutting off Mom's words.

At the same time, the whole room went dark.

FIFTY

EMMA

"Did you know this would happen?" Emma hissed at Joe in the darkness. "Did you know they'd shut off the electricity to shut up Mom?"

"No!" Joe protested. "I thought—"

"Finn!" Chess called, reaching out.

His hand brushed Emma's arm just as Finn shoved past them both, toward the door to the stage.

"We've got to get to Mom before the guards do!" Finn called back over his shoulder.

Usually Emma's brain worked as fast as Finn could move,

but now she wanted an extra moment to think, an instant to figure out the consequences of every action.

Behind her, the crowd went from shocked silence to a loud buzz. Did they believe Mom? Whose side were they on now?

Emma couldn't tell. She couldn't make out any individual words, just a deafening roar of . . . more anger? More fear?

"Finn's right! We can use the darkness!" Natalie called. "It helps us!"

In the next instant, some kind of emergency backup lights switched on. They were so minimal they only cast shadows—they seemed to emphasize the darkness, rather than fighting it. But now Emma could make out the dim shape of her little brother beyond the door, halfway up the towering stairs to the stage.

He looked so small, so defenseless. And that made Emma forget everything else: logic, Joe's plan, the crowd. . . .

"Finn, wait for me!" Emma called after him.

She pushed her way through the door, letting go of any worry about security systems or alarms.

Wouldn't a security system need electricity, too? she told herself. *Or is there a backup generator for that, also?*

She didn't touch the doorknob, and no alarm sounded, so

it didn't matter. She took the stairs two at a time. She didn't look back, but she thought maybe Chess, Natalie, and Joe followed.

She caught up to Finn right at the edge of the stage and pulled his head down beside hers.

"At least look before we climb on up!" she whispered in his ear.

Together, they peeked over the rim of the stage.

The dark shape of someone in a long robe stood over Mom behind the wall of her witness stand.

It was Judge Morales.

"Never . . . hello?" Mom was saying doubtfully, probably speaking into the microphone.

"Give up," Judge Morales sneered. "Can't you tell all the mikes are off now? And there's a practically soundproof wall between you and the crowd—no one could hear you, even if they weren't all shouting."

Emma realized the crowd noise seemed dimmer now, more distant. Maybe she could only hear it at all because they'd left the door open.

"I—I—" Mom stammered.

A cluster of guards rushed up beside Judge Morales.

"You want us to guard the prisoner?" the man in the lead asked. "Search her? *Punish* her?"

"There'll be time for that later," the judge snapped. "*She's* not going anywhere. We can look for accomplices later, too. The priority has to be subduing the crowd. This is a Protocol Six-Oh-Two situation. All of you—go!"

She led the guards to the other side of the stage, past the large wooden structures of the judge's podium and the empty jury box.

Now Mom was alone.

And again Finn was a step ahead of Emma, scrambling up over the edge of the stage and scurrying toward Mom.

Emma wanted to scream as she took off after him: *Mom! Mom! We're here!* She wanted to yell, *We love you!* and *Aren't you proud of us for finding you?* and *Oh, Mom, I thought we'd never see you again. This is the happiest moment of my life!* But she pressed her lips together and held it all in because they were still running through darkness, and Judge Morales and the guards were just on the other side of the podium and jury box, and the whole angry crowd was just on the other side of the wall.

And Mom wasn't free yet.

Still, as Emma caught up with Finn, she threw caution to the wind and launched herself around the wall of the witness box and into Mom's lap. Finn did, too. The two of them tumbled together into Mom's arms.

"We're saving you!" Emma whispered, just as Finn sighed happily, "Oh, Mom."

And then Mom gasped and began laughing and crying all at once, and alternately holding her hands over her mouth and holding on to Emma and Finn.

"*My* Emma?" she whispered in disbelief. "*My* Finn?"

And Emma understood why Mom might be confused in the near-total darkness, when she'd thought her three kids were still safely back in the other world, and only the Gustano children had been brought into this one. Mom began running her hands over their faces, as though she could identify them solely by touch.

"Yours," Emma assured her. "All yours."

It wasn't fair that she couldn't see Mom's face in the shadowy darkness. She wanted that so badly—not just to see Mom, but to see Mom seeing *her*. At least Emma could snuggle close; she could hold on tight.

"Mom?" Chess whispered behind her, moving around to the side of Mom's chair. Dimly, Emma saw that Natalie and Joe had arrived with him, and Joe was already bending low, diving toward the shackles that trapped Mom in her chair.

"You're all here?" Mom said numbly, reaching for Chess, too. "But—"

"We figured out your codes," Finn bragged. "Well, some of them. *I'm* the one who found the butterflies on your websites!"

"What? I never thought you'd see that until later,"

Mom whispered. "*Years* later. If ever. It was really meant for other—"

"Probably better not to talk much right now," Joe muttered. He seemed to be lying on the floor beside the witness box, his arms outstretched. Emma was pretty sure he had a screwdriver out to pry off the shackles, but she couldn't actually see it in the darkness.

"Joe?" Mom whispered, looking around. She let out a strangled cry, and her voice turned strangely bitter. "Funny how I know your voice so well, though I've never seen your face . . . *you* brought my children here? Into danger? How dare—"

"I *found* them here, Kate," Joe corrected. "They were a step ahead of me. And they even taped over the doorway to the tunnel, to try to guard it."

Emma thought that should make her feel proud—or proud of Natalie, anyway—but it didn't. There was something wrong with how Mom and Joe were talking, almost as though they were still using code.

Mom buried her face in her hands.

"I'm sorry," she whispered. "I've made a mess of things. But you *came*, and now you're all here, and—"

"And we've got Natalie, too," Finn interrupted. "She—"

Emma put her hand over his mouth, because if it was a mistake to talk about codes right now, it would be a really bad idea to talk about Natalie being their secret weapon. Finn pushed back at her.

No—he was falling toward her, because the platform beneath Mom's chair gave a little jerk.

"Something's happening," Natalie hissed from the other side of the witness box. "Everybody down!"

FIFTY-ONE

CHESS

"Kids, save yourselves!" Mom whispered. "Hide! Now! Away from *me*!"

Chess wanted to argue, *We're not leaving you behind! We're not going anywhere without you!* But the words stuck in his throat. Joe was still working on the shackles on Mom's legs that bound her to the chair, but he hadn't even managed to pry away the first one.

Still, Chess crouched down behind Mom's chair, so that even if the lights came back on, no one would be able to see him from the crowd.

"Natalie's standing lookout for us," he assured Mom.

"We've got time. And even if someone sees her . . ."

Surely Mom knew that Natalie could just impersonate the Natalie Mayhew of this world; surely she knew that those two would look like exact doubles.

Mom turned her head toward Chess, and even though Mom's face was completely in shadow, he could feel the anguish in that one motion.

"Natalie's not . . . Have I just endangered another woman's child, too?" Mom moaned. She raised her head toward the crowd, and Chess understood: *What if this world's Natalie was already standing somewhere out there?* She *would know that the other world's Natalie didn't belong. So would everyone around her.*

The odds were, this world's Natalie was somewhere in the crowd.

"Natalie! You hide, too!" Chess whispered out into the darkness.

What other problems had he missed, because there hadn't been time to think?

Finn and Emma hadn't left Mom, either. If anything, they were holding on tighter.

From the other side of the stage, Chess heard Judge Morales's voice—so uncannily like and unlike the kind Ms. Morales's voice, all at once—as she called out, "Yes, we have enough power for that, even if we're making it look like a total outage otherwise. The plan's a go as soon as everyone's in place."

The platform beneath Mom's chair jerked again and began sliding away from the witness box, out toward the front of the stage.

"They're going to show me to the crowd!" Mom whispered. "Kids! Go!"

She pushed away at Finn and Emma, and turned and shoved at Chess, too.

None of them let go.

"Mom, it's still dark," Finn protested. "We're okay."

"Joe, hurry!" Emma whispered. "Do you have another screwdriver? I could help!"

The platform they were on had totally separated from the wall of the witness box now, sliding closer and closer to the front of the stage. If the lights came back on, all of them would be in plain sight.

"Chess!" Mom called. "Help me! Take care of Finn and Emma!"

There was a sob in her voice. There was a sob in Chess's throat, too, and it was threatening to burst out. And that would endanger everyone, even if lights and guards and evil judges didn't.

Chess reached down and began pulling on Finn's and Emma's arms.

He began pulling them away from Mom.

FIFTY-TWO

FINN

"Chess, *stop,*" Finn moaned, because he didn't understand what was happening, and the only thing holding him together right now was being able to hold on to Mom.

The hard metal of her handcuffs dug into Finn's wrist, but he just clutched her hand tighter.

"Finn, Joe's doing everything he can for me," Mom said, and she had the same super-calm Mom tone she'd used that time Finn had broken his arm. "I need you to be brave, too."

I can't, Finn wanted to wail. But Mom was whispering something to Emma, and *Emma* started tugging on Finn, too.

Finn burrowed his face harder against Mom's side.

"Citizens, calm down," Ms. Morales's voice—no, *Judge* Morales's voice—boomed out over the crowd.

"Mom, if her microphone works again, won't yours work, too?" Finn whispered excitedly.

Even in the near-total darkness, Finn could see Mom shaking her head.

"They're using some sort of auxiliary system," Mom whispered. "They—"

Judge Morales's voice kept booming around them in the darkness, drowning out whatever else Mom was going to say. It seemed to silence the crowd, too.

"We apparently have saboteurs who believe they can shut this trial down simply by cutting an electrical line," Judge Morales said. "After they tried to throw us off with a fake recorded voice."

That was how she was trying to explain what Mom had said? Finn wanted to yell back at Judge Morales, just the way he'd yell at a playground bully, *You're the one with the fake recording! You're the one who shut off the electricity!*

"Believe me, all the guilty parties will be found and punished accordingly," the judge continued, her voice overpowering everything. "But right now, we all need to show the saboteurs that the will of the people is not to be tampered with. We have working microphones again, and in a second, we'll have the spotlights back. Even without our projection screen, it's time to call other witnesses alongside Kate Greystone."

The crowd buzzed again, this time with excitement.

"Mom!" Finn whispered. "They're not going to use the screen! They'll have to show you and your answers for real! No matter what anyone else says, all you have to do is tell the truth!"

"I can do that better if I'm not worried about you, Finn," Mom whispered back.

Was that true?

Finn still didn't understand everything, but he didn't want to be the reason Mom had to lie.

"What game are they playing now?" Joe whispered from below. "I don't see how—"

He broke off, because a blinding light appeared at the back of the auditorium.

"Run!" Mom whispered, shoving even more urgently at Finn and Emma and Chess.

But the light wasn't trained on Mom. It wasn't even swinging toward her. It was aimed at a pack of guards at the back of the auditorium. A pack of guards—and three small, huddled shapes.

And one of the shapes was calling out pitifully, in a voice

that sounded a lot like Finn's own, "Mom? Mom? Are you there? Please, somebody—they promised! They said they were taking us to our mom!"

It was the Gustano kids.

FIFTY-THREE

EMMA

That's how they think they're going to control Mom, Emma realized. *They still think those are her kids. Whoever's in charge doesn't know why she dared to tell the truth a few minutes ago, but they're reminding her whose lives are at stake.*

A chill ran through her, because *all* their lives were at stake, and had been all along.

A moment ago, Mom had whispered into Emma's ear, "Logic *and* love are going to triumph in the end, and in the meantime, I need you to take care of your brother. *Both* of your brothers. Trust me." And Emma had believed her. But now Mom sagged back against the chair she was trapped in, and Emma could feel her mother's despair like it was something contagious.

"I thought your message meant those kids were safe!" Mom hissed at Joe. "Otherwise, I wouldn't have—"

"Shh!" Joe begged. "I'm sorry! I had a plan!"

Had, Emma thought. *Past tense.*

Was he giving up, too?

"Joe, don't you have any more electronic devices to fool them with?" Emma asked. "Maybe we could record *our* voices and throw them out into the crowd. Or . . ."

"That device I dropped was just a fake," Joe protested.

"You built a drone lizard!" Emma reminded him. "Isn't there something else—"

"Anything like that takes time!" Joe whispered back. "And there isn't any left!" He seemed to be holding out his coat pocket, helplessly. "I have wires and screws and a few of *my* kids' things I thought I could build something with—sparklers and smoke bombs left over from the Fourth of July, Lego pieces and rubber bands and string . . . You tell me what good any of that does us now!"

If the situation hadn't been so dire, Emma would have thought, *Sparklers and Lego pieces? Joe's so much like me!*

But now she could only think, *He's totally losing it.*

Natalie came racing back to the others, even as Chess, Emma, and Finn reluctantly backed away from Mom and Joe.

"They're bringing those kids up to the stage," Natalie reported. "I heard fake Mom—I mean, the judge—she said that they won't put the spotlight on Mrs. Greystone until the kids are right beside her. They want the dramatic effect. But we can't let anyone see all of you here. Do you want me to run over and try to talk to . . . to fake Mom, to buy some time?" Her voice shook. "I don't know what I'd say, but—"

"Oh, Natalie," Mom said, her voice awash in helplessness. "We can't ask that of you. There's too much of a risk . . . a mother would see the difference. All of you—Joe, too—save yourselves!"

Joe kept stubbornly lying on the floor, working the screwdriver against the shackles. Emma liked him more than ever.

"What kind of a woman—what kind of a *mother*—doesn't answer even when her own children call out to her?" the judge taunted over the loud, booming mike.

But the judge didn't give Mom a working mike, so no one could hear her even if she did *call back to those kids,* Emma thought. *The judge is just trying to make Mom look worse and worse!*

Quivering, Mom bent her head low.

"There's still hope for me," she whispered with a sad little laugh. "They'll keep me alive because there are still things I know that they want me to reveal. But those kids, they're only valuable to the leaders if . . . if . . ."

She meant the Gustano kids were only valuable to the leaders as long as the leaders thought the Gustanos were truly Mom's children.

And the Gustanos would lose that protection if the leaders saw Chess, Emma, and Finn Greystone.

What if the Gustanos themselves give away everything once they're with Mom? Emma wondered.

Mom did *look* like the Gustanos' mom. If they really were two different worlds' versions of the exact same woman—and as much as Emma hated the idea, it did seem true—then Mom and Kate Gustano were probably genetically identical. It made sense the same way that there would be two Natalie Mayhews, the same way that Ms. Morales and Judge Morales undoubtedly held the exact same genes.

But Ms. Morales and Judge Morales were *not* the same otherwise. And probably there'd be some differences between Mom and Kate Gustano, too. Probably Kate Gustano and her kids shared some special code words and special, silly memories that were different from the ones Mom and the Greystone kids shared, just because they'd lived in different places and had different lives.

And the Gustanos would notice if Mom didn't act like their mom. If Finn Gustano was anything like Finn Greystone, it wouldn't take him long to blurt out, "Hey! This isn't really our mom! She just looks like her!"

And if Finn Gustano—or Emma Gustano, or Rocky—said something like that, it would be like signing their own death warrant.

Emma watched the three struggling Gustanos in their circle of light, as the guards around them prodded and shoved them up toward the front of the auditorium, up toward the stage. The crowd parted for them too easily. The crowd wasn't just terrified of the guards—it looked like they were terrified of the Gustanos, too.

Because of Mom, Emma thought, her heart sinking. *Because they think any kids of a horrible criminal like Mom would be horrible, too.*

The crowd didn't have any sympathy for sobbing little Finn Gustano, with his trembling lip and the bubble of snot in his nose. They didn't have any sympathy for the fierce way Emma Gustano held on to her little brother's arm, holding him up, or the protective way Rocky Gustano kept his arm draped around both his siblings' shoulders, even as they were already connected by handcuffs and chains.

The analytical part of Emma's brain wanted her to just keep staring at the Gustanos, to study and classify their every feature and move: *Oh, that's so much like us Greystones,* or *Hmm. That's not like us at all. Is that something that came from their father's genes, or is it because they lived in Arizona and we lived in Ohio?*

But the Gustanos and the guards—and the portable spotlight the guards carried—were getting closer and closer. It was only a matter of minutes before they'd be climbing the stairs, only a matter of minutes before the spotlight would shine on them and Mom together.

And on the Greystones and Natalie and Joe, too, if they didn't move quickly.

"Kids!" Joe hissed. "Go back down those stairs! Let Natalie take you—"

He pulled Natalie down beside him, and seemed to be whispering something in her ear. But Natalie sprang back, shaking her head no.

"We can't!" she protested. "There are guards beside that door now—I saw them! And they'll know we don't belong up here, they'll know I'm not really this world's Natalie Morales. . . ."

Natalie was practically sobbing. Emma saw everything in the slump of the older girl's shoulders. She saw how Finn had gone back to clutching Mom's arm, how Chess huddled helplessly on the floor, how Mom held her face in her hands. And, worst of all, how even Joe seemed to have dropped his screwdriver.

All of the others were giving up.

Emma decided to hold her breath again.

At first, she told herself, *I'm just testing a hypothesis. That's all. If everything's hopeless, it doesn't matter what I do. And if this world is going to kill me, I at least want to know as much as I can about how and why.*

It'd been a while since the bad smell of the alternate world had bothered Emma, but that didn't mean it wasn't there.

Maybe we've been immersed in this world's stink for so long we don't even notice it anymore? Maybe that's true for everyone in the crowd, too? And maybe the effects . . . build up?

Emma held her breath for so long that her head swam and dots appeared before her eyes. It wouldn't do anyone any good if she just passed out.

But she still didn't let herself breathe.

Logic and love, Emma told herself, remembering her mother's words. *Love and logic.*

Love was the reason Emma, Finn, and Chess had come all this way to rescue their mother.

In another way, love was the reason Mom had wanted to rescue the Gustanos. She knew the love the Gustano parents had for their kids, because of how Mom loved Emma, Chess, and Finn.

Love was what mattered most.

But logic was *how* Emma could make love win.

When Emma had been holding her breath for so long that she swayed with dizziness and her eyelids sagged down over her eyes, she finally thought, *We just need to buy more time. Just enough time for Joe to finish freeing Mom. And we* can *do that with the bits and pieces and kids' toys Joe has in his pocket.*

Her eyes popped open and she took the very, very smallest breath of air she dared. But she was still clearheaded enough to hiss down to Joe:

"Did you say you had string and rubber bands and Lego? And smoke bombs? I *really* want those smoke bombs! *I've* got a plan!"

CHESS

The guards and the Gustano kids reached the door in the clear wall between the stage and the crowd. Now they were through the door and climbing the stairs. Now they were at the edge of the stage.

And Chess could only watch in frozen horror as the beam from the portable spotlight in the guards' arms swung closer and closer.

Then Emma was nudging him and shoving something into his hands.

"Throw these out on the stage," she whispered. "Hurry!"

Tiny wires poked Chess's fingers, but as far as he could

tell, Emma had handed him nothing but junk.

"You think we're going to hold off the guards with wires and rubber bands and bits of string?" he asked incredulously. "And . . . *Legos*?"

"It's dark! We could make them trip!" Emma whispered back.

Chess wanted to cry, that she could still sound so hopeful. Over nothing.

"All we have to do is confuse them," Emma whispered. "And when they see the smoke . . ."

Emma reared back her arm and threw something into the air. Chess heard a muffled thud a few feet away. Evidently Joe's smoke bombs were the type that splatted and set off smoke instantly, because Chess's next breath brought in an ashy odor.

And . . . somehow it brought him courage, too.

He blindly tossed the handful of trash toward the guards surrounding the Gustanos.

"Let me have some of those smoke bombs!" he whispered to Emma.

Chess sensed, more than actually seeing, that Finn and Natalie were throwing smoke bombs, too. And Joe had gone back to struggling with Mom's shackles with renewed vigor.

The guards screamed, and Finn Gustano wailed louder than ever.

"You're under attack!" Emma screamed at the guards. "Lots more rebels are coming to fight you! Run while you still can!"

And it was crazy, because anybody could tell Emma's voice belonged to a little girl. And the smoke bombs were just kids' toys. They did little but pop and fizzle and stink.

But maybe in the darkness the guards heard them as terrifying weapons; maybe the thin columns of smoke seemed to be the first sizzlings of a larger explosion. The guards reeled backward, clutching their heads as if they couldn't figure out what to do. One of the guards dropped the portable spotlight, and all the man needed to do was pick it up again. But he let the light careen about, shooting its beams out wildly.

Behind the guards, the crowd began to shriek and wail and shove their way toward the exits. In the crazily veering flashes of light, Chess saw dozens of other guards step out from behind the pillars and push the crowd back.

But the guards on the stage—the ones closest to the smoke bombs—just stumbled about, barely even managing to hold on to the Gustano kids.

"Joe!" Chess cried. "What was in those smoke bombs? Are they—"

"Magic" was the word he wanted to use, but that was silly. It didn't make sense that the little puffs of smoke made the guards crash into each other and mutter "Why am I doing this?" And "What should I do next?"

"I think it's just that they have air from the other world!" Emma hissed. "From the *better* world! It's like an antidote! I didn't know it'd work like this but—let's use it!" She smashed a smoke bomb down right in front of Chess. "Breathe deep, everyone! Breathe in as much of the good air as you can!"

Chess sucked in the ashy air, and it smelled different now that he viewed it as belonging to the other world. This air made him think of bonfires on autumn nights, of logs crackling in a fireplace, of Mom lighting candles on his birthday cake every single year, every single birthday.

This air made him think of home.

Behind him, Mom let out a sound that might have been a laugh and a cry all at once.

"Kids, kids, I love you so much!" she cried. "But you have to save the Gustano kids for me! And yourselves! You have to go! Now!"

"You, too, Natalie!" Joe yelled. "Run! Remember what I told you . . . Kate and I will be right behind you!"

"We'll meet you!" Mom added. "Back at the house! On the *other* side!"

Chess stood, torn even now. He'd come to rescue his mother. That was all he wanted.

But she wanted him to save the Gustanos. And she knew a lot more about this world than he did.

The beam of the spotlight swung closer than it had before, throwing a glow onto Mom's face. Everybody else ducked down out of sight, but Mom was still trapped in her chair and couldn't. And so Chess saw in stark detail that Mom was staring straight at him, her desperate wince full of not just anguish but hope—and maybe even faith as well—as she pleaded, "Kids, *please*!"

It was the "*please*" that did it. She wasn't ordering them anymore. She was begging. And . . . trusting them. Trusting them to make the right choice.

Chess looked down at Finn and Emma, both of them so little and so brave. He looked over at the Gustanos, weeping and wailing and reeling about blindly and helplessly, just like the guards.

He grabbed Emma's arm and Finn's hand and took off running.

FIFTY-FIVE

FINN

Finn was having so much fun.

The more smoke bombs he threw, the more he felt like himself again. What had they all been so worried about? They could ward off these guards with *toys*.

So when Mom yelled, "Go!" and Chess grabbed Finn's hand and pulled him along, Finn raced directly toward the guards.

"Finn, Emma, and Rocky Gustano!" he shouted. "Come with us! *We'll* save you!"

The guard beside Other-Finn was staring down at his hands as though he couldn't quite understand why he was clutching a little boy's arm. So it was easy for Finn to shove the man away and yank Other-Finn forward.

"W-what? Why . . . ? Rocky, what's going on?" Other-Finn screamed. His eyes were wide and terrified as the crazily rolling beam of light struck his face; the handcuffs slid back and forth on his wrists as he reached back for his older brother.

"We're getting you out of here," Chess was telling Rocky. Rocky squinted at Chess, then yanked on Other-Finn's arm the same way Chess was tugging on Finn.

Behind them, the crowd screamed and Judge Morales's voice boomed uselessly, "Silence, everyone! Guards, follow the protocol!" So Finn couldn't hear what Emma or Natalie told Other-Emma to get her to run. Maybe they didn't need to tell her anything; maybe she was like Emma: smart enough to figure out everything on her own. But the three Greystone kids, the three Gustanos, and Natalie began moving as a pack through the darkness, jumping past guards who did little but stare helplessly into the smoke.

"This way!" Natalie called, running ahead. "Away from the judge! There should be a door at the side—"

"Good idea!" Emma hollered back.

Finn threw his last smoke bomb over his shoulder, just in case any guards tried to follow.

"And don't kidnap anyone ever again!" he yelled.

He wanted to see if Mom and Joe were running yet, too, but the rolling light pointed the other way now; the rising smoke stung his eyes. He started to trip, and Chess yanked him up.

"Keep going!" Emma yelled.

Or maybe it was Other-Emma; it was hard to know.

They crashed through a curtain at the side of the stage and kept going, into more darkness.

And then Finn's shoulder hit a door, the kind that opened with a bar across the middle. He shoved hard, and there was light on the other side.

Light, and a new set of double doors.

These doors were surrounded by two rows of guards. They were still in formation, looking strict and tall and mean in their crisp, dark uniforms.

"Somebody throw more smoke bombs!" Finn called back over his shoulder. "I'm out!"

Behind him, Emma let go of Other-Emma's arm and held up both of her hands.

They were empty.

Finn whipped his gaze over to Natalie and Chess, who had their palms out, too.

Their empty palms.

Everybody was out of smoke bombs. They had nothing left to fight these guards.

The first guard stepped forward, reaching out to grab Finn.

FIFTY-SIX

EMMA

"Natalie!" Emma yelled. "Help!"

It was impossible to say in front of the guards what Natalie needed to do. Not when the guards could hear everything.

And not when one guard already had his hands around Finn's arm; not when a second guard was already reaching for Emma.

Emma stopped and pulled back and put her hands on her hips. It was time to speak in code.

"Don't you know who her mother is?" Emma demanded, pointing back at Natalie.

Behind her, Chess and the three Gustano kids were

jumbled together. Chess's face was red and sweaty as he struggled to keep a grip on the chain that linked the Gustanos' handcuffs. The three Gustanos were screaming and scrambling away from these new guards in a panic. Other-Finn's mouth was open so wide Emma could see his tonsils; Other-Emma shoved Chess away while Rocky yanked back on his handcuffs.

Rocky crashed back into Natalie, almost knocking her over. She threw her arms up helplessly and struggled to stay on her feet.

She did not look powerful.

But then Chess said, "That's Natalie *Mayhew*," pronouncing her name the same awed way he'd spoken it back in the basement the afternoon after Mom left, when he'd told Emma that Natalie and her friends practically ran the elementary school.

And that was all it took. A second later, Natalie whipped her hair back over her shoulder and thrust her chin high in the air and shoved past the Gustanos and Chess. She marched straight to the guard who was reaching for Emma and looked him square in the eye.

"My mother said for me to take these children out this door," she said, her voice ringing with bossiness. "All of them. The prisoners in chains *and* my helpers."

Emma suddenly understood what Chess had meant

about Natalie running the school. Now Natalie sounded like she could run the *world.*

"Er, miss, we don't have authorization for that," the guard replied. He sounded apologetic, though. And maybe a little uncertain. "Our orders were to let no one in or—"

Natalie made her back very straight. She was probably six inches shorter than the guard, but Emma suddenly felt as though Natalie was taller than everyone.

"Maybe it's too dark for you to see very well," Natalie said.

Sarcasm, Emma thought, because the emergency backup lights here were brighter than the ones on the stage. *But she's making it seem like the guard can't see well enough to do his job. Like he's not even* capable *of doing his job.*

"Oh no, miss, we—we—" one of the other guards started to stammer.

"I *am* Natalie Mayhew, and in an emergency situation like this, that is all the authorization you need," Natalie finished.

The guards looked at each other. They weren't bumbling like the ones on the stage. They still stood stiff and proud and stern. Emma wanted to blurt out, *Natalie, can't you say something else? Can't you do something to prove who you are?*

But that would be like a code, too. Emma couldn't make it look like *she* was telling Natalie what to do.

Natalie only tapped her foot impatiently. Like she was just waiting, and she knew the guards would obey. Eventually. If they knew what was good for them. And then . . .

The guards stepped aside. The one who'd been reaching for Emma let his hands drop. So did the one who'd been holding on to Finn.

"Do you need a detail of guards to accompany—" the first guard began.

Natalie whirled on him.

"Don't you think I have my own security force waiting outside?" she snarled. "My own *superior* guards?"

"Yes, miss. Of course, miss," the guard rushed to reply.

How did she do that? Emma wondered. *How was she so . . . perfect?*

The funny thing was, Natalie had sounded a little like she was just arguing with her mom. Like all that yelling at her mother had only been practice.

Now Natalie was making the Gustano kids and Chess, Emma, and Finn march through the door. She stood beside them like *she* was their guard.

The first door led to a dark, empty hallway and another set of doors.

And then they were all outside the building, blinking at their escape from darkness. The air out here was only slightly less murky than it had been in the auditorium, and it made

Emma feel almost as strange. But at least there was enough light to see by. For a moment, she just wanted to take in everything: the puzzled, terrified expressions on the Gustano kids' faces; the strange, ugly buildings around them; the emptiness of the street before them. And, most of all, the determination on Natalie's face.

Has anybody ever told you that you look a lot like your mom? Emma wanted to ask her. *That you act a lot like her, too, trying to fix everybody else's problems?*

But Natalie was still giving orders.

"Now run!"

FIFTY-SEVEN

CHESS

Chess ran.

It was amazing that his legs and feet worked, because his brain didn't seem to be functioning.

Maybe we should . . . If . . .

For a few blocks, none of them did anything but run, pell-mell, straight down the middle of the deserted street. Then it occurred to Chess that eventually someone was going to start chasing them, and they should probably try harder to hide. Just as he started to pull back to tell the others that, Rocky yanked his brother and sister away from the group.

"This is . . . crazy," the oldest Gustano gasped, slowing to a trot. Other-Finn and Other-Emma huddled beside him, their chains and handcuffs clanking. "We just need to find a *phone.* Was that . . . was that some sort of cult? And we're away from it now, so . . ." He appealed mostly to Chess and Natalie. "I guess you're trying to help, but . . . can we borrow a phone? To call the police?"

"The phone we have doesn't work here," Emma said. "And we think the police are bad guys, too."

The three Gustano kids just gaped at her.

Of course, Chess thought. *We're confused, and we've been working on figuring out everything for the past week. The Gustano kids don't know anything.*

"Are we in some foreign country?" Other-Emma asked. Her "I've got to make sense of this" squint looked awfully familiar. "With a corrupt government?"

"That's probably the best way to think of it," Chess said, trying to make his voice gentle. "We're taking you to safety. We promise. Then we'll explain."

The thin wail of a police siren rose behind them.

"Keep running!" Natalie screamed. "Faster!"

They took off again, full speed—or, at least, full speed for Finn and Other-Finn. The two little boys seemed to be struggling valiantly to keep up, and Chess saw that Rocky and Other-Emma kept having to force themselves to slow down to their little brother's pace. Of course, they were handcuffed to their brother, but Chess stayed by Finn, too. Natalie and Emma ran slightly ahead, in the lead.

So if the police come, Emma's going to be safer than Finn or me, but . . .

As the police siren seemed to draw nearer—was it just one siren? Two? Three?—Chess got an image in his head of a whole row of police cars pulling up behind them, maybe picking off Finn. . . .

None of us can outrun police cars, Chess told himself. *We have to find a route the cars can't follow.*

They were still blocks and blocks away from the abandoned house. Nothing around him looked familiar, though at least they'd gotten past all the towering buildings with their horrid blue-and-orange banners. Chess was pretty sure that the only landmark he'd recognized before—the retaining pond—was just ahead on the right.

Oh, the retaining pond . . . And behind it . . .

"Listen!" Chess screamed. "When we get to the pond, we run off the road and take the bike path behind it!"

"*Is* there a bike path in this world?" Emma shouted back at him.

"I don't know!" The police sirens were getting closer and

closer. The walls of fences and unpassable hedges rose around him. "It has to be! Or else—"

He couldn't say it, but the words rang in his head.

Or else we don't have a chance.

FIFTY-EIGHT

FINN

This is just like running home from the school bus after school, Finn kept telling himself. *It's just a slightly longer route. Keep running.*

Except, running home from the school bus always meant running home to see *Mom*, who would be waiting with chocolate-chip cookies or apples and Goldfish crackers or . . . or just a hug.

Finn was always hungry, and he liked food a lot. But sometimes what he wanted most was the hug.

But Mom said she'd meet us at the house today, Finn told himself. *So, see? It isn't different! She'll hug us all when we get there!*

"This way!" Chess shouted, veering off the street. He

pulled on Finn's arm, then Other-Finn's arm, too, tugging them both along with him.

"No confined spaces!" Rocky growled at Chess. "You can't take us anywhere we—"

"Just a bike path!" Chess shouted back at him. "Where we'll be out of sight!"

Rocky glared at Chess, but he threw a quick glance over his shoulder and followed along.

"Please let it be there. Please let it be there," Finn heard Chess repeat again and again.

Finn surged ahead, catching up with Emma and Natalie.

"It is!" he yelled back to Chess. "Just a little overgrown!"

The bike path was a *lot* overgrown. Branches whipped out at them, slashing at their arms and legs and faces and catching at their hair. A clearing appeared ahead, but Natalie held them back.

"Wait, just wait, shh, don't let anyone hear us . . . ," she whispered. She peeked past a thorny bush. "Okay, it's clear. Come on! Hurry!"

All seven of them dashed across a street and then back onto the rest of the overgrown path.

Why isn't anybody out? Finn wondered. *Why isn't anyone calling to us, "Oh, is something wrong, kids? Can we do anything to help?"*

Was it possible that every single person in this town had

been in that awful Public Hall?

The roar of police sirens behind them reminded Finn that even if that had been true before, it wasn't true *now*. The police were coming. And the police here were bad guys, too.

The sirens seemed to multiply and echo. Now it sounded like the police cars weren't just behind the kids, but ahead as well.

Can't be, Finn told himself. *Just keep running. . . .*

Beside him, Other-Finn kept glancing up at Rocky and Other-Emma. Finn wanted to say something encouraging: *You're doing great!* or *We're almost there!* But he found he didn't have enough air in his lungs. It was hard to breathe when the air smelled this bad. And when the air itself seemed to whisper, *You're not going to make it. You should just give up now.*

Emma fell back to run alongside Chess and Finn and ask, "Isn't it going to be hard to see the house from the path?"

Chess faltered, almost tripping.

"Oh, right, nothing looks the same, and there are all those fences . . . ," he murmured. "What if we miss it?"

"Should we go out to the street at the last block? At Chestnut?" Emma asked. "Or whatever they call Chestnut Street here?"

Finn didn't know all the street names in his neighborhood—it was just "the street where Tyrell lives" or "where that one old lady lets us pick raspberries" or "where they have that house that *I'm* going to buy someday, because it has a swimming pool."

When this is all over, I'm never going to any of those places again, he thought. *Maybe I won't even go to school. I'm just staying home with Mom.*

They burst out into the open again, and Chess and Emma screamed together, "This way!"

The broken-down street before them seemed a million miles wide and a million miles long. It should have been a relief not to have branches tearing at his clothes and hair constantly, but now Finn felt too exposed. Unless he could scale an eight-foot-high fence on one side or another of the street, there was nowhere to hide if someone showed up. The police sirens seemed to have faded in the distance, but maybe that was because Finn's ears had gotten used to them. Or maybe his ears weren't working right at all. The street before them seemed, if anything, too silent. The handcuffs on the Gustano kids' wrists clanked as they ran, and that suddenly seemed too loud.

And then someone stepped out from a gap in the fences. A woman.

Ms. Morales. The *real* Ms. Morales. He could tell, because she was wearing the same neon green exercise shirt she'd had on when she'd dropped them off at their house earlier that morning.

Finn decided neon green was his new favorite color. Definitely better than dark blue or orange.

"Natalie? Finn? Emma? Chess?" Ms. Morales called, her face a mask of concern. "I finally found you! But—"

It didn't matter that the concern on her face was almost immediately replaced by anger. Or maybe fear. It almost didn't matter for that moment that she wasn't *his* mom. She was *a* mom, and she'd always been nice to him, and right now he just needed a grown-up who would hug him and tell him everything was going to be okay.

He put on a burst of speed and took off running toward her.

In the next instant, he heard Ms. Morales scream, "Watch out!"

FIFTY-NINE

EMMA

Everything happened at once.

Emma had just turned her head to ask Chess, "That *is* our Ms. Morales, isn't it?" and Chess had replied, panting, "Neon green shirt, so, yes, I *think* so. It has to be."

At the same time, Rocky, Other-Emma, and Other-Finn had whipped around in the broken-up gravel of the street, as if they were about to run in the other direction.

And then, as Finn raced faster than ever toward Ms. Morales, she suddenly screamed, "Watch out!" and police officers appeared at the tops of every fence and started dropping toward the street below.

Finn skidded to a halt. All the other kids froze.

We're so stupid, Emma thought. *Those boys told us that first day there were SWAT teams everywhere on this street who captured Mom. We're going to be captured the exact same way. . . .*

Then Ms. Morales screamed, "Stay away from those kids!" and all the police officers froze.

"Ma'am?" One of the men gulped. He was a tall man with imposing muscles, but in that instant he sounded cowed and confused. "Did you say . . ."

"Mom! We've got to get out of here!" Natalie yelled. "I'll explain later!"

"Mom?" One of the police officers nearest Emma muttered under his breath. He seemed to be trying to peer past the tangled, twig-strewn hair hiding Natalie's face. "*Is* that the daughter? Or an impostor? And the orders we received, are they . . ."

Natalie flipped her sweatshirt hood up over her hair again, but it didn't matter. Now all the police seemed to be staring at her. While they were distracted, Emma took a testing step forward, closer to Ms. Morales and the gap in the fences behind her. The police didn't do anything.

That gap . . . Is that where the abandoned house is? Emma wondered. *Are we that close?*

Ms. Morales stepped farther out into the street, closer to all the police.

"I demand to know what's going on here," she said. Her eyes seemed to take in not just the police and Natalie and the three Greystones, but the Gustano kids cowering together, their handcuffs clinking in the sudden silence. "Why are those children—"

Natalie hurled herself at her mother, crying, "I did what you told me. Isn't that all that matters?"

Natalie plowed into her mother's side. Emma hoped it looked more like a hug than a tackle to the police officers. But Ms. Morales was knocked sideways, and she would have fallen if Natalie hadn't clung to her so tightly.

"Come on!" Emma called to her brothers and the Gustanos. The Gustano kids hesitated, seeming equally terrified of Ms. Morales and the police surrounding them. Then Chess grabbed Finn in one arm and Other-Finn in the other and took off running. Rocky and Other-Emma bounced along behind him, half running, half dragged.

"Mom, you better not have unpropped that door," Natalie muttered, pulling her mother along, too.

Emma raced around the corner of the fence, and, yes! The abandoned house stood before her. She sprinted for the front door. The can of corn was still there, holding it open. Emma crossed the porch in one step, burst through the door, and swung it open wide, making room for the other kids and Ms. Morales behind her.

"No! No! No!" Other-Emma screeched. "We'll be trapped! Again!"

"There's a tunnel!" Emma yelled back over her shoulder. "We'll escape!"

"A tunnel?" Some of the police who'd hesitated before began running after the kids.

Do they know about the other world? Emma wondered.

Then a worse thought occurred to her: *What if these awful people follow us into the other world?*

As soon as Natalie and Ms. Morales scrambled from the porch into the house, Emma reached out and yanked the door shut, slamming it as hard as she could.

Locked, she thought disjointedly. *It locks automatically. Now no one else can come in.*

She turned and sprinted toward the basement stairs alongside Natalie and Ms. Morales.

A second later she heard a crash and the sound of splintering wood.

The police officers were hacking their way into the house.

SIXTY

CHESS

Chess shoved Finn toward the basement stairs and screamed, "Don't stop until you get to the other side!"

Chess wanted to turn around and grab Emma, too, so he could make sure she was safe. Maybe Natalie and Ms. Morales as well. But he still held Other-Finn in his arms, and the little boy was struggling to get away. Rocky and Other-Emma were trying to pull Other-Finn away, too.

"I'm taking you to safety!" Chess screamed at them. "I promise!"

"We're not going into another dark basement!" Other-Emma sobbed. "We're not!"

Then a horrid thud sounded behind them. Daylight streamed in through a crack in the wall that hadn't been there a moment before. Chess looked back and saw the blade of an ax coming through the drywall.

A matching echo came from the kitchen, and then, from the other corner of the living room. Were the police smashing their way into the house from all sides?

"This is the only way!" Chess screamed, dragging all three Gustanos toward the stairs.

They screamed but didn't resist. Emma and Natalie came up from behind and shoved the Gustanos as well.

It was a wonder everyone didn't just fall down the stairs. Chess pulled and tugged and pushed as he ran, and he lost track of whose elbow he yanked forward, or whose handcuff smashed against his face. The lights came on when Chess was about halfway down the stairs, and he realized that Finn must have hit the light switch. In the sudden glow, Chess saw that Finn had also swung the door of the little side room open.

"Come on! Come on!" Finn called from beside the door.

"Keep running!" Chess hollered back. "Don't wait for us!"

Then they were at the bottom of the stairs. Chess heard footsteps from above. The police were in the house now.

"Go! Go! Go!" Chess screamed.

His voice blended with Finn yelling, "Come on!" and Emma and Natalie shouting, "Hurry!" and the Gustanos shrieking in such panic and fear that Chess couldn't make out any exact words.

He couldn't hear Ms. Morales.

He turned around and she was running, too—mostly, it seemed, because Natalie was pulling her. But she had such a dazed expression on her face, she didn't even look like herself.

"Make sure the next door is open!" Emma shouted ahead to Finn, and Finn disappeared into the little room. Chess and the whole jumble of everyone else followed along, aiming for the door back into the tunnel.

"It's dark in there!" Other-Finn wailed, and Chess was surprised to realize that he was still mostly carrying the little boy, still dragging him along.

"There's light on the other side!" Emma called back.

Chess kept running. Before, stepping back into the tunnel from the alternate world had felt so odd, almost as if he'd ceased to exist. But this time as he crossed the threshold, Chess felt his mind clearing.

Because I understand what's happening? Chess wondered. *Because I'm shaking off the alternate world, and that's* worse *than the tunnel?*

He could still hear the police in the abandoned house behind him.

"Shut the door!" he screamed over his shoulder to Natalie. "Lock it if you can! Or jam something against it!"

But the police had axes. What would stop them from hacking away at the door to the tunnel, too?

Blindly, Chess kept running forward, deeper and deeper into the tunnel. Two lights suddenly glowed around him—the flashlights from Natalie's and Ms. Morales's phones. Those lights provided just enough glow that Chess didn't trip or run straight into a wall. The whole group ran in silence now, as if everyone had lost words, or lost the breath to speak words. Chess's mind kept spitting half thoughts at him: *If they follow us . . . to our house . . . we should . . .*

What if there wasn't an end to that thought? What if there wasn't anything they could do?

Somehow, suddenly, there was more light around him, and Chess could see shelves lining the walls. Familiar shelves: the ones they'd been so surprised to see that Mom had stocked with cans of food and shoeboxes full of cash.

Mom . . . , Chess thought. *Where's Mom now? Did she escape, too?*

Chess heard footsteps behind him, but they were too heavy to be Mom's. And there were too many of them.

These footsteps had to be the police.

They were in the tunnel, too.

"Hurry!" Natalie gasped, breaking into the brighter,

more open space behind Chess. "That man—Joe—he said there's a secret way to shut off the tunnel if anyone follows us. He said we get to the area with the shelves, and then—"

"Don't let them catch us!" one of the Gustanos shrieked in terror. Chess was a little surprised to see that it was Rocky.

"Don't worry. We won't," Emma said, patting his back. "Natalie, how—"

"Oh, this is ridiculous," Ms. Morales said. She had an expression on her face like she'd just awakened. "What was I thinking? Running like that just makes us *all* seem guilty. No matter what happened out there, this isn't the way to handle it. I just need to talk to—"

"Mom, no!" Natalie said, grabbing her mother's arm. "You don't understand!"

"Natalie! The secret!" Emma called.

"It's the same lever as before," Natalie called, even as she tugged back on her mom's arm. "You pull it straight out from the wall like you're trying to break it, not just turning it side to side. But—"

"Chess, help!" Finn called.

He was already trying to climb up the shelves toward the lever. But it was too high over his head.

Chess heard the footsteps behind them getting closer and closer. How much time did they have? What if the secret lever didn't even work, and they still had to run and run and run? He saw the Gustanos on the floor, weeping. Would he have to carry all *three* of them up the basement stairs next? He saw Emma scramble toward the lever, too. He saw Ms. Morales shake off Natalie's hand and turn around, as if she still intended to solve everything by talking to the police. She took a step back into the darkness.

In one huge stride, Chess crossed the floor and grabbed the lever. He jerked it straight out from the wall, and it broke off in his hand.

A split second later, everything exploded.

SIXTY-ONE

FINN

Finn blinked and blinked and blinked. Dust settled around him, blocking his view.

"Chess!" he screamed. "Emma!"

"Finn?" Two voices answered: his brother's and his sister's.

No, it was three voices—there was an echoing "Is that you, Finn?"

Other-Emma.

And then a fourth, slightly deeper: "Are you all right? Is everyone okay?"

That was Rocky.

Finn lifted his head, still blinking. He was jumbled up on the floor with Chess and Emma: Her elbow was in his ear; Chess's knee was in Finn's rib cage. Beside them, the Gustano kids were equally tangled together.

But no one looked hurt. No one was bleeding. No one had any broken bones sticking out.

"Natalie?" Finn called.

"Over . . . here."

Her voice sounded weaker, but maybe that was just because she was farther away. The air seemed clearer now: The dust had settled, and the stench was gone. Behind Natalie, shelves leaned and sagged. A pile of cans and jars lay beneath the shelves, all of them dented and squashed and broken, scattered across the floor. While Finn watched, another can slowly dropped to the floor, a delayed reaction. He blinked again, trying to make sense of what he saw. In a few places, the wood of the shelves had splintered and cracked, and dirt and bits of drywall sifted down through the holes, as if the earth behind the shelves was straining to fill the entire basement.

There hadn't been shelves behind Natalie before. There hadn't been dirt either. There'd been a huge, hollow tunnel.

And Ms. Morales.

"Mom?" Natalie called. She sat up straight. "Where's Mom? She was right here!"

"She . . . she stepped back. . . ." Chess seemed to choke on his own words. He looked at the metal lever in his hand, and scrambled to his feet. He hit the broken lever against the wall. "There's no place for it to fit anymore! No sign that it was ever attached! It's like—"

"Like there was nothing here but a hidden room," Emma said, her voice stunned. "Like it wasn't a tunnel to anywhere."

Natalie whipped out her phone.

"I have service again!" she cried. She hit her finger against the phone's screen, then screamed into it, "Mom! Answer!"

A ringing came from beneath a pile of smashed jars at the bottom of the shelves.

"Her phone's here, but she isn't?" Natalie cried incredulously. She let her own phone drop to the floor. She stood and began digging her fingers into the dirt trickling through the broken shelves. "Mom!"

"The phone must have mostly been in this room," Emma said. "Ms. Morales mostly . . . wasn't."

Finn went over and wrapped his arms around Natalie's waist.

"Your mom," he said. "My mom. And Joe. They'll find . . ."

Each other, he wanted to say. *Another way out. Us.*

Emma and Chess limped over to the broken shelves,

too. They patted Natalie's shoulders and pressed their hands against the shattered wood and the wall of dirt. Both Emma and Chess moved with the same air of disbelief as Natalie.

"We went to rescue our mom," Chess said dazedly. "And . . . we lost your mom instead."

Natalie collapsed against the broken wall and splintered shelves, her face buried in her arms. Now it was more like Chess, Emma, and Finn were holding her up.

"We're sorry," Emma whispered.

Finn had never heard his sister sound like that before, so utterly defeated. So utterly lost.

He turned his face to the side, because he couldn't bear to look at her, couldn't bear to see her and Chess and Natalie reaching out again and again to touch the dirt that had replaced the tunnel. He couldn't bear to watch them trying to understand what couldn't be understood, or accept what couldn't be accepted. He couldn't even bear to watch the cans still rolling off the last shelf and dropping to the floor one . . . by . . . one.

But Finn caught a faster movement out of the corner of his eye: Rocky, Other-Emma, and Other-Finn on the floor behind him, all of them scrambling for the phone Natalie had dropped.

"Look," Finn whispered, and Natalie, Chess, and Emma turned around.

Before them, Rocky stabbed his finger against the screen, hitting numbers. Then all three of the Gustano kids clustered around the phone, screaming into it, "Mom! Mom! We got away from the kidnappers!"

"We're free now!"

"Come get us! Oh, please, come get us!"

Finn couldn't hear the voice on the other end of the line, and that was probably a good thing. It would have made him cry. He looked back, and Natalie had tears streaming down her face as she watched the Gustano kids. Emma and Chess did, too.

"We saved *them*," Emma said.

"We did what Mom wanted," Chess whispered. "And she said . . . she said she's protected by what she knows, and those kids weren't protected at all. . . ."

Finn realized that he'd been trying to say things wrong before.

"And next time we'll save *her*," he corrected himself. "And Ms. Morales. And Joe. We'll find another way in. Another tunnel. Next time."

He expected the big kids to get that look in their eyes that meant they were going to lie to him. He expected them to pat his head and put on fake cheer to assure him, "Of course! Everything's going to be fine!"

But Chess only straightened his spine. Emma lifted her

chin in the air. Natalie clutched his hand. It was like Finn had helped *them*.

And then Other-Finn tugged on Finn's arm. He smiled his gap-toothed smile, and behind the snot and tears and dirt smeared across his face, his eyes glowed. They were the exact same shape and color as Finn's. And for now, they held the exact same hope and confidence.

"You can do it," Other-Finn said. "If you could rescue us, you can do *anything*."

EPILOGUE

CHESS, EMMA, FINN, AND NATALIE

The kids emerged from the Greystone house into a neighborhood swarming with police and firefighters. Yellow tape was everywhere, stretching from tree to tree carrying the words, "POLICE LINE DO NOT CROSS." The Gustanos stiffened at the sight of the police, but Finn, whom they seemed to trust the most now, whispered to them, "No, no, *these* police are good guys. Everything's okay."

And somehow the Gustano kids had the sense not to ask questions in front of the adults, who were all shouting questions of their own.

"Did you smell any natural gas odor in there?"

"Did you see any flames?"

"Has everyone from your house been evacuated?"

Emma was the only one who managed to get a question in edgewise: "You think we just went through a *natural gas* explosion?"

One of the firefighters took pity on her and answered, "Well, that or an earthquake. Plain old sinkhole's another possibility—right now nobody's getting the story straight."

And then one of the cops noticed the handcuffs on the Gustano kids, and Natalie and the Greystones had to focus on getting *their* story straight.

"We've been away because our mother's out of town on business, and we came back to check on our cat, and *these* kids were trapped down there," Chess said.

"They said they'd been kidnapped in Arizona, and the kidnappers kept moving them around—they just arrived here today," Natalie added.

"Please, can you take care of them?" Finn ended, smiling his most innocent smile. "Get them back to their parents as soon as you can?"

And then the Gustano kids were whisked away, and the Greystone kids and Natalie only had to deal with firefighters for a while.

"I'm sure *your* parents are going to want to know that the

four of you are safe," one of the kindliest-looking firefighters said.

"Well, my mom dropped us off, and then she was just sitting in that SUV over there waiting for us, and . . ." Natalie did not have to use any acting skills at all to make her eyes widen at the sight of the empty SUV. She took off running toward it, crying, "Mom! Mom! Where are you, Mom?"

The firefighters ran after her, and for a moment, Chess, Emma, and Finn were left alone. They could hear the firefighters speaking gently to Natalie: "Young lady, can we call someone for you?" "Oh, your father . . . can you give us his number?"

Chess put his arms around his little brother's and sister's shoulders.

"They'll be asking us that question soon, too," he warned them. "And when they can't find Mom, we have to be ready to . . ."

"Go live with strangers," Emma finished for him.

Chess was surprised that she'd reached that conclusion so quickly, without first suggesting their old babysitter, Mrs. Rabinsky (who, he had to admit, always seemed tired out after just one night with them) or some neighbor like Mrs. Childers.

Finn was surprised that Emma had said that in front of

him, instead of making up some comforting lie.

Both of them could tell that Emma was only trying to sound brave when she squared her shoulders and added, "We'll be fine. We'll have each other." She gulped. "Just . . . just like Mom told us . . ."

But then Natalie was back, putting her arms around all of them, and telling the firefighters who trailed after her, "And these kids will come home with me, too. My dad will take care of all of us."

While the firefighters conferred about this, Chess whispered, "Natalie, there are *three* of us. All he'll know is that our mom has totally disappeared. He'll never . . ."

And Natalie jutted her jaw into the air and countered, "He'll agree to this because I tell him to. That's how it works with my dad. He lets me do anything. It drives my mom crazy." For a moment, her chin trembled. "Mom is the only one who . . . who . . ." She swallowed hard and dropped her voice to a whisper. " . . . *cares*."

Finn nestled in close, wrapping his arms around her waist.

"We'll find her," he reminded Natalie. "Her and our mom and Joe. We will."

Emma started to add, *We figured out the first part of Mom's coded message. Maybe all we need to do to find our way back is to solve the rest of the code.* She wanted to assure Natalie, *I'm really good at codes and secret messages. You know that, right?*

But maybe that wasn't what Natalie needed to hear. Emma thought hard as she hugged Finn and Natalie tight, then reached back to draw Chess in, too. The four of them stood together for a long moment. United.

"And in the meantime," Emma finally said, "until we get our mothers back, we'll *all* have each other."

ACKNOWLEDGMENTS

About thirty years ago, a newspaper columnist named Rheta Grimsley Johnson wrote about a sad, odd, *true* coincidence so compelling that the story has haunted me ever since. It took me almost three decades to realize it, but that column planted the first seeds of this book. So Rheta Grimsley Johnson is the first person I need to thank.

I'd also like to thank my agent, Tracey Adams, and her husband and co-agent, Josh Adams, for their belief in this book and this series at a time when I wasn't sure what I had.

Likewise, I owe my editor, Katherine Tegen, a great deal for her faith in this book and this series and me. Thank you as well to everyone else at HarperCollins who worked on the book, especially Allison Brown, Ann Dye, Mabel Hsu, Christina MacDonald, Aurora Parlagreco, Bethany C. Reis, Mark Rifkin, and Amy Ryan. And thank you to Anne Lambelet for the amazing cover art.

I'd also like to thank my niece Meg Terrell and my sister, Janet Terrell, who's a teacher, for their help with thinking about life in elementary (or intermediate) school. A shout-out as well to my daughter, Meredith, who helped with my research trip to the National Cryptologic Museum.

And I'm always grateful to my friends in my two Columbus-area writers groups, who provided love and support and listening when I needed it most: Thanks to Jody Casella, Julia DeVillers, Linda Gerber, Lisa Klein, Erin McCahan, Jenny Patton, Edith Pattou, Nancy Roe Pimm, Amjed Qamar, Natalie D. Richards, and Linda Stanek. My friend and fellow author Lisa McMann lives in the wrong place (though she says *I'm* the one who lives in the wrong place), but she provided moral support at a critical time, too, while I was working on this book.

And thanks as always to my family, especially my husband, Doug. A dinner with Doug and our friends, journalism professors Beverly and Mark Horvit, helped me figure out an important part of this book, so this is both a thanks and a "Sorry for completely zoning out for a while."

Finally, thanks to my friends Janis and Dan Shannon for showing me certain unique features of their new house, while our friends Sarah and Mark Fox and Barb and Gary Munn stood there saying, "Margaret, you're going to put this in a book, aren't you?"

People say that to me all the time, about all sorts of things. But this time . . . they were right.